Warwickshire County Council

Lea 7/18			
9·5·19			

This item is to be returned or renewed before the latest date above. It may be borrowed for a further period if not in demand. **To renew your books:**

- **Phone the 24/7 Renewal Line 01926 499273 or**
- **Visit www.warwickshire.gov.uk/libraries**

Discover • Imagine • Learn • *with libraries*

Warwickshire
County Council

Working for Warwickshire

D1420200

014232976 X

Inferno

Julie Kagawa

YOUNG
ADULT

HQ
An imprint of HarperCollins*Publishers* Ltd
1 London Bridge Street
London SE1 9GF

This paperback edition 2018

1
First published in Great Britain by
HQ, an imprint of HarperCollins*Publishers* Ltd 2018

ISBN: 978-1-84845-686-0

MIX
Paper from
responsible sources
FSC™ C007454

To Tashya. Together we can slay dragons.

PART I

Spark

EMBER

Tramping through the jungle for hours on end was not my idea of a good time.

It was hot, insanely so. Normally, heat didn't bother me, but the humidity level beneath the canopy had been cranked up to like two hundred percent. It felt as if I was walking, and breathing, through a wet, heavy blanket. My clothes—the olive drab shirt, cargo pants, even the socks in my combat boots—were damp with sweat, and tying my hair back did not prevent it from hanging in my eyes and sticking to my forehead. Insects droned in my ears, in the trees, everywhere around us—a constant, high-pitched buzz that faded into background noise unless you concentrated on it.

Behind me, Garret moved like a shadow, making virtually no sound as he glided through the undergrowth. I couldn't see him without turning, but I knew he was there. I could sense him—the steady rise and fall of his breath, the heartbeat thumping quietly beneath his jacket. Lately, I didn't even have to look at him to know where he was; his presence, both in my thoughts and in the world around me, became more prominent with every passing day. I knew he was worried. Not for us and our situation, though as always he remained hypervigilant and alert to our surroundings. But I knew his thoughts were back home, with the Order and the people we'd left behind. I couldn't blame him. Across a continent, a war was brewing. Back in the States, Talon was on the move, and though we didn't know their plans, we did know they had a massive clone army, a huge force of dragons bred for war, programmed to follow orders without fail. They had already used that army to wipe out the Order of St. George, striking a devastating blow against their greatest enemies, nearly destroying them completely. The Order, what was left of it, was in shambles. Talon stood unopposed to do whatever horrible thing they were planning. And where were we? Tromping through the deepest, darkest parts of the Amazon jungle, fighting bugs and vines and heat exhaustion, searching for something that should not exist.

Ahead of us, Riley followed our guide down a narrow, winding trail that could barely be called a path, cutting through vines and undergrowth with machete in hand. Though the rogue was putting up a good front, he was worried, too. Garret wasn't the only one to leave people behind. Riley's underground—his network of rogues and the hatchlings who'd escaped Talon—was in danger, too, as the organization was systematically eliminating every dragon who didn't conform to Talon. This trip almost hadn't happened. Riley had been extremely reluctant to leave his underground, consenting only when Wes and Jade both told him to go, that they would take care of the hatchlings and the rogues. In the end, Riley had agreed, but I could tell he wanted to get this over with as soon as possible and return to the network he'd left behind. I knew Garret felt the same about the Order.

But this was important. Whether we liked it or not, the war with Talon had come, and the organization was poised to unleash destruction upon everything we cared about. We needed all the allies we could get, and if this lead turned out to be real, then it just might give us a chance. Not a great one, but it would level the playing field a bit.

The guide, tall and rawboned and carrying a machete much like Riley's, suddenly paused. The trail ahead had been blocked by a tangle of vines and branches, so with a quick "One moment, please," he went to work hacking through the undergrowth. Riley, rather than standing back, joined him, and together they started slicing through the tangle in short order.

After stripping off my rucksack, I rummaged in the pocket and pulled out a canteen, feeling the heat and humidity pulsing from my skin. I took a few sips, then handed the container to Garret, who accepted it with a nod of thanks.

"Well…" I sighed, leaning back against a thick, gnarled tree. Above me, the trunk soared into the air until it joined the canopy far overhead. Insects flitted through the branches, and only a few patches of sunlight made their way down from the blanket of leaves above us. "This isn't the way I thought I would spend my weekend." I took a breath, and it was like breathing the air in a steam room. "Air-conditioning is a wonderful, wonderful invention, Garret," I told him. "How did we ever get by without it?"

Garret offered a faint smile as he handed the canteen back. He looked natural out here, in his boots and camo jacket, pale blond hair cut short. He looked like a soldier. "I thought dragons liked the heat," he said with a glance at the guide, still whacking vegetation with Riley. I sniffed, crouching down to stuff the canteen back in the rucksack.

"Yes, well, most people think we like sitting on piles of gold in dark, dreary caves. You don't see us doing that anymore, do you? Especially since we can track our funds from a computer, in the comfort of an air-conditioned office." A mosquito the size of my thumb landed on my arm, looking hungry, and I slapped it away. "And maybe it's made us soft, but I for one am glad that we've caught on to the conveniences of modern life. Air-conditioning and indoor plumbing beats sitting in a cave full of treasure any day."

Garret's voice turned serious. "Not all dragons think that apparently."

"No." I shivered a little as I rose and pulled the rucksack over my shoulders once more. The jungle seemed to close around us, reminding me why we were here. "I guess not."

Riley walked back to us, breathing hard. He had tied a bandanna around his head to keep his hair back, but a few dark strands had poked out and stuck to his forehead. The white tank beneath his open, long-sleeved shirt was streaked with moisture. For the briefest of moments, in the shadows of the canopy, his eyes glimmered gold.

Warmth fluttered somewhere deep inside me, like a candle dancing in the breeze. The *Sallith'tahn*, the life-mate bond, telling me that Riley—or rather Cobalt—was my Draconic other half. But it was weaker now. Barely a flicker, when before it had been a rushing, surging inferno of heat and desire. I had broken the *Sallith'tahn*. I, as a dragon, had decided to be with someone else. To choose love over instinct. I suspected the *Sallith'tahn* thing would never truly go away, and I doubted Riley would ever forgive me for rejecting him but, for now at least, the war and the threat of Talon took precedence over our petty squabbles and jealousy. We had to work together to survive. Alone, we didn't stand a chance.

"Our guide says we're almost there," Riley informed us, unscrewing the cap of his own canteen. "Another forty-five minutes to an hour, according to him." He took a few quick swallows from the container, then raked a sleeve across his face. "Man, I forgot how sucky the jungle is. Good thing Wes isn't here. He'd never stop complaining. Still have that compass, St. George?"

"Yes." Garret frowned slightly. "Why? We have a guide."

"Not anymore." Riley turned to glare at the guide, who was still hacking through vegetation and deliberately not looking at us. "There's some kind of statue marking the trail about a mile from here, and from then on, we're on our own. He says the path keeps going, but he flat-out refuses to venture beyond that point."

"He's leaving?" I scowled. "That wasn't the deal."

"Apparently it was." Riley replaced the cap and slung the canteen over his shoulder, his own expression disgusted. "He said he would take us as far as he could. Well, that's as far as he's willing to take us."

"Why?"

"Because, in his own words, beyond the statue is the territory of a god."

A chill crept up my back, even in the suffocating heat, and I swallowed. "Then I guess we're on the right trail."

"Yep." Riley rubbed the back of his skull, looking both nervous and annoyed about being nervous. "Never did like the idea of meeting a god. Somehow, I get the feeling gods just don't like me very much."

"You?" Garret asked, the hint of a smile crossing his face. "With your complete disdain for authority figures? I don't see why that would be."

"Ha, ha, laugh now, St. George. We'll see how funny it is when we're all piles of dust being scattered by the wind."

We started off again, walking single file down the narrow path, following our guide toward the territory of a god.

If possible, the jungle got even thicker, more tangled, with branches and vines clawing at us from either side of the trail. Our guide came to a sudden stop and murmured something I couldn't understand. Ahead, sitting to one side of the tiny path, a stone statue rose out of a cluster of vines and roots, the snarling visage of some scaly, horned creature peering out at us.

Riley cocked his head at the statue. "Huh," he remarked. "Is that supposed to be a dragon? It looks like a wild pig had a baby with an alligator."

I shook my head at him. "Can you be any more irreverent? I haven't been struck by lightning on this trip yet."

The guide turned, his dark face solemn in the shadows of the undergrowth. "This is as far as I go," he said. "From this point on, you only have to follow the path. I will wait here until your business is complete."

Riley frowned. "I thought you said you served this master or god or whatever you call him."

"I do. But I am simply his voice outside of the jungle. Only those who have been invited can step into his territory unharmed. Therefore, I will wait for you here. If you do not return by sunset, I will know you are not coming back. Now, go." He nodded down the trail. "My master is not a patient god. It would be unwise to incur his wrath."

We went, slipping deeper into the jungle, venturing into the unknown. Into the territory of a god.

Almost immediately, I knew something was wrong. My dragon instincts stirred, edgy and restless, though I couldn't see anything unusual. But I could feel eyes on me. I could sense something watching us, stalking us down the trail, keeping just out of sight.

Garret moved closer, walking by my side, even down the narrow path. His eyes were hard as he murmured, "Something is following us."

"Yeah," I whispered back. My hand twitched, wanting to reach for the Glock hidden beneath my shirt, but I didn't want to give away that we knew we were being stalked. "Should we tell Riley?"

"He knows," Garret replied, keeping his gaze straight ahead. His posture was calm, but I could sense the tension in him, ready to explode into action. "Stay alert. Be ready to move when it happens."

As he said this, we entered a clearing, and figures melted out of the undergrowth. Tall, slender, with only a strip of cloth tied around their waists, they moved like ghosts, making virtually no noise as they stepped forward. Before we could say anything, they had surrounded us, and a dozen bone-tipped spears were leveled at our hearts.

GARRET

Two weeks earlier

I stood in Gabriel Martin's office, watching as the lieutenant walked into the room with a slight limp. He shuffled around the desk, then sat down with a grimace and eyed me across the wood. I stood calmly at attention, mostly out of habit, until he waved me into a seat.

"Sebastian," he greeted as I settled into the chair. "You've come from the infirmary, yes? How is St. Anthony?"

"The same, sir," I replied. Tristan St. Anthony still lay in a coma, unmoving and unresponsive, much as he had the past two days. The fact that he was still alive at all was either a testament to his hardheadedness or his extremely good luck, for many of his severely wounded brothers had not survived that first night.

"Stubborn bastard. He would have to make things difficult. The medic is going to give me an earful about moving him, I'm sure." Martin half smiled, then shook his head with a sigh. "We're leaving, Sebastian," he went on, sobering as he looked

at me. "We're too exposed here. Our numbers have been depleted, our defenses broken, and Talon still knows where we
are. If they attack again, there is no way any of us will survive
another round."

"Yes, sir," I replied. I'd suspected as much. Martin was right
to leave, to gather the remaining soldiers and retreat to fight
another day. We couldn't stand against Talon, not like this. I
didn't like the idea of abandoning the base to the enemy, but
I knew we had little choice. "Where will you go?"

"Somewhere Talon won't find us." Martin sighed. "The
Order has several locations throughout the country, emergency safe houses that are meant to be used as a last resort.
We've never had need of them, until now. I plan to fall back
to one of them, regroup and see about contacting the rest of
the Order. If anyone in St. George survived, they'll be doing
the same."

"Do you think there could be other survivors?"

"God, I hope so," Martin said. "We can't be the only ones
left. There have to be others—even a handful is better than
none. Talon couldn't have destroyed every single soul in St.
George. What about your dragons?" he asked. "What will
they be doing?"

"Riley is planning to leave, as well, sir." For the past two
days, the rogue leader and the other dragons had been staying
in the empty officers' quarters at the far end of the compound.
There were too few St. George soldiers left alive to even think
about harassing them, but the dragons stayed deliberately isolated from the rest of the base. Dragons being allowed on St.
George soil was still an alien concept to most of the soldiers,
and neither Martin nor Riley wanted to take any chances. Soldiers were not allowed to venture to the "dragon's side" of the

compound, and the rogue leader had forbidden any contact with the rest of the base. Riley himself stayed as far away from the soldiers as possible, his inherent distrust of St. George and the desire to protect his underground making him reluctant to interact with humans, even Martin. Only Ember went between the two sides without fear, acting as a liaison between dragons and St. George, relaying messages and updates to them both. There had been hard eyes and wary glances whenever she walked across the yard or into a room, but so far there had been no real problems with having a dragon stroll freely through Order territory.

Of course, the remaining soldiers having seen the red dragon lead a counterattack against the horde that would have otherwise destroyed the base didn't hurt. Perceptions *were* changing. Slowly. Many of the soldiers' attitudes had downgraded from openly hostile to merely suspicious. No one but Martin had spoken to Ember or the rest of the dragons since they'd arrived, but no one had openly threatened or mocked them, either. It was the best I could hope for.

Sadly, there were a few whose hatred had not waned, who despised the dragons and thought the Order should shoot them, and me, in the head while they had the chance. Thankfully, Martin's authority over the Western Chapterhouse was absolute, and he was respected enough to be obeyed, even in the face of what would be considered extreme blasphemy. It didn't stop the men from talking, but it did prevent an all-out rebellion.

Martin rubbed his forehead. "Go to your dragons, then," he stated. "Talk to them. Find out what they intend to do. I wish I could promise them protection if they came with us, but you know the Order as well as I do. The soldiers here are one thing, but if we meet other survivors, I'm uncertain I can convince them to listen to me, regardless of what happened."

"Which is why we'll be leaving before we start getting shot at."

We turned. Ember and Riley stood in the doorframe, gazing at us. The rogue leader had a grim, almost defiant expression as he faced Martin. Ember gave him a brief, annoyed look before slipping around to stand beside me.

"What Riley means to say," Ember broke in as Martin's eyes narrowed, "is that our people are nearly healed, and we should probably find a safe place for them before Talon comes after us again. If you are going to try to bring the Order together, it's not a good idea for us to stay around, at least not initially. I don't think they'll be as...understanding as you have been, Lieutenant."

Riley smirked. "I thought that's what I said."

We ignored him. "That's what I suspected," Martin replied, nodding. "Understandable, of course, given the circumstances. When do you intend to leave?"

"Tonight," Ember replied. "In a few hours actually. Jade and the others are well enough to travel, so we'll be leaving after sunset and driving through the night. You won't have to worry about us anymore."

Martin pondered this, then looked at me. "And you, Sebastian?" he asked, as I'd known he would. "Will you be going with them?"

His voice wasn't angry or accusing, but my stomach tightened all the same. I could hear the hidden meaning behind his words. *You are a soldier of St. George. This is your home, with the people who raised you. You belong here, with your brothers. You belong with us.*

I hesitated only a moment, then nodded. "Yes, sir."

"There is no way I can convince you to leave with us?" Martin continued, and before I could say anything, he added, "We could really use your help, Sebastian, especially now. Your knowledge and expertise on the enemy is what kept us alive that night. Well, that, and the arrival of your dragons." One corner of his mouth quirked, very slightly, but just as quickly, he sobered. "I'd like to have you with us, Sebastian. I can't order you to come, of course, but St. George—what's left of it, anyway—could use all the help it can get."

"I'm sorry, sir," I answered firmly. "But I don't intend to join the Order again." I'd chosen my side, and St. George was no longer home. Though a small part of me wished I could go with him, if only to be a voice for the dragons, to continue the call for change, I knew beyond a doubt where my loyalties lay.

"I see." He sighed again, but nodded. "Well, take care, Sebastian. I don't know what the Order will do after this, if there is an Order around to do anything. But…" His eyes shifted to Ember. "I do know that things are going to change. For better or worse, I'm not certain yet." He reached into his desk and pulled out a burner phone, then handed it to me over the surface. "Take this," he said as I reached for it. "It has one number on it. Use it if you need to contact me for any reason. Somehow, I have the feeling our paths will cross again."

Before I could answer, there was a knock, and Martin's gaze rose to the door. "Yes?"

"Sir!" A soldier stepped into the room, pausing to give Ember, Riley and me a wary look, before turning to Martin. "Lieutenant," he continued, "the guards intercepted a man outside the gate. He won't say who he is or where he came from. All we could get out of him was that he has a message…" His gaze shifted to Riley and Ember. "For the dragons."

RILEY

Well, this day had gotten weird.

A man was sitting quietly at the table in the conference room, flanked by soldiers of St. George. He was lean and bony, wearing a simple shirt and dark pants, and his skin was tanned and leathery. His hands were folded in front of him, his dark gaze staying fixed on the wooden surface until the four of us—myself, St. George, Ember and the Order lieutenant, Martin—approached and stood at the table's edge, facing him.

"I am Lieutenant Martin," the officer began in clear, official tones. "Current commander of the Western Chapterhouse of St. George. Who are you? What is it you want here?"

At his voice, the man finally raised his head, his expression calm. But his gaze wasn't for the lieutenant, but for the red hatchling standing beside St. George.

"Ember Hill," he said in a soft but perfectly audible voice. His dark gaze slid to me. "Ex-Agent Cobalt. My master sends his greetings."

Ember tensed, as did St. George. The two guards did, as well, hands straying toward their weapons. The man at the table, however, remained as serene as ever. I stepped forward, feeling Cobalt rise, responding to a potential threat. "And who would that be?" I growled.

"Forgive me, ex-Agent." The man bowed his head. "But my master would rather not discuss business with the soldiers of St. George within earshot." His gaze flicked briefly to Martin and the soldier. "This message, and the terms that come with it, are for you and Miss Hill alone. Sebastian may stay, if he likes," he went on, and I stiffened. That he knew the soldier's name, as well...who *was* this human? And who was this mysterious master who knew us all? "But the rest of St. George must leave. My master was quite insistent that this was for your ears alone."

"I don't think so," Martin said. "You're in Order territory, sitting in a St. George chapterhouse. Anything you want to tell the dragons, you can inform us of, as well."

"Come now, Lieutenant," the man went on in a reasonable voice. "Surely you can see I am not a threat. I am no dragon, no soldier. I am not armed. Your soldiers have already determined that I am wearing no wires or transmitters. Two dragons and a former soldier of St. George should have no trouble with a frail old man." His thin lips twitched. "But feel free to shackle me to the table, if you are that worried."

"Who are you?" I growled. Frail old man, my ass. He obviously knew far too much to be harmless. "How the hell do you know who we are, or that we'd be here, for that matter?"

"I will tell you," the stranger said, and refolded his hands to the table. "Once St. George is out of the room."

I looked at Martin. He stood for a moment, rigid and silent, his jaw set, before he nodded once and jerked his head at the soldiers flanking the man. They gave him worried looks but immediately turned and walked out. Martin watched the stranger a moment more, dark eyes appraising, before he turned to Sebastian.

"We'll be just outside. Call if you need us."

"Yes, sir," the soldier replied.

The officer gave the figure at the table one last glance and walked out of the room. The door closed behind him, and we were alone with the stranger.

The man didn't move. "All right," I said, stepping forward. "You got your wish. St. George is gone. So start talking, human. You obviously know who we are, what we are and probably why we're here. There's only one possible group I can think of with that kind of information."

"I am not from Talon," the man said. "Let us get that suspicion out of the way right now. You have no reason to fear me. I represent a single individual, not an organization. Though Talon is part of the reason I have come. My master has sent me here with a message. He wishes to meet you, ex-Agent Cobalt. You and Miss Hill. There are things he wishes to discuss."

"Uh-huh. And we're supposed to drop everything and go meet with this mysterious individual right now, am I correct? Sorry, but I'm going to need a little more than that. Especially since we don't even know this person's name, or yours, for that matter."

"My name is not important," said the stranger. "I am simply his voice. His name, however, you might have heard before, ex-Agent Cobalt. My master calls himself Ouroboros."

Ouroboros?

The bottom dropped out of my stomach. I felt Ember and

St. George watching me, and suspected I looked as stunned as I felt. "That's not possible," I stated. "Ouroboros is…"

"A legend?" the old man answered with the hint of a smile. "A myth?"

"Dead," I said flatly. "The dragon known as Ouroboros is supposedly dead. After he went rogue, no one has seen him—"

"In over three hundred years," the stranger finished. "Yes, that is what Talon would have you believe. However, Ouroboros is very much alive, ex-Agent Cobalt. And he sent me here to find you and the daughter of the Elder Wyrm." His gaze shifted to Ember, who straightened quickly. "He has something to discuss with you. In person."

Ember glanced from the old man to me. "I take it this… Ouroboros is important?" she asked. "Who is he, anyway?"

I took a deep breath. "Ouroboros," I began, hearing the awe in my own voice, "is a Wyrm. An old, *old* Wyrm. Right behind our infamous leader of Talon, he's the oldest dragon in the known world."

Ember's brows arched. "Oh," she said.

"Yeah." I nodded. "So, he's kind of a big deal. Even though he's not supposed to exist. A long time ago—and I'm talking over *three hundred years*, mind—Ouroboros and the Elder Wyrm had a disagreement. Everyone has forgotten what it was about, but they think it had something to do with Talon, and the direction the Elder Wyrm was taking it. The stories say the fight was everything from an argument to a full-blown, Godzilla versus Mothra–style throw down, but in the end, Ouroboros left Talon and went rogue. The very first dragon to do so. He just…disappeared. The official consensus in Talon was that he'd died, but there is a legend, among rogues especially, that claims that somehow Ouroboros survived and is still out there. Hiding from Talon, managing to stay off their radar all this time." Riley shook his head. "Of course, it was always just a myth. No one has seen or heard anything from Ouroboros since the day he fled Talon."

St. George looked at the man sitting at the table. "Not so much of a myth, it appears."

"No." I narrowed my gaze at the stranger, suspicion rising up like dark flame. "So if what you say is true," I said, "and Ouroboros is alive, where the hell has he been all this time? Why hasn't he done anything? Does he not care that we've all been dying, thanks to Talon and St. George? He's probably the only one who can go head-to-head with the Elder Wyrm and have a sliver of a chance. Why hasn't he ever made himself known, contacted the rogues at the very least? Why now?"

"I do not presume to know the mind of Ouroboros," the human stated. "I have come to deliver his message, nothing more. I do know that contacting anyone by modern means, such as phones, computers, and the like, has never been his preference. Phones can be traced. Computers can be hacked. Ouroboros is a bit of a…traditionalist, if you would. If you wish to know the answers to your questions, you will have to go to him and ask him yourself."

I growled in frustration. "Fine. Where is he?"

The man blinked. "Forgive me, ex-Agent," he said, still in that supremely calm voice. "I'm afraid I cannot tell you that." He raised a hand as I stepped forward. "You, of all people, should know the lengths to which a rogue will go to keep their location a secret."

"Then how are we supposed to find him?" Ember wanted to know.

"If you agree to meet my master, I will take you to where you must go. I warn you, however. It is a lengthy journey. Ouroboros is not here, in the United States. Hiding himself so well meant cutting himself off from nearly all of civilization. The trip to meet him will take some time."

"Time we really don't have," I snapped. "There's a war happening now, and Talon is on the move. I can't leave the hatchlings to go traipsing halfway around the world for a chat."

"Even if that chat is with Ouroboros?" the stranger asked mildly. "The First Rogue? One of only four great Wyrms in the entire world? Who knew the Elder Wyrm centuries ago, who is the second most powerful dragon your kind has ever known? I would think that you, ex-Agent Cobalt, with your network of dragons trying to hide from Talon, would be especially eager to see why Ouroboros has called for you."

"Hey, don't get me wrong." I held up a hand. "I would love to meet Ouroboros and pick his brain a little. Particularly on how he's stayed off Talon's radar for the past three hundred years." I raked a palm over my scalp. "But this is a really bad time. I can't leave the hatchlings now. Talon is still after us, and there's probably not much time until they launch their second phase of attack, whatever it may be. I have to get my underground as far away as I can before that happens."

Ember looked at me, then back to the man at the table. "Do we have to give you an answer now?" she asked.

"No, Miss Hill." The man shook his head. "Please take your time. Talk among yourselves. Decide what you want to do. But...remember that Ouroboros is not a patient Wyrm, nor one that forgives or forgets." His voice remained the same, serene and matter-of-fact. It was not a threat, merely a statement, but I felt the warning reverberate through me all the same. "He has no tolerance for those who waste his time. If you refuse this offer now, it will not be made again in your lifetimes. So please choose carefully."

★ ★ ★

"Bloody freaking hell," Wes remarked. "Ouroboros? The First Rogue? That's bloody impossible. I thought he was... I mean, isn't he supposed to be..."

"Nonexistent." This from Mist, leaning against the far wall. Leaving the stranger under the dubious watch of a couple soldiers, Ember, St. George and I had retreated to our temporary quarters on the other side of the base. Now, the three of us were gathered in Wes's room, along with two other dragons who had joined us recently: Mist, a former Basilisk agent whose motives for being here were still shady as hell, and Jade, an Adult Eastern dragon with a fondness for tea and being aloof.

"Ouroboros is a myth," Mist said. "An urban legend the rogues keep alive to give them hope." Her long silver hair glowed dully in the shadowy corner she'd claimed as hers. Even though there were still a few hours of daylight left, the curtains were drawn and the lights were turned off. The only luminance came from the screen of Wes's laptop on the desk, because my human hacker friend seemed as allergic to sunlight as a vampire.

"He isn't real," the girl insisted. "Everyone in Talon knows Ouroboros died long ago. After all this time, we would have seen or heard something."

"Yeah, well, tell that to the human sitting in St. George's conference room," I said, jerking my thumb back at the closed door. "Because he's either eaten too many magic mushrooms, or he says that the First Rogue is not only real, he wants to meet with us."

Jade, standing quietly beside a wardrobe, regarded me with interest. "If Ouroboros indeed lives and has called for you, it would be wise to go. One does not receive a summons from an ancient Wyrm often, if ever."

"Yeah, but…" I scrubbed both hands through my hair, frustration warring with curiosity. Of course I wanted to go. This was *Ouroboros*, the First Rogue. The legend who had hidden his existence from Talon so well that everyone, inside the organization and out, had thought he was dead. For *three hundred years*. I would kill to learn his secrets.

But if I left, what would happen to my underground if Talon came for us again? My network was brave; they had fought Talon's clone army and had turned the tide for St. George. Without our intervention, the Order would have been slaughtered.

The cost was high, far too high. Some of them hadn't made it. Five hatchlings were dead, buried in the desert sand with the soldiers they had fought beside. I knew them all by name; I remembered the day I'd taken each of them away from Talon, with the promise of a better life, one that was free.

"You're worried about the others," Ember said quietly.

"Of course I am," I answered. "I can't leave them alone now. It's too dangerous. Talon is actively trying to kill us, and they have a huge clone army to do it. I don't dare send them back to the safe houses—the nests have all been compromised. I have one place left for us to go, and I can only hope Talon hasn't found it."

"I take it we're going back to the farm," Wes stated, and I nodded. He sighed. "Well, hell, Riley, I can take them there. It's not rocket science to drive a bloody van."

As I stared at him in shock, Jade broke in, as well. "And if you are worried about their safety," she said, "put your mind at ease. *I* will remain with them until you return. Talon will not threaten any of the hatchlings while they are under my watch."

"I… Are you two feeling all right?" I wondered, aghast. What the hell was going on here? Wes hated people, and teenagers especially. And Jade barely knew us. "What's gotten into you two?" I asked, frowning. "If I didn't know better, I'd say you were doing everything to get me to leave except physically pushing me out the door."

"Riley." Wes gave me one of his patented *I'm surrounded by idiots* looks. "Think about it. Ouroboros is the second-oldest dragon in the world, and he's at odds with the bloody Elder Wyrm. What would happen if we convinced him to fight for us?" The hacker shook his head at me. "If you can't see the potential there, mate, then I really have no hope for you at all."

"Yes," Jade added with a somber nod. "Know thyself, know thine enemies. A thousand battles, a thousand victories."

"What the hell does that mean?"

"That we *are* at war." The Eastern dragon gave me a look that was nearly as impressively disdainful as Wes's. "And knowing our enemy will be the key to overcoming them. Knowledge is the greatest weapon we have, and who better to obtain this knowledge from than one who has lived longer than nearly everyone else on the planet?"

"And I know you, Riley," Ember broke in. "You want to meet with Ouroboros. If you miss this chance, you're going to be kicking yourself for the rest of your life."

"Agreed," Mist added. "If I was summoned by a legend, I would make that a top priority, but that's just me."

I sighed. "I wonder if you people realize that I'm the leader of this underground," I remarked. "Just throwing that out there, in case you've forgotten." As expected, no one seemed impressed, and I shook my head in defeat. "All right, I suppose we're going to see what the First Rogue wants with us. Wes, Jade, if you're *sure* you've got the hatchlings…"

"Oh, will you just go already," Wes said. "You sound like a bloody nursemaid."

EMBER

The present

The humans surrounded us, silent as wraiths in the darkness of the jungle. There were close to a dozen of them, dark skinned and mostly naked, wearing loincloths and necklaces of shell and bone. Most carried crude wooden spears, which they'd pointed at us in a bristling ring of spikes. A few outside the circle held bows and arrows. None of them spoke, or made any sound at all. They simply watched us with unreadable black eyes.

"Okay," Riley murmured, gazing around. "That's a little worrisome. Do you think this is the welcome party?" His voice was amused but held a hint of warning. Garret had drawn his weapon and was keeping the muzzle pointed at the ground, ready to respond with lethal force if he had to.

"What do you think they want?" I asked, keeping my gaze on those sharp points hovering very close to my face. Garret had moved behind me, and I could feel the tension lining his muscles, his hard gaze as it swept the crowd. Riley shrugged.

"No clue, but I'm not too keen on getting skewered to find out." His gaze slid to me, and a hard smile pulled at his mouth. "You have a change of clothes, right?"

"You want us to Shift? In front of all these humans?"

"Who are they going to tell? The news monkeys?" He rolled his eyes before his attention focused on the crowd again. "I figure this way we won't even have to fight anyone. They'll just drop their spears and run."

"And if they don't?"

"Then I'd rather be in dragon form if they try to shove a spear up my ass."

The crowd in front of us suddenly parted, and an old man stepped through, stopping just a few feet away. He was thin, nearly skeletal, with twig-like arms and only a few strands of wispy white hair stuck to his head. He regarded the three of us with eyes that were still sharp and clear, then raised a clawed hand to point at me.

"You," he rasped in a thickly accented voice. "Name."

"My name?" I asked. Around us, the warriors remained silent, still keeping their spears pointed at us. The old man didn't answer, just continued to watch me with piercing black eyes. "Ember," I said quietly. "My name is Ember Hill."

He nodded once and stepped back, and the men surrounding us lowered their spears. The old man raised a withered hand and beckoned, indicating for us to follow.

We did, trailing him down a narrow path that soon disappeared as we went deeper into the jungle. Even for Garret and Riley, it was difficult to keep up. The old man, and the men surrounding us, moved like ghosts through the trees and vegetation, silent and nearly unseen. They blended perfectly into their world, unlike us, the noisy intruders, stomping through the undergrowth in our rugged boots, hacking at vines along the way. The jungle closed in around us, becoming darker and even more tangled, as if offended by our presence and our attempts to clear a path. After only a few minutes, I was lost, and all sense of direction had vanished into the canopy. Which made me nervous. If our mysterious guides decided to disappear and leave us stranded in the middle of the jungle, we might never find our way out.

"Where do you think they're taking us?" I whispered to Garret after a few silent minutes. The soldier had holstered his weapon but his posture was still tense, his eyes constantly scanning our surroundings and the men slipping noiselessly through the trees beside us.

"I don't know," he replied, glancing at something overhead. I looked up and saw a small yellow monkey on a gnarled branch, peering down at me with large black eyes. "But they knew your name," Garret went on. "That means they were waiting for us."

We continued into the darkness. The men and our guide never slowed down or said anything, either to us or each other. The one time Riley tried talking to our guide, the old man simply shook his head and put a finger to his lips. After a couple hours of walking, I was starting to wonder if this hike would ever end, if the jungle just went on forever, when Garret suddenly nudged my arm and pointed to something in the trees ahead.

At first, I didn't see anything different or unusual: just looming trunks, undergrowth, vines and shadows. Then the outline of a wall, stony and ancient, appeared through the trees, nearly invisible with moss, vines and gnarled roots. As we got closer, I spotted a crumbling archway in the wall, flanked by a pair of statues so weathered and moss covered that they were entirely featureless. Beyond the barrier, rising toward the jungle canopy, a huge stone structure, as weathered and moss-eaten as the statues, towered among the trees.

My brows rose. Was this where these people lived? A hidden village deep in the jungle, surrounded by the ruins of an even older civilization? I was amazed. It was hard to believe that there were still places in the world this untouched by modern conveniences, where humans had lived without electricity or phones or computers for hundreds of years.

As we approached the archway, however, the old man stopped and turned, holding up a hand. I looked around and saw that the warriors surrounding us had backed away and were standing several yards from the entrance, as if reluctant to step close.

The old man looked at me, then Riley and Garret. He took a step back, pointing at us, then to the archway beyond. I frowned.

"You're not coming with us?"

No answer, just the repeated motion of pointing at us, then to the gate, a little more vigorously this time. Riley looked at us and shrugged.

"Guess we go on without him. Be on your guard, though. I'd hate to walk into an ambush of archers firing at us from every nook and cranny."

We stepped toward the archway, moving cautiously as we approached the gate. I glanced over my shoulder once, and saw that the old man and the rest of the warriors were gone. Like they'd never existed.

We continued through the gate. Beyond the wall, the arch opened into a massive courtyard. Moss and vegetation had swallowed half of it, with weathered stone tiles poking up from the green and walls crumbling under the weight of gigantic roots that snaked over them like monstrous pythons. They slithered through the courtyard between uprooted stones and piles of rubble, making the footing treacherous. Crumbling buildings covered in moss and vines stood at the top of the steps, and trees pushed up through the stone, splitting roofs and walls as they reached for the sky. Between the steps and the buildings, more streets snaked off into parts unknown.

"It's awfully quiet," Riley remarked as we ventured warily through the sprawling courtyard. Insects scurried away from us, fleeing over rocks and vines, but they were the only sources of movement I could see. "And I'm not just saying that to be cliché. You guys can feel it, too, right?"

I nodded. He was right. A few minutes ago, the jungle was teeming with sound: buzzing insects, calling birds, howling monkeys in the treetops far overhead. Now the canopy was dead silent, as if every living creature for miles around was afraid to make a peep.

"I don't like it," Garret began as, at that moment, a tremor went through the ground under our feet.

We froze in the center of the courtyard, weapons out, bodies tense as we gazed around. The tremor came again, a faint vibration that made the rocks tremble, accompanied by a muffled boom. And another. Insects scattered in every direction, and a few pebbles went tumbling and bouncing down the wall, as the footsteps grew steadily louder, and my heart beat faster and faster. It nearly stopped when I saw a ridge of spines moving behind the roofs—roofs that were at least forty feet tall.

"Aw, shit," Riley breathed. And then words failed us as a dragon the size of a building walked calmly between the ruins and into the light.

He was old; even without his massive size, I could tell that much. His scales were a dull blackish-green, the color of swamp water, and his enormous wings were tattered and full of holes. Moss and vegetation grew along his back and shoulders, giving him a shaggy look, and I suspected that when he laid down, he could blend perfectly with the jungle floor. His curved black claws were longer than my arms, and bony horns swept forward from a narrow, skull-like face, eyes burning orange-red in the sockets. Those piercing eyes now fixed on me, as the great Wyrm Ouroboros raised his head, towering over us all, and flashed the most terrifying smile in the world.

"Ember Hill." His voice was the deep growl of thunder, shaking the earth and reverberating in my bones. "Daughter of the Elder Wyrm. We meet at last."

My legs were shaking, and my voice had gotten caught somewhere between my heart and my throat. For a moment, I had the crazy, horrifying thought that perhaps Ouroboros had drawn us here, to a forgotten temple in the middle of nowhere, to kill us. Or, more specifically, *me*, the daughter of his ancient rival, the Elder Wyrm. Perhaps with the thought that disposing of the Elder Wyrm's blood would somehow aid in Talon's destruction. Or maybe he just wanted revenge and he couldn't strike at the leader of Talon directly, so he would kill her daughter instead.

Well, if that's the case, the joke's on you. I'm not the favored twin. If you eat me, all you'll be doing is...

...denying the Elder Wyrm immortality. My blood turned to ice. I was the Elder Wyrm's vessel, created to house her memories so she could essentially live another thousand years. Was that why Ouroboros had called us here? Did he somehow know

of the Elder Wyrm's ultimate plan to become immortal and want to end it for good?

Ouroboros, I realized, was still watching me, like a king waiting for his slave to lift his face off the floor. I glanced up into the ghoulish, reptilian face and saw amusement in his burning eyes. He knew the effect he was having on us, and was probably reveling in it.

Come on, Ember. You're the daughter of the Elder Wyrm. Even if he does plan to kill you, don't let him see you sweat.

I took a furtive breath, raised my head and took one step forward, toward the second-oldest dragon in the world.

"Ouroboros." I concentrated on keeping my voice calm, collected. Like *she* would. "It's a pleasure to finally meet you."

Ouroboros laughed, the deep, booming sound making my heart skip and probably startling every bird for miles into the air. Beside me, Riley flinched, and Garret went for his gun, though I saw him force his hand away from his weapon a moment later. There was nothing we could do against a dragon this size. We would need a missile launcher to even put a dent in his armored scales. This was the king of the realm, the undisputed god of the jungle, and everyone here knew it.

I had to wonder: if Ouroboros was *this* huge—close to eighty feet from snout to tail, if I had to guess—how big was the Elder Wyrm?

That was a scary thought.

"Ah." Ouroboros chuckled, shaking his massive head. "It is refreshing to actually talk to someone who will hold a proper conversation," he stated as his voice sent tremors down my spine. "My subjects—the people you met on the way here— all they do is bow and scrape and press their faces to the dirt. When they do venture past the wall, I can't even get them to look at me. I was hoping the daughter of the Elder Wyrm and the infamous rogue Cobalt would be less easily cowed." He glanced at Riley and cocked his head.

There was a split-second hesitation on Riley's part, as if he, too, had to take a breath to center himself, before his lip curled in a faint smile. "I wouldn't want to presume," he said, sounding like his defiant self. "You were having a nice conversation with Ember, and I didn't want to interrupt. Not certain if the penalty for that kind of thing is death around here."

Ouroboros snorted, and a smoke cloud the size of a small car went curling away toward the canopy. "So you are exactly as they say," he mused, sounding pleased. "And I can see why Talon despises you so much. Perhaps you will survive what is coming, after all. But…" His expression darkened, and it was like a wall of clouds dropping over the sun, ominous and terrifying. "Before we go any further, there is one matter I will put to rest, right now."

Through all of this, Garret hadn't moved or said anything, and the Wyrm's attention finally shifted to him. "St. George," Ouroboros growled, his voice making the ground tremble. "The last I saw of your kind, I was crushing a pair of lance-wielding knights on horses. Now you hunt us with guns and vehicles and modern weapons. I might have separated myself from Talon and the rest of civilization, but I still hear the goings-on of the world. Your Order has brought much death and destruction to dragonkind. You have hunted us relentlessly for centuries, and have done your best to make us extinct." The Wyrm's huge body sank into a crouch, talons digging into the stone as he lowered his head, regarding the soldier with glittering red eyes. "Dragons do not forget, St. George," he rumbled.

"Nor do we forgive. I do not see how you thought to come into the lair of a great Wyrm and leave alive."

My stomach dropped. Garret faced the dragon calmly, no sign of fear on his face, though his expression was resigned. "St. George was wrong," he said, not moving as those massive jaws shifted closer, wreathing him in smoke. "What we did to your people…" His gaze flickered to me and Riley. "There's no excuse for the slaughter we caused. But I'm not part of the Order any longer. I'm here because I want the fighting to end."

Anger flared, and I clenched my fists. Why was Garret's loyalty in question anymore? Hadn't he done enough, proven his commitment? He had risked his life on multiple occasions, been threatened, captured, abused and shot in the back by his own Order, all to keep dragons safe. To show St. George that their ancient enemies were not the demons they believed them to be.

Of course, that was before Talon released their mindless dragon army on the Order and nearly destroyed them in one fell swoop. So, they weren't helping things at all. But a few in the Order *were* starting to listen. Like Lieutenant Martin. If he could allow a bunch of rogue dragons into his base, then there was hope, after all. Hope for a future without war, where dragons didn't have to live in fear. Where teenagers weren't trained as killers and assassins. And where a former soldier of St. George and a dragon could be together without both sides trying to tear them apart or kill them.

Frighteningly, Ouroboros didn't look impressed or appeased. "I'm afraid that's not good enough, dragonslayer," he said, making my heart pound with terror. "Are you telling me a murderer should not be punished just because he is repentant?

That remorse will erase all the blood on his hands, all the lives he has taken?"

"No." Garret's voice was a whisper, though he quickly composed himself, gazing up at the monstrous dragon looming overhead. "But I can do more good alive than dead. At least until this is over. I know it will never be enough, but I can try to make up for my past."

"Can you?" The great Wyrm curled a lip, showing a flash of yellow fangs the size of short swords. "You are one human. Your life is but a heartbeat. A flap of a butterfly's wing. If I destroy you here, squash you like an insect, no one will know. No one will mourn you. One less human in the world will not make any difference."

"Hey, now." Riley sounded nervous. "I admit, the guy was a bastard when he worked for St. George, but he's been pretty useful to us."

The Wyrm ignored him. With a terrifying smile, he sat up, towering over us. "I'll make this sporting, St. George," he said, and nodded back toward the gate, in the direction we came in. "Run. Now. We'll see how far you can get before my flames catch up to you. And, human, I haven't had to chase anything for over a hundred years. Do try to make a fight of it, won't you?"

Garret didn't move. I saw his gaze flicker to me for the briefest of moments, saw the countless emotions burning in his eyes, before he faced the Wyrm once more. "No," he said calmly. "I'm not running. I have nothing to hide anymore."

"Well." Ouroboros sniffed, sounding faintly peeved. "You're no fun at all, are you? I guess I'll have to be content with a quick snack, then. Don't worry, though, human." He reared back like a snake, jaws opening to show his fangs and enormous maw. "I'll make it quick."

I lunged in front of Garret, feeling my body explode into dragon form as I did. The great Wyrm pulled up in surprise as I spun to face him, spreading my wings in a desperate attempt to shield the soldier from the massive creature before us. I knew nothing I did would help; one swat from Ouroboros would easily kill us both. But I wouldn't stand there and watch Garret die in front of me.

There was another ripple of energy, and a lithe blue dragon stepped in front of the ancient Wyrm, as well. Stunned, I glanced at Cobalt, but he wasn't looking at me, his narrowed gold gaze was on the huge dragon overhead.

"This isn't why we came, Ouroboros," the rogue said, the tremor in his voice barely noticeable. "And you didn't call us here just for a snack. What do you really want?"

Ouroboros looked amused. Sitting back, he cocked his head, regarding us with ancient red eyes. "Well," he rumbled. "I suppose that answers my question. The girl's actions are not terribly unexpected, now that I have met her, but I will admit, Cobalt, you've surprised me today. Considering how long you've fought against St. George, I would have thought watching one of your enemies crushed in front of you would be gratifying."

"Oh, don't get me wrong." Cobalt's voice was light, but his body was still a tense, coiled wire between the Wyrm and us. "It was mostly for a certain red hatchling who has a tendency to leap in front of the lunging dragon before she looks." He shot me an exasperated glance before turning to Ouroboros again. "But I don't risk my hide for just any human. The soldier has fought Talon and St. George with us, and in this day and age I'll take all the allies I can find."

The great Wyrm nodded. "Excellent," he said, confusing the hell out of all of us. "That's what I wanted to find out.

"I wanted to test how far you would go to help each other," Ouroboros explained. "Two dragons and a soldier of St. George might not be enemies, but it is hard to believe they are allies, even harder to believe they are friends. I wished to see if you were truly a team who thought and acted together, or a random group of strangers simply thrown together by circumstance. If it was the latter, I would be wasting my time here. Because I doubt you would survive what is to come."

"Then…you weren't really going to kill him?" I asked, relieved that my voice was working and not frozen in terror at the back of my throat.

"Oh, I definitely would have killed him," Ouroboros said. "Had you not moved to defend the soldier, he would be nothing but a dissolving lump in my stomach right now." He paused, running a tongue along his teeth. "Mmm, it has been a long time since I've eaten a mortal," he mused in a longing voice. "Perhaps I should start demanding sacrifices again."

I shuddered, and beside me, Cobalt curled a lip. Ouroboros didn't seem to notice. "You want to strike a blow against Talon," he continued. "But guts and determination alone do not win wars. If you are going to fight the organization, you'll need soldiers, allies to assist in the struggle. I can help with both."

"How?" Cobalt asked. "Will you be joining us?"

My heart beat faster at the thought. If we had a Wyrm like this on our side, the second-oldest dragon in the world, we might have a chance of bringing Talon down for good.

But Ouroboros snorted. "It has been over three hundred

years since I have spoken to any of my kind, and in that three hundred years, Talon and the Elder Wyrm have finally forgotten that I exist. Or, at the very least, they have concluded that I am dead. If I returned with you, I would be letting all of Talon know that I am very much alive, and the Elder Wyrm will not stand for that sort of competition."

"But...you're a Wyrm," I protested. "You could help us win this war. Countless dragons are being used and destroyed by Talon. How can you sit back and do nothing?"

"Nothing?" The Wyrm's voice held the hint of a growl, warning me to watch myself in the lair of a god. "I am doing something, hatchling," he went on. "I have called you here. Because an opportunity has arisen, and I see a chance to strike at the Elder Wyrm and Talon. But the future is hazy, and Talon is on the move. It is not yet time for me to reveal myself. Especially as I am unsure that you will survive this war, or indeed the next encounter.

"I called you here," Ouroboros continued, "because I have information that may be helpful to your cause. I think you, in particular, will find this very interesting, ex-Agent Cobalt. As you stated earlier, a war is coming. You cannot take on an organization as large as Talon with a ragtag group of hatchlings and rogues. You're going to need allies willing to fight the organization, and you have very few at the moment."

You *could still help us*, I thought stubbornly, though I knew better than to say it out loud. Best not to annoy the giant Wyrm that could flick you over the wall like a bug. Still, it was infuriating. We'd come all this way, leaving behind friends and those still in danger from Talon, to meet with the world's most legendary rogue. Only to have him say he couldn't be bothered to fight Talon with us.

I felt my spines bristle. Cobalt gave me a warning look, as if he knew what I was thinking, and turned to face the Wyrm again.

"I take it you happen to know where we can find a few," he said.

Ouroboros chuckled. "Oh, you could say that. The dragons there are quite unhappy with the organization, and some of them have been there for a *very* long time. They would be more than eager to join the fight against Talon, I would think. If you can get to them."

I looked at Cobalt, saw him frown slightly as he pondered what the Wyrm was saying, then draw in a slow breath as he figured it out.

"The facilities," he breathed, staring at Ouroboros. "You know where Talon is keeping the breeder dragons."

My stomach twisted. There was so much hope and longing in Cobalt's voice, even after all this time. After years of searching, countless traps, false leads, betrayals, failures and disappointments, he still held out hope that, one day, he would find the place Talon kept their breeder females and rescue them all. It was one of his life goals, probably the biggest one, the white rabbit he kept chasing no matter how many dark holes it led him down. Maybe this time, Ouroboros would give Riley what he desperately wanted. But I couldn't help but be skeptical. The last time we'd followed a lead to where the facilities were supposedly located, it had been a clever trap that had nearly killed us all.

"Yes," Ouroboros said. "I do."

RILEY

"Where are they?"

Ouroboros tilted his head slightly. I suspected that if he'd been in human form he would've arched an eyebrow. What would he look like in human form—if he even *had* a human form? Maybe he'd been out here so long, away from everyone except the natives who worshiped him, that he hadn't Shifted in the three hundred years he'd been out of Talon.

Realizing that the self-proclaimed god of the jungle probably wouldn't appreciate having answers demanded of him by some cocky Juvenile dragon, I hurried on. "I mean, I've searched for those facilities for years, but everything I've found has been a dead end or a trap. Talon has hidden them so well that if I wasn't part of the Basilisk branch myself, I would've thought they didn't exist."

"Oh, they exist," Ouroboros said. "And the reason you haven't been able to find them is because you weren't look-ing in the right places. That, and the location is very difficult

to get to. The facilities are located on a privately owned, unnamed island."

"An island," I breathed. Of course, why hadn't I thought
of that before? A privately owned island was isolated, hard to
reach and cut off from the rest of the world: the perfect place
to hide a large number of captive female dragons.

"Yes." Ouroboros nodded. "Talon owns the island, of course,
so no one is allowed to set foot on it. Not that anyone would
attempt it. Because here is the interesting part. The island is
located a few hundred miles east of the Caribbean, in the area
known to humans as the Bermuda Triangle."

"The...Bermuda Triangle?" I choked out.

"Indeed. That is where you'll find Talon's breeding facilities,
ex-Agent Cobalt. Though getting to it is going to be a challenge. It won't be like breaking into a single office building.
You must circumvent the security of an entire island. And if
you somehow manage to get to the breeders, how will you get
them out again? How will you even get them off the island?"
Ouroboros folded his claws in front of him, regarding me with
appraising red eyes. "If you can accomplish this, young Basilisk, you will have pulled off what dozens of rogues around the
world could only dream of." One corner of that narrow maw
pulled into a smirk. "As such, I myself have very little hope
that any of you will survive. But I will wait, and see what happens. Perhaps you will surprise me."

He chuckled and rose to his feet, engulfing everything in
his shadow. "Well," he stated, "I believe our business is at an
end. It has been entertaining, if nothing else." He paused, and
the subtle warning that crept into his voice made my stomach writhe in fear. "Of course, it goes without saying that you
will not mention my name, or my location, to anyone. What

transpired here does not leave this jungle." His red eyes narrowed, glittering coldly, and I resisted the urge to shrink into the temple floor as the Wyrm loomed over us like a Titan. A massive, unstoppable force of nature. "I am placing a great deal of trust that you will keep this meeting strictly confidential," he rumbled, making tremors ripple through the ground. "But if word that I am alive does happen to reach the organization, do not believe that I won't find you. And if that happens, you and everyone who has ever known you will be consumed, until there is no one left who remembers your name.

"Ember Hill." Ouroboros glanced at the red hatchling, who met his gaze calmly despite the subtle trembling in her wings. "Daughter of the Elder Wyrm. I am pleased that we could meet face-to-face. But know this—I see much of *her* in you, and that can be both a blessing and a curse. Choose your path wisely—it would be a shame to kill you before you reach your full potential."

Ember raised her chin, standing tall as she faced the giant Wyrm. "Are you sure you won't join us, Ouroboros?" she asked. "The war is going to affect everyone, even you, whether you like it or not. Stand with us. This could be your chance to finally strike back against Talon and the Elder Wyrm."

He snorted a laugh and began walking away, back toward the maze of ruined stone and crumbling towers. Pebbles bounced and vibrations ran up my legs as Ouroboros drew away, his long tail swaying behind him. "I have been patient for three hundred years," he said without looking back. "I can be patient awhile longer. Go to the island. Free the breeder females, if you can. We will see if you are successful, or if Talon proves to be too much for you to handle, after all. Perhaps you will die, and Talon will continue their plans unopposed. Maybe all of this will have been for nothing."

He turned a corner, sliding behind stone walls and jungle foliage, until only his tail was left. His final words echoed as the tail disappeared, and the ancient Wyrm vanished back into legend and rumor.

"But maybe not."

DANTE

"I have a task for you, Dante."

I stood in the Elder Wyrm's office, waiting silently as the CEO of Talon finished whatever was on her computer and turned to me with piercing green eyes. Even now, after numerous meetings, being summoned to her side, knowing my heritage and carrying out her orders, that ancient, unyielding stare could still make my knees tremble and my insides squirm in terror. I was getting better at controlling it, though, to appear calm and poised as the heir to Talon should be. Now, I politely averted my gaze and nodded, keeping my voice deferent but calm, to let her know I was suited for whatever task she required.

"Of course. What would you have me do?"

My heart pounded. This would be my chance to redeem myself, to make up for my failure and inability to complete the last mission, which was the complete destruction of St. George's Western Chapterhouse. Victory should have been assured; the Order was in shambles with the death of the Patriarch, and they'd cut themselves off from each other as a result. We had greater numbers and surprise on our side; we should have completely wiped them out, to the last man. Ironically, I had failed because of my own sister's interference; her sudden arrival with Cobalt and a small army of rogue dragons was enough to turn the tide and save a handful of soldiers. *Enemy* soldiers. Soldiers of the Order of St. George, who had hunted dragons toward extinction for hundreds of years. Why Ember was helping our sworn enemies I had no idea, but lately my sibling's actions had been so frustrating and completely unreasonable that I wondered if it was just to spite me and give Talon the middle finger.

It didn't matter in the long run. The Order had still been broken; they were no longer a threat to Talon or any of our operations. But because of Ember, the Elder Wyrm's faith in me had been shaken. And that was something I could not forgive. I had worked too hard, and come too far, to lose this position because my reckless, defiant twin refused to cooperate.

I was almost to the top. One more step, and then I would truly be free.

"Our enemies have been scattered to the winds," the Elder Wyrm said, rising from her seat. "The Order of St. George threatens us no more. But there are still dragons out there who refuse to ally with Talon. Cobalt and his rogues have proved surprisingly resilient, though they will not be able to stand against us much longer.

"However..." The Elder Wyrm turned and walked to the window, observing the city below as she often did. "There are other dragons, older, very powerful dragons, who could be instrumental in the coming conflicts. We have received word that a few Eastern dragons survived the Night of Fang and Fire, that their lairs were empty when our forces came for them. It is likely that the Eastern dragon who currently aids Cobalt and Ember was able to warn them of the attack, which is another small thorn that must be removed. So be it." She turned from the window, fixing me with a piercing stare. "Dante, you will go to China, to the council of Eastern dragons, and you will give them a message. Join Talon, or die. There will be no compromise."

My mouth went dry. Destroying the Order of St. George was one thing. Threatening an entire race of dragons, especially when they simply wished to be left alone, was another. I forced myself to speak calmly. "Of course. Although, if I may, the Eastern dragons have long been known for their reclusiveness and their unwillingness to take part in the war. Would it not be better to leave them alone, rather than expend lives and resources to hunt them down?"

"Perhaps." The Elder Wyrm turned back to the window, looking thoughtful. "Certainly, the Eastern dragons would prefer to remain neutral and unopposed, as they always have. But that time is done. All dragons must unite under one banner, one organization. We offered to make a place for the Eastern dragons before and they refused, but now they have seen our strength, and they know they cannot stand against us. I would prefer to have our proud cousins willingly join our cause, but if they do not, they declare themselves enemies of not only Talon, but the rest of dragonkind. We cannot have any opposition in this new world we are creating, Dante. There can be no loose threads hanging in the wind, not this late in the game. No, you will stand before the Eastern council, and you will deliver Talon's message. This is their final chance. Be certain that they understand."

I took a furtive breath and nodded. "It will be done."

The Elder Wyrm turned from the window, and her eyes glittered as she continued to regard me across the room. "This is a test for you, as well, Dante," she said quietly, making my stomach curl and my pulse thud in my ears. "The Eastern council is comprised of the oldest, most powerful dragons in all of China. You will be far from home, far from the protection of Talon. And the Night of Fang and Fire has decimated their numbers. They will be angry. Neutrality and pacifism aside, they are still dragons—they will want revenge for themselves and their people. If you speak to them as a mere hatchling, demanding they join us or die, they will destroy you without a thought. And neither I nor anyone in Talon will be able to save you."

I felt a stab of very real fear, imagining myself surrounded by ancient dragons, eyes blazing with anger and hate as they loomed over me. If even one of them decided to end the life of Talon's representative, there would be nothing I could do about it. Even taking Gila bodyguards would be useless against dragons that old and powerful; they would crush us all without a thought.

"However," the Elder Wyrm went on, "you are not a mere hatchling. You are the heir to Talon, the prince of an empire, and the Voice of the Elder Wyrm. If you convince them of that, they will not dare to touch you." The ghost of a smile touched her lips as she turned and walked back to her desk, her final words causing a chill to settle at the base of my spine. "Now go, and take Talon's message to the Eastern council. We will see if you are truly worthy of your title."

RILEY

"This is bloody impossible, Riley." Wes sighed.

I glared at him. The six of us—myself, Ember, St. George, Mist, Jade and Wes—stood in what had once been the tornado shelter of the old farmhouse. It had been repurposed as the command center, mostly because it was the only room that could fit four dragons, a hacker and a soldier of St. George without curious hatchlings wandering in. And that was a good thing, because my temper was running very short, and I was likely to snap at the first teenager who poked his head in wanting to know what we were doing.

The rest of the trip from Brazil had been uneventful. No ambushes, no vessels or agents of Talon leaping out to kill us in the middle of the jungle. No ancient Wyrm swooping in to swallow us in one bite. Though Ember had ranted a bit about spending more time in airport lines than the meeting with Ouroboros. We'd left the Amazon, caught a ride back to civilization and flown home as quickly as we could. I'd arrived at the farmhouse half dreading Talon had already come and that nothing remained but charred, blackened skeletons of both buildings and hatchlings in their wake. But nearly everything was as I left it, and everyone was accounted for: twelve hatchlings, one human hacker and two female dragons. As she had promised, Jade had taken over in my absence, and the hatchlings had developed an almost fanatical respect for the Asian woman.

Mist had been with them, as well, though no one could tell me what *she* had been doing while we were in Brazil. I'd told Wes what we'd learned as soon as I could reach him, and Mist had gotten ahold of that information, too, because *somehow* she had been able to acquire an old map of the island, one that detailed the layout of the facility, the buildings, the fence line, everything. When I'd demanded to know where the hell she had gotten it, she'd told me her employer had been able to dig up the old blueprint and send it to her. She wouldn't say anything more, except that her mystery employer wished us luck with our mission, that he approved of us taking down the facility and would send us more information as he acquired it.

Of course, I'd been suspicious as hell, but I couldn't argue that having a map to the unnamed island in the middle of the Bermuda Triangle was a godsend. I wouldn't look a gift horse in the mouth, but I couldn't decide if having the Basilisk around was worth the paranoia. I would have to deal with her eventually, but rescuing the breeders came first.

Unfortunately, after studying the map and discussing the security Talon would likely have set up around the island, it was becoming increasingly clear that we didn't have a chance.

"Dammit," I snarled, slamming a palm onto the table where the map had been laid out, smoothed over, pointed at and argued about. We'd been stuffed into this dimly lit hole for several hours, trying to come up with some sort of plan for storming a Talon-owned island facility without getting killed, and we were no closer to rescuing the breeders than we'd been when we first started. The problems were always the same. How were the six of us going to sneak onto a heavily guarded island, make our way past the security and defenses and numerous Talon employees, to get to the breeders? And even if we did get to them, how were we going to sneak them off again? There could be several hundred dragons on that island, some of whom were likely to be pregnant and unable to Shift to human form. We certainly couldn't herd them all down to the water and tell them to swim for it.

I raked a hand over my scalp, feeling like I was beating my head against a wall as the truth slowly crept over me. There were too few of us. Six individuals, no matter how skilled, stubborn or determined, would not be able to pull this off. We didn't have the bodies, and we didn't have the resources. If we attempted to rescue the breeders on our own, we would all die.

Still, I couldn't give up. I had spent too many years searching for the facilities to stop now. I knew where the breeders were; I'd promised myself I'd free them all if I ever found them. I wasn't going to stop until I figured this out.

"There has to be a way," I growled, staring at the map again, as if a solution would suddenly make itself clear. "Something we're missing. Something we haven't thought of."

"Riley," Wes said. "It's in the middle of the bloody ocean, mate. You're not going to float there on a raft. And who knows how much armed security is between you and the breeders? Not to mention all the normal Talon employees, all the people who actually take care of the dragons, the facility and the island. It'll be like assaulting an amusement park."

"I don't want excuses," I snapped at him. "I don't want you to tell me it's impossible. I want you to figure out a way to rescue the dragons Talon has been using as fucking broodmares for years. There has to be a way to do this."

"There is."

Ember's voice floated to me through the darkness. I looked up and saw the red hatchling standing quietly beside the soldier, one fist against her chin in thought. Her green eyes were narrow and solemn as they rose to mine. "There is a way," she continued. "But...you're not going to like it.

"We can't do this alone," the red hatchling went on, looking to the others, as well. "I think everyone has realized that. It will be next to impossible to get to the breeders, and even if we do, we don't have a way to get them all off the island. We need help." She glanced at St. George beside her, and her jaw tightened. "We're going to need the Order."

Oh, fuck that.

I was about to follow up the thought with the actual words when Jade cut me off. "Listen to her, Riley," the Asian dragon urged. "We cannot do this ourselves, that is very clear. We have allied with the Order in the past. So far they have kept their word and have not hunted us down."

"That was different," I said. "We were saving their hides back then. They didn't have much of a choice. I sure as hell am not giving the Order of St. George the location of Talon's breeder females. What do you think will happen if we take a bunch of dragonslayers onto that island, where there will be countless female dragons with no way to escape? What do you think the *breeders* will do if they see St. George storming the facility? It'll be a fucking massacre."

"Normally, I would agree with you." Shockingly, this came

from the soldier, making Ember frown at him. He stood quietly at the edge of the table, gazing down at the map. "Giving the Order the location of the facility..." His brow furrowed. "It's a risky move. Riley is correct—St. George has always suspected Talon has a place where they keep many of their female dragons. In the Order..." He hesitated, as if reluctant to continue, before saying in a grave voice, "The highest priority was always taking out the female dragons, because without them, the race couldn't survive. In any other circumstances, I wouldn't go to the Order. Martin may be honorable, and some of his soldiers are beginning to realize that not all dragons are the same. But if St. George discovers that the largest population of female dragons is together in one spot..." He shook his head. "Riley has every right to be concerned.

"But," he added before I could feel vindicated, "these *aren't* normal circumstances. Ember is right—there are too few of us to fight a war. We need allies, and the Order of St. George might be the only ones who can help. They're scattered and broken, but they still have resources we could leverage. If we can get to the Order and convince them that we're better off standing together, we might have a chance to pull this off."

I tried very hard not to snarl at them both. "If they listen to us at all," I said. "And decide not to shoot us in the back of the head the second we set foot on that island."

"What else are we going to do, Riley?" Ember asked in a reasonable voice. "We don't have many choices. Talon is still out there trying to kill us and probably the Order, as well. They don't want any survivors, and if this keeps up, there will be no one left who can stand against the organization. How long before they decide they don't need the breeder dragons, too?"

"Dammit," I growled, clenching a fist. They were right; we

were out of options, and time was running out. As much as I hated it, it seemed we were going to have to ally with the dragonslayers one more time. "All right." I sighed. "But if this turns into a slaughter, that's it, do you hear me? I've already lost too many hatchlings to this stupid war. If St. George decides it would rather shoot us than try to stop Talon, I'm done with them for good, understand?" Neither of them answered, though Ember gave a solemn nod. "All right," I muttered. "So, how exactly are we going to get the Order of St. George to listen to us again without taking off our heads? Teaming up to survive the Night of Fang and Fire was one thing. How the hell are we going to convince an army of dragonslayers to rescue an island of dragons?"

"I'll contact Lieutenant Martin," the soldier said. "He, at least, will hear me out. And for the rest of the Order, we'll just have to play it by ear."

"Fine. Make the call, St. George. And let's hope this doesn't turn into a massacre."

Mist stirred, glancing at the ladder leading out of the storm cellar. "If we're done here," she said, and it was more of a statement than a question, "I'll excuse myself."

I raised an eyebrow at her. "Got somewhere to be, Mist?"

She gave me a somewhat evil smile that said she knew exactly what I was thinking. "Nowhere in particular," she said. And without waiting for me to reply, she walked across the room, swung onto the ladder and disappeared through the hatch.

Suspicion flared. I wanted to ask again about the mysterious employer that she was obviously going to contact. That he could so easily "acquire" the map to a top-secret island run by dragons seemed too good to be true. You didn't just happen to have those things lying around. But I knew Mist would never reveal his identity unless he gave the order himself, and that worried me. The ex-Basilisk wasn't working for Talon, but she wasn't working for us, either. This employer of hers might be helping us now, but if he suddenly decided to have her sabotage everything we were fighting for, she would do so without hesitation.

I needed to find out what she knew. Who her employer really was. And if Mist wasn't going to volunteer the information herself, then I would just have to get it some other way.

EMBER

"This is it," Garret murmured.

From the backseat I peered past his shoulder to gaze up at the church in the middle of the clearing. Not a tiny wooden thing with a single room, either; this was a large stone building with a high steepled roof, soaring arched windows and a bell tower. Its walls were covered in moss, the roof tinged green, but the windows were all intact, and despite the emptiness of it all, it looked like it had been somewhat taken care of.

"Martin and the others are inside," Garret said, gazing up at the building, too. "This is one of the Order's safe houses. If any of the other chapterhouses survived, they would rendezvous here."

"Great." Riley opened his door with a grimace. "All right, then, three dragons and an ex-soldier knocking on the Order's door. Let's get this over with."

"Have fun, kiddos," Wes said, waving cheerfully beside me in the backseat. "I'll just stay here and keep the car warm, in case the bullets start flying."

We piled out of the Jeep, the three dragons in question—
me, Riley and Mist. The only one missing was Jade, who had
offered to stay back at the farm and watch the hatchlings,
much to Riley's relief. I knew he would have been even more
reluctant to come if he'd had to leave his underground alone.
Following Garret, we walked toward the large wooden doors
at the top of the steps, where a guard waited beside the frame,
watching us approach. He wore normal clothes instead of a St.
George uniform, and would've looked like a regular person, if
not for the M14 held in both hands.

"Sebastian," he said as we stopped at the top of the stairs.
His voice and stance weren't overly hostile, but they definitely
weren't welcoming.

"Williams," Garret returned. "Are you here to escort us in?"

The other soldier snorted. "The lieutenant ordered me to
let you pass, you and your lizards." He jerked his head through
the door. "So get going. Last door on the right. He's waiting
for you."

We did as he instructed, ducking into a dim, cool hall that
soared high overhead. Light streamed through the tinted windows, casting colorful shadows over the floor, and a hush hung
in the air. It was almost peaceful here, despite the tension on
the faces of the few soldiers we passed, their gazes suspicious.
We reached the last door on the right without being challenged, and Garret knocked on the wood.

"Enter."

Lieutenant Martin stood in the corner of a tiny office, book-
shelves lining the wall and a worn-out desk beneath them.
He was speaking to a tall, lean soldier with short black hair,
and my heart leaped as I recognized him. Garret drew in a
short breath.

"Tristan," he said, his voice soft with relief. "You made it."

"Surprised?" The other soldier smirked at him. He had a bandage square taped to his temple, and the shadow of a bruise under one eye, but he was alive and on his feet, not motionless in a hospital bed. "I couldn't let you take all the glory, could I?"

"Sebastian." Martin came around the desk, and Tristan fell silent. His black eyes flicked over me and the others. "So, you're back with the lizards," he said in a neutral voice. "Has Talon made their move yet? Do we need to prepare for another attack?"

"No, sir," Garret said. "We…have a request this time. For the Order." Martin raised a brow, and Garret stepped aside. "I think it's best that Riley explain it."

Tristan and Martin looked to the rogue, who gave a heavy sigh, as if he still couldn't believe he was doing this, and came forward.

"We have a problem," he said without preamble. "And frankly, you have the same problem, St. George. We're in a war, but we are completely outnumbered and outgunned. We can't do anything against Talon, because we don't have enough bodies to take up the fight."

"I am well aware, dragon," Martin said. His voice was calm, not angry or indignant, even when speaking to his ancient enemy. I suddenly realized why Garret respected this man so much. "But the Order of St. George is stretched rather thin at the moment. Am I to assume that you know where we can find more allies?"

The rogue leader nodded. "That's pretty much the gist of it."

The lieutenant regarded him solemnly. "And am I also to assume that these…allies…are dragons?" he asked.

Riley sighed again. "Yeah," he muttered reluctantly. "They're dragons. Talon has an island, in the North Atlantic Ocean. It's...where they keep their breeder females. How many are there is anyone's guess, but they're the dragons they've chosen to produce fertile eggs for the organization, so at least a few."

Behind Martin, Tristan straightened, eyes widening. "Then it's true?" he asked in a breathless voice. "There really is a place where Talon keeps all its females."

Riley glared at him. "Yeah, St. George. There is, and it's a pretty shitty setup. Dragonells who fail in some way, or who defy the organization, get sent to the facility, to become broodmares for the rest of their lives. They never leave, never get off the island, never have the chance for a normal life. They're basically prisoners whose only purpose is to pop out eggs for Talon. That sound like a cushy life to you?"

"Dunno." Tristan smirked. "Private island, all meals provided, nothing to do but sleep, eat and breed? Sounds like heaven to me."

"St. Anthony," Martin warned before Riley could explode. "If you cannot behave yourself, you can leave." Tristan held up both hands, falling silent, and Martin turned back to Riley. "So, these breeders," he went on. "From your description, I would assume that they are unhappy with Talon's treatment of them, and would fight the organization if they could?"

"We hope so," I said as Riley still looked like he might snap Tristan's head off. "If we can get to the dragonells and free them, we think a few at least will take up the fight with Talon. But we don't have the numbers to stage a rescue. We can't get to the island on our own."

"And that is where you need us," Martin finished.

"Yes, sir." Garret nodded. "We hope that the Order would be willing to ally with us, on a more permanent basis. If we combine our people and resources, we'll have a better chance against Talon."

Martin didn't say anything, standing there with his arms crossed and his brow furrowed in thought. "Allying with the rogues would be tactically sound," he finally agreed, frowning. "However, there are those who would think the Order is being used, that you came to us solely for our help in rescuing these breeder dragons, and when that is done, you will either leave or turn on us."

"You know that's not true, sir," Garret said.

"I know," Martin agreed. "But I'm not the one you'll need to convince. I might lead this chapterhouse, but the soldiers are the ones who will be going into battle with you. And if others from St. George show up, what then? How will you convince them that you are not enemies, that you mean the Order no harm?"

"How about not burning this place to the damn ground?" Riley growled. "Or not tearing some idiot's face off when they keep threatening us? That feels like a pretty good indicator to me."

Martin's voice was flat. "It's not."

"What do you suggest, Lieutenant?" I asked.

He glanced at me. "If you could do a small task for the Order," he replied, "work with a few of the soldiers, that would be a sign of goodwill. At the very least, it would be a start."

"A small task," Riley repeated. "Of course. And let me guess, you have just the thing in mind, don't you?"

Martin turned and stepped back around his desk, where several sheets of paper lay across the surface. "The Order took a massive blow when the clones attacked," he said, picking up one of the documents. "We've been scrambling for supplies, resources, anything that will help defend us when we're attacked again. Recently, I received word about an item that could specifically help our cause. A weapon capable of firing shots with such velocity that it can punch through damn near anything. A high-powered rifle meant to pierce through tanks, armored cars, bunkers...and possibly the chest plates of a full-grown Adult dragon."

My eyes widened, and Riley gave an incredulous snort.

"Oh, a *dragon-killing* gun," he said, his voice thick with sarcasm. "That's definitely something the Order needs. We'll get right on that."

"If we are to fight Talon, we need all the resources we can get," Martin said firmly. "You said so yourself—we are vastly outnumbered and outgunned. We all saw the Adult clone the night the base was attacked. What if Talon has more of them? This might give us an edge against such enemies."

"Sadly, it doesn't exist quite yet." This came from Tristan, indicating the two of them had been discussing the weapon before we came in. I wasn't surprised. Tristan was the Order's best sniper; he would certainly be interested in a rifle capable of punching through the armor of a dragon. "It's a prototype, being designed by the military. But they're transporting it to another base tomorrow night. And since it's top secret and they don't want anyone catching wind of the prototype and possibly stealing it, they're doing it by train."

"By *train?*" Riley repeated. "Why?"

"Possibly to keep it hidden. Military escorts draw attention." Tristan shrugged. "And a train is harder to hijack, especially if there are armed guards in every car. Which there probably will be."

"So, let me get this straight." The rogue leader crossed his arms. "You want us to track down a train guarded by the US military, steal a prototype weapon specifically designed to kill dragons and hand it over to the Order of St. George?"

"Basically?" Tristan looked at Garret, who said nothing. "Yeah."

"If you do this," Martin added, "you will be sending a message to the rest of the Order that you are willing to help us, to stand with us. And we will be more inclined to help you, in return."

"Or we get ourselves killed, and you don't have to worry about it," Riley muttered. "No skin off your nose. I don't see you volunteering any of your men to help."

"That is not true," Martin replied calmly. "St. Anthony will be going with you."

"I... Sir?" Tristan glanced at the lieutenant in surprise.

Martin's lip curled in a faint smile. "You wanted to see the prototype, St. Anthony. Now's your chance." Tristan looked like he wanted to argue, but he was too well disciplined to talk back to his superior officer. Martin narrowed his eyes. "The dragons cannot be the only ones making the sacrifices, soldier," he said. "The Order of St. George, and this chapterhouse, is more honorable than that. We must meet them halfway at least. Go with Sebastian, procure the weapon and aid them in any way you can. That is an order, St. Anthony."

Tristan saluted. "Yes, sir."

"Uh, one question," Riley said. "How are we supposed to get on this armed train? I assume it'll be moving. And they'll certainly notice a car pulling up alongside it."

Martin gave that faint smile. "A stealthy approach is definitely recommended," he replied, and I suddenly realized what he was implying. "If I were to plan an attack, I would suggest a drop from above."

GARRET

"It's late," Tristan muttered. "That's not a good sign."

I glanced at him. There were four of us, sitting on or around an old black jeep, about two hundred yards from the tracks. Me, Tristan, Ember and Riley: two soldiers of St. George and two dragons waiting side by side. I could feel the subtle tension in the soldiers around me, both dragon and human; both sides uncomfortable with having the other so close. Riley and Tristan, in particular, seemed especially agitated. Probably because the first part of the mission involved dropping onto the train from dragonback, and to say neither seemed thrilled with that idea was a gross understatement. But as much as they might hate it, and each other, they would carry the mission through. Tristan because Martin had ordered it, and Riley because he knew we had to secure the Order's help to reach the facility. I just hoped we could get through this night with no incidents. Missions were difficult enough when your team liked and respected each other; forcing two lifelong enemies to work together was a much riskier operation.

Beside me, Ember was quiet, watching the tracks as we waited on the passenger's side of the jeep. Like me, she was dressed in black: black sweater, pants and a dark ski cap pulled over her bright red hair. Though for her part, she wouldn't need them much longer. She seemed calm, far calmer than Riley or even Tristan, though my ex-partner hid his anxiousness well. I could feel the subtle heat of her body next to mine, tempting me to pull her close, but I stifled those urges for now. The mission took priority. I could feel Tristan watching us sometimes, stealing a glance when he thought I wasn't looking, his expression caught between confusion and doubt. Like he was trying to puzzle something out, and neither of us were giving him the answers he expected.

Abruptly, Tristan's phone buzzed. He pulled it from his pocket and held it to his ear, then muttered a short "Roger that" a moment later. Lowering his arm, he glanced at me. "Ryan just gave the heads-up. Train's on its way now. We're about ten minutes from go time."

Ember took a deep breath and looked at Riley. "Guess that's our cue."

Riley gave a curt nod, and the two dragons moved into the shadows, ducking behind the copse of trees at our backs and vanishing from sight. Tristan let out a furtive breath and glanced at my side of the Jeep.

"This is crazy. You realize that, right?"

Apparently, his enthusiasm for the heist had dulled when he'd realized he had to be part of it. "Yeah. I know."

"We're robbing a train—a freaking train—on dragonback. Two soldiers of St. George, flying in on *dragons*, to pull off a train heist in the middle of nowhere. I mean, stop for a second and really think about how ludicrous that sounds."

I gave a half smile. "My whole year has sort of been like that." Pushing myself off the car door, I walked forward a few steps and gazed down the tracks, looking for the telltale glimmer of the train. Briefly, I thought of all the things that had happened to me since I'd fled the Order in the company of dragons. Meeting the rogues. Being kidnapped by an ancient Eastern dragon. Discovering Talon's clone army. Going to Brazil to meet the most powerful rogue in the world and the second-oldest dragon in existence. Any one of those things might give a normal soldier of St. George a nervous breakdown. All because I'd committed the strangest crime of all: falling in love with the enemy. "Actually, this is pretty far down the weirdness scale for me," I told Tristan, who arched his brows. "I'm so desensitized to it now I don't think I can be surprised anymore."

Tristan shook his head. "Damn, Sebastian," he muttered. "I don't even want to know what *you've* been doing the past few months. Living with the lizards." He snorted. "I can't imagine what that's like."

"They're not that different from us," I told him. For a moment, a small, tired part of me wondered if I was wasting my breath, but I stomped on that voice. Convincing the Order was not going to be done overnight. We had made an amazing amount of progress already; I couldn't expect Tristan to start trusting dragons after twenty-two years of trying to eliminate their entire race. "It's not like I was living with robots or wild dogs," I went on.

"You've said that before," Tristan muttered.

"And I'm even more certain now." I turned, narrowing my eyes at him. "I've lived with these dragons for months," I said, holding his gaze. "I've fought beside them, argued with them, rescued a few from Talon and the Order and had my own ass saved a few times. I've spent more hours with these dragons than anyone else in the history of St. George ever has. I think I should know them, and their intentions, by now."

"Easy, tiger." Tristan held up his hands. "I'm not disagreeing with you. And...holy shit."

I glanced calmly over my shoulder as two long, scaly forms prowled out of the shadows under the trees, their eyes glowing yellow and green in the darkness. They appeared without noise or warning, silent despite their relatively large size, wings and claws making no sound as they glided over the dirt. Tristan straightened, one hand dropping to his sidearm, making Cobalt curl a lip at him.

"Don't be stupid, St. George," the rogue growled, breaking the silence. With a snort, he stalked around the other side of the jeep, subtly putting the vehicle between himself and the soldier. "I'm already hating this enough as it is."

My ex-partner blinked, probably from hearing the sarcastic voice and tone coming out of a dragon's mouth. Another reminder that Riley and the dragon were the same—same creature, same personality—just wearing different forms.

Ember padded up behind me and laid her chin on my shoulder as she gazed at the tracks. Her scales were warm, not heavy or uncomfortable, and I could see the reflection of her glowing dragon eyes in the corner of my own gaze. I felt Tristan staring at us again, and wondered what he thought about having a dragon's fire-breathing jaws and lethal fangs a breath away from your throat. I could almost hear him squirming uncomfortably against the jeep, thinking I was tempting fate. I felt nothing. Nothing but the calm stillness before a mission. If anything, the steady breathing of the dragon beside me, her dark wings casting us in even more shadow, only made me certain of our success. She knew what she had to do. This wasn't anything new or strange. We'd been through so many crazy circumstances together that having a large crimson dragon leaning against me felt perfectly normal. Ember the dragon was no different than Ember the human. I trusted her with my life.

Now, if Tristan and Cobalt could tolerate each other long enough to get this done, and not kill each other on the way, things would be perfect.

"There it is," Ember murmured.

My senses sharpened, and I raised my head, followed her gaze. A distant spotlight was cutting through the darkness, winking in and out through the trees. I could hear it, suddenly, the clank of metal on iron tracks, the rattle of dozens of cars, and I breathed slowly to control my heartbeat.

"All right," Cobalt growled, and took a breath, as if he was psyching himself up to do something horribly unpleasant, like plunge his head into a bucket of spiders. "I guess it's time. Let's get this circus show on the road."

I double-checked to make certain I had everything I needed as Ember stepped forward and lowered her wings, crouching slightly as she did. Careful to avoid her spines, I swung onto her back, settling in front of her wing joints. For a moment, I felt a weird sense of déjà vu. The last time I'd done this was the night Ember and Cobalt had broken me out of the Western Chapterhouse hours before my execution could've taken place. This was a very different scenario. So much had changed.

I glanced at Tristan, who was standing next to Cobalt with an uncertain look on his face, as if contemplating the best way to mount a dragon. Cobalt, for his part, was making it as easy as he could; his wings were lowered and the frill that went down his back and neck had been folded flat to his spine. The blue dragon stared straight ahead, unmoving, only the tip of his tail beating an irritated rhythm in the dust, as Tristan struggled with the problem. Finally, Cobalt let out an impatient hiss.

"Are you waiting for a saddle, St. George? Our ride is almost here. Let's go."

"Shit," Tristan muttered, and threw himself onto the dragon's back. He scrabbled gracelessly for a moment, trying to find the best position, before settling in front of the wings as I had done. "Ow, dammit, watch where your spines are poking," he growled as Cobalt smirked back at him. "I'm not planning to have kids, but I'd still like the option."

Cobalt snickered. "I'll try not to come to any sudden stops."

Ember raised her head and peered at me, her eyes a solemn green in the darkness. "Ready?" she asked. I nodded.

The train approached, rumbling along the track, its single light piercing the darkness before it. I felt Ember's muscles coil, felt the ripple of power that went through the dragon as her wings unfurled to either side of me like sails. She crouched, and I braced myself as she launched herself into the air with one powerful downward flap. Wind blasted me, tearing at my hair and clothes, as we rose into the air, the ground falling swiftly away into blackness. I kept myself pressed low over Ember's neck, gritting my teeth as we climbed, my arms wrapped tightly around her neck.

Ember leveled out, her wing beats becoming less frequent and powerful as she eased into a glide, buoyed on the wind currents. Carefully, I sat up and looked around for Tristan.

Cobalt soared alongside us a few yards to the right, wings outstretched, tail streaming behind him. It was hard to tell from the distance and the movement of the dragons, but I thought there was a smirk on his scaly face. Behind his shoulders, Tristan was still flat against the dragon's body, arms wrapped around his neck in a death grip. His eyes weren't closed, but his jaw was clenched, and his gaze was fixed firmly to a spot between Cobalt's horns, as if he were refusing to look down. I bit the corner of my lip, not knowing whether to feel sympathy or amusement. Abruptly, his gaze flickered to me, a death glare shooting from his eyes. The howling wind would blow away our voices, but I didn't have to hear him to know what he was thinking. *Laugh and I will kill you.*

The train snaked away below us, cutting a silent path to the north. Ember angled a wingtip down, and we glided after it.

I bent forward, pressing close to the dragon's neck as she dropped lower, wings beating occasionally to stay aloft. Winds buffeted us, and Ember wobbled in the gusts coming off the train, but we soared over the caboose and dropped even lower, skimming just ten or so feet from the moving rail cars.

The prototype is in the sixth car from the engine, I thought, remembering Martin's instructions to us before we left. *According to my sources, the prototype and the cars immediately adjacent to it will be under guard, but the rest of the train should be empty. If you want to get the drop on them, the best way is to go through one of the roof hatches of the cars before it.*

The engine and tinder car loomed ahead of us. Ember drew up, then back-flapped her wings three times and dropped from the air. Her talons hit the roof with a metallic thump, and she instantly splayed her feet to keep her balance on the moving car.

Carefully, I slid off the dragon's back and took a moment to find my balance, as well. The train wasn't moving very fast, but the rooftop was narrow, and the car shook and rattled as it continued down the tracks. I crouched next to Ember as

Cobalt and Tristan landed behind us, the scrape of claws on the metal roof echoing over the wind.

Ember swung her head around to face me, concern shining from her green dragon eyes. "You got this, soldier boy?" she asked, her breath warm even through the shrieking wind. "I still don't like the thought of leaving you here. What if you need backup?"

"We'll be fine." I glanced at Tristan as he slid down and crouched low as I had done. "This is part of the plan. We're not here to fight the whole train. We just need to get in, get to the prototype and get out quickly. It shouldn't be too heavily guarded—no one is expecting an attack, especially one where people drop onto the roof from dragons." I half smiled at her, and she rolled her eyes. "Just follow the train and stay close," I continued, putting a hand on her shoulder. "Be ready to come swooping in when it's time. If everything goes according to plan, we'll be leaving the train from car six in approximately ten minutes."

Her eyes narrowed. "And if everything does not go according to plan?"

Tristan snorted, keeping his body bent horizontal to the roof as he joined us. "Then we'll still need that extraction," he told the dragon. "Just double time."

"Oh, sure, we can do that," Cobalt added, creeping behind him like a giant blue cat, his wings fluttering wildly in the wind. "Go ahead and hurl yourself off the roof of the train, St. George. I promise, I'll try my best to catch you."

Ember sighed. "Be careful, Garret," she whispered, drawing away. The wind ripped at me almost instantly, cold and eager to push me off the edge. "Don't get killed over this. We'll be close. If you're not on the roof in ten minutes, I'm coming in after you."

"Ten minutes," I told her. "See you then."

Ember crouched, half opened her wings and sprang off the car, blasting me with wind as she rose into the air. A second later, Cobalt did the same, and the two dragons soared up into the darkness until they were lost from sight.

I glanced at Tristan, and he nodded. Now it was our turn. Ember and Cobalt had done their part in getting us here unseen. It was up to us to find the prototype, subdue any opposition guarding it and get out before the rest of the guards discovered what was going on.

We crept along the roof, keeping our footsteps light and our shoulders braced against the wind, until we reached the hatch at one of the corners. Our objective was two cars down, but there was a guard car between us, with armed soldiers inside. Even if Ember and Riley had been as quiet as they could, two dragons with a pair of riders landing on the roof of a metal car with soldiers still inside would have drawn attention and given us away. We couldn't swoop onto the prototype car, not without alerting the US military to the existence of dragons. We had to take care of the guards before we went after the prototype.

As Tristan pulled open the hatch and shined a flashlight into the pitch-blackness within, a shadow overhead caught my attention. I glanced up to see two dragon-shaped blurs against the night sky, dark wings outstretched as they glided after the train. Ember and Cobalt, right where they'd said they would be.

"Clear," Tristan said at my shoulder. "Let's move."

I switched on my flashlight, pulled out my weapon with my other hand and dropped through the hatch.

I hit a metal floor in a crouch, then quickly scanned my surroundings for enemies. The narrow space was empty, the walls bare. I stepped aside as Tristan landed next to me with a barely audible thump, and we crept toward the door at the end of the box. The metal barrier was latched but not locked, and we quickly slipped through onto the platform of the next car, pressing ourselves beside the doorframe. After a moment of silence, I knelt at the door and opened a compartment on my vest to pull out a long black tube, while Tristan stood at the frame and watched my back.

Silently, I fed the snake cam through the crack beneath the door, watching the screen as I turned the night vision lens to scan the room beyond. There were two soldiers standing in the room about fifteen feet from the door, talking to each other. Their postures were relaxed, though both carried M16s in their hands. They obviously weren't expecting an attack, but we'd have to be quick. If we ignored these two guards, they would engage us while we were trying to make our escape.

I pulled the snake cam out and held up two fingers to Tristan, indicating the room beyond. He nodded and swung out of his pack, then pulled out strips of breaching charges before handing them to me. When the charges had been placed over the locks and hinges, we retreated back to the first car, and Tristan held up three fingers. Two. One.

Both of us turned away as the boom of an explosion rocked the night and sent smoke billowing from the door. Before the smoke had even cleared, Tristan rushed to the frame, kicked in the crippled door and tossed a flashbang into the room.

Shouts of alarm came from inside, just as a retina-burning flash pierced the darkness, followed by a muffled boom of energy. I lunged through the frame and saw a pair of dazed, reeling soldiers just before Tristan and I slammed into them. My soldier didn't resist as I snaked an arm around his throat and sent him into unconsciousness.

Lowering the limp sentry to the floor, I looked up at Tristan, who nodded grimly as he released the second unconscious guard. That took care of this car, but the one with our objective in it was surely going to be more of a challenge. Any soldiers in it had certainly heard the explosions caused by charges and flashbangs and would know that they were under attack. They'd be ready for us.

Swiftly, we moved to the other end of the car. As we pressed to either side of the frame, Tristan nodded at me, and I quickly pushed open the door.

A hail of machine gun fire rang out. I jerked back as a storm of bullets peppered the frame, sparking off the railings and metal walls. Apparently, the guards had decided to take the initiative and not wait for us to kick in the door. From the sounds of the weapons, two soldiers stood to either side of the frame, firing M16s in sharp three-round bursts at us. Tristan and I pressed back behind the doorframe, sparks flying around us, and waited for an opportunity to move. I had a flashbang in hand, but the soldiers were giving us no chance to counterstrike. If I poked any body part out of cover now, I would get a bullet through it.

There was a roar overhead, a swooping of leathery wings, and a curtain of fire suddenly appeared between us and the soldiers. It blazed against the darkness, blindingly hot and intense, and the storm of gunfire ceased amid loud cursing and cries of alarm. The shadow swooped up and out of sight, too fast to be seen clearly, but for a few seconds the soldiers gaped after it, stunned. Long enough for me to pop out and hurl the flashbang at their feet.

The force of the explosion threw one soldier into the wall, where he collapsed, motionless. The other staggered back, reeling, and Tristan leaped over the space between cars, kicked him in the stomach and followed with a savage right hook to the guard's temple that knocked him senseless.

The way to our objective was clear. Quickly, we ducked through the door, wary for more soldiers lying in ambush, but the car was empty save for a narrow wooden table in the middle of the floor. A lamp sat atop it, bathing the table in a dim orange glow, and in the center of the light lay a long case of glimmering metal.

Tristan let out a breath, reached out and pulled the case toward him. It was almost certainly our objective, but we had to make sure. The case was padlocked shut, but a pair of heavy-duty bolt cutters took care of that problem. The latch released with a click, and Tristan yanked it open.

"Oh, yes," he murmured as the lid fell back. A long, *long* black barrel lay gleaming in the cutout foam padding, much larger than a standard rifle barrel and three times as thick. It was obviously meant to be fired from a stand or tripod, as it would be far too heavy for a single person to lift, much less aim. The rest of the weapon had been disassembled and lay in pieces in various foam cutouts, but Tristan stroked the length of the barrel with an almost maniacal glint in his eye. "Hello, beautiful," he purred. "Would you like to come home with me?"

I rolled my eyes. "Hey, Romeo, ask it to dinner later. We gotta move."

Almost at the same time, a bang came from the door at the

far end of the car, and angry voices echoed through the barrier. More guards were on their way.

"Shit." Tristan closed the case with a snap, then hauled it off the table. It was almost too big for a single person to carry, but he set his jaw and started for the door. "Let's go."

We left the car, hurried to the ladder and together managed to drag the prototype case onto the roof. Wind buffeted us, cold and savage, and the tops of the empty train cars stretched on in either direction.

"All right," Tristan panted, holding tightly to the case as he scanned the sky. "Where the hell are those lizards? We're sort of sitting ducks out here."

"They'll be here—"

"Freeze!"

I looked up. Three soldiers had ascended the roof of the car from the other side, and a pair of M16s were now pointed in our direction. One of the men, the one out front, looked to be a captain or sergeant, for he was dressed differently than the near-identical soldiers behind him. I raised my hands as he approached, the two guards flanking him, to give me a hard smile.

"Well, well. End of the line, it seems." His voice had a trace of a Southern accent, breathy and somewhat smug. "I guess I'll have to give you props for this ballsy little heist. Though, for the life of me, I don't know where you thought you were going to go, unless your plan was to sprout wings and fly away."

Tristan snorted, managing to turn a laugh into a rather painful-sounding cough that didn't fool anyone. The officer's eyes narrowed, and pointed a black handgun at my face. "Put down the case and step away, now," he demanded. "Nice and slow, and keep your hands where I can see them." When neither of us moved, his voice turned hard. "Boy, don't make me shoot you," he said as the soldiers behind him took aim. "It's over. There's nowhere to go. Your choices are either death by jumping or death by lead poisoning. Or you can surrender now and live awhile longer. Personally, I'd take the last option."

There was a ripple of shadow over the trees, and I smiled. "One more," I said, making the officer frown. "There is one more choice."

"Yep," Tristan agreed, the smirk on his face indicating that he'd seen it, too. He kept a tight hold of the case as he nodded to the soldiers. "Time to go. Sorry, boys, but we're doing you a favor, trust me."

The officer's frown turned to a scowl. "All right, that's enough of that. Shoot—"

A roar boomed overhead. The two soldiers whirled, and managed to prostrate themselves on the roof as the two dragons came swooping in. The officer screamed, raising his gun to fire, but was hit by a passing wing and knocked to his back, barely stopping himself from going off the edge. Cobalt didn't slow; I heard Tristan's yelp of surprise as the blue dragon grabbed both him and the weapon case and flapped away over the trees. A half second later, talons closed around my arms, my feet left the roof and I watched the train fall away beneath me as Ember rose into the air, beating her wings furiously, and we soared over the tree line and disappeared into the night.

EMBER

"You should have had them destroyed!"

That was the first thing we heard upon returning to Order headquarters, a loud, angry voice echoing down the hall to the command room. I paused, as did Garret, Riley and Tristan, listening as the indignant, hate-filled words carried through the corridor.

"What has gotten into you, Lieutenant? Speaking to dragons? Letting them into our ranks? Promising to *help* them? Can you be any more blasphemous?" The voice turned into a sneer. "You might as well sacrifice a goat and try to summon the devil himself."

I sighed and, beside me, felt Garret tense. We did not need this right now. We'd just gotten to the point where at least some in the Order didn't view us as soul-sucking demons. For the first time, dragons and the Order had worked together on something that wasn't a life-or-death situation. The last thing we needed was someone trying to destroy the very shaky truce we'd established.

I shot a glance at the others, all of whom looked as grim as I felt. Garret and Tristan were tense and had that look of wondering if they should go forward or not. Riley's mouth was twisted into a smirk, but it was one of his dangerous ones, and his eyes were hard.

"That's Lieutenant Ward," Tristan mused, sounding like he'd just stepped in something nasty on the sidewalk. "I didn't know he survived. He must've just gotten here." He and Garret shared a somber glance, and Tristan blew out a breath. "Well, this is going to be interesting."

"Who is this bastard?" Riley wanted to know.

"He's the lieutenant of the Eastern Chapterhouse," Garret answered. "He can be very...verbose in his beliefs."

Tristan snorted. "That's putting it mildly. When you graduate the Academy, the Eastern Chapterhouse is where you're sent if your teachers didn't like you." A particularly loud portion of the rant echoed though the hallway, and he winced. "Maybe this isn't the best time to announce we just robbed the military," he suggested in a wry voice. "I say we do a tactical retreat and come back when Ward has cooled off a bit."

The officer's voice rang through the corridor again, berating Martin for not shooting us all in the back of the head as he should have done, and I narrowed my eyes. "No," I said. "If we let this continue, word could spread. The other soldiers might start to listen, and then everything we've accomplished so far will be for nothing. We'll be back to square one." I gazed down the hallway and set my jaw. "Besides, I want to talk to him. I want to look him in the eye and have him say those things to my face."

"He will, Ember," Garret warned softly. "Ward's hatred for dragons is something even the Order takes note of, and he doesn't mince words. It's probably going to be very ugly, if he doesn't try to shoot us on the spot. Not that Martin will allow that to happen, but I do want to warn you."

"I know." I nodded at him. "And I'm not expecting to change his mind. I just want him to see us. Even if it's just to hurl insults, he'll be talking to us instead of trying to slaughter us on sight. I want him to know that there's actually a person on the other end of his bullets, not a mindless animal."

"Oh, good." Riley sighed as we started down the hall again. "That's what I wanted to do today. Get screamed at by a dragon-hating fanatic. This is going to be all kinds of fun."

"For you and us both, dragon," Tristan muttered. "Being known as a dragonlover around here is almost as bad as being a lizard. Just ask Garret. He knows, isn't that right, partner?" Garret shrugged, but Tristan continued to watch Riley, the corner of his lip curling in a smirk. "The trick is not to stare directly at them when they're screaming in your face, and think happy thoughts."

Riley snorted. "Like melting their face off with fire?"

"Well, I think of girls, but whatever floats your boat."

As they were talking, Garret reached down and took my hand, strong fingers curving around mine. He squeezed once, gently, before letting go—a quiet reassurance that he was still there, that he had my back. I smiled at him, and we entered the command room.

"Lieutenant." Martin's voice, calm and resolute, drifted to us as we stepped through the frame. "I understand your concern, but there is no cause for—"

"Oh, you understand my concern, do you?" interrupted another voice, the same one that we'd heard in the corridor. It belonged to a tall, muscular man with cropped blond hair and a pale mustache beneath a very large nose. He wore the black-and-gray uniform of the Order, the familiar red cross on a white shield standing out on one shoulder. Though I noticed the sleeves were slightly singed and torn at the cuffs. "You understand my concern that one of our lieutenants has apparently turned into a dragonlover? That he has allowed demons into the Order's sacred affairs? That, in our darkest hour, the hour we must stand fast against our enemies and not bend, our sanctum has been violated and our soldiers are in danger of corruption because their superior officer has betrayed them, and the Code, to the very creatures we swore to wipe out?"

"Man, he sure likes to hear himself talk, doesn't he?" Riley muttered. "I feel like he needs a pulpit and a choir behind him screaming, *'Hallelujah!'* every third sentence."

Beside him, Tristan had a quiet but very intense coughing fit, turning away and putting a fist to his mouth. It did not go unnoticed, as the men finally looked up and spotted us.

"Sebastian." Martin's tone was as calm as ever, nodding to Garret and the other soldier. "St. Anthony. You've returned." He nodded at the glowering man standing across the table. "I think you know Lieutenant Ward of the Eastern Chapterhouse?"

"Yes, sir," Garret said as Tristan echoed him. "I believe we met last year."

Lieutenant Ward stared at Garret, pale eyes glittering with contempt. "Garret Xavier Sebastian," he announced in tone of mock grandeur. "The Perfect Soldier. The traitor who ran off with dragons." His fat lip curled as he stared Garret down, ignoring me and everyone else in the room. "And now you're back, and it appears that your taint is spreading. That this foul brand of lunacy is affecting even those who are supposed to lead." Ward shot Martin a quick glare of contempt before turning on Garret again. "Were it up to me, Sebastian, I would execute you on the spot," he said, making me stiffen. "That is what the Order demands of traitors and dragon converts. That is what you deserve. But it appears I have been voted down. That you have somehow convinced Martin and the rest of your chapterhouse to welcome evil into your ranks. So be it." He made a vague gesture, as if washing his hands of all of us. "I have no choice but to go along with this travesty. But make no mistake." One thick finger rose, pointed in Garret's face. "Once the Order is back on its feet, once we have dealt with Talon and have slaughtered these demons that have been sent against us, you and all your sympathizers will be brought to justice. I will make certain of it."

Garret's voice was quiet, unruffled. I was amazed he could speak to this disgusting human without swearing in his face. "The Order of St. George has been scattered, sir," he stated. "There is virtually no one left but us. Talon is on the move, and St. George, what's left of it, cannot stop them alone. We're going to need all the allies we can get."

Ward snorted. "Where are your lizards, Sebastian?" he demanded. "Where are the devils that Martin claims are helping us? Are they afraid of a true son of the Order? Bring them to me. I would like to see these dragons who would have us believe they are working against Talon."

"You're looking at them," I said, trying very hard to keep the growl out of my voice. "There's no need for threats, Lieutenant. We're standing right here."

Ward's gaze jerked to me. For a moment, his pale eyes widened as he took me in. "You?" he said in disbelief as I raised my chin and stared him down. "You're a girl. A child."

"Yes, because dragons hatch fully formed out of the egg," Riley broke in, the smirk on his face not quite able to mask his anger. "Already grown and hungry for human souls. They certainly don't start life as innocents. Where would the Order be if they knew half the dragons they're slaughtering are kids who haven't hurt anyone?"

"Innocents?" Ward's face twisted so hard I thought he might be having a seizure. "That's like saying fire is cold or a wolf is a vegetarian. There is no such thing as an innocent dragon. I don't care if they're five or five hundred, every soulless lizard will get the exact same treatment—a bullet to the back of its skull. If I can kill them while they're young, that's one less dragon to plague humanity when it's an Adult."

I felt Riley's fury rise like an inferno, felt the subtle shift of energy that said Cobalt was very close to the surface, ready to burst out and char this insufferable human to ash. "You wanted to see us," I said quickly, before things spiraled out of control and someone ended up shot or incinerated. "Here we are. Was it actually for a purpose, or did you just want to throw insults in our faces?"

Ward's jaw tightened. "I would prefer bullets to insults, but that will have to wait for the moment." His pale eyes narrowed, and he stepped around the table, looming over me. I felt Garret lean close, as well, his presence bolstering me as I stared up at the lieutenant. "Why are you here, dragon?" the officer demanded. "Martin says you are not part of Talon, but even if that were true, it does not explain why you have chosen to seek out your enemies. Why did you risk coming here? What do you hope to gain from the Order of St. George?"

I met his gaze. "Hasn't Martin told you?"

"Some things." The officer's voice was unyielding. "But I

want to hear it from the dragon's mouth. I want to hear it from you."

"Well, that's too bad," Riley broke in. "Because I don't feel like telling you a damn thing, St. George. Maybe if you hadn't called me a soulless demon we'd be more inclined to share. As is, I'm not about to reveal anything to someone who might shoot us all in the head, or the back."

I hesitated. I could feel Riley's gaze burning the side of my face, hard and angry. *Don't tell him anything,* it was saying. Certainly I could understand his reluctance. Letting this man set foot on an island of breeder dragons seemed like a very bad idea, as was letting him know that we now had what could be a very powerful weapon in our possession. How much had Martin already revealed? If he hadn't told Ward our plans, I didn't want to be the one to fill him in.

I exhaled. If we refused to say anything, that would only foster more mistrust and enmity between dragons and St. George. I didn't like this man; in fact, I was pretty sure I hated him. He was everything that was wrong with the Order, all their the bigotry, elitism and narrow-mindedness rolled into one awful human being. I didn't want to answer any of his questions. But that wouldn't help our cause. It wouldn't help the numerous breeder dragons trapped on Talon's horrible island. I knew that, around this human, I had to be very cautious, but I could still attempt to be civil.

I felt a slight brush against my arm—Garret, quietly letting me know he was still there. I drew strength from his touch. *Garret would be able to do this,* I thought. Even in the face of constant, blatant hatred from the very people he used to know, when they were screaming for his execution and calling him all sorts of terrible things, he could still be calm and polite.

I would never have his patience, but I knew that there were issues larger than myself and my feelings. For now, anyway, I would be the bigger person and not tell this human what he could go do with himself.

I took a furtive breath and met the officer's gaze again. "We came here because we need the Order's help," I said, ignoring Riley's disgusted growl. "Because Talon is after us, too, and we thought combining forces with St. George would give us both a better chance at survival." There, that was answering the question without revealing any details. Unfortunately, Ward was smarter than he looked.

"That tells me nothing," he stated. "Dragons would not seek out the Order of St. George on a whim, not without some sort of plan. Not without some kind of negotiating power. If you came to us, you either have something we want, or you're planning something and you need the Order's help. Why risk it otherwise?" His gaze suddenly went to Tristan, as if he'd just noticed the large black case the soldier was holding, and his eyes narrowed. "What are you not telling me, dragon?"

"Lieutenant Ward." Fortunately, Martin broke in at that moment, gesturing to a seat at the table. "If you would—I was just about to explain the situation." Ward glowered, but he finally backed off. Martin spared a glance at Tristan, then turned to Garret.

"Am I to assume that the mission was a success?"

"Yes, sir." Garret nodded once. "We have the prototype."

"Good." Martin gestured to Tristan. "Leave it on the table, St. Anthony."

Tristan complied, giving the case a final longing glance as he walked away. "So, does this mean the Order is going to help us?" I asked, and Ward made a strangled noise of disgust, eyes flashing contempt as he glared at the other officer. Thankfully, he didn't say anything, though Martin sighed heavily, bowing his head as he braced his arms on the table surface.

"It appears so," he murmured, almost too soft to be heard. "Dragons and the Order, working together. Heaven help us all." There was a pause, as if he was taking a deep breath, or making peace with that notion, before looking up. "Lieutenant." He turned to Ward. "As you have already guessed, the Western Chapterhouse has accepted the aid of a group of dragons not allied with Talon. The reasons for this are severalfold—we need more bodies than we currently have to stand against the organization. These dragons have inside knowledge about Talon and how it works. They have already proved instrumental in acquiring something that could help us greatly in the war effort."

Not to mention, we did save you from the first wave of Talon's clones, I thought, though it seemed petty to voice it out loud. Ward made a disgusted noise and crossed his arms. Martin ignored it.

"As part of this deal," the lieutenant went on, "the Western Chapterhouse has agreed to aid them in their efforts against Talon. You don't have to be part of this, Lieutenant," he added before Ward could say anything. "The Eastern Chapterhouse can refuse to help, and it will be well within your rights to do so. But know that the dragons here are under my protection, and I will not permit anyone, soldier or otherwise, to harm, threaten or harass them in any way. Please make that known to your men. The last thing we need is a battle within our own walls."

"You goddamn fool," Ward growled. "You've made a deal with the devil, and have dragged the rest of us into it, as well.

What is this aid you've promised, because I'll be damned if I'm letting a group of lizards out of my sight."

"A rescue mission," Martin said calmly. "We're going to free a group of dragons Talon is holding captive."

I thought Ward might explode. His neck bulged, his eyes got huge and his face turned an interesting shade of red. "Are you…fucking serious?" he roared, making me wince. "Not only are we accepting help from these monsters, we're going to free them, too? Turn more dragons loose on the world, that's what you're planning?"

"You don't have to come," Riley said, that dangerous smirk crossing his face again. "If rescuing a bunch of soulless lizards is against your moral code, feel free to stay behind. In fact, I encourage it. It would be such a crying shame if you didn't make it back."

Ward shot him a look of black hatred, and I winced. Riley's anger, though justified, was not helping things. "Lieutenant Martin," Ward continued, his voice stiff and ugly. "Just so we are perfectly clear. Do you truly intend to help these monsters?"

"Yes," Martin replied firmly. "I gave my word, and the Order is in desperate need of allies, Lieutenant. These dragons have agreed to help us fight Talon, and right now, I will take their aid and the hope of survival over following the Code of St. George."

"Very well," Ward growled. "Then I have no choice but to be a part of this. Someone must be there to make sure these things don't slit our throats from behind. Though let it be on your conscience when they inevitably turn on us."

"Funny," Riley said. "I was just thinking the same thing."

Ward didn't deign to answer. Spinning on a heel, he marched

from the room, slamming the door behind him. The frame rattled in the wake of the lieutenant's exit, and he was gone.

Martin sighed.

"Sebastian," he continued, as if determined to ignore everything that had happened in the past five minutes. "Good work on retrieving the prototype. I did some research while you were away. The island you've described does indeed exist, and appears to be privately owned. Look here." He pointed to the table, where the map of the island lay unfolded at the center. "Judging from the map," Martin continued as we crowded forward, "it has a docking station at the west point for food and supplies, and a guard tower at the north, south and east points of the island. But as far as I can tell, the rest of the fence line is unpatrolled."

"So getting in won't be an issue," Riley guessed. "The challenge will be leaving the island with a bunch of dragons in tow, some of whom might not be able to Shift into human form." He grimaced and looked at Martin. "Did you happen to find a solution to that little problem? How we're going to safely transport a large number of dragons across the ocean without anyone seeing them?"

"The Order still has a few resources at its disposal," Martin replied with a thoughtful look at the map. His brow furrowed, and he nodded slowly. "It will be difficult, but I think I have a way." He paused, as if thinking, then glanced up at Riley. "I assume you'll want this done as soon as possible."

Riley nodded. "As soon as we can."

"All right." The lieutenant stepped back from the table. "I'll need to make a few more calls, phone in a few favors, but if everything works out, we'll be ready to go in under a week. I can't promise anything more than that."

"You've already agreed to more than we'd hoped for," I said, making him raise a brow at me. "Thank you, Lieutenant."

He gave a grim smile. "Don't thank me yet, dragon. If this mission is to succeed, *all* its members must work together without fail. That means dragons and soldiers of St. George. Talk to me afterward, if any of us are still alive. St. Anthony..." He looked at Tristan, who snapped to attention. "If you would kindly join me in my office with the prototype. I would like to hear the mission details while we are examining this weapon in private. Sebastian?" He glanced at me. "Join us when you can."

"Yes, sir."

They left the room, Tristan retrieving the prototype from the desk, leaving me to think about the upcoming mission, and how unlikely it was that everyone would get along, work together and pull this off without a hitch. Ward's arrival and insistence upon coming with us to the island certainly threw everything into question.

Riley shook his head and stepped back. "Well, I need to find Wes," he announced, glancing at me and Garret. "Let him know what's going on, see if he can uncover anything useful. If that Lieutenant Loudmouth and his men are coming with us, I want to know everything we can about that island so we can at least be prepared if they decide to shoot us in the back."

"What about Mist?" Garret suggested. "She's the one who gave us the map. Maybe she knows something."

Riley's face darkened.

"Yeah," he muttered, not sounding at all convinced. "Mist. An ex-Talon agent with a mystery employer backing us up with the soldiers of St. George. That gives me all sorts of confidence that this mission is going to go well." He ran a hand down his face, grimacing. "Maybe you can talk to her, Firebrand," he suggested, glancing at me. "See if you can find out who this mystifying employer of hers is. I haven't had any luck dragging it out of her."

"Me?" I asked. "You're the fellow Basilisk. What makes you think I'd have a better chance?"

"Because you're the one with the knack for making people do things they don't want to do."

"Thanks," I said sarcastically.

"Not a criticism, Firebrand." Riley gave a wry grin and gestured to the door Martin and Ward had gone through. "Look around you. Do you think any of us want to be here? Do you think any one of us are happy having to work with people whom we've considered our enemies for hundreds of years? Dragons allying with the Order of St. George? If you suggested that to anyone a year ago, they'd either be horrified or they'd think you'd gone completely bonkers." He shrugged. "And yet, here we are, working together. Trying to save more of us. Because of you.

"So, yeah," he finished, stepping toward the door. "If anyone has a shot of pulling information, kicking and screaming, out of Mist, I'd give you a better chance than me. Of course, if you don't want to feel like you're beating your head repeatedly against a brick wall, that's fine, too. She'll slip up someday."

"Watch yourself out there," Garret warned. "Lieutenant Ward won't try anything directly, but a lot of his men have the same convictions he does. If they know there's a dragon walking around..."

"Oh, don't worry, St. George." Riley smiled grimly. "I always watch my back around genocidal maniacs. And I'll try not to eat anyone who tries to fuck with me. Best I can promise at the moment." His gaze slid to me and turned grave. "You be careful, too, Firebrand," he cautioned. "All it takes is a single loud voice to start a riot, and this place feels like a tinderbox right now. One spark, and everything will go up in flames."

With that dire warning, he left the room, leaving me to wonder if I'd done the right thing in seeking the Order's help, after all.

GARRET

I'd never actively disliked Lieutenant Jacob Ward, until now.

I'd heard the stories, of course. We all had. His reputation was infamous among the soldiers of the Order, fed by rumor and egged on by the man himself. Drills that routinely made soldiers pass out from exhaustion, pain or dehydration. Punishments ranging from cleaning his boots with your tongue to doing push-ups in full gear for three hours straight. How his personal goal was to make every new recruit cry at least once during their first week at the chapterhouse. In the past, I'd never looked forward to missions where we had to partner with Ward's men, because the soldiers of the Eastern Chapterhouse eventually developed the cruelty and ruthless nature of their lieutenant. They were superb dragonslayers, brutal and efficient in the field, but their insatiable bloodlust, and the way they treated anyone smaller or weaker than themselves, sometimes made them difficult to work with. I had been the target of their hazing once, when a pair of soldiers took personal offense to my growing reputation and tried to "put me in my place." Two broken jaws and a dislocated elbow later, they'd known I was someone to leave alone, but I'd had to be just as brutal and vicious as them to get my point across.

I wondered how many of those soldiers had survived and were here right now. I wondered what would happen if they did try to start something with any of the dragons here, particularly Riley.

I grimaced. It wouldn't end well, for either side. Not that I doubted my dragon teammates could take care of themselves when faced with a soldier of the Order, but if tempers were lost and violence erupted, it could shatter everything we were trying to accomplish. We needed the Order's help, but you could only push a dragon so far. And, former comrades or not, if any one of them hurt the girl across from me, they would end up in the infirmary with a lot more than a broken jaw.

Ember, I noticed, had grown quiet. She hadn't moved from the edge of the table, but was gazing at the map spread across the center. Her fingers reached down, tracing the edge of the paper.

"Did we do the right thing?" she mused, her voice solemn. "Did I do the right thing, insisting we come, that we seek out the Order? Maybe Riley was right, after all." She pulled her hand back, still staring down at the map as if it could give her answers. "What if the Order isn't ready for this?" she murmured. "For hundreds of years, St. George has hunted us. We've been demons and monsters to them for centuries. They're not going to change their beliefs in a few days. And I didn't even think of the breeders. What's going to happen when they see the Order of St. George arrive? They're just as likely to panic and start fighting out of fear and desperation." She sighed, bowing her head. "Dammit. If we go to that island, and a dragon is hurt or killed because of me…"

I moved behind her, slipping my arms around her waist. "It won't be your fault," I told her. "You have done everything you can to prepare both sides for this. You're right, the Order won't change their beliefs in a few days. And as long as St. George exists, dragons will continue to fear and hate us. But we have to start somewhere." She leaned back, resting her head on my shoulder, and I tightened my grip, content not to move. "This is a huge first step, Ember," I said. "You have no idea the magnitude of an officer of St. George agreeing to ally with dragons. They're starting to listen. We just have to trust that they'll keep their word. And that they'll eventually realize the truth."

"Martin, perhaps." Ember's hands came to rest on my arms, squeezing gently. "I could see him finally accepting us, or at least realizing that some dragons don't want what Talon wants. But Lieutenant Ward…" She sighed, a shadow crossing her face. "I'm afraid of what he'll do," she whispered. "What he might order his soldiers to do. We'll be in the middle of nowhere and there will be no place for the breeders to run. What if his real goal is to get to that island and slaughter every dragon there? Riley would never forgive me." Her voice dropped, becoming nearly inaudible. "I'd never forgive myself."

"That won't happen," I told her firmly. "We'll stop him. I'll stop him, Ember, I promise. Even if I have to shoot him myself."

Ember shivered. "I hope it doesn't come to that."

I hoped it wouldn't, either. I was weary of fighting my former brothers, sickened by their blood that stained my hands. I would protect the rogues, the underground and the dragon

I loved, but that didn't mean I didn't hate myself each time I had to pull the trigger against the men I'd once fought beside.

"Garret?" Ember's voice was contemplative, her fingers tracing small circles on my forearms. "Do you think…the war will come to an end in our lifetimes?"

I gazed down at her. It was hard to imagine. I'd known nothing but war my entire life. Everything I could remember was fighting, blood, battles and death. Except for one brief memory of a small town called Crescent Beach, and a summer that changed everything.

"I don't know," I murmured. Certainly the Order allying with rogue dragons was a huge step in the right direction, but it almost seemed to come too late. When Talon was poised to destroy everything. "Why?" I asked her. "What got you thinking of this?"

"Oh, I don't know." Ember reached back and slipped her fingers into my hair. "I was remembering that summer, I guess." She didn't have to say what she meant; it was seared into both our memories forever. "I was thinking it would be nice to go back to normal again. Where we're not running or fighting for our lives. Do you know how long it's been since I've even thought about surfing? Or anything that doesn't involve bullets and guns and crazy suicide missions?"

I chuckled. "I thought that *was* normal for us." She swatted my arm, and I grinned, pulling her closer. "Maybe someday," I murmured, making her sigh. "Someday this will be over, and then you can drag me to parties and dancing and all the normal things people are supposed to do together." I gave a wry grin, brushing her hair from her shoulder to place a kiss on her neck. "You'll probably have to teach me, though. I still don't have a great grasp of what normal is supposed to be." *I'm in love with a dragon. I'm as far removed from normal as anything can get.*

"Honestly?" Ember whispered. "I don't even care about those things anymore. I just… I want us to be alive at the end, all of us. You, Riley, Jade, Mist, the rogues… Dante." She swallowed hard. "The longer the war goes on, the more likely it is I'm going to lose someone. We've gotten lucky so far. I can't even remember how many close calls we've had, but I know it can't last forever." Her hands tightened almost painfully on my arms. "That's all I want," she whispered. "I'd rather die fighting beside you than spend normal alone."

I gently turned her to face me and ran a thumb over her cheek. "I can't promise you that, dragon girl," I told her softly. "I wish I could. I wish I could protect everyone, but war doesn't ever give you that luxury." She nodded sadly, and I drew her closer, lowering my head. "But I can promise you this—as long as I have the breath to keep going, I won't give up. I'll keep fighting for that normal life. As long as this war doesn't kill me, I plan to be right beside you when this is done." She blinked, and I offered a small smile. "What do you say when this is all over we find a beach and go surfing again? I'll bet money you fall off your board more than I do."

Her eyes flashed, and a grin finally crept across her face. "I'll take that bet, soldier boy," she said, looping her arms around my neck. "And you're going to eat those words, along with all that sand and seawater, when you wipe out."

"Oh?" I tightened my arms around her waist, feeling heat start to flicker through my veins. "And what if I don't? What do I get if I win?"

"The love and reluctant admiration of a dragon."

"I thought I had that already."

"Don't push your luck, soldier boy," Ember said, and kissed me. I closed my eyes, feeling the heat spread to all parts of my body, melting away the worry, stress, nervousness and fear, at least for the moment. We could still die. In war, it was all too easy; you'd blink, and someone else would be gone. But as long as I was killed fighting for her, for a future I would probably never see, I would have no regrets.

Of course, that didn't mean I'd go down without a fight.

"Lieutenant Ward?"

Footsteps sounded outside the door, clipped and hurried, making us pull back. "Lieutenant Ward," the voice said again as someone swept into the room. "I have those papers you wanted—"

He stopped short, blinking in surprise as he spotted me and Ember in the center of the room. I met his gaze, feeling a ripple of shock and recognition go up my spine, seeing the instant he recognized me, as well.

He hadn't changed much since the time we'd last seen each other. It had been a couple years ago, and only in passing; I'd made certain to avoid him whenever I could. Since then, he'd gained a few inches, and that scar across his bottom lip was new. But everything else, from his hard blue eyes, to the set of his jaw, to the way his mouth twisted into a sneer when he saw me, was exactly as I remembered.

"Well, well," Peter Matthews said, his voice that same smug taunt from when we were new recruits trying to scrape by at the Academy. "Look who it is. The lizard-loving traitor himself."

"What do you want, Matthews?" I asked steadily, ignoring the instant flare of anger that shot through my veins. Not for his words; I'd been called far worse of late, by both friends and enemies. Nothing he said could anger me. I'd heard it all before. It was Matthews himself, the long years of torment and abuse, the competition and mutual hatred we shared for each other.

He doesn't matter, I tried to tell myself. We were no longer in the Academy, competing for approval, trying to prove our worth. I was no longer eleven years old, trying to defend my-self from being pummeled in the bathrooms. We were both soldiers, and he was no longer someone I needed to fear.

But something was building inside, a simmering heat that flickered through my lungs, rising in intensity. Heat and anger and a savage, almost primal urge to protect the girl beside me. I breathed out slowly, and the air in my throat felt scalding hot.

"Lieutenant Ward already left," I told the other soldier, and jerked my head toward the exit. "You'll probably catch him if you hurry."

Matthews didn't answer. His cruel gaze shifted to Ember standing beside me, and the sneer twisting his face turned even uglier. "And that must be your little dragon whore. I can see why you're so infatuated—she's almost cute. For a soul-sucking lizard. Tell me, Sebastian..." He shot me an evil grin, baring his teeth. "I'm curious. Does she take it from the front, or the back?"

The heat in my veins exploded. Fire roared through me, searing and furious, turning my vision red. I felt myself mov-ing forward, muscles tensing, intending to drive my fist all the way through Matthews's sneering mouth and out the back of his skull.

"Garret, don't!"

Something caught my arm from behind, jerking me to a stop. "Don't fight him," Ember said, eyes narrowed and angry as I glanced back. "That's what he wants. He'll take any excuse to draw us out, to make everyone see that we're violent and can't be trusted."

I took a deep breath, controlling the heat and the fiery rage that came with it. She was right. I couldn't let Matthews draw me into a brawl now. Too much depended on everyone working together. One scuffle could ruin any chance of dragons and soldiers getting along. Ember knew that. *I* knew that.

Matthews, however, didn't.

"Don't give him too much credit," I told Ember, straightening and casting a hard look back at the other soldier. "He can't plan that far ahead. There's no ulterior motive here. He's just an asshole."

Ember blinked, perhaps more stunned by my hostility toward the other soldier than the use of the word itself. I couldn't blame her. I usually let insults roll off my back; life in the Order—where polite obedience was expected even if your superior officer was screaming in your face—taught you to take nothing personally. Words couldn't hurt you; as long as you didn't believe them, they meant nothing.

But Peter Matthews could get under my skin like no one else. There were too many memories, too many years of mutual dislike, that simmered into resentment and loathing. Too many incidents where Matthews did his best to threaten, harm or humiliate me. Graduating the Academy had been a relief on many levels; I could start killing dragons as I had trained to do my whole life, but it also meant that I had finally escaped the constant torment of Peter Matthews.

But now, it wasn't about me. I had something more important to protect. And the whole Order would burn to the ground before I let him lay a finger on the girl at my side.

"Oh, what's the matter, Sebastian?" Matthews said. "Still afraid of me?" He smirked, blue eyes glittering. "You were always a squirrelly little shit, even in the Academy. Still can't look me in the eye, even now. Or does your dragon bitch not want her toy broken?"

A growl, faint but audible, rumbled deep in Ember's throat, and the pupils of her eyes went razor-sharp. Despite her resolve, Matthews was treading on very thin ice right now. And he was either too arrogant to know the dangers of poking a dragon, or he was stupidly hoping something would happen. "Come on," I told Ember, taking her hand and stepping away, toward the back door. "Let's get out of here." *Before we both do something we'll regret, and that idiot ends up in the infirmary with a shattered jaw. Or his face burned off.*

"That's right, run away, Sebastian," Matthews called as we fled the room, his mocking voice following us out the door. "Just like you always did. Still the pissant little coward, huh? Even when you have a lizard to hide behind. That's okay." We slipped into the hall, but his last threat still echoed behind us. "I'll find you. You and your lizards. Count on it."

"Who the hell is that douchebag?" Ember muttered as we walked swiftly down the corridor. She was shaking, probably with anger and the effort of not Shifting into her true form and blasting the sneer off Matthews's face.

"Peter Matthews," I replied. "I went to the Academy with him. We were in the same class. He...never liked me much."

Ember snorted at the understatement, casting a disgusted look back down the hall. "Has he always been such a jackass?"

"Actually, he's worse. He was made squad commander a couple years ago, and has Ward backing him up. They share some similarities, if you hadn't noticed." Ember frowned, a grim shadow crossing her face as she put the two together. "Before, Matthews was just a bully. Now…" I shook my head. "He might actually be dangerous."

"Great." Ember crossed her arms. "I was nervous enough with Lieutenant Ward coming along. But if his whole squad is like Matthews…"

I nodded. "We're going to have to be extra vigilant, and make sure the soldiers of the Eastern Chapterhouse don't put the mission at risk." How we were going to do that, I wasn't exactly certain, but I did know that I wouldn't let Matthews or any of his soldiers hurt the dragons we were trying to save. "We need to inform Riley and the others, let them know the situation," I went on. "Matthews hates dragons as much as Ward does. If he and Riley ever get into it, it'll be bad."

She sighed. "Yeah. I'll go find Riley and warn him about Commander Jackass. Where will you be?"

"I should join Tristan and Lieutenant Martin." They would be in Martin's office now, with the weapon we'd stolen. *The dragon killer.* I wanted to know more about it, if it was really as potent as Martin believed. If it could really take down a dragon with one shot. And if it could, what that would mean for us, both dragons and St. George, in the future.

★ ★ ★

Martin's office door was locked when I got there, and the murmuring voices I heard through the room stopped instantly when I knocked. "Who is it?" came Martin's gruff voice through the wood.

"Sebastian, sir."

"Hang on."

The locks clicked, and the door swung open to reveal

Tristan's unsmiling face on the other side. Martin stood behind his desk, looking grim, the weapon case open in front of him. I stepped through the frame, and Tristan locked the door behind me.

"Sebastian." Martin nodded as I joined Tristan at the edge of the desk. "St. Anthony has given me the details regarding the heist. He says there were two soldiers of the United States Army that saw the dragons before you could escape."

I nodded. "Yes, sir. It was unfortunate, but unavoidable. If Ember and Riley hadn't showed up when they did, we'd either be dead or captured."

Martin's jaw tightened. "I doubt the eyewitness accounts will be taken seriously, even if the soldiers themselves believe what they saw. Still, it is concerning." He frowned, folding his arms to his chest. "One of the main purposes of St. George is to ensure that the general public know nothing of the existence of dragons. If we are to start working with these rogues, we must be more cautious." His eyes narrowed. "Especially now that Lieutenant Ward is here."

"Yes, sir." I understood Martin's concern. Ward would take any excuse not to cooperate with us, to insist that working with dragons was not only immoral, it was dangerous. "But the dragons don't want to be discovered, either, sir," I added. "These rogues in particular have had plenty of experience keeping their heads down and off Talon's radar. They understand it's for the best that no one knows they exist."

Martin nodded. "But you managed to get the weapon," he said, gazing down at the open case on his desk, where the long length of the barrel glinted under the dim light. "Well done."

Tristan edged forward, unable to keep the eagerness from his voice as he stared at the weapon. "Can this thing really one-shot a dragon?" he asked, sounding like he'd give anything to try it out. I frowned at his enthusiasm.

"We won't know until it's tested," Martin replied. "It is a prototype, after all. All we have right now is theory." Reaching out, he closed the case with a snap, making Tristan slump in disappointment. Martin smiled faintly. "Put it from your mind, St. Anthony," he urged. "At this moment, we have larger issues to deal with."

"Sir," I ventured as Tristan gave the weapon case one last longing gaze. "How many from the Eastern Chapterhouse survived the attack?"

"A half dozen, including the lieutenant," Martin replied, and I blinked in shock. Only six soldiers had made it through the Night of Fang and Fire. Six, out of what had been the largest St. George chapterhouse in the United States. I thought back to the attack on our own chapterhouse a few weeks ago. It had been savage, violent and overwhelming, and even though we had prepared for it, we'd nearly been wiped out. Only the arrival of Ember and the rogues had been enough to turn the tide. Without them, it would have been a massacre.

"I'm counting on you both to help me keep the peace," Martin said, glancing at Tristan, as well. "Sebastian, talk to your dragons. They should try to avoid any contact with the soldiers for now. St. Anthony, keep an eye on our men. I don't want them getting into fights with Ward's boys, nor do I want them listening to whatever rhetoric will be going around the barracks. We can't fight a war with Talon if we're constantly battling our own people."

"Yes, sir."

"And, Sebastian." Martin looked at me. "You know you're likely to be a target. From what I hear, a few of the men have already singled you out. But we'll need every able body we can get for the upcoming war, so you are forbidden to put anyone in the infirmary unless it's a matter of life or death, is that clear?"

I suppressed a wince, wondering if Martin knew Peter Matthews was here. I'd never told him about my old rival, but it wouldn't surprise me if the lieutenant somehow knew of our history. "Yes, sir."

"Good." Martin looked down at the closed weapon case on his desk. "Because it appears that our next mission will be rescuing a colony of dragons in the middle of the ocean."

RILEY

The next few days, things were tense. I went out of my way to avoid the soldiers, and I noticed Sebastian doing the same, particularly when the soldiers of the other chapterhouse were around. Ember stayed near me or St. George when she wasn't in her room, and Wes ventured out only to use the bathroom across the hall.

And then there was Mist. Or, more accurately, the lack of her. I knew she was around; sometimes I'd catch a glimpse of her slipping out of a room, or hovering in a corner, watching and listening, while everyone talked. It worried me; she was an ex-Basilisk and shady as hell. If she was sending Talon vital information about us, we'd be dead before our little rescue operation ever got off the ground. But Mist was either too good to be caught, or she was just a naturally cautious person, because I never saw her in the act of something overtly suspicious.

One night, I was more restless than usual. I lay on the hard mattress, listening to Wes snore in the corner, the million thoughts swirling around my head making sleep impossible.

Per normal, I wondered if my underground was all right; Wes had checked their status as soon as he'd woken up, and every couple hours thereafter until we went to sleep. They were fine for now, but they were still just kids and I worried for them constantly, hoping Jade could keep them safe while I wasn't there.

I thought of Ember a lot, still feeling the ache of the severed life-mate bond deep inside. It wasn't as sharp as before, where Cobalt had raged and mourned the loss of his *Sallith'tahn*, but it was still there. I'd buried it under work and planning, keeping myself deliberately busy so I wouldn't have to think about it, but in the quiet hours of the night, it crept up again, reminding me of what I'd lost. Strangely enough, I didn't hate the soldier for it. If Ember didn't want him, there'd be nothing he could do to change her mind. But watching them together... Ember truly seemed content with her human, so who was I to interfere?

I *did* think she was being shortsighted and setting herself up for heartbreak; humans didn't live very long compared to dragons, even if there wasn't a war going on. Sixty years, eighty years; it was a heartbeat to us, the blink of an eye. Even if the soldier didn't get his head blown off in the next year or so, he would eventually grow old, wither and die, as all humans did. And Ember would still have her whole life ahead of her like the rest of us. That was another reason dragons rarely formed attachments to humans; they just weren't around very long. Even my friendship with Wes was a bit of an anomaly. I was sure that Jade or Mist didn't have a best girlfriend that was human.

Mist. I shifted on the mattress, putting my hands under my head to stare at the ceiling. Mist had been on my mind a lot lately. Mostly because I *knew* she was up to something, and yet

I could never pin her down long enough to prove it. Infuriating Basilisk. It was all the more aggravating because I should know her tricks; I had been doing this far longer than her. I knew she thought she was smarter than me; maybe this was a game to her, see how far she got before I finally caught on.

Annoyed and knowing I wouldn't get any sleep tonight, I swung my feet off the cot and sat up. Wes's snores vibrated through the room as I checked my watch—3:22 a.m. Still too early for even the soldiers to be awake. I wished I knew what that Martin guy was planning, and what the damn holdup was. Organizing a raid on a heavily armed facility in the middle of the Atlantic Ocean wasn't something you could pull out of your ass, but still. We were wasting time; the breeders weren't getting any younger, and Talon wasn't getting any less powerful.

A rustle in the hall just outside the room made the hairs on my neck stand up. It was barely audible, especially through the locked door and the snores of my hacker friend, but my dragon instincts stirred. Something, or someone, was out there.

I stood up and glided to my door, opening it just enough to peer through the crack.

A glimmer of pale, silvery hair vanished around the corner at the end of the corridor, making my gut clench and my suspicion flare to life. *Mist.* The Basilisk was up and on the move. This was my chance. Now we would finally see whose side she was really on.

I pushed the door open as smoothly as I could, careful not to make it creak, and slipped into the hall after the girl. Barefoot, I followed that faint shimmer of silvery hair through narrow, pitch-black corridors, the stone floor cold against my feet. Mist moved swiftly through the underground bunker, silent as a ghost, thankfully not looking back. She might not have seen me in the darkness and shadow—I'd be difficult to spot in my black jogging pants and T-shirt—but she was an ex-Basilisk. Naturally wary and suspicious.

Then again, so was I.

I followed her up the steps to the old church, across the room and out one of the back doors into the hazy moonlight. Now Mist started to act nervous, glancing over her shoulder, even pausing to scan the trees behind her. But the woods surrounding the church had plenty of places to hide, and human eyesight could not pierce the shadows well enough to spot a person crouched at the foot of a tree. The challenge was moving when she moved so that my footsteps, rustling through leaves and bushes, didn't give me away. Still, I'd been trained for this, and was able to follow the pale form through the woods fairly easily, a shadow trailing a ghost.

About a half mile from the church, Mist finally came to a stop in the center of a small clearing. As I knelt behind a gnarled tree, watching her, she pulled her phone from a pocket and held it to her ear. With the distance and shadows, it was nearly impossible to see her lips move, but I thought she muttered the words, "I'm here," before lowering her arm. I took a deep breath, then let it out slowly.

All right, then. Mysterious meeting outside in the middle of the night. This isn't suspicious at all. My jaw clenched in anger. *What have you been doing, Mist? Who are you selling us out to?*

A few minutes passed, and then someone melted out of the trees across the clearing and began walking toward Mist. A human, dressed in a nondescript black suit and tie, the kind many Talon agents wore. He carried a black briefcase in one hand and didn't hesitate as he walked toward the dragon waiting in the clearing.

Dammit, Mist. Briefly, I closed my eyes. *I don't want to have to kill you. But if this is anyone from Talon, I can't let this go on. Whatever you're up to, it has to end tonight.*

Opening my eyes, I squinted to see their lips as the human drew close. But Mist stepped forward and turned just enough that their faces were blocked from view. They spoke quietly, too far away to be heard, and then the mysterious agent handed Mist the briefcase, turned and disappeared into the trees again. Mist watched until he was gone, then began walking back the way she'd come.

She had just reached the edge of the trees when I stepped out, grabbed her by the shoulders and slammed her back into a trunk. She grunted at the impact, and then icy blue eyes flashed up to meet mine.

"Hello, Mist." I smiled coldly. "Fancy meeting you here."

"Cobalt." The other Basilisk matched the chilliness of my smile. She didn't seem surprised to see me, though I knew she wouldn't reveal such emotion. Or the fact that I had finally taken her off guard. "So that *was* you I felt following me. Congratulations for being able to stay out of sight. I guess your skills aren't completely overexaggerated, after all."

"Thanks. I try." I stared into her eyes, seeing my own reflection gazing back, grim and dangerous. "Surprisingly, thinking one of my teammates is going to betray us to Talon is a pretty good motivator," I went on, and tightened my grip, pinning her harder into the tree. "So, now comes the part where you're going to tell me everything. Who you met with, what's in the briefcase and, most importantly, who the hell you're working for."

"Interesting." Mist met my gaze, unrepentant. "And if I don't give you what you want?"

"Then I'm going to have to force it out of you, one way or another."

I felt bad for threatening her, but enough was enough. This was some seriously shady crap she was pulling, and there was too much at stake to leave anything to chance. "You can either tell me now," I warned, "or in an interrogation chair. I'm done playing games, Mist."

"Oh, Cobalt." Her smile turned brittle. "You make it sound so easy."

Her knee came up, hitting me between the legs, sending a blinding stab of pain through my groin. I convulsed with a grunt, staggering away, and she followed it with a savage kick to my temple. I threw up my arm, taking it on the shoulder instead of the noggin, but the impact still rocked me sideways and made my head ring. During the second roundhouse that followed, I managed to grab her leg, turn and throw her to the ground. She rolled with the impact, coming up on her feet, but it was enough time for me to take a breath and get my balance again, and for the shrieking pain of my sensitive bits to fade somewhat.

I shook my head and grinned at the other dragon, who was balanced on the balls of her feet in a fighting stance, still holding the briefcase in one hand. "Playing dirty, Mist? Why does that not surprise me?"

She smirked. "It sure as hell surprised you a moment ago."

"Fair enough." I stepped forward, letting my muscles relax and my senses sharpen, taking in my surroundings and the girl in front of me. "Let's see if you can do it again. No Shifting, though." Fighting as humans was a lot safer than fighting as dragons. You could pummel your opponent senseless, but fists and feet were still less dangerous than claws and fangs. Once we Shifted, the tone of the fight changed into something far more lethal. And, shady or not, I didn't want to kill her.

Mist shrugged. "Fine," she agreed, and tossed the suitcase to the forest floor. "I can take you down just as easily as a human."

"You talk a big game, hatchling." I edged closer, smiling. "Let's see you put your money where your mouth is."

"Actually, I'd rather put my foot where your mouth is," Mist replied, and lunged, kicking straight up toward my chin. I jerked my head back, feeling her leather boot miss my nose by about a centimeter, and dropped low, sweeping her other leg out. She tumbled backward, somehow turned the fall into a backflip and landed on her feet again like a damn cat. I had about a second to be impressed with her flexibility when that leg shot out again, side-kicking me in the gut and driving most of the air from my lungs. As I staggered, bent nearly in two, I saw her bring her foot up, almost touching the side of her face, right before her heel slammed into the back of my head.

My chin struck the ground, clacking my teeth together painfully, and the world went fuzzy for a moment. Instinctively, I rolled to the side, hearing her foot slam into the ground where my head had been a moment before. Before she could pull it back, I grabbed that slim ankle and yanked hard, jerking her off her feet. She landed on her back, and this time I heard the explosion of air leave her body as she hit hard and lay there for a moment, stunned.

I lunged forward before she could recover, straddling her waist and pinning her wrists to the ground. She froze, and for a moment, we stared at each other, panting. Mist gazed up at me, defiant, silver hair spilling around her head like a cloud.

She felt…suddenly fragile. Her wrists, clamped beneath my fingers, were long and slender; I felt I could snap them if I squeezed hard enough.

"Well." Her voice came out breathy, and for some reason, I felt my stomach prickle. "Here we are. Now what?"

I licked suddenly dry lips. "You could always tell me who you're working for."

"Are you going to hold me down until I do?"

"I'm sure Wes or Ember will miss me eventually." I smirked down at her, settling my weight fully. "I'm a dragon. I can be patient. Or you can just tell me now and get it over with. Because you're going to tell me eventually." I tightened my grip on her arms, and she grimaced. "Who is your employer, Mist?" I demanded, my voice hard. "Tell me. Give me a reason to believe you're not selling us out to Talon. I can't let you go until I'm certain."

She slumped, closing her eyes. "If I tell you," she said, her voice barely above a whisper. I leaned closer to hear. "You have to promise me one thing."

My heartbeat picked up, thumping in my ears. "What's that?"

Abruptly, her head shot forward, the top of her skull striking me square in the nose. I yelped and shot backward, my hands going to my face, and Mist kicked me in the chest, shoving me off.

"Don't assume the fight's over until it is."

Through blood and tears of pain, I looked up and saw her foot coming at my head, aimed at my temple. Knowing that if it landed I'd probably be knocked senseless, I lunged forward instead, catching her around the waist. She threw a couple quick elbows into my face, making my already abused nose scream with agony, but as we toppled backward I some-how ended up behind her. Snaking an arm beneath her jaw, I tightened my grip, putting her into a rear-naked choke, using both arms to cut off the supply of blood to her brain. She tucked her chin, trying to save her neck and give herself a few seconds as we struggled in the grass. An elbow hit me in the ribs, hard enough that I felt something crack, but I gritted my teeth and hung on.

Briefly, it flashed through my head that, if she were to Shift right now, I'd be in trouble.

Beneath me, Mist shuddered, her struggles growing more frantic. I knew that, if she didn't break free, she was seconds away from passing out. Dragon or no, six to eight seconds was all it took for someone to go unconscious once the blood flow to the brain was cut off. Again, Mist jabbed me in the ribs with an elbow and threw her head back, attempting to bash me in the face. I ducked my chin, setting my jaw. I didn't enjoy this. Choking out a girl half my weight was not high on my list of things I was proud of, even if she was a Basilisk who could easily kick my ass if I wasn't paying attention.

The girl slumped in my arms, and just as I was tensing for the Shift, her hand came up, tapping my elbow three times in rapid succession. Signaling surrender.

I let her go immediately, not pausing to think that this could be a ruse, that she could be lying to get me to lower my guard. If she wanted to escape, all she had to do was change forms, and I'd be unable to hang on. Though her comment about making assumptions was still echoing through my brain, mocking me. Mist fell forward, coughing and gasping, one hand going to her throat as she sucked in air. Panting, I sagged against a tree, watching her recover.

"Why didn't you Shift?" I asked after a moment.

She shot me a confused look. "We agreed...to no Shifting, didn't we?" she asked, still breathing hard.

"Yes, but...you're a Basilisk. Lying is in our job description. If I didn't let up, you'd be unconscious right now."

Her brow furrowed. "If I had Shifted, you would've been forced to change form, as well. And like you said before, that would have upped the lethality of the fight by a great deal. One or both of us could have sustained serious injuries, and that would have been counterproductive to what I'm supposed to do here." She blinked, and the slight frown deepened. "Do you really think so little of me that you believe I would try to kill you to protect my secrets?"

"I don't know, Mist," I said truthfully. "I don't know anything about you. I have no clue why you're here, who you're working for or what your real agenda is. You assure me you're not my enemy, but you go sneaking off in the middle of the night to meet with suspicious people in secret. How can I be sure they're not part of Talon? How can I trust anything you say if you're only telling me half-truths?"

She held my stare for a moment, then sighed, bowing her head so that her silver hair slipped forward to cover her face. Her next words were soft, barely audible, even in the stillness.

"All right," I heard her whisper. "If this is the only way I can get you to trust me...

"I work for the Archivist," she said, sending a jolt of shock up my spine. *The Archivist?* Mist's mysterious employer, the one who'd ordered the ex-Basilisk to rescue us from Talon, travel with us and aid us where she could, was the freaking Archivist? "I believe you have already met him," Mist continued, glancing up at me. "In Chicago. Do you remember?"

"You mean the Wyrm that guards the Vault below the library?" I rasped out. "Yeah, I remember." How could I not? You did not just forget a meeting with the third-oldest dragon in the known world. No wonder Mist could provide us with seemingly impossible-to-get information; the Archivist was the literal guardian of all the organization's dirty secrets. He had access to knowledge I could only dream of.

There was just one small problem.

"Mist," I began, "correct me if I'm wrong, but the Archivist works for Talon."

A flicker of a smile crossed the girl's face. "Yes and no," she said in that cryptic way that made me want to strangle something. "Yes, the Archivist guards the Vault and protects Talon's secrets. No, he will not openly oppose the Elder Wyrm. But he keeps his own network of spies and Basilisks, a handful of dragons whom he trusts will not betray him to the organization. We are his eyes and ears within Talon, accessing secrets where he cannot."

"Why?" I asked. "Is he planning a coup against the Elder Wyrm?" That would be interesting, to say the least. As the second-oldest dragon within Talon, the Archivist could command a lot of respect. He might have the support to at least challenge the hierarchy and the Elder Wyrm. Though I wasn't certain what kind of leader he would be. For all I knew, he might be just as corrupt and power-hungry as the current CEO.

But Mist shook her head. "No, the Archivist has no interest in ruling Talon," she said to my vague disappointment. "And even if he did, the Elder Wyrm has far too many resources and is still far too powerful for him to take down alone. He's made that very clear."

"Then what the hell does he want?" I asked.

"I don't know." Mist shrugged as I frowned at her. "I don't question orders," she said calmly. "I just do my job. That's how it's always been."

I snorted. "So he's no different than Talon. Protecting his interests and expecting everyone beneath him to do their job, no questions asked."

"Perhaps," Mist said, unconcerned. "But he has always been a neutral observer. This is the first time he has offered aid to a cause directly opposing the Elder Wyrm." Her lips quirked as she met my gaze. "Maybe he actually thinks you can change something."

I smirked back. "Well, we'll try not to disappoint him."

Mist shook her head, rose and walked to where the black case lay, forgotten when the fight began. I stood, as well, a little slower due to at least one bruised rib, and maybe a broken nose. Damn, the girl hit hard. My face felt like a dagger had been jammed below my eyes.

"So are you going to tell me what's in that thing, or do I have to steal it from you later?" I asked as Mist walked back with the case in hand. She gave me a resigned look, put the case on the ground and clicked it open.

"I'm not certain myself," the Basilisk admitted, pushing back the top. "I was just told it was important, and that it could greatly aid us in our upcoming mission..."

She trailed off, her eyes widening. Even more curious, I walked around to her back, just as the girl reached into the case and pulled out a dark piece of clothing. Pitch-black, it sucked in the light and looked like it was made out of ink. I drew in an awed breath as I realized what it was.

"Well, damn. He sent you a Viper suit."

I stifled a tiny flutter of envy that went through me as I stared at the fabric. Ember might not have realized it back when she'd had one of her own, but it was a high honor to possess a suit, as only a few dragons were ever given the infamous black outfit that let you change between forms without the suit tearing or being destroyed. Only the top agents in the organization were gifted with Viper suits. They were reserved for the fearsome assassins, though I'd heard of a couple exceptional Basilisks who were given them, as well. But they were stupidly hard to get ahold of, and the process of making them was a heavily guarded secret. Knowing what I did now, it made sense that Ember, the daughter of the Elder Wyrm, had been given a Viper suit. *I* had never gotten one while I was in Talon, despite being the best Basilisk in the organization at that time.

Not that I was bitter or anything.

I gazed at the slinky fabric in Mist's hands and forced a grin. "Guess the Archivist wants us to succeed, after all," I said. "That, or he doesn't want his favorite spy getting killed. Must be nice, working for someone who can give you fun toys like that."

"I would think so," Mist said, and pulled an identical suit out of the case. "Because there are three of them here."

Holy shit. *Three* Viper suits? I stared at her to make sure she wasn't joking, then looked down at the open case. It was hard to tell them apart, but there were indeed two more folded Viper suits in the case. Three suits, three dragons. Me, Ember and Mist.

And the second most powerful dragon in Talon backing us up.

"Okay," I said, nodding as Mist watched me with that knowing smile. "So, you're working for the Archivist, and he wants us to take down that island. This might not be such a bad thing, after all."

EMBER

I should've seen this coming.

I mean, I'd known it could happen. Tensions were running high, and from what I could tell, there was a silent battle going on between the soldiers of the Western Chapterhouse, and the soldiers of the Eastern Chapterhouse. Nothing overt; the soldiers had been told that fighting would not be tolerated, and if nothing else, they were disciplined and followed orders well. But within the church walls, the enmity and mistrust between both dragons and soldiers was palpable. Ward's men, the soldiers of the Eastern Chapterhouse, condemned the other soldiers for sympathizing with dragons, and their contempt was obvious. For their part, the men of the Western Chapterhouse seemed balanced on a razor's edge. They had seen us, a few had even talked to us, but the vitriol and hatred toward dragons from their peers, and from Lieutenant Ward in particular, made them uncertain and confused. Having two lieutenants so at odds with each other was throwing everything they knew into chaos.

We dragons kept our heads down and remained mostly out of sight, not engaging the soldiers unless we absolutely had to. Personally, I didn't like the idea of hiding from our supposed allies, especially since we could be trying to convince them that dragons weren't evil. It seemed like a wasted opportunity. Still, I understood that it was a lot to ask of the Order—allying with their ancient enemies when their Code, their very religion, told them that dragons were soulless monsters that must be destroyed. It wasn't a good time to convince them otherwise. Especially since some of the soldiers were more vehement in their hatred than others.

"Where ya going, dragon?"

I stared at the soldiers who were leaning against the wall in the middle of the corridor. They were big and muscular, with buzzed heads and matching smirks. The one who had spoken was none other than Peter Matthews, Garret's old rival. His blue eyes were hard as he glared at me.

I tensed, feeling the heat start to rise in my veins. Inside the church, the stone hallways were tight and narrow, with little room to maneuver and no other ways around. If I wanted to get where I was going, I would have to pass these two. Beneath my clothes, the slick material of my new Viper suit flattened to my skin, sensing hostility, anticipating a sudden, violent change of body. I took a deep breath to cool my lungs.

"I'm just looking for someone. Excuse me."

"For Sebastian."

I didn't answer. I *was* looking for Garret, because he had texted me a few minutes ago with instructions to meet in the command room. It had sounded important, like maybe they had finally figured out a way to get to the island. But judging by Peter Matthews's expression, his mind had gone straight to the gutter.

At my silence, his smirk twisted, becoming a sneer as he turned to the other soldier, jerking his head in my direction. "Joseph, that's Sebastian's little dragon bitch," he told him. "Watch them together sometime—she can make him dance, sing, beg and roll over. He eats right out of her hand. It's pretty fucking hilarious."

"Yeah?" the other soldier gruffed, staring at me. "So it's that good, huh? Hey, dragon, how much of my soul would I have to sell to get some of that?"

Well, this conversation had gotten disgusting in a hurry. I pushed down my anger and walked forward, determined to ignore them.

Abruptly, Matthews's hand shot out, slamming into the opposite wall, blocking my way. I froze, clamping down on the knee-jerk reaction to Shift and bite his arm off.

"Joseph asked you a question, lizard," Peter Matthews said, his voice full of menace as he loomed over me. "Don't you know it's rude to ignore someone? Or is common decency as foreign to you animals as everything else?"

I bit my lip to keep the flames under control, to stifle the instinctive desire to Shift in the face of an obvious threat. My anger and disgust with these humans was reaching dangerous levels. *Keep it together, Ember. You can't start a war right now.*

"Good God, you two are stupid."

The deep, mocking voice echoed behind us. The soldiers jerked up, and I spun around to see Tristan St. Anthony's lean, wiry form standing at the end of the corridor. His arms were crossed, and he was staring at the other soldiers, ocean-blue eyes crinkled in disgust.

"And here I thought I'd seen it all," Tristan said, strolling up casually. He shot a disdainful look at Peter and shook his head. "Do you have a fucking death wish, Matthews? You know, there are easier ways to kill yourself than harassing a fire-breathing dragon in a very tight hallway."

"St. Anthony." The other soldiers straightened so they were no longer in my face, but they didn't move back. Peter Matthews's sneer faltered but came back quickly. "Did Sebastian send you to rescue his scaly mistress? That's what you Western Chapterhouse pussies are all about now, right? Rescuing the enemy? Cozying up to lizards?"

The other soldier, Joseph, snickered. "Maybe she holds his leash, too."

Tristan raised an eyebrow at the pair. It was a small motion, but the amused contempt he could project with it was impressive. "Rescue a dragon," he said slowly. "Right. Clearly, that's what I'm doing here. I'm certainly not saving a pair of class-A morons from being turned into steaming piles of stupidity when the dragon decides she's had enough and fries your asses."

Matthews snorted. "It can't touch us," he stated with smug confidence. "Not if it wants our help to rescue its scaly friends. If it even singes one hair, Lieutenant Ward will put a bullet through its head and slaughter every lizard in this place. That's why it won't lay a paw on me, isn't that right, dragon?" He gave me a cruel smile. "I've got your number," he said as I seethed and dug my nails into my palms to stop the flames from exploding. "You dragons are all about manipulation, but we can play that game, too. The Eastern Chapterhouse isn't full of blind, bleating sheep. You won't corrupt us like you did Sebastian." His eyes narrowed, mean and challenging. "So what'dya say to that, *lizard*?"

A thousand answers sprang to mind: angry, sarcastic, petty, defiant. For a split second, I almost went with the tried and true response of a foot to the groin. *I wouldn't be changing into a dragon. They couldn't fault me for staying human, right?*

Matthews was watching me, his sneer triumphant. I could feel Tristan at my back, waiting to see what I would do. The third soldier had gone tense, as if he just realized how volatile the situation had become, and how close to an angry dragon they really were. He was afraid, I realized with a jolt. Afraid that I would Shift and tear them both to pieces. He knew a pair of humans stood no chance against a dragon, even if they were trained to kill them. They would need guns and a lot more men, and they certainly wouldn't start the battle right in the dragon's face. Peter Matthews was either very stupid or smarter than I gave him credit for. He knew, and he was counting on my not being able to Shift.

I met Peter Matthews's gaze. "You're a coward," I told him calmly. "You hide behind protocol, because you know I can't retaliate. You know that if I respond at all, the soldiers here will turn on us in a heartbeat, and we can't afford that now. That's fine. Play your hateful little games. I have bigger problems to deal with." Peter Matthews sneered, but a spark of anger flickered across his face. I narrowed my eyes, letting a sliver of heat rise to the surface, tinting the air with the scent of smoke. "But let me make one thing very clear. If you hurt or threaten any of my friends, it won't matter where we are or how many soldiers are around. By the time I'm done, there won't be enough left of you to fill a shot glass."

Matthews's lip curled up. "Who do you think you're talking to, lizard?" he growled. "I've killed more of your kind than you can even imagine, and you'd be no different. Don't threaten me."

I brushed passed him, continuing down the hall. I didn't look back, or slow down. Only when I was around a corner and out of sight did I stop and press my forehead to the cold stone wall, breathing hard to calm the inferno within.

Okay, so this was bad. I knew the soldiers of St. George hated us, but this was taking it to a whole new level. And as far as I could tell, those two would be going to the island with us. How were we going to rescue the breeders and get everyone out safely when I had to watch my back around my supposed teammates?

Footsteps came around the corner and I looked up with a growl, both hoping and fearing it was Matthews.

"Just me," Tristan said, holding up his hands. I relaxed, taking a final breath and pushing myself off the wall. Tristan stepped closer, his mouth pulled into a wry grimace.

"Sorry about that," he offered, surprising me. I looked up at him with a frown, and he shrugged. "We're not all raging assholes like Peter Matthews. Most of us know how to be civil, even to our enemies."

Enemies. Suddenly tired, I leaned back against the wall, feeling his cool gaze on me. *Are we still enemies, then?* I wanted to ask. *How much longer will it take for you to trust us?* After everything Garret had told him, even after working with us himself, if Tristan St. Anthony still saw us as monsters, how would we ever convince the rest of the Order?

"So," Tristan said after an awkward silence. His voice was hesitant, as if he were debating whether or not to say anything. "You and Garret..."

He trailed off, watching me. I knew what he was asking. *What are you doing with my friend? What does he mean to you?* I could hear the questions in his voice, the concern that I was using the soldier. The fear that Garret had given his heart to a soulless demon, and I would someday rip it to shreds and leave him bleeding in the dust.

There were a lot of things I could tell Tristan. Promises and assurances that I would never hurt the soldier. Reasons that he trusted us, that we trusted *him*, with our lives. But, in the end, I went with the truest, easiest explanation.

"I love him," I said, and felt Tristan's astonishment. Whether from my admission, or that I, a dragon and a monster, could feel such a thing. Glancing at the other soldier, I smiled at him sadly. "Hard to believe, isn't it? I had trouble believing it myself."

"I…" For the first time since I'd known him, Tristan seemed at a loss for words. "I didn't realize," he finally said. "I didn't think dragons could…"

Love. "Yeah, well." I sighed, raking my hair back. "Until recently, I didn't think we could, either." *And now I can't imagine being without him.* "The organization… Talon, they told us a lot of lies," I went on. "Lies that we believed, as an entire race, for a long time."

"And that's why you left?"

I nodded. "Among other reasons." *Freedom, happiness, the ability to make my own choices, to name a few. Oh, and not being forced to murder my own kind when they disagree.* "We just want a normal life," I said, seeing Tristan from the corner of my eye, watching me. "One that Talon doesn't control. Where we don't have to fight a war we didn't want in the first place."

Tristan pondered this. I could sense him gearing up to ask more questions, but at that moment, my phone buzzed. I pulled it out and stared at the new text message that flashed across the screen.

Meeting is about to start. You okay?

Garret. I smiled and texted back: Yeah. On my way, before glancing at Tristan. "I have to go," I told him. "They're wait-ing for me in the command room."

"For both of us," Tristan replied with a wry grin, and indi-cated the way forward. "After you."

★ ★ ★

Garret and Lieutenant Martin were waiting patiently at the large table in the center of the floor when I came in with Tristan. Lieutenant Ward, standing across from Martin with his arms crossed, gave us both a look of blatant contempt that I did my best to ignore. The dragon half of my team was pres-ent, as well; Riley loomed over Wes in a corner chair, both staring intently at his laptop, while Mist hovered in a corner, watching everything in silence.

Garret blinked, looking surprised as I entered the room with Tristan. His gaze sought mine, gray eyes questioning, as I circled around to his side of the table.

"Everything all right?" he murmured as I slid in beside him.

There was no suspicion in his tone. No jealousy, just puz-zled concern. I realized I was still radiating heat; the anger and adrenaline from the encounter with Peter Matthews hadn't dissipated. For a moment, I considered not telling Garret what had happened with the soldiers in the hall. Given his history with Peter, I wondered if it wouldn't be better that he didn't know. Garret wasn't the vengeful type, not like Riley, but he just might make an exception for his old rival. Perhaps it was better to keep this hidden for now.

I decided against it. *No secrets, Ember.* This wasn't a case of playground bullying. This was a war, and these were the soldiers who would be aiding us on our mission. Garret needed to know, in case Peter Matthews did decide to shoot us in the back.

"I'm fine," I whispered back, and gave his arm a brief squeeze. "I'll tell you everything after the meeting." He nodded, and I turned my attention to the table, where the map of the island facility was laid out in the center. "What's going on?"

"We think," Garret began, "we have a way to get the breeders off the island."

PART II

SMOLDER

DANTE

I had never climbed so many steps in my life.

This is ridiculous. Why didn't anyone tell me that this council was held at the very top of a mountain, and the only way you could get there was climb or fly? With a groan, I pushed myself to my feet, secretly wishing, for perhaps the first time, that I could make this journey in my real form. Around me, the rocky cliffs rose straight into the air, soaring to jagged, impossible heights. The winding trail up the side of the mountain was narrow at the best of times and completely treacherous otherwise. The stone steps were slick, crumbling with age, and there were no railings, handholds or barriers of any kind between me and a sheer drop down the side of the mountain. The temple was isolated, as far from civilization as you could get. If I had known I would be climbing what felt like a few thousand steps to reach my objective, I might've saved myself the trouble and flown there. Sadly, I had only the one suit, and I wasn't inclined to ruin it by Shifting. Besides, though I had no way of knowing, I suspected this was a test of some sort, that they were watching to see what the impatient hatchling would do. If I showed up at the council of ancient Eastern dragons in my real form, they would know I had failed, and I hated failing.

Overhead, the sky was mottled with clouds, and some of the peaks had vanished into the blanket of gray and white. The temple, I hoped, would be just beyond the cloud bank.

Checking my watch, I took a deep breath and continued climbing.

The clouds closed around me, a solid wall of white that muffled everything, and the trail shrank to a sliver of stone between the side of the cliff and open air. Setting my jaw, I pushed upward, concentrating on putting one foot in front of the other and not losing my balance.

And then, the steps ended, the clouds disappeared and I was staring at a magnificent temple perched at the very top of the mountain. Weathered gray walls and a sweeping, clay-tiled roof stood against the blue of the sky, with one of the balconies overlooking a sheer drop down the side of the cliff face. The temple looked as ancient as the mountain itself; I wondered how old it really was…if it had been built with the intent to house a dragon.

A single monk, bald and dressed in somber black robes, stood beside the doors as I approached. I hoped he wouldn't try to speak with me—my Mandarin was all but nonexistent—but he silently bowed and stepped aside for me to pass. I walked down a very long corridor, lit only with flickering candles in nooks or atop brass stands, until deep, ancient voices began vibrating the stones at my feet.

Outside a pair of enormous wooden doors trimmed in gold, I paused, taking a moment to breathe, to calm the emotions fluttering inside. *You are not just a hatchling*, I told myself. *You*

*are the heir to Talon, the Voice of the Elder Wyrm herself, and
they will respect that position or face the wrath of the organization.*

Opening my eyes, I raised my head, pushed back the doors
and strode into the chamber, smiling as I did.

Six pairs of ancient, all-knowing eyes turned on me. A round
stone table stood in the center of the room, surrounded by pillars, candle stands and a half-dozen Adult Eastern dragons,
all in human form. They wore long flowing robes of various
colors and billowing sleeves, and the weight of their combined
stares nearly knocked the air from my lungs.

As the doors groaned shut behind me, I faced the roomful
of dragons and bowed, feeling their gazes on the back of my
neck. "Please forgive my tardiness," I said, holding the bow.
"The climb up the mountain was...steeper than I first imagined. I hope I have not kept you long."

"You," one of the females said, her smooth voice tinged with
anger. She was an older woman, smaller than me by several
inches, with silver-gray hair braided down her back and piercing dark eyes. "How dare you come here, demanding an audi-
ence with the council, mere days after Talon brutally attacks
our kind for no reason? You slaughter our people, burn our
temples to the ground, send those...*abominations* to destroy
us, and now you have the audacity to stand before us in the
name of peace and cooperation." Her eyes started to glow an
ominous yellow as the outline of her true form—a massive red
dragon with a golden mane and horns—flickered overhead for
a split second. "Tell me, hatchling, why shouldn't we kill you
here and now? What can you possibly do to stop us?"

I kept my voice polite, nonthreatening. As if this were a perfectly normal meeting, and I felt no fear whatsoever. "There
is nothing I can do, should you decide to end my life," I said

calmly. "However, that course of action is not advisable. If you kill me, Talon will show you no mercy whatsoever."

The woman gave a brittle laugh. "That is supposed to frighten us?" she mocked. "Talon has already shown us the extent of its 'mercy.'"

"Forgive me, but I have to disagree," I said, joining them at the table. "Everything you've seen so far? That was only the tip of the iceberg. Right now, Talon's attention is dispersed—our operations in the US and England are taking much of our time. If you kill me, it will turn the full force of its gaze on this temple and everyone in it." I met the woman's eyes, un-challenging, but unafraid. "I am the blood of the Elder Wyrm and the heir to the most powerful organization in the world," I stated calmly. "You do not want the Elder Wyrm to make this personal."

"Enough," said one of the others, an old man with a white beard and thin mustache down the front of his chest. Ancient black eyes gazed at me across the table. "You did not come to us simply to test our patience," he said. "If Talon sent you here alone, they must be very confident in whatever you are about to say. Speak, then, and let us be done with it."

I bowed my head respectfully. "Thank you." Facing them all, their expressions ranging from anger to distrust to calm indifference, I took a furtive breath.

"You have all seen the power Talon now commands," I began. "The Night of Fang and Fire struck not only here, but at all St. George bases around the world. Our forces took them by surprise, and the dragonslayers fell before the might of Talon. The Order of St. George has been wiped out. The war is finished, and the dragonslayers are no more."

If the Eastern dragons felt surprise or dismay at the news,

they hid it perfectly. "Our enemies have been put down," I went on. "St. George will no longer threaten us. The rogue dragons will no longer threaten us. The only opposition Talon has left...is right here.

"We shouldn't be enemies," I continued before they could mount an argument, or accuse me of threats. "We are the same, and all dragons should be united under one banner. Join us. Accept the gift the Elder Wyrm is offering your people. With your wisdom and Talon's power, we can make our race even stronger."

"And if we do not?" Another dragon spoke, a beardless man with his hair pulled into a long tail that reached the small of his back. He was the youngest dragon at the table, and probably older than me by several centuries. "If we refuse this 'gift'?"

"You've seen what Talon can do." My voice didn't falter; *I* could not falter, even in this. "You know that our power rivals even yours. The Elder Wyrm does not want this to be a fight. She believes we can come to an agreement that will benefit both sides. But if you refuse, you declare yourselves enemies of Talon, and we will respond accordingly."

"And you will have 'no choice' but to destroy us," the old male dragon said, and smiled humorlessly. "So, it is the most ancient of ultimatums—*join us or die*. That is what you are really saying, is that not correct, hatchling?"

"Yes," I said, no longer willing to sugarcoat it when the intent was obvious. "It is."

No one seemed surprised by this. Most of them simply nodded, as if that's what they'd figured all along. "We will need time to think on your offer," the male dragon said, and gestured to a door off to the side. "If you would give us a few minutes to speak among ourselves, we will call for you when we have an answer."

I bowed and stepped away. "Of course."

"Before you go, Dante Hill," another dragon said, the younger male with the ponytail down his back. "I believe this is for you."

Surprised, I watched as he gestured to a monk, who approached me and held out a rolled piece of parchment. "One of our own was here a short time ago," the dragon explained as I took the scroll. The paper was dry and cracked, yet surprisingly strong. "She urged us to join with the rogue dragons of the West, against your organization. I cannot help but think that she was correct all along."

"Shen." The older male dragon frowned at him. "We discussed this. For days. It was put to a vote, and the council made its decision."

"Regardless," the younger man went on, a brief flash of annoyance going through his eyes, "after she left, she contacted us a few days later, with a message to pass on to you. Specifically you." My confusion must've showed on my face, for he gave a small shrug. "Do not ask how she knew you were coming—*merely a hunch*, she told us. But she wanted to make certain that, should you ever arrive, you received that letter." The dragon shook his head in what could almost be awe. "Her intuitions are rarely incorrect. Were I you, Dante Hill, I would pay careful attention to what she has to tell you."

★ ★ ★

The room the monk led me to was stark and empty, a cold wind blowing in from an open window. I dared a peek outside and saw the staggeringly long drop down the side of the mountain. There weren't any chairs or even a stool to sit on, so I stood at the window with the mountain air cold against my back and unrolled the scroll. It was written in a fine, elegant script, and my name, in the blackest of inks, graced the top of the page.

Dante Hill,
If you are reading this letter, it means a gamble of mine has paid off, and that Talon has sent someone to speak to the Eastern council one last time. I suspected that it would be you. I regret that I cannot be there in person, but I must return to those who need me most.

   You don't know me; we have never met in person, but we share a common connection: your sister, Ember. I met Ember when I traveled to the United States to investigate the Order of St. George. She is a remarkable young woman. Intelligent, determined, resourceful—traits I'm sure she shares with you. My heart aches for the burden that she carries, that you both carry; war is painful enough without having to fight your own family.

I felt a strange lump rise to my throat. I never meant for Ember and I to be on the opposite sides of a war. Even now, with everything that had happened, I couldn't think of her as the enemy. But I was the heir to Talon, and I had responsibilities I could not ignore, even for family. This person, whomever she was, seemed to understand that.

Swallowing hard, I continued reading.

   You may choose to ignore my words; we are on opposite sides, after all, and I am the enemy of Talon, according to the Elder Wyrm. But, for your sister's sake, I ask that you consider what I'm about to tell you very carefully. The Elder Wyrm has plans for Ember, plans that she does not share with you, Dante. There is no easier way to say this, so I will come out with it directly: Ember Hill was created to be the Elder Wyrm's vessel. She intends to use your sister to extend her own life, to achieve immortality.

The scroll shook in my hands. For a moment, I considered crumpling the paper and hurling it out the open window, but I forced myself to continue reading the last few lines on the page.

If you wish to know more, I'm certain you can uncover the truth when you return to Talon; much like your twin, you are intelligent and resourceful, and the only way for you to truly realize what the Elder Wyrm plans for Ember is to discover it for yourself.
A friend of your sister,
—Jade

I folded the scroll and tucked it into my suit pocket, feeling numb.

My first reaction was that this was a trap, a scheme of Cobalt and the rogues, to target me and make me question the organization. Of course it had to be a trick. I was the heir of Talon and the second in command, poised to take over the company in a few years. The Elder Wyrm wouldn't keep something like this from me.

And yet... I knew that was a lie. I wasn't so naive as to think that the Elder Wyrm, the oldest, most powerful dragon in the world, would share all her secrets with me. And if this *was* true, what then? I couldn't defy Talon, and I certainly couldn't challenge the Elder Wyrm, not if I wanted to keep my position. Or even my life. I'd come too far, worked too hard, to give up everything now.

The door to the room opened with a creak and the monk stepped inside. "The council is ready for you," he announced. "Please follow me."

My mind spun as I walked the long hallway into the inner chamber again. Six ancient dragons waited for me with their answer for the Elder Wyrm, but I could barely focus. Besides, I knew what they were going say even before I set foot in the chamber.

"Dante Hill." The oldest-looking dragon rose from his seat, observing me over the table. "Blood of the Elder Wyrm. You can return to Talon with this message—the Eastern council has come to a decision, and the answer is no. We will not be joining Talon, now or anytime in the future. If this results in our destruction, then so be it. Your organization will have to survive without us."

"Very well." I bowed to them all and stepped away, suddenly eager to leave. "I will return to the Elder Wyrm with your answer. I am sorry that we could not come to an accord, that we could not change the world together."

The old dragon's eyes glittered. "The world the Elder Wyrm envisions is not a world for us," he said, and his last words followed me out of the chamber, haunting my steps. "I wonder if you yourself realize what type of world you are helping to bring about."

EMBER

I stood on deck of a large container ship, the wind snapping at my hair as the vessel plowed through the waves, and watched the moon rise over the edge of the world. The sky was clear, the moon an enormous yellow eye hovering over the water, seeming to watch us as we sailed straight into the Bermuda Triangle.

It had been nearly two days since we'd shoved off from the Florida coastline and headed due east into the North Atlantic Ocean. I didn't know what resources Lieutenant Martin had called upon, but they appeared to have come through, for this empty, midsize container ship had been waiting for us off the coast. It was inconspicuous, able to traverse vast ocean distances at a fairly good speed—Garret told me the average cargo vessel could average fourteen to seventeen kilometers per hour—and, best of all, it was perfect for holding a large number of pregnant Shifted dragons.

"I thought I might find you here."

I turned as Garret came up the steps, his boots making almost no sound on the metal rungs. He was dressed head to toe in black combat gear, and had pulled a dark ski cap over his pale hair, leaving only his face uncovered. He looked, as always, like a soldier, but one with a slightly different mission than normal. Infiltration, rather than assault. For the first part, anyway.

"We're about twenty minutes from the island," Garret said, joining me at the rail. I felt his hand brush my arm as he gazed down at me. "Are you ready for this?"

I nodded. "Ready as I'll ever be, I guess." We'd be stopping about a kilometer from the island, whereupon we would take two pairs of Zodiacs—low-slung, fast-moving rubber rafts—the rest of the way. I gazed over the water, trying to spot our destination in the darkness and moonlight, but we were still too far out. And even though I hated to ask, I felt I had to know. "What about the rest of St. George?"

"This is a mission," Garret replied. "It's what we've trained for. The target is different, but the trappings are the same. The soldiers have been conditioned to follow orders, even if it conflicts with what they believe. Even if their mission is to save a group of dragons and not slaughter them."

"And Lieutenant Ward?" He, unfortunately, was coming with us, as well. In fact, it was a fairly sizable force we were talking to the island: three dragons and two dozen soldiers of St. George, not to mention the lieutenants of the Order. Wes was staying behind with the ship, but would be in radio contact the whole time, providing support in navigating the island. We all knew what we were doing.

But a lot could go wrong, and I was trying not to think about it. I hoped Garret was right about the soldiers of the Order. We had enough to worry about without Peter Matthews, or Lieutenant Ward for that matter, going crazy in the presence of so many dragons and opening fire.

Garret eased closer, his warmth melting away the chill of the wind. "Ward is still a soldier," he reminded me in a soft voice. "He'll follow the mission, and he'll be able to keep the others in line. But if he can't…" His eyes glittered under the moonlight, filled with dark promise. "We'll do what we have to do."

I shivered, remembering his face when I'd told him about my encounter with Peter Matthews. For the first time since I'd known him, I'd been afraid Garret would lose it, that he would stalk out of the room, hunt down the other soldier and calmly break all his limbs. Thankfully, he'd controlled himself, and we'd both avoided the soldiers of the Eastern Chapterhouse until now, but I knew he was worried about Ward and his men.

I leaned into him for a moment, hearing his heartbeat echo mine. His arms slid around my waist, drawing me closer, and I sighed. "Let's hope it doesn't come to that."

"Hey."

Footsteps echoed on the stairs, and Riley appeared, walking across the deck to join us. Garret didn't release me, but Riley barely gave us a second glance as he leaned his elbows against the railing and stared over the waves. The wind tossed his loose hair and jacket, and his eyes glowed a subtle yellow in the darkness. As I often did, I could see Cobalt there, long neck raised to the sky, wings fluttering behind him in the wind.

"Gotta hand it to you, St. George," Riley murmured, his gaze still on the distant horizon. "I didn't think your Order would actually come through, but here we are. On a ship in the middle of the freaking Bermuda Triangle." He shook his head, but it wasn't in anger or disgust; he seemed truly amazed. "After all this time, the facilities are within reach. I can finally get those kids out of there, and then burn that whole place to the ground."

"We haven't rescued anyone yet," Garret said quietly. His arms were still around my waist, and he seemed content to leave them there. And strangely, I sensed no jealousy from Cobalt; it was like he didn't even notice.

"Yeah, I know." Riley gave the soldier a sideways look, then returned his attention to the sea. "Point is... I know when I'm outmatched," he muttered. "I wouldn't have been able to do this on my own. Not way out here. I wouldn't even be able to get close." He snorted and shook his head again, this time in wry disgust. "It's hilarious to think that the only way I have a chance of rescuing these dragons is with the fucking Order of St. George backing me up. If you'd told me that a year ago, I would've laughed in your face or thought you'd sailed right into crazy town. But now..." He paused, as if he couldn't believe he was saying this. "We might actually pull this crazy thing off. If the Order remembers which side they're supposed to shoot, anyway."

"Yeah," I agreed. And that was the problem; we couldn't fully trust half our team in a mission where trust was vital. For Riley's sake, and for the sake of the breeders he'd fought so hard to find, I hoped this mission would not end in tragedy.

A rumble went through the ship, the shudder of engines as the vessel slowed. Not stopping, but cutting through the waves at about half our former speed.

Garret raised his head, a flash of steely determination crossing his face as he gazed over the ocean. "There it is," he whispered, making my stomach do a couple backflips before settling. I followed his gaze and saw a distant silhouette against the blue-black of the sky.

"Yup." Riley pushed himself off the railing, that defiant smirk mirroring the gleam in his eyes. "It's showtime."

RILEY

I sat at the front of the Zodiac raft, the wind and salt spray in my face, watching the looming silhouette of the island get larger and larger. Mist sat beside me, her long hair stuffed under a ski cap, her body hidden under her Viper suit. Not for the first time, I glanced down to make sure the sleek black outfit was still under my clothes; no one had told me how the Viper suit, after a few minutes of sucking at your skin, seemed to mold to your body, until it felt like you were wearing nothing at all. When I first put it on, it was creepy as hell, and I'd wondered if I'd be able to stand the clinging sensation, which had amused Ember and Mist to no end. Now, I repeatedly forgot I was wearing it.

Six soldiers of St. George were crouched at our backs, heavily armed and dressed for battle. All of them were of the Western Chapterhouse, and Lieutenant Martin was here, as well. We, apparently, had gotten the good raft. Ember and St. George had to ride in the raft with Lieutenant Windbag and his thugs. I had no love for the Order, but I would admit that Martin, at least, could see the bigger picture.

Still, that both lieutenants of the Order were accompanying us on the mission was frustrating. This was *my* operation. I had planned it for years. The soldiers of St. George cared nothing for these dragons. In fact, under normal circumstances, this wouldn't be a rescue mission at all; it would be a strike to slaughter each and every one of them.

But I couldn't do this alone. And I understood why the lieutenants had to be here. None of these soldiers would take orders from a dragon, at least not willingly. We were barely allies. For a mission this large and volatile, where one wrong move could spell disaster for everyone, dragon and soldier alike, we couldn't take any chances.

The island loomed closer, a massive black giant against the stars. I gazed up at the huge shadow, felt excitement, anticipation and fear rip through my stomach, and took a deep breath. This was it. The location of Talon's breeding facilities. After all these years, decades of rumors, dead ends, frustration and disappointment, I had found it. The lives of countless captive dragons hung in the balance tonight. I sure as hell wasn't going to fail them.

Martin's voice cackled through my earpiece, low and commanding: "This it is. From here, we split up. See you on the other side, gentlemen."

I glanced at the lead raft and caught Ember's gaze. She sat next to St. George, the wind tossing the red curls that had escaped her cap. Her eyes were bright with determination as she gave me a nod and a faint smile, which I returned. *See you soon, Firebrand.*

The rafts veered apart. Three of them swerved sharply to

the left, heading for the northwest side of the island. My raft turned east and began following the cliffs, alone.

After several silent minutes, a small beach appeared between the foreboding cliff faces, a tiny strip of sand that was the only break in the seemingly endless wall of rock. We drove the raft onto the shore, hopping out to pull it onto the sand. After we'd dragged it out of reach of the waves, I straightened and looked around. About a hundred yards up the beach, dense jungle formed an ominous barrier between us and our targets. If anyone shipwrecked on this tiny beach, they'd have no clue that a huge, multi-million-dollar facility lay beyond that menacing tangle of vines and trees. Though I had no doubt the jungle was the least of our obstacles. The real security would be farther in.

"Wes," I said quietly into my throat mic. The hacker was back with the ship, huddled over the map on his computer, tracking our movements. "We've landed."

"Hang on," Wes muttered in my ear. "Just trying to pick up your location. Okay, I've got you. Can you hear me, Lieutenant?"

"Loud and clear," Martin replied.

"Looks like you're about two and a half miles from the first fence line," Wes continued. "Head northwest and you should reach it."

"Roger that." I nodded once and turned to Mist. "Okay, Mist. You're up."

She gave me a tight smile, took a few steps away from the soldiers and began to change. Her black Viper suit seemed to melt into her skin as the girl's body stretched and shimmered, unfurling into the sleek, silver-white dragon that was her true self. I kept a careful eye on the soldiers as she changed, hoping none of them would forget themselves and start shooting. Their eyes were wide as they stared at her, and I realized none of them had likely ever seen an actual Shift before. A couple, I saw, gripped their weapons tightly, as if fighting their instinctive response to kill any dragon they saw.

Mist ignored the soldiers, nodded at me and glided up the beach toward the jungle. Without so much as a rustle, she vanished into the shadows and undergrowth, where she would scout ahead, silent and deadly, to warn us of any potential guards, patrols or ambushes.

"All right, people." Martin's voice cut through the stunned silence. "Get it together. You've all seen dragons before, so wipe those vacant looks off your faces. Remember, this is recon and rescue, not assault. Be on your guard, and don't shoot anything unless I give the order. I don't care what it is—unless I tell you to kill it, I'd better not hear you *thinking* about pulling the trigger. Let's move."

The soldiers snapped into mission mode. Dragons or no dragons, this at least was familiar to them. Flipping our tac lights on, white beams cutting faintly through the grasping shadows, we crept silently up the beach and pushed our way into the jungle.

It closed around us, thick and menacing. The branches blocked out the sky and what little light there was, so the shadows beneath were nearly impenetrable. It was also ominously silent, much like the jungle in Brazil had been when we'd approached Ouroboros's domain. Except for our own footsteps and the rustle of vegetation as we pushed through, this jungle seemed eerily empty of life.

About ten minutes into the trek, we discovered why. The trees opened into a large clearing. A wide strip of open ground, probably fifty yards across, stretched away to either side, seeming to form a ring around the inner island.

Crouching at the edge of the trees, I scanned the clearing warily, searching for patrols and hidden sentries. But the open space was empty and still, no guards, towers or anything as far as I could see. So why an open area smack-dab in the middle of the island? Something wasn't right; I smelled a trap, even though I couldn't see one.

"Thoughts?" I muttered to Martin, crouched a few feet away. The lieutenant shook his head.

"I don't like it. But I don't see anything, either."

Mist glided out of the trees, silent as a damned ghost, appearing next to me without a sound. "There are no patrols or guards on either side of the perimeter," she announced. "It's clear."

"How certain are you of that, dragon?" Martin asked.

Mist frowned. "Very," the Basilisk answered. "Unlike you, Lieutenant, I can see in the dark. I can also smell a human from a great distance if the wind is blowing right. There are no signs that anyone has been in the vicinity for a very long while. There are no tracks, no patrol paths, no disturbed vegetation. No movement. I know how to do my job, human."

"Easy, dragon," Martin said quietly. "Not questioning your abilities, but this seems suspicious because it's so out of place. And I don't like being out in the open."

"Well, we certainly can't sit here all night," I said, and rose to my feet. "Mist, keep scouting ahead. The rest of us will follow."

With Mist leading the way, we started across the open field. And for the first minute or two, everything was normal. I was beginning to think we'd actually reach the compound without too much trouble, but of course Talon never made things that easy.

"Oh, no," I heard the Basilisk whisper from up ahead, before whirling around. "Stop!" she hissed. "Everyone, freeze!"

We froze. A couple of the soldiers raised their guns, glancing around as if expecting an attack, though the night remained silent and still. "Mist," I said in a low voice, feeling my heartbeat roar in my ears. "What's happening?"

"I just figured out the reason this place isn't guarded," Mist said. She stood like a statue in the long grass, wings half-spread, tail held stiffly over the ground. "It doesn't have to be. Look down, Cobalt, about twelve inches from your right foot. Carefully."

I followed her instructions, and my stomach gave a violent lurch as I saw a glint of metal in the weeds. "Shit," I breathed. "This is a fucking minefield."

The soldiers, who were beginning to relax, went rigid again. Martin took a quiet breath and looked at Mist, frozen in the same spot. "Can you lead us through it, dragon?" he asked in a low voice.

"I think so." Mist looked around, narrowing her eyes. "If we move very slowly, I can tell where the mines have been buried. For the most part. Step exactly where I step, and we should be fine."

"Single file," Martin told the soldiers beside us, and they moved, very carefully, into position. "No one goes forward unless the dragon tells us to."

I pressed close behind Mist, and we inched our way across the field. It was an agonizingly slow crawl, with Mist staring hard at the ground in front of her, sometimes standing motionless for long periods of time while she debated whether or not to go forward. Every time I moved or put my foot down, I held my breath, hoping I wouldn't step on a hidden mine and trigger an explosion.

Finally, after several tense, heart-pounding minutes, we reached the other side of the clearing. As we stepped into the tree line, I collapsed against a trunk in relief, as a couple soldiers did the same.

"Well," I muttered as Martin sank to a knee, gazing back over the field, "that probably shaved a good fifty years off my life. I vote we not do that again."

"Agreed," Martin said dryly. "Though I think this isn't as much about defense as it is about keeping the captives on the island."

"Yeah, I imagine so," I said. "More to discourage the breeders from trying to run away than to keep anyone out." I gazed back over the seemingly innocuous clearing and shivered. "I sure as hell wouldn't want to risk it, especially in human form."

"Unfortunately," Mist remarked, sounding worried, "it's going to make getting the breeders out challenging. At the very least, it's going to slow us down."

Dammit. I didn't think about that. Let's hope we don't have to flee a bunch of guards on our way out.

"Contact Sebastian," Martin ordered, glancing at me. "His team should know about this."

I bristled. *Contact him yourself, Lieutenant*, the immature, defiant part of me thought. *I'm not one of your damn soldiers.* But this was not the time to play "you're not the boss of me." With a sigh, I turned the mic to the soldier's private channel. "Hey. St. George."

"Riley?" came Sebastian's voice immediately. "What's your status? Everything all right?"

"We're fine. On target so far, but...ah, we've run into some potential problems." Briefly, I told him about the minefield and our brush with death. "So if you come to a large open area, proceed with caution," I advised. "One wrong step, and someone is going to have a really bad day."

"Understood." Per normal, the soldier's voice was obnoxiously calm, as if I'd told him we'd just passed a troupe of monkeys, not woven our way through a lethal minefield. "Thanks for the warning. I'll let the rest of the squad know. Where are you?"

"Close. By my estimate, we're about a half mile from the fence line."

"Let us know when you're in position."

"I will. Riley out."

I lowered my arm and looked at Mist, waiting quietly in the shadows. "All right," I said, forcing a grin. "Into the jungle of death we go. You know, if this was a movie, we'd all be dropping like flies any second now."

Mist blinked, twitching her tail. Clearly, she didn't appreciate the movie reference. "If this was a movie," she replied, "you'd be the funny smart-ass who gets tragically killed."

"Ouch. I always thought I was the ruggedly handsome hero."

She rolled her eyes and slipped into the trees again. The rest of us followed, long shadows closing around us, and we continued into the jungle.

GARRET

"That was Riley," I told a frowning Lieutenant Ward as I cut contact with the rogue. "His team just ran into a minefield on their way to the compound. No incidents, but we should proceed with caution ourselves, in case there are more."

He grunted, giving a brief nod before turning to relay the information to the rest of the squad. His voice was clipped and matter-of-fact as he told everyone to keep their eyes open for mines and other hazards and to watch where they put their feet. No mention was made of Riley and the other team, and I didn't expect there to be. Ward didn't want to be here; the idea of rescuing dragons was abhorrent to him. He'd come along only to make sure his own soldiers made it out alive and to lead the assault on a Talon facility himself. Our job tonight was to create a big enough distraction for Riley and the others to sneak away with the breeders in tow, but Ward saw it as a chance to kill Talon servants.

Probably better that way. At least here, on the front lines, Ward was good at what he was required to do. I doubted he would have been so eager if he were on the other team.

Beside me, Ember moved silently through the grass, in human form for now, the slick material of the Viper suit making her a featureless shadow. As the only dragon in the group, she was remarkably calm, surrounded by the soldiers of the Eastern Chapterhouse, all of whom watched her with combinations of suspicion and dislike. Peter Matthews, especially, kept giving her sidelong looks, his lips twisted in a sneer. I stifled the simmering heat and anger burning in my chest, but kept a close eye on him. Should he decide to act on his thoughts and go after the lone dragon in our party, he would have to get past me first.

Fortunately, the impending mission was taking priority over the dragon walking among us, and except for the dirty looks, the soldiers ignored Ember. We moved silently through the undergrowth, heading due north toward our target, until the trees thinned out and the outline of a wall could be seen at the top of a rise.

Ward halted, holding up a hand, and the squad came to a full stop. At his signal to take cover, they melted into the brush and behind trees. I huddled in the ferns, Ember beside me, and peered at the gates a few hundred yards away. Even from this distance, it looked like the entrance to a prison, a pair of watchtowers flanking the iron doors and spotlights raking the ground. We had our target; now we just had to wait until Riley's team gave the signal that they were in.

"So far, so good," Ember whispered, huddled close to me in the ferns. "Nothing has blown up or exploded in our faces, and no one has tried to shoot us in the back. I hope Riley and the others are okay."

"They're trained for this," I murmured back. "Riley knows

what he's doing, and Martin will keep the others in line. We just have to back them up when the time comes."

"I know. And I trust them." She nodded, then took a deep breath. "We have to succeed here, Garret," she whispered, staring at the wall with narrowed green eyes. "This is Riley's White Whale. He's been searching for the facilities for so long we can't let him lose this now. And for the first time, dragons and the Order are truly working together, not for survival, but for something that will change everything." She clenched a fist on her leg. "This mission is so important. We absolutely cannot fail."

"We won't." I put a hand over her fist. "No matter what it takes, or what we have to go through, we'll get the breeders off this island and take them home."

"Together," Ember added, turning to give me a piercing, almost challenging look. "No dying tonight, Garret. No crazy sacrifices. Whatever happens, we go home together."

I gave a wordless nod, and she pressed close, igniting the heat within. Crouched together, fingers intertwined, we watched the moon climb higher over the wall and waited for the coming chaos.

RILEY

Another obstacle stood between us and our objective.

This one, while not quite as lethal, was just as imposing—a twenty-foot wall of concrete, with wooden watchtowers on the corners. From where we crouched, my binoculars revealed a single guard manning the closest one. A large spotlight sat at the top of the tower, dark for now, but we certainly couldn't afford to alert anyone to our presence. If even one guard sounded the alarm, the mission would be screwed.

"Okay," I muttered, staring up at the tower. "Guess it's my turn, then. Mist?" I glanced at the white dragon. "You know what to do?"

She gave me a Draconic look of disdain. "Climb the other watchtower and take out a guard without being detected," she replied. "It's almost as if I've trained for this exact sort of thing."

I smirked. "Did the sarcasm come with the class?"

"You should know," she replied, and slipped into the darkness like a wraith.

Staying low to the ground, I ghosted up to the wall. Pressing close to the rough surface, I gazed at the top.

Twenty feet. Not too bad. Years of training with the Basilisk branch made scaling even sheer concrete walls a piece of cake. Digging my fingers into whatever cracks and holes I could find, I started climbing.

A few minutes later, after hauling myself to the lip of the wall, I got my first real look at the facilities.

Son of a bitch. The place looked like a prison camp. To the left were several large buildings, including what was probably a headquarters office and the apartments for the humans living here. I could just make out the flat plate of a helicopter pad behind the biggest square building, confirming why there were virtually no roads to and from the compound. Their supplies were likely flown in. There were a few smaller structures that could be anything from storage to the main power building, but they didn't really concern me. My attention was on the other half of the compound.

Another fence, this one made of steel and topped with coils of barbed wire, surrounded a pair of large white buildings near the eastern side of the wall. Beyond the fence, the place reminded me of an institution or rehab facility, with meandering walkways traversing a large green lawn, benches and a small pond in the center of the yard. A basketball court and a tennis net stood to one side of the smaller white building, which was still a good three stories high. There were rows of windows on every floor, none of them barred, and the whole place seemed spotlessly clean and well maintained. But the barbed-wire fence, guard towers and spotlights sliding across the yard made it very clear that this was just a fancy prison, and everyone here had received a life sentence.

The larger of the two buildings only confirmed that. It was six stories high, made of solid steel and concrete, with double iron doors tall enough to let an airplane through. I took a deep breath and let it out slowly, dispelling both rage and excitement. I could not afford to be careless now. I was here, at the facilities. And they were about as horrible as I had imagined. I would free my fellow dragons tonight, every single one of them, or I would die trying.

Preferably the first option.

I shimmied up to the platform of the first tower and eased into the room with the guard. He sat in a chair with a pair of earphones on, bobbing his head to whatever was playing on his phone. It was easy enough to slip behind him, slide an arm around his neck and send him into unconsciousness. I grabbed what looked like a key card from around his neck, stuffed a gag into his mouth and zip-tied his hands behind the chair as Mist's voice came to me over the channel.

"Target has been neutralized. Watchtower B is clear."

"Got it." I fished a rope out of my pack and tossed it over the wall to let Martin and the rest of them scale the barrier and drop to the other side. As we converged again, Mist slipped out of the shadows in human form, her black Viper suit making her blend perfectly with the night. She gave me a short nod as she rejoined us. Another obstacle cleared. One more to go.

"Wes," I muttered as we crept toward the prison fence, keeping to the shadows and along the dark sides of the buildings. "We're over the main wall. Approaching the prison yard now. What's the security like outside?"

"The spotlights are on a random rotation," Wes replied. "Electronic locks on the outer door, but I should be able to get you through that, no problem."

"Don't worry about the locks," I told him. "I grabbed a key card from one of the guards. It should get us through the door."

"Oh, well, bully for you. The challenge will be getting across the yard. Right now, I can program the spotlights to do a patterned sweep for a few seconds, but you're still going to have to get through without blundering into one of them. Think you can do that?"

I peered around the corner of the apartment buildings. The barbed-wire fence sat about eighty yards away, spotlights gliding lazily across open space. The watchtowers on the corner would be manned, but the night was dark enough to hide a group of soldiers in black slipping over the ground. If we didn't hit a spotlight. "Do we have another option?"

"Well, it's not too late to say bugger this, turn around and get off the bloody island of Dr. Moreau. But since that's about as likely as the Elder Wyrm taking up tap dancing, I'd have to say...no."

"Yeah, well, if we do this again, try to say 'no' more quickly. We're on a time limit."

"Keep your bloody pants on. I'm already working on it."

The spotlight movements changed. Very slightly; if you weren't watching them, you wouldn't notice. But before, where you couldn't predict where the circle of lights were going, now both spotlights fell into a pattern. I studied the lights for a minute, memorizing the rotation, before turning to Mist.

"You got it?"

"The pattern?" The other Basilisk looked past me to the circling lights. "Yes."

"Think you can get up there and cut a big enough hole in the fence for the rest of us before the lights come around again?"

A faint smile tugged at her lips. "I think I can manage that."

"Lieutenant." I looked at Martin. "Once Mist creates a hole, we have to get across the yard while avoiding the spotlights. So that means your men have to follow close and do *exactly* what I do. Screw this up, and the whole compound will be on us in a heartbeat."

Martin nodded. "I understand."

"All right, Mist." I handed a pair of bolt cutters to the girl. "It's all you."

She took the tool and, without hesitation, slipped across the open space to the fence. I held my breath as the spotlights swept closer, until the girl darted back again, just avoiding the edge of the light, and beckoned to us with a hand.

"Wes? Security cameras?"

"One above the front door and a few in the halls. Taking care of them now."

"All right. I'm going in. Riley out."

I crept forward, getting as close as I could without venturing into spotlight territory, then waiting until they swept around once more. As soon as they glided past, I moved, scurrying up to the fence, sliding through the hole Mist had made and hurrying across the yard while trying to stay as low and quiet as I could. The soldiers followed at my heels, moving in perfect unison, and we swept across the open ground in total darkness.

Mist was crouched by the front door as we exited the yard. A security camera hovered over the frame, winking at us ominously, but I trusted that Wes had either temporarily blacked it out or put it on a playback loop. The Basilisk gave me a grim look as I joined her.

"Door is electronically locked. Let's hope you grabbed the right key."

Without answering, I pulled the key card I'd taken from the tower guard and slid it through the slot, which beeped and turned green a second later. After yanking open the door, we slipped through the frame and closed it behind us.

I wasn't quite sure what I'd expected when I was finally inside the facility. Perhaps rows of prison cells or individual locked rooms. Certainly not what looked to be a comfortable lobby, with sofas surrounding coffee tables, a Ping-Pong table in the corner and a television on the wall. I *was* expecting the lone security guard inside the entrance, who blinked at us in shock for a half second too long; obviously *he* was not expecting a group of armed strangers to come waltzing through the front door. I lunged forward and silenced him, then dragged him behind one of the sofas.

"Now what?" Mist asked as I straightened.

I glanced at Martin. "Secure the perimeter," I told him. "Make sure there aren't more guards wandering around, and if there are, take them out quietly. Mist and I are going to find the breeders. I'll let you know when we've located them." I narrowed my eyes. "It goes without saying, but don't let any of them see you until I've explained the situation. I don't want a bunch of armed soldiers of St. George surprising them in their sleep. Then this will be less a rescue mission and more a 'get out before everything burns to the ground' mission."

Martin nodded briskly. "I'll await your signal," he said, and gestured for the soldiers to move out. They filed out of the lobby, into the dark corridors beyond, and disappeared.

"Riley." Wes's voice echoed over the com again. I crouched behind the sofa with the unconscious guard, Mist kneeling beside me, and tied his hands behind his back. "I've got a camera feed on the second floor of the place. Looks like there's a bunch of individual dorm rooms up top. I'd say that's where they're keeping the breeders, mate—the not-pregnant ones, anyway."

"Got it." I gagged the unconscious human, then carried him to a nearby closet and stuffed him inside. "On our way now."

"So, how are we going to do this exactly?" Mist wanted to know as we crept up the stairs. "Go to each individual room, one by one, and explain what we're doing to every dragon on the floor? That will take forever, even if we knew how many dragons are in this place, which we don't. We don't have that much time."

"Yeah, I know."

"And what happens if some of them don't want to leave? What if they mistake what we're doing here and sound the alarm?"

"Mist," I growled as we reached the top of the stairs. "You're not really helping with the devil's advocate stuff."

"Just want to be sure that there is an actual plan in place," she countered as we continued down a short hall and rounded a corner. A dimly lit hall stretched away before us, with numbered doors lining the walls like apartments. "And this whole daring rescue in the middle of one of Talon's biggest operations isn't relying solely on luck and your gut intuition."

"I *have* a plan—"

The soft click of a door interrupted us. Instantly, we melted back around the corner, pressing our backs to the wall, as one of the doors opened and something shuffled into the hallway.

Peeking around the corner, I set my jaw. It was a dragon, all right. A hatchling, probably in her late teens, her dark hair cropped short. She wore an oversize T-shirt that hung to her knees, and from where I stood, I could see the glint of a metal anklet above her left foot. Most likely a tracking device. My blood boiled at the thought of these dragons being held prisoner, living their whole lives on this island, simply because they didn't meet Talon's expectations. Worse, being forced to produce offspring so that Talon and the Elder Wyrm could expand their reach and become even more powerful, all under the pretense of "saving our race from extinction."

I clenched a fist. No more. That ended tonight. I might not be dealing a crushing blow to the organization anymore; now that they had their monstrous vessel army, they could simply clone mindless slaves, instead of brainwashing them from the beginning. But the dragons here, at least, would not spend another day in Talon's crushing grip. We didn't know what was coming; hell, maybe we would *all* die soon. But, for me, anyway, better to die free than live as a slave. I hoped these dragons felt the same.

The girl stepped forward, bare feet making almost no sound on the carpet. I waited until she was almost to the corner before I lunged out, clamping a hand around her mouth and pushing her back into the wall.

She stiffened, eyes going wide, as I put a finger to my lips. "I'm not here to hurt you," I whispered, hoping the kid wouldn't freak out. I suspected the non-pregnant breeders were regularly dosed with Dractylpromazine to prevent Shifting, but I didn't want to deal with a hysterical teenager, either. "My name is Cobalt, and I've come to get you out."

If possible, the girl's eyes got even bigger. I took that as a good sign and hurried on. "We're leaving," I told her. "All of us. I have a boat waiting outside that will take you and everyone else off this island. You'll never have to work for Talon again. I'm getting all of you out tonight, but we have to be quick and quiet about it. Do you understand what I'm saying?"

The girl nodded against my hand.

"And if I let you go, you won't scream and alert every guard in the place?"

She shook her head.

Okay. Holding my breath, I released her.

"Omigod," the girl blurted as soon as she was free. "You're Cobalt!"

I winced. "You wanna scream my name a little louder? I don't think the guards outside heard you."

"Oh, sorry," the hatchling said, pitching her voice to a much softer level. "It's just...you're really here." Her eyes watered, years of hope and disappointment welling to the surface. "They tell stories about you," she went on. "Some of the older dragons. They say there's a dragon on the outside who can get you out of Talon, if you're lucky enough to meet him." The sheen in her eyes grew brighter, and her lip trembled. "Director Vance told us that you don't exist, that no one has ever discovered the location of the facilities and that we're here for our own safety. But some of us still held out hope. That you were really out there, and that maybe this was the year you'd find us."

A tear slid down her face, making the guilt churning inside about a million times stronger. "I'm sorry," I said. "I came as soon as I could."

"Cobalt." Mist appeared beside me, looking stern. "There is no time for this. We need to wake the rest of the breeders and let them know what is going on, without alarming them and alerting the guards."

"I know." I turned back to the hatchling. "Where is everyone else?" I asked urgently. "Are they here, in this building?"

"Most of them." The girl glanced at Mist, saw she was a

dragon and relaxed. "The pregnant ones are next door, in the medical facilities."

"How many?"

"Five, I think."

"Shit." I raked my hands through my hair. Five pregnant dragons that couldn't Shift to human form would make sneaking out of here even more difficult. We had prepared for this scenario, so it wasn't unexpected, but having a confirmed number made the stakes more real.

I looked back at the hatchling. "What's your name?"

"Sera."

"All right, Sera, can you wake the rest of the dragons here and let them know what's going on? Get them up and ready to move out when I give the word?"

The girl paled, but nodded. "I think so."

"Good enough. Mist." I looked at the other Basilisk. "Stay with her and help. You know the plan. Don't forget to warn them about the soldiers. We don't want anyone freaking out before it's time."

Mist nodded. "I assume you're going after the pregnant breeders."

"Yeah. So you have about fifteen minutes to make sure everyone here is ready to move. Once we give the order, it's go time. Wes…" I spoke quickly into the throat com. "I'm heading into the medical facility next door. It's where they're keeping the pregnant dragons. I need to know what I'm up against."

"Hang on" came the voice on the other end. "I'll see if they have any cameras inside."

The hatchling hovered at the edge of the corridor, watching me. She was trembling slightly, worrying her bottom lip. I put a hand on her arm.

"Take Mist with you," I told her. "You can trust her, and the soldiers in the building. They're here to help. Once I get the breeders, we're all leaving together. But I need you to keep calm and make sure everyone understands what's happening. Can you do that?"

Sera took a deep breath, and nodded.

"All right." I took a step back, glancing at Mist. "I'm counting on you. If you don't hear from me in fifteen minutes, keep with the plan. I'll let Martin know what's going on."

"Cobalt." Sera met my gaze. "Be careful of Director Vance," she said, a current of fear underlying her voice. "He's the one in charge of everything, and he spends a lot of time in the medical bay. If he sees you…"

I nodded. "Thanks for the warning. I'll be careful."

I crept back down the stairs, found Martin guarding the front doors with the soldiers and explained the situation. He nodded.

"Do you need us to cover you?"

"No," I said. "Better that I talk to the breeders alone. A half-dozen pregnant dragons aren't going to take an invasion of St. George soldiers very well. Stay here, watch the building and be ready to move. Once I give the go-ahead, things are going to get crazy."

"Understood." The officer gave a grim smile. "We'll be ready."

I slipped out the door and back into the yard, easily avoiding the spotlights as they swept the perimeter. Ducking into the shadows between the buildings, I gazed up at the brick-and-mortar walls. "Wes? Anything?"

"Bugger all," Wes muttered. "Yeah, I'm in. This place is locked down tight, Riley. At least three guards, and they're all carrying these massive bloody elephant rifles. The dragons are in individual cells—two hatchlings, two Juveniles and one Adult. Also, there's some bloke in a suit walking around—looks like he could be straight from Talon."

"Got it." I slipped up to a window on the ground floor and peered in. A darkened room with white counters and medical equipment lay beyond the glass, part of the hospital bay attached to the building if I had to guess. Fishing a glass cutter out of my belt, I made a tiny circle in the window, just enough to reach my hand through and unlock the pane. Pushing up the window, I glanced around warily before slipping inside.

"I'm in the medical bay, Wes. Looks like some sort of exam room."

"Right. You shouldn't have any problems until you get to the main enclosure. Let me know when you're close, and I'll take care of the cameras."

I crept through a series of hallways that for all the world looked like part of a normal clinic. White tile floors, individual rooms with counters and shelves of equipment, a couple wheelchairs sitting against the wall. Until I reached a single door that was outlined in yellow and black stripes and read Danger! Authorized Personnel Only.

I snorted in quiet contempt. *That's a bit dramatic. It's not like we're dangerous wild animals that will bite someone in half for no reason.* Then again, if I were an imprisoned, pregnant dragon that couldn't Shift into human form, I might be a bit cranky and inclined to take it out on my human captors, too.

The door was locked, but the key card I'd taken from the guard opened it easily. As the door hissed back, I slipped into a vast, cavernous room, the roof soaring up to about sixty feet overhead. Metal walkways lined the walls, passing over rows of large enclosures about fifty feet high, with steel walls that were probably a foot thick. The temperature had skyrocketed; the air was hot and damp, and I felt like I'd stepped into a sauna. The room smelled of wet vegetation, and beneath my heavy combat jacket, the Viper suit felt uncomfortably slick.

"Wes," I muttered into the com, "I'm in the main room by the medical bay door. Can you tell me which cells are holding the breeders?"

"Hang on." There was a short pause, and I slipped between a pair of standing shelves that held things like shovels, hoses and bags of fertilizer. "Okay," Wes told me, "looks like they're in cells three, eight, thirteen, sixteen and twenty-two."

I peered at the walkways between two five-gallon buckets. "Where are the guards?"

"One patrolling the walkway, two guarding the doors on opposite ends of the room."

"And the Adult? Where is she?"

"In the last cell, mate. Twenty-two."

On the other side of the room. Of course. "Right," I muttered. "Looks like I'm headed to cell twenty-two."

As I scoured the walkway and open floor beneath, searching for the best route across the room, voices and approaching footsteps caught my attention. I ducked behind the shelves, hunkering down behind several bags of topsoil, as two figures appeared, walking toward the door I'd just come through.

I swallowed a growl. One was a dragon, a tall man in a business suit, with short brown hair and a perfectly groomed goatee. He was also an Adult, given the way my instincts shrank back, wanting me to crawl beneath the shelves to hide. This must be the famous Director Vance, the one in charge of this island of atrocities. He was speaking to a balding human doctor–type with glasses and a white lab coat, the smaller man nervously tapping a pencil against his clipboard as they walked.

"Scarlett should be ready to lay any day now," the human was saying as they got closer. "She just started nesting behavior this morning, so I stopped her food and ordered her habitat be put in isolation mode until the egg arrives. Which should be sometime tomorrow or the next day, if I had to guess."

"Good," the dragon said. "I've just received word from Talon. This is to be Scarlett's final hatching. Once the egg has been sent to the organization, terminate her name from the schedule."

The human chewed his lip. "Forgive me, Director," he ventured, and those cold dark eyes fixed on him, unblinking. "I understand Talon's desire to scale back production," the human went on as the pencil resumed its anxious tapping against the clipboard. "But Scarlett has always produced healthy, fertile eggs. Now that we've reduced the number of resident females by nearly half, she is one of the only breeders left who is a known quantity. I'm not one to question the organization's motives, but—"

"Then don't." Director Vance narrowed his eyes, seeming to loom over the smaller human, who cringed away from him. "You are not paid to question Talon, Dr. Miles. You are here to keep our breeders healthy and happy, and to make certain the eggs arrive safely and on time, a task that you are paid exceptionally well to do. What Talon does with the members of our organization is not your concern. I suggest you put it from your mind and follow orders before you find yourself out of work, on a small raft, in the middle of the Bermuda Triangle."

His voice raised the hair on the back of my neck. I'd heard

his kind speak many times before, but that cold, clinical detachment never ceased to infuriate me. As if he were discussing the inner workings of a car, rather than a living, breathing, sentient creature. I remembered the fear in Sera's voice when she spoke of Director Vance, and my resolve hardened even further.

"Yes, Director." The human's voice trembled, but there was a hint of sullenness there, too. "As you say. I'll remove Scarlett from the list and prepare her for deportation." The medical bay door opened with a hiss, and the pair vanished from sight as it closed behind them.

As soon as they were gone, I hurried across the room, careful to locate the three guards and time my approach so that I passed out of sight of each of them. Thankfully, the room was dim, with heavy shadows making stealth a bit easier. As I reached the cell labeled twenty-two, I saw that a single large window had been set into the front of the otherwise solid steel walls. Through the glass, a junglelike habitat greeted me, heavy vegetation and indoor trees growing along the inner wall. Beside the window sat a pair of huge, dragon-size doors that looked thick enough to hold up to a tank, but a normal-size door was also set into the wall to the left of the window. A single lightbulb glowed a warning red beside it, probably to indicate the cell was occupied.

"Wes?" I crouched in the shadows under the walkway, ready to make that final dash. "I'm about to break into cell twenty-two. Where are the cameras?"

"Give me a second" came the terse reply, followed by a moment of silence. "Okay, the one in twenty-two shouldn't be a problem now. But…" And a slow whistle came through the earpiece. "Bloody hell. I'd be careful if I were you, mate."

That sounds ominous. A familiar key card slot blinked at me as I eased up to the human-size door, and I grimaced as I pulled out my stolen card. *Let's hope this thing works here, too,* I thought, and swiped it through the reader.

The light beeped green, and I slipped into the habitat of a pregnant Adult dragon.

It was even warmer in here, and humid, reminding me again of the jungle where Ouroboros had staked his territory. I felt sweat form on my brow and run down my neck. My boots squelched in soft dirt as I turned carefully, searching the vegetation. *Okay, so where is this dragon Wes is so worried about—?*

I felt her approach before I saw it; a low growl rippled through the air, and the branches rattled as a twenty-foot crimson dragon stalked out of the shadows and came right at me.

I stood my ground, holding up my hands to indicate I wasn't a threat, as the Adult female prowled close and stopped, her muzzle just a few feet away. Her teeth were slightly bared, and smoke curled from her nostrils as we stared at each other. Golden eyes narrowed as they met mine, puzzled and suspicious but not entirely hostile. I didn't move, keeping my hands raised and empty, but careful not to show any fear. I didn't think she would attack and savage me like a mother bear, but I was a stranger, and I *had* invaded the territory of a nesting female dragon; her protective instincts would be very high right now. Add imprisonment, restlessness and poor treatment at the hands of her human captors, and that probably wasn't doing a lot for her disposition.

On second thought, she was showing remarkable restraint

not biting me in half like a twig. Maybe I should've had a little more foresight before barging in unannounced.

The dragon stared at me, then curled her lip back, just enough to show fangs. "Who are you?" she demanded, though she kept her voice low and quiet. Well, as quiet as a twenty-foot dragon could be. "You don't work here. I've never seen you before." Her eyes glittered, the tip of her tail swishing an agitated rhythm behind her. "Have you come from Talon? What do you want with me?"

"Scarlett." I stretched a hand toward her, keeping my movements slow and my tone soothing. "My name is Cobalt. I'm not here to hurt you. I came to get you all out of here. Tonight."

"Cobalt." The dragon's voice was flat. Sitting back, she raised her head with a sniff, then peered down at me with sorrowful eyes. "So, you're not a myth, after all."

"No," I agreed. "I'm not. Sorry it took me so long, but it's over now. We're leaving this place, and you'll never have to see it again."

The dragon sighed. "Maybe for everyone else," she said, sounding weary all of a sudden. "But it's too late for me. There's no way off the island. I'm too close to nesting, so I can't fly very far. And I certainly can't swim to the nearest continent."

"You won't have to," I told her. "I didn't come alone. There's a ship waiting about two hundred yards off the western side of the island. You won't have to swim far."

"We'll never make it," Scarlett insisted. "You're going to get us all killed before we ever reach the water."

"Do you not want to get out of here?" I asked, frustrated.

"Of course I do!" Her tail lashed, causing a handful of leaves and twigs to flutter to the ground. "But have you seen what lies between us and the beach?" She shook her horned head, curling her talons in the dirt. "We'd have to go through an army of humans and guns. And Director Vance. He's not going to let us just walk out." She shivered, folding her wings tight to her body. "I've been here longer than almost everyone now," she whispered, a haunted look going through her eyes. "I've seen what happens to dragons who try to escape. I've talked a few of them out of it myself. We won't get past the fence before we're gunned down. Talon would rather kill us all than let us go free."

"Scarlett, listen to me." I stepped forward and put a hand on one scaly foreleg. She blinked and gazed down with resigned gold eyes. "I know what I'm doing," I told her softly. "There is a plan in motion as we speak. I have friends, well, not exactly *friends*, but people, both on the island and outside, who are committed to getting you all out of here." I didn't want to go into the details of how we had convinced the Order of St. George to help us, and there was no time to explain even if I did. "We didn't go into this expecting it to be easy, but we didn't come unprepared, either. Right now, I need you to trust me. Can you do that?"

The dragon sighed out a long, writhing cloud of smoke and bowed her head. For a moment, she stood there, huge body coiled and tense, her talons curled in the dirt. Finally, she relaxed and looked at me, her voice becoming a growl. "If there is really a chance to leave this place," she rumbled, "I will take it. And maybe I'll bite some heads off on my way out. What do you need me to do?"

Relief flickered, but I couldn't be distracted now. "When I give the order," I said, "things are going to get crazy. I don't have time to sneak around to every cell and let the others know what's going on, not without being spotted by the guards. When the shit hits the fan, I need you to rally the other dragons. You're the biggest and oldest here—they'll listen to you. Let them know what's happening, and then be ready to move on my signal. Will you do that?"

Scarlett nodded, but then a soft beep jerked my attention behind me. I spun, just as the door opened and a man walked into the room, the same doctor who had been speaking to Director Vance earlier.

"Scarlett," the doctor was saying as he came forward. "I've just received word from the director. You are to be..."

He stopped, eyes going wide as he saw me, but I was already moving. Lunging, I grabbed the human by the collar and shoved the barrel of my gun in his face, pressing him back to the wall. The human gasped, and his clipboard dropped to the floor.

"*Shh*, Doctor," I growled, smiling at him over the firearm. "Don't make any stupid decisions. I'd hate for this to go off at such a short range."

"Who are you?" The human's voice trembled; he stared at me, then glanced over my shoulder at Scarlett. A sheen of sweat covered his brow, but that might've been from the heat. "How did you get in here? If you've hurt any of these creatures—"

"Hurt them?" I bared my teeth in a vicious smile. "Trust me, human. I'm not like you. I'm taking your 'creatures' out of here, far away, where you and Talon will never get your filthy hands on them again."

"Cobalt, wait." Scarlett strode forward, her shadow climbing the wall as she loomed over us. "Don't hurt him. Dr. Miles is a good man. He's not like the other Talon servants. He really does look out for us, as much as he can."

I gave a dubious snort, but the human stared at me, his eyes going even wider behind his spectacles. "You...you'll really take them away?" he whispered. "All of them? You have a plan to get them out of here, without being killed?"

I nodded warily.

"Good." The human gave a fervent nod, gripping my shirt. "Good! Take them. Do what you want with me, but get them as far away from Talon as you can. They don't deserve to be here. Nothing deserves the kind of treatment the organization inflicts on their own kind. If you can really get them all away from Talon..." He shook his head, his eyes a little watery as he looked at Scarlett. "Your name is on the deportation list," he told her, and I felt the dragon stiffen behind me. "And we both know that dragons who leave the facility are never heard from again. If there is a chance for you to escape Talon, you must take it."

"Will you help us?" Scarlett asked before I could say anything. I wanted to glare back at her, but didn't want to take my eyes of the doctor, either. "You can get to places we cannot, Doctor. Will you help us, one last time?"

"Hang on a second," I growled. "What makes you think I'm about to trust this guy? If he alerts any of the guards, this operation is done. None of us are getting out alive."

"Then knock me out, or leave me here," Dr. Miles said. "I won't stop you. But..." He closed his eyes for a moment, then continued in a strained voice. "I can get to the security room, and open all the cells at once. That would make things easier for you, wouldn't it? Leaving the island, however..." He met my gaze. "I don't know how you're going to get everyone past the guards and the security, but you made it this far, so I assume you have a plan for escape."

"Dammit," I muttered. I was going to have Wes try to unlock the cell doors, but if this human could open them all at once, that would make getting out of here a lot easier. If he didn't sell us out.

"We can trust him, Cobalt," Scarlett said, as if reading my thoughts. "I trust him. He won't betray us to Talon."

I set my jaw. "Fine," I muttered, and stepped back, lowering the gun. "But if you double-cross us, let all their deaths be on your head, and know that I *will* come for you even if it kills me. How soon can you get to the place you need to be?"

"Two minutes" was the reply. "How much time do *you* need?"

"That should be enough. I'll give my team the two-minute warning. Don't throw the locks until you hear it start."

"Hear...what start?"

I smiled coldly. "You'll know when it begins. Trust me."

The human paled but pushed himself off the wall and hurried to the door. "Give me two minutes from the time I walk out," he said over his shoulder. "And Scarlett...good luck to you. Tell the rest of them I hope their lives will be better."

"I will," the dragon said solemnly. "Thank you, Doctor. For everything."

He nodded once more and vanished through the frame.

"Mist," I growled into the com as soon as the door had closed. "We're about to start. Where is everyone?"

"All here" came the instant reply. "Everyone is gathered, and the soldiers are ready. Waiting on your order."

"Good." I checked my watch. One minute, thirty-nine seconds till go time. "Stand by." I switched channels and growled, "You there, St. George?"

"Yes."

"In position?"

"Ready and waiting."

"Okay." I counted down the last few seconds and took a deep breath. "Light it up."

GARRET

"Bravo is in position." I raised the night vision binoculars and saw the large front gate, flanked by two watchtowers, that led into the main compound. Ember crouched beside me, in human form for now, though I could almost feel the buzz of energy surrounding her, ready to explode into wings and scales. I looked behind me at the soldier with the RPG aimed at the compound, and nodded. "Fire."

With a deafening hiss and a line of smoke, the rocket-propelled missile slammed into the heavy iron gates, and the explosion that lit up the sky could probably be heard for miles. Almost immediately, spotlights flared to life in the towers, sweeping down to rake the ground in front of us, and shouts of alarm echoed through the ruined gates, getting closer every second.

Here we go. I glanced at Ember, who caught my eye and offered a grim smile, as the soldiers around us raised their guns and dug into position. "Don't get killed, soldier boy," she ordered, reaching down to squeeze my arm "We're going home after this. All of us."

I smiled. "Count on it."

Men poured through the shattered gates, and the soldiers around me opened fire, filling the air with the howl of machine guns. I raised my weapon and joined the fray as Ember Shifted and launched herself skyward with a blast of wind. Her chilling battle cry rose over the screams and roar of gunfire, and everything dissolved into chaos.

I knelt behind a tree, firing short, controlled bursts at the enemy before ducking back into cover to avoid retaliation. The enemy guards, once they realized they had been ambushed, quickly sought cover behind the walls and shattered gate. There were more than I'd first thought, and they wisely did not press forward to engage us in the open, returning fire from the safety of their walls and towers. The spotlight raked over the ground, pinning a soldier in its glare one second before he was torn to pieces by gunfire.

"We need to take down those towers!" Ward's voice hissed in my ear. "Sebastian, you're close. See if you can draw its fire. Matthews, be ready to take the gunners out when he does."

I gritted my teeth. For a split second, I couldn't help but wonder if this was a ploy to get me killed. But I was a soldier, and he was my commanding officer. I had to trust he knew what he was doing.

I popped out of cover, firing several rounds at the closest watchtower, trying to see past the blinding circle of light as it swung around. Just before it reached me, I dove behind the tree again, and a storm of bullets peppered the trunk, tearing chunks from the wood and showering me with splinters.

I huddled against my vanishing cover, expecting a round in my back at any moment.

There was a Draconic roar of fury, a flare of orange light that lit up the forest, and the storm of bullets abruptly ceased. I peeked around the shredded trunk to see the watchtower on fire, flames pouring from the roof and out the sides, as a small crimson dragon wheeled around to strafe it again. Cries of alarm rang out, and shots were fired after her, but Ember twisted in midair and darted into the trees.

"Press forward!" Ward snapped, sounding grimly pleased. "All units, take the wall. Don't give them a chance to recover."

We converged on the gate, using Ember's distraction to gain ground quickly. But as we approached the wall, a shiver ran up my spine, and the hairs on the back of my neck stood straight up. Something was coming...

I glanced up just as a massive shadow fell from the sky, landing in front of the gate with a crash that shook the ground. Spreading its wings, a huge, dark green Adult raised its head and glared down at us, hatred and loathing shining brightly in its yellow gaze.

"St. George." Contempt dripped from the dragon's voice as the rest of my unit fell back, raising their guns. "How dare you butchers come here. Is there no place we can be free of you?" With a snarl, it lowered its neck and spread its wings, as if blocking the path to the compound. "Your assault ends here," it growled, and I saw the telltale swelling of its sides that made my adrenaline spike. "I will kill you all before I let you touch our females!"

I threw myself aside as the dragon's jaws opened and the inferno rushed forth like the blast of a rocket engine. The dragon swept its head around, searing the ground and catching a pair of soldiers in the flames. They cried out and reeled away, blazing like torches, before crumpling to the grass.

"Kill it!" Ward snarled, unnecessarily, as the remaining soldiers opened fire. The Adult roared, rearing up as bullets tore into its body or sparked off its armored chest plates. "Kill it now!"

With a roar and a blast of flame, the dragon lunged into the midst of the soldiers. One swipe from a huge forepaw sent several of them flying. Its jaws snaked down, grabbed another soldier and hurled him into the wall with a sickening crack. I rolled to my feet in the embers and smoking grass, sparks and burning debris drifting all around me, and raised my weapon, but gunfire rang out from behind the wall as the enemy guards pressed their advantage, and I had to duck behind a tree to avoid taking fire. Between the raging dragon and the guards, we were forced to fall back, giving way under the relentless assault of fire and lead.

"Tristan!" I hissed into the com as bullets peppered the tree I crouched behind. "Do you see this?"

"Yeah." My partner's voice was tight with frustration. "I do, but the thing's staying back behind the wall. I only have a bead on its front, which might not do anything even if it does hit. I can't get a clean shot."

I looked back toward the battle. Ward was still shouting orders over the bark of his own rifle, standing his ground even as the dragon sliced through his unit like paper. It lashed out with a claw, knocking the last of the soldiers away, and suddenly it was just Ward, standing alone in front of an Adult dragon. The dragon lunged, and Ward leaped back to avoid the snapping fangs, but hit a chunk of broken wall and fell, sprawling to his back. Still firing his weapon, to no avail. The

Adult stalked forward, ignoring the rounds that sparked off its chest plates. I could see the triumph in the dragon's eyes as it took a breath, and I knew I was about to watch the strike team commander get incinerated.

The flames roared from the dragon's jaws, blazing a hellish orange-red, and Ward disappeared into the blaze. I clenched my fist against the trunk, angry that I hadn't been able to do anything. Despite my personal feelings and his blatant hatred for me and my dragon friends, his death would still be a blow to St. George, and we couldn't take much more of them.

The inferno flickered and died away, and my eyes widened. Ward still sprawled over the ground, head turned away as if bracing himself to die, the grass around him charred to a crisp. Ember stood over him, head lowered and wings spread, glaring up at the Adult dragon with defiant green eyes. She'd used her own fireproof body to shield the lieutenant, and the Adult snorted in surprise as the flames disappeared.

"Ember Hill?" Cocking his head, the Adult regarded her, puzzled. "You…why are *you* here? Did you come to assault this base with St. George? But I thought you and Cobalt…"

He trailed off, yellow eyes suddenly widening with realization and alarm. "Cobalt," he muttered, turning back toward the buildings. "He's here. On this island. He's come for my breeders!"

Ignoring us all and the shots still being fired in his direction, the huge Adult opened his wings, launched into the air and streaked back the way he came. Toward the facilities, Cobalt and the females.

RILEY

I heard the explosion even through the walls of Scarlett's habitat.

The dragon jerked her head up, teeth bared, eyes dilating in alarm. "What was that?"

"Our signal to leave," I said, striding to the front of the cell. "Let's hope your doctor friend did what he said he would do and unlocked all the doors, otherwise this will be a really short prison break. Mist," I said, speaking into the com as I turned. "I have the pregnant dragonells. Start the evacuation—I'll meet you outside in two minutes. And don't forget the minefield. Lead them through one at a time if you have to, but don't get anyone blown up. The soldiers should be taking care of any guards that would come after us."

"Roger that." A moment's pause, and then: "Good luck, Cobalt."

"You, too."

I looked back. The red dragon was still standing in the middle of the habitat, listening to the sounds of rising conflict, wings half-flared and trembling. "Scarlett!" I snapped, making her jump. "You can't freeze up on me now," I said. "I need your help to gather the rest of the dragonells. My team is out there, launching a distraction so we can get the hell out, but if everyone here panics, we're all going to die. We need to let the others know what's happening. Are you with me?"

She blinked, and a steely look crossed her reptilian face. "I'm with you," she growled, and strode forward, toward the large iron doors at the front of the cell. I had to scramble out of the way as the large Adult dragon barreled past me and struck the double gates with the force of an oncoming semi. There was a crash that sounded like two vehicles colliding, and the doors flew open with a bang.

"Shit!"

A shot rang out from the room beyond, sparking off the metal frame, and Scarlett hissed with fury. Sprinting out behind her, I raised my gun and fired several shots at the guard overhead on the walkway who was aiming his very large rifle at the dragon who had come bursting out of her cell. At the same time, a gout of flame hissed through the air as Scarlett spat fire at the guard, and he tumbled from the railing like a burning torch.

I looked around. Dragons were emerging from cells around the room, confused and bewildered and much smaller than Scarlett. A yellow-green hatchling with brown stripes down her neck and back spotted me and gave a hiss of alarm, baring her fangs.

"Intruder!" she snarled, and crouched down as if unsure whether to flee or fight. "You don't work here. Did you kill Dr. Miles? Who are you?"

Her outburst attracted the attention of the three other drag-

onells—two Juveniles and another hatchling—who stared at
me with wary eyes. But before I could say anything, a shadow
fell over us as Scarlett marched forward, raising her head to
glare down at them all.

"His name is Cobalt," she said without preamble. "We can
trust him. He's here to get us out."

"Out?" The yellow-green hatchling blinked at the Adult in
disbelief. "What do you mean, out?"

"I mean I'm here to get you off the island," I broke in. "What
you're hearing outside…that's my team launching a distraction
so the rest of us can escape. I have a container ship waiting
just off the northern beach. It's a bit of a swim, but once we
get there, you'll be free. You can leave Talon and this hellhole
and never look back."

"All of us?" one of the Juveniles asked. "What about everyone in the building next door?"

"They're being taken care of. I have people moving them out
as we speak." I pointed back toward the entrance. "We go out
the front, meet the rest of them on the other side of the wall
and leave while the guards are dealing with the other team."

"What if we're shot at?"

"We'll protect you." I gazed around at them, seeing fear, un-
certainty and a very cautious hope. "It'll be risky, but this is
the best way to get you all out. If someone does try to stop us,
fight back however you can. Don't let them capture you—I'm
not leaving anyone behind."

"We could be killed!"

Above me, Scarlett snarled, her booming voice making
the rest of them jump. "What would you rather do?" she demanded. "Stay here, in this prison, for the rest of your lives?
Give up your choice, your free will and your bodies to Talon, so

the organization can raise more dragons that think like them? Do you want your offspring to go through that? And, if they don't meet Talon's requirements, end up here?"

The hatchling cringed, and one of the Juveniles shook her head. "No," she growled. "Fuck that. I'm done with this place. I'd rather die trying to escape than live here another day. Let's get out of here."

Relieved, I nodded. "Okay, then. Follow me."

As we hurried to the large double doors of the front entrance, an explosion echoed from somewhere outside, flaring through the windows. Hoping that these doors were unlocked, as well, I put my shoulder against the iron surface and shoved it as hard as I could. The heavy steel door groaned as it swung back, opening onto a war zone.

Oh, boy.

I could see the battle in the distance, the flare of dragon-fire and gunshots lighting up the darkness. The yard, except for the roving spotlights, was eerily vacant, though it was obvious where all the guards were. Shouts and screams rose into the air over the howl of gunfire, and the unmistakable roar of an Adult dragon made me shiver.

"Director Vance," Scarlett growled behind me. "He's a real bastard. I hope your people came prepared."

"Don't worry about them. They can handle it." *I hope.* An explosion pulsed through the air, followed by an enraged snarl, and I winced. *Ember, St. George, be careful. Don't either of you get yourselves killed.*

Directly ahead of us, the gates to the yard hung open, a pair of dead or unconscious guards lying between the posts. "Mist?" I growled into the com. "Status report. Where are you?"

"We just made it over the wall" was the reply. "There are

twenty-four confirmed breeders, about two-thirds of them hatchlings. They've been given regular doses of Dractylpromazine, so they won't be able to Shift for several hours. The soldiers had to kill two guards on our way out, and one breeder was injured when a bullet grazed her arm, but otherwise everyone is fine."

Better than I could hope for. "Head for the beach. Don't wait for us, just get going. We're on our way."

"Understoo—"

"Riley!" Sebastian's voice rang over the com, urgent and almost frantic, making my blood chill. "Wherever you are, get out of there! The Adult is coming back."

"Shit." Spinning around, I pointed east, toward the gradually lightening sky. "Run," I told the dragons, who stared at me wide-eyed. "Get out of here! Fly west until you hit the beach. You should be able to see the ship from there."

"Alone?" the yellow hatchling asked, her eyes going huge. "What about you? Aren't you supposed to lead us—"

"The director is coming," I snapped, making them all jerk up. "He's on his way now, and I sure as hell am not going to lead him to everyone else. You five get out of here—I'll slow him down at least."

Scarlett shook her head. "Cobalt—"

"This isn't negotiable," I said, cutting her off. "I promised to get you out of here, and I will. Once you're over the wall, stay low, below the tree line, so you won't be seen from the air. There is nothing between you and freedom now, as long as you decide to step out and meet it. So, get going." They still hesitated, torn between flight and staying behind, and my voice became a snarl. "Move!"

The hatchlings went first, taking to the air in a flurry of

wings. A heartbeat later, the Juveniles followed. Only Scarlett remained behind, her eyes hard and defiant as they stared at me, as if daring me to make her move. I gave a weary smile in return.

"Go on," I said, nodding my head at the sky. "Don't worry about me. This is why we came, Scarlett, to make certain we got you out. So get going. I'll be fine."

Her tail thumped against the dirt, and she took a step back. "Don't die," she ordered as her wings finally unfurled, sweeping red curtains that caught the wind. "We still need you."

"I'll give it my best shot," I promised. "Now get out of here already."

She launched herself into the air, whipping cyclones of dust that buffeted my hair and clothes, and soared away after the others. I watched until they had cleared the outer wall and quickly dropped out of sight.

I turned back, took off my gun belt and shed my human form. Wings and tail uncurled as Cobalt rose up, breaking through my skin. For a split second of distraction, I wondered what the Viper suit would do; if I would feel anything as it molded to my body. There was a moment of discomfort, the sensation of a too-small shirt being pulled over my chest, then nothing.

A low growl vibrated the dirt at my feet. Heart pounding, I looked up as a fifty-foot, dark green dragon prowled around a building and came to a stop between the gateposts. He was breathing hard; blood from numerous bullet wounds ran down his scales and dripped to the ground, but he still looked healthy enough to squash me like a cockroach. Slowly, he gazed around the empty yard before stopping on me. I dug my talons into the dirt as he stepped through the gate, his voice rippling through the air like a thunderstorm.

"Where are they?"

"Gone," I replied, forcing myself to meet the stare of an ancient Adult. "Safe. Somewhere you'll never find them."

"Ex-Agent Cobalt." Vance came to a stop in the middle of the yard, close enough that his enormous shadow still fell over me. Close enough for me to feel the power radiating off his scales. "The organization told me you were dead."

"Yeah. I get that a lot."

The Adult dragon ignored that statement. "Rest assured, I will find my breeders," he said, sounding confident and assured. "There is no escape, no place on this island that they can hide. Save me some time. Tell me where they are, and I'll make your death painless."

I curled my muzzle in a sneer. "Oh, didn't you know? I stole them away to *my* magic island, where I'm the king and they're all part of my harem. Sorry, but I don't really feel like giving them back."

"Very well." Vance smiled coldly and took a step closer. "Then I suppose I'll have to pull your limbs off one by one, until you feel more cooperative."

I took a deep breath. No way in hell I was going to win this fight. That was fine; I just had to keep him here, keep him distracted, until the breeders reached the ship and the evacuation was complete. Maybe I'd even come out of this alive.

And then, a shadow fell over us, a second before Ember swooped down with a flash of metallic red and landed beside me. Stunned, I blinked at her, and she shot me a sideways grin.

"Garret and the others are on their way," she told me in a near-whisper. "They just have to get through the rest of the guards. We can hold out until then, right?" Turning, she stepped forward, toward the Adult looming above us, and raised her voice. "This guy isn't that scary."

Vance snorted in contempt. "Your bloodline will not save you, Ember Hill," he growled, and stalked forward. I tensed, lowering myself into a crouch, and saw Ember do the same. "You have no idea what you've done. Do you think the breeders will be able to survive without Talon? That this so-called 'freedom' is worth risking your lives over?" He curled a lip. "They were safe here. If you take them into the world now, they will all die when Talon launches the final stage of their plan. I will not allow that to happen." His eyes narrowed, zeroing in on Ember. "Even if I must kill the daughter of the Elder Wyrm myself!"

EMBER

He lunged at me, covering the space between us in a leap, jaws gaping to bite me in half. I sprang into the air to avoid it, hearing his jaws snap shut below me, and immediately dove at his back, landing between his wings and sinking my claws into his scales.

He roared and spun on me like a snake, frighteningly quick for his size. I saw his head whip around from the corner of my eye, and I leaped out of the way, barely dodging his fangs a second time. As I flew off his back, I saw Cobalt lunge in and rake his claws down the Adult's leg and shoulder. There was a faint metallic screech, and Cobalt darted away as Vance lashed out at him. I spun in midair and came back for another attack, but the Adult swung his head around again, bashing me in the side with his horns. I heard something snap as I tumbled from the air and hit the earth, then rolled to a painful stop at the base of a tower.

"Ember!" Cobalt raced toward me, but Vance whirled and lashed out with a talon, swatting him into the fence. The blue dragon went through the barrier and collapsed to the ground, dazed and tangled in wire.

The Adult prowled forward, half-open wings draping me in shadow. "Insects," he murmured, watching me stagger upright, an amused smile on his face. "Hatchlings. You cannot hurt me. You are a vague annoyance at best." I lunged at him with a snarl, but a stab of pain went through my ribs, slowing me down, and a clawed forepaw smashed into my shoulder like a sledgehammer, sending me tumbling over the ground. "Where are my breeders?" Vance rumbled, stalking toward me. I staggered upright, but a heavy claw slammed into my back, crushing me to the ground again. I gasped for breath as the world went fuzzy. "Tell me," the voice overhead growled. "I know they are still on the island. Point me in the direction they went, and I will let you live to face the wrath of the Elder Wyrm."

"*Rnesh karr slithis,*" I spat at him, and he chuckled.

"Such language," he said, and casually bent my wing backward. There was a snap, and I shrieked in agony as the Adult let the broken limb drop. "You try my patience, Ember Hill," he said as I panted through clenched teeth and tried not to pass out from the pain. "I will ask again. Where are my breeders? I encourage you to make it easy for yourself. I have at least five more limbs I can break before I start peeling off scales."

Garret, I thought, squeezing my eyes shut. *Where are you?*

"Still not talking?" The Adult sighed and gripped my other wing. "Then I suppose we'll have to do this hard way."

"Director!"

A roar echoed above us. I looked up, just as another Adult with dark red scales slammed into Vance, knocking him off me. The two Adults crashed to the dirt, making the ground tremble like an earthquake. Vance let out a bellow of fury.

"Scarlett! You traitorous bitch! What are you doing?"

The other dragon smiled, golden eyes shining with hate. "Something I've wanted to do for years," she growled, and lunged at the Director. Vance reared up to meet her, and the two behemoths collided with the screech of metallic scales and claws.

I staggered to my feet, still dizzy from the throbbing pain of my broken wing. Gritting my teeth, I stumbled away from the battle, watching as Scarlett lashed out and raked a gaping wound across the larger dragon's neck. With a furious hiss, the director plowed into her, using his greater bulk to knock her over, trying to pin her down to end the fight. Snarling, Scarlett rolled onto her back and used her hind legs to rip and gouge at the other dragon's stomach. Blood ran down the scales of both dragons, staining the ground crimson.

"Ember!"

Cobalt appeared beside me, panting, his yellow eyes bright with pain. "Are you all right?" he asked anxiously. His gaze landed on my wing, hanging uselessly at my side, and narrowed furiously. "That son of a bitch! I'll kill him."

"We have to help Scarlett." I looked back at the raging Adults. Scarlett, still under Vance, was putting up a good fight; blood streaked his underside and shoulders from where her talons clawed at him. But Vance was larger; he still had her pinned and appeared to be biding his time.

"Ember, you're hurt…" Cobalt began, but I'd already started across the yard, ignoring the shrieking pain in my wing. With a growl, he bounded after me.

As I got close, Vance abruptly snaked his head down, dodging a blow from Scarlett's talons, and clamped his jaws around her neck, right below her chin. My stomach dropped, and Scarlett screamed, slashing and clawing furiously, trying to throw him off. Vance dropped his full weight onto her, crushing her to the earth, and the red dragon's struggles grew weaker and weaker.

I hit the Adult dragon as hard as I could, sinking my talons into his shoulder, tearing through scales into flesh and muscle. Vance jerked, his huge body shuddering, but he couldn't turn to deal with the annoying hatchling dragon without letting go of Scarlett. I dodged a swat from his tail and went for him again, leaping to his back to assault the base of his neck, biting and clawing wherever I could reach. I saw Cobalt leap at him, as well, sinking his talons into the dragon's side and raking several long furrows down his ribs.

With a roar, Vance turned on us, releasing Scarlett to whip his head around. I felt jaws close on my hind leg a second before I was hurled through the air, the ground rushing up at me. I struck the earth and rolled, and everything fractured into blinding shards of agony.

For a few seconds, it was all I could do not to pass out. Through my hazy, darkening vision, I saw Vance swat Cobalt away and turn on me with murder in his eyes. He took a step forward...

And a shot rang out somewhere close, causing the dragon to jerk up with a snarl. Blearily, I turned my head. A handful of soldiers swarmed into the yard, the chatter of M14s echoing off the buildings. As I struggled to stay conscious, one pale-haired soldier leaped over a pile of rubble, spun to face the dragon and fired a flurry of shots into its side.

"Garret," I whispered as Vance bellowed with rage. As the soldiers spread out, surrounding him, he drew back, nostrils flaring, to unleash a column of fire at his enemies.

He didn't see Scarlett stagger to her feet, eyes burning, and make one last, desperate lunge. As the director's mouth opened, glowing red with imminent flames, the crimson dragon struck him hard, knocking him off balance, and clamped her jaws around his throat.

This time, the dragon's booming roar was strangled. He turned on Scarlett, raking with his claws, trying to jerk free. His blows opened terrible wounds all over her body, but as I watched, unable to stand or even move, Scarlett closed her eyes and clung to him with stubborn determination. The soldiers surrounded the pair, continuing to fire on the director, whose struggles finally began to slow. I saw Garret sprint forward, dodge beneath Vance's long tail and aim his weapon at the dragon's side. Right behind the foreleg where the heart would lie. At such short range, the bullets finally pierced through the dragon's scales and slammed deep into his body.

Vance convulsed, tail and wings thrashing, and Garret dove out of the way. With Scarlett still clinging to his neck, the huge dragon staggered, swayed and finally collapsed, hitting the ground with a crash that sent tremors through the earth. His sides heaved, his tail beating a weak rhythm in the dirt until, slowly, both stopped moving. With a last groan, the massive Adult dragon shuddered and went limp, the light fading from his yellow eyes, as he finally relinquished control and slipped away into death.

RILEY

The bastard was finally dead. I watched as the director of Talon's infamous facilities—the dragon in charge of this island, who knew exactly what two dozen female dragons went through, day after day, and remained coldly indifferent to their suffering—shuddered once and gave up the fight. Relief, triumph and a sadistic glee blossomed in my stomach as the Adult finally went still. I had never in my entire life been so happy to see another dragon die.

But that didn't erase my failure, or the price of our victory. While the soldiers of St. George cheered and pumped their fists in the air, I limped across the broken ground to where the two Adult dragons lay entwined together. Vance stared sightlessly upward, jaws parted and his tongue lolling out of his mouth. Even in death, he looked surprised, as if he couldn't believe he had lost. Scarlett lay motionless beside him, eyes closed, her jaws still locked around his neck. She was still alive, though her breaths were labored and shallow, and the gaping wounds all over her body told me she wasn't going to leave the island tonight. Or ever.

I swallowed the helpless anger and gently prodded her with a forepaw, careful not to touch any torn flesh or broken scales. "Scarlett," I said quietly, and her eyes opened, gazing blearily up at me. "You can let go now," I said, my voice coming out slightly choked. "We won. Vance is dead."

A look of triumph passed through her eyes, and she released her death grip on her foe, smiling as she gazed up at the stars. "Worth it," she said in a smug, quiet voice, reminding me of yet another crimson dragon who would've likely done the exact same thing if she had the chance. "You'll take care of them, right?" she added before I could say anything else. I swallowed hard and nodded.

"Yeah," I husked out. "I'll take them as far from this place as I can. They'll never have to live under Talon again, I promise."

She relaxed. "Good," she said, though her voice was barely audible. "I'm glad I came back. They deserve a chance...to be free."

She didn't move again.

Numb, I stepped back and looked around. The soldiers were still celebrating their victory, clustered around the pair of bodies in the center of the yard. For a moment, I felt a stab of anger. St. George didn't understand the sacrifice that had just happened, what the cost of this victory really was. All they saw was two dead dragons, and for them, that was reason enough to celebrate.

All except for one, who knelt at the side of a small red dragon a few yards away.

Ember. Guiltily, I trotted up, ignoring the soldiers who smiled and grinned and slapped each other on the back for killing a dragon. Ember was struggling to her feet as I approached, her jaws clenched in pain and her pupils razor-thin slits against the green of her eyes. Her right wing still hung at an awkward angle, making my stomach curl at the sight of it.

"Riley," she panted as St. George put a hand on her shoulder to steady her. Her gaze traveled past me to the bodies in the center of the yard. A pained look crossed her face, and she glanced back at me, hopeful. "Scarlett?"

I shook my head. Ember sighed, slumping into St. George, who took her weight without pause. "Dammit," she muttered, closing her eyes. "I didn't want... I was hoping there wouldn't be any casualties, but I guess that was too much to ask."

"What about the rest of them?" St. George asked, turning to me without letting go of the red dragon. "Did the other breeders make it out?"

"Yeah," I said. "Mist was able to lead them away and get them over the wall. They should be heading to the beach now. Give me a second—I'll change back and tell her to wait for us."

A shout came from the center of the yard. I turned to see the other officer, Lieutenant Ward, stride forward to yell at the soldiers, ordering them to stop standing around congratulating themselves and to secure the rest of the buildings. With hasty "yes, sirs," the soldiers complied, heading toward the apartments and medical building behind us. Glancing around, Ward spotted us, and a stony expression settled over his features. Setting his jaw, he came toward us.

I tensed, subtly moving in front of Ember as the officer marched up, his back stiff and his stride rigid. He wasn't looking at me or St. George, his gaze fixed on the red dragon between us.

For a moment, he appeared to teeter on the verge of saying

something; his jaw clenched and unclenched, as if he were unwilling or unable to voice what he was thinking. Ember gazed calmly at the lieutenant, seemingly aware of what was going on, though it was confusing the hell out of me. Finally, the human gave up. With a scowl, he wrenched his gaze from Ember and looked at St. George, ignoring me and the fact that I had been glaring at him ever since he'd begun stomping toward us.

"Sebastian," he said briskly. "Contact Lieutenant Martin and let him know that we have secured the facilities. Inform him that all hostiles have been eliminated, and that we will be joining him as soon as we clean up here." His gaze flickered to me, then at the empty buildings behind us, his lip curling slightly. "I take it the target lizards were evacuated safely?"

"Yes, sir," St. George answered, ignoring the demeaning term for us. "What should we do with the workers who survived?"

"Don't kill them," I growled, remembering Dr. Miles and the way Scarlett had spoken of him. Yes, they worked for Talon and they were part of this whole hateful facility, but I still didn't like the thought of St. George gunning down unarmed, unresisting doctors and scientists. "They're unarmed, and some of them are just doing their jobs. They don't deserve to be slaughtered in cold blood."

Ward's eyes glittered. It was clear he didn't appreciate being given orders by a "lizard," and his voice was cold as he answered. "They're Talon minions who knowingly serve the organization. Our Code is clear—all who sell their souls to evil must be executed."

"You've already broken your Code a dozen times tonight, Lieutenant," Ember said, surprising us all. "Break it one more time. We've won. The mission is over. There's no reason for more needless death."

Ward stared at her, anger radiating from him. I tensed, and on Ember's other side, I saw St. George do the same. But, shockingly, Ward nodded once and stepped back, his posture stiff.

"As you say, dragon. This once." He turned on a heel, preparing to stride away but paused, adding over his shoulder, "Do not expect it to happen again."

I turned on Ember as Ward marched off, calling orders to his soldiers. "Okay, what the hell was that about?"

She just smiled. "Nothing. It doesn't matter. It's over now." The relief in her voice was palpable as she leaned into the soldier, who gazed down at her with worried eyes. "You did it, Riley," she murmured. "The facility, the breeders…you finally found them. And now we're going to take them away from this awful place and make sure Talon never gets their claws into them again."

"Yeah." I took a quiet breath as the realization finally hit. "Not just me, though," I told Ember, and gazed over my shoulder to where the soldiers of St. George were sweeping across the yard. I could never have done this alone. It had taken all of us, dragons and soldiers, to pull off something this huge. "The Order of St. George teaming up with dragons to rescue dragons," I muttered, and it still sounded ludicrous. "The world is either a very funny place, or it's about to end."

Ember gave a painful chuckle. "Probably both," she gritted out. "But this was a huge blow to Talon, you can be sure of it." Raising her head, she observed the buildings and the soldiers moving between them, her gaze solemn and bright. "Now, the question is, how is Talon going to react, and what are they going to do next?"

DANTE

"Welcome back, sir."

I nodded absently to the guard as I strode through the doors of Talon headquarters, both relieved and apprehensive to be home. I'd destroyed the letter from Ember's mysterious friend long before I left China, but the words written on that page had haunted me the entire journey back to the States.

The Elder Wyrm intends to use Ember to extend her own life, to achieve immortality.

It couldn't be true. I'd thought—I'd always assumed—that the Elder Wyrm would leave Talon to one or both of us when she finally left the world. I'd been working toward that ever since I discovered my true heritage, preparing for the day I would take over. It would obviously be me; Ember had no head for business or politics and no desire to manage a giant conglomerate of dragons. She would still be part of Talon, however, and I would make sure she was safe and taken care of.

But if the Elder Wyrm was trying to become immortal…

I strode through the building, giving short, one-word answers to any who tried to engage me. In the relative privacy of the elevator, I pulled out my phone and tapped a familiar number, then held it to my ear. Someone picked up on the first ring.

"Hello, Mr. Hill," said the Elder Wyrm's personal assistant. "Welcome back. How was your trip overseas?"

"Fine, thank you," I replied automatically. "Where is the CEO?"

"The Elder Wyrm is in an emergency meeting right now and cannot be disturbed. I will inform her of your arrival as soon as she is finished."

Emergency meeting? I frowned. What was going on? It wasn't like the Elder Wyrm to keep me in the dark. Though this might work out perfectly; she would be distracted for a bit. I really did not want to face her right now. "That's fine," I told the assistant. "No hurry. I just wanted to inform her that I was back."

There was one guard standing at the elevators on the ground floor and a pair watching the hall as I stepped onto my office floor. More security; something had definitely happened while I was away. After informing my personal assistant that I was not to be disturbed unless it was a summons from the Elder Wyrm herself, I slipped into my office and locked the door behind me.

I sat at my desk and stared at the computer screen for a long moment, debating with myself. Did I really want to do this? Go poking around the Elder Wyrm's private affairs? What if I confirmed something horrible, something I could not ignore? What would I do? Confront the Elder Wyrm? Demand answers from the leader of Talon, the oldest, most powerful dragon in the world? I almost laughed out loud at the thought.

This is for Ember, Dante.

Ember was created to be the Elder Wyrm's vessel, the letter had claimed. It was a place to start. I certainly couldn't ask the Elder Wyrm about it, but there were others who might know the truth. I could think of one human in particular who'd helped develop the vessel program and had been involved with the clones from the beginning.

Snatching my desk phone I buzzed my personal assistant, who answered instantly. "Yes, Mr. Hill?"

"Contact Dr. Olsen," I told her. "Let him know I wish to speak to him immediately via our private channel. Tell him it cannot wait."

"Of course, sir."

Immediately was a relative term when it came to the head scientist, I'd come to realize. Fifteen minutes passed in silence, while I sat alone with my thoughts and wondered exactly what I was doing. Finally, my computer warbled, announcing an incoming call. I hit a button, and Dr. Olsen's lined, slightly agitated face filled the screen.

"Mr. Hill," the scientist greeted with a pathetic attempt at a smile. "Welcome back. I trust this interruption to my work is very important." His gaze flickered toward the exit, as if he were impatient to be gone. "I was in the middle of a very delicate procedure with one of the vessels, and I really must return as soon as possible."

"Forgive me, Dr. Olsen," I said, smiling broadly. "I won't take much of your time. I just have a few questions regarding your work with the vessels, if I may."

He relaxed. Talking about the vessels, his created "children," was something he never tired of. "Of course, Mr. Hill. What did you want to know?"

"You were one of the first scientists to develop the vessel program, is that right?"

He puffed up. "Yes, that is correct. My work in cloning and genetics was essential in creating the program. Why do you ask?"

My heart pounded. I had to play this exactly right. "You are the only one I can trust in this matter, Dr. Olsen," I replied. "Strict confidentiality is vital, so listen carefully. I need you to forward me all the data you have regarding the research, development and experimentation on the Elder Wyrm's vessel."

His brows shot up. "I wasn't aware that you knew about that, Mr. Hill," he stated, making my heart plummet. It was true, then. The Elder Wyrm's vessel was indeed a thing, and Dr. Olsen was a part of it. "I was under the impression that you and your sister's origins were never to be revealed," the scientist went on. "The organization made very certain we understood that."

I felt numb, but forced myself to keep talking, smiling. "In light of recent events," I continued, "the organization has decided it needs to review all data on Ember Hill to find a way to deal with her and the growing rogue conflict. Perhaps there is something in her files that we have missed. As her brother, and the one who has lived with her the longest, I've been tasked with reviewing all possible angles, including the ones pertaining to her origins. So, if you would send me what I need, Dr. Olsen, I would appreciate it. Discretion is, of course, essential. The Elder Wyrm does not want this information getting out."

He stared at me for a long moment, his expression strained. My uneasiness surged, but I continued to speak calmly. "Did you hear me, Dr. Olsen? Is there a problem?"

He shook himself. "No," he said quickly. "No problem. Apologies. I forget, sometimes, how different our species are. But no, the organization comes first, even over family. I understand that." He paused, a shadow crossing his face for the briefest of moments. "I understand that all too well," he almost whispered.

"You'll have your information, Mr. Hill," the scientist finished, drawing back. "I'll send it over now. Is there anything else you require before I return to work?"

"No," I replied. "Thank you, Dr. Olsen."

The scientist nodded briskly, and the screen went dark.

I sat there, dazed. Dr. Olsen had confirmed what the letter told me, that Ember was intended to be the Elder Wyrm's vessel. That she had been created specifically for the leader of Talon. Which meant that, as her brother and twin, I, too, was a clone of the Elder Wyrm.

My computer chimed, indicating new email.

My hand shook as it touched the keyboard, and I took a steadying breath. Did I really want to see this? Would it shake the very foundations of what I thought I knew? And if it did, what was I prepared to do about it?

I opened my email to find that the new file had come in. *Project Nephilim*, the attachment read, making my stomach dance and curl in on itself like a nest of snakes. The arrow hovered over the file as I struggled with my decision. I could delete the email, destroy it and erase any knowledge about the project and what it could mean for Ember and myself. I could continue rising in Talon, always pushing upward, toward the summit. I was so close. Just one more step to the top, and then everything would be mine for the taking. I would finally be free.

But then, I might never know the truth. And this wasn't just about me; it was about Ember. Even now, when we had grown so different that we were almost strangers, she was still my sibling, my twin, and my family. I had always looked out for her, no matter what.

I clicked the button.

GARRET

The semi's front wheels bounced as I turned onto the narrow gravel road, making me wince. Not for myself, but I hoped it wouldn't jostle my very sensitive cargo in the back. Five female dragons—four pregnant and one who was still healing from a broken wing. Dragons recovered quickly and, according to Riley, any injury to their wings healed especially fast, as they were essential to a dragon's survival. Ember had recovered enough for her to be able to Shift back, but it had been a strained few days from the North Atlantic Ocean back to the States. And the lack of heavy-duty painkillers was not helping.

I worried for her. She put up a good front, but I knew she was in pain and was trying to hide it as best she could. I wished I could comfort her, stay by her side, but there were so many things that required my attention. Both Lieutenant Martin and Lieutenant Ward wanted my report about what happened at the facility, and Martin required me to act as a liaison between the Order and the rogues, as Ember could not and Riley was insanely busy taking care of more than two dozen frightened female dragons.

Thankfully, the journey was almost done. I knew I wasn't the only one who would be relieved to be on solid ground again.

Ahead of me, the first semi came to a stop with a squeaking of brakes and a billow of dust. Beyond it, I could see the familiar blue roof of the farmhouse, two stories high, with numerous rooms and enough space, inside and out, to host a large group of renegade dragons. In normal times. With a few hundred acres of privately owned farmland surrounding it, this was the safest place for us to hide from Talon and the rest of the world. But there were already twelve hatchlings on the property, all of them rogues Riley had gotten out of Talon. Now we were arriving with twenty-six more. Things were going to be *very* cramped the next few days. And that didn't even count the dozen or so soldiers of St. George who would be arriving, as well.

I suppressed a grimace. With everything that had happened on the island, and with a reprisal from Talon almost a certainty, it had been decided that the alliance between the rogues and the Order of St. George would continue, at least for now. None of us were particularly happy about it, especially Riley and Lieutenant Ward. But even they recognized the advantage in numbers, that we were stronger as allies than enemies. If Talon did send their vessels after us again, at least together we stood a fighting chance.

Glancing in my rearview mirror, I saw the van that had been trailing behind me pull around and roll up the drive. Lieutenant Martin was in the driver's seat, with Ward sitting beside him with his usual scowl on his face. I cast a nervous glance at the front porch, where several faces peered curiously out the windows, watching the convoy pull into the yard.

Riley had sent word ahead, warning Jade and the others that the Order of St. George were coming, instructing them not to panic when the soldiers arrived. Hopefully, no one would.

The van pulled to a stop beside my door, and the passenger's side window buzzed down. "Sebastian." Martin gazed at me, his voice tired. "Where do they want us?"

"The farmhouse is full," I answered, which was putting it mildly. With the arrival of the dragonells, the total number of rogues in the farmhouse now totaled thirty-four, and that wasn't counting Ember, Riley, Mist and Jade. It was a big house, but every available room, couch and pullout bed would be taken over by dragons. Dragons who were exhausted, shaken, confused and still understandably terrified of the Order. Adding a dozen soldiers of St. George to a crowded, already volatile situation was asking for trouble. "There's a bunkhouse around back," I told Martin, who gave a solemn nod. "According to the owner, it hasn't been used for years, and all the bedding has been taken by the rogues, but it'll be a roof over your heads at least."

"We'll make do." Martin glanced behind him at the soldiers waiting quietly, and sighed. "This isn't the worst we've endured."

"Not a very defensible position, Sebastian," Ward remarked. Glancing at the farmhouse, his eyes narrowed in disdain. "If Talon attacks us here, we'll be at a severe disadvantage. What measures have the lizards taken to ensure we won't be overrun in the night?"

"Talon doesn't know about this place," I replied. "After the Night of Fang and Fire, there was nowhere else to go. The rest of Riley's safe houses had been compromised. Plus, it's the only location that can hold a large number of dragons without them being seen by the general public."

"Still." Ward shook his head. "No guards. No defensives. Not even a lookout. How do these lizards expect to fight if they are attacked?"

"They're not soldiers, sir." I nodded to a pair of faces in the window peering out at us with wide, anxious eyes. "Many of them are teenagers. With few exceptions, none of them have been trained for war. Until very recently, if anyone did arrive on their steps with the intent to kill them, they ran. Because that's all they could do. They didn't stay to fight a battle they would lose, and they knew talking would be useless. We—St. George—taught them that."

Ward grunted. "That is still no reason to lower your guard," he stated, unappeased. "Especially now. Talon is trying to destroy us all, and has an unlimited number of soulless abominations, or whatever you call them, to do it. If we must stay here, I want some measure of warning before Talon strolls in and slaughters everything." He blew out a short breath and curled a lip, as if preparing to do something abhorrent. "I'll have to speak to that blue lizard, and see if we cannot correct this oversight."

"His name is Riley. Sir."

Ward's jaw tightened, but before he could say anything, Lieutenant Martin broke in. "We'll be in the bunkhouse," he stated. "Give us an hour to settle in, and then come speak with me, Sebastian. If you would."

"Yes, sir."

The windows buzzed up, and the van continued around the farmhouse and out of sight.

As I ran a tired hand down my face, a hollow thump came

from the back of the semi, sounding suspiciously like a tail had been smacked against the wall in impatience. Ember, it seemed, had had enough of waiting around. Not that I could blame her; spending hours in the back of a tractor-trailer couldn't be pleasant for anyone. Even though she'd been able to Shift back to human form, she had opted to stay with the four pregnant dragonells so they wouldn't be alone for the journey. Of course, that also meant she'd spent two days in a dank, poorly lit shipping container as we'd sailed back to the coast. I hadn't seen her in human form since we'd assaulted the facility, and I knew the accommodations for the dragons, while necessary, had not been ideal. I just hoped the red dragon had not reached the point of snapping at anything that got close to her.

I opened the door and exited the rig, seeing Riley ahead of us, dropping down from his seat with Mist close behind him on the passenger's side. He gave me a nod as he strode around the back of the semi. I returned it before walking to the doors of my own truck and pulling them back with a rusty groan.

A cloud of warm, stale air billowed out of the opening, smelling of rust, grease and the faint, musky scent of dragon that was unlike anything else in the world. Ember stood in the frame, in human form and wearing the black Viper suit that masked her from head to toe. Her arms were crossed, and she gazed down at me with half teasing, half exasperated green eyes.

"Jeez, Garret," the girl stated as my heart jumped in both worry and relief. "Were you aiming for the potholes? You must've hit every dip from here to Florida."

I masked a relieved smile and held out my hand. Without pause, Ember took it and hopped down from the truck, right into my open arms. I pulled her close as her arms circled my neck, and we stood like that for a moment, the late-afternoon sun beating down on us.

"We made it," she breathed into my neck. "We're home."

"Yeah," I murmured. *Home.* That was a strange thought. For years, the Order had been home, the soldiers of St. George my family. And then, for a while, I hadn't known where I fit in. I was adrift, an outsider, mistrusted by dragons and hated by the Order that raised me. Now, I was certain I'd found my place. This was where I belonged, with Ember and Riley and a bunch of rogue dragons.

Ember pulled back to gaze at the farmhouse over my shoulder. "And the house is still standing," she remarked. "It didn't explode or burn down while we were gone, so that's a good thing."

Four scaly bodies were curled up at the back of the container, so entwined with each other that it was impossible to tell them apart. "Everyone okay?" I called into the darkness.

Glowing dragon eyes peered at me, wary and mistrustful. I spoke as gently as I could, opening the doors a bit wider so that the light spilled into the truck. "Come on," I urged. "Everyone follow me. I'll show you where you'll be staying. Don't worry about being seen—we're pretty much in the middle of nowhere. You're safe here, I promise."

Slowly, the pile of dragons uncurled. Cautiously, they edged out of the truck, then gazed around in wonder, eyes wide as they took everything in. I reminded myself that they hadn't left the island in years, perhaps decades. The tight confines of the facility was all they knew, so the outside world was probably very strange and exciting. Ember watched them from a few feet away, her expression shadowed with sympathy and understanding. Perhaps she saw herself in them, wide-eyed and eager, from very long ago. Before her world was consumed with fighting and war, blood and death. Before she was forced to leave that ordinary girl and ordinary life behind and become a soldier.

"This way," I told the group, and they followed us across the yard to the barn sitting at the edge of the pasture. Shoving the doors open, I led the small group of dragons into the cool barn. The individual stalls had already been prepared, and fresh straw, water and blankets lay in each of them.

Upon seeing the inside of the barn, the dragonells relaxed. Without any prompting, they each took a stall and began rooting around in the hay, as if making a nest. Nothing was said about the lack of proper accommodations, of being forced to stay in a barn. I suddenly had the feeling that such housings were normal for them, as normal as a room with a bed. I saw Ember clench her fists at her sides, anger radiating from her skin.

"Last time," she whispered, as if making a promise. "This is the last time you'll have to do this, I swear it."

A shadow fell across the doorway a moment before Jade entered the barn. The dragonells jerked up, their eyes going wide with fear and awe, recognizing a much older, vastly powerful Adult. The small Asian woman gazed back at them serenely and inclined her head.

"Don't be afraid," she said, her soothing voice flowing over them like water. "You have nothing to fear from me, or any of the dragons in this circle. We will do our best to protect all of you, so rest easy. You are safe here."

Once again, the dragonells relaxed, sinking back into the straw, though they still kept an eye on the Eastern dragon as she turned to face me and Ember. "I'm glad you're safe," she told us, returning Ember's smile. "And that the mission was a success. I only regret that I was not there to aid you. The loss of any life is a heavy burden. I would have shared it with you if I could."

Ember's face darkened, probably remembering Scarlett, as I thought back to the other soldiers who hadn't made it off the island. Nine men had been killed in the assault when the monstrous green dragon showed itself. Nine soldiers we had to leave behind. Three of them had been from the Western Chapterhouse, men I had known and fought beside. It was a relatively small number, but now with the Order so scattered and broken, the loss of every soldier was devastating.

"Thanks for staying here, Jade," Ember said. "And for looking after the rest of them. Any trouble with Talon?"

"No. The organization has been unnaturally quiet the past few days. It is worrisome." The Eastern dragon furrowed her brow. "I believe this is what you call the calm before the storm."

I had the dark, ominous feeling she was right.

DANTE

"The Elder Wyrm has called for you, sir."

I barely heard the voice coming through my speaker. I was numb. Nothing felt real anymore as I stared at the words on my computer.

True. It was all true. The experiments, the start of the vessel program, everything the letter hinted at. Ember and I were clones of the Elder Wyrm. But it was worse than that. According to the scientist's notes, Ember was the one they'd wanted to create: a near-perfect replica of the Elder Wyrm. I was an afterthought, a backup plan. Something that was allowed to exist only to give my twin a better chance at life. Because Ember was the vessel intended for the Elder Wyrm to achieve immortality. Or at least another thousand years.

"Sir? Sir, are you there?"

I shook myself out of my daze, answering the call out of habit. "Thank you, Ms. Brooks. Please inform the Elder Wyrm that I am on my way."

Slumping back, I stared at the file for a few seconds longer, then deleted the entire thing. No point in keeping such incriminating evidence sitting on my computer, and I had confirmed what I'd set out to find. It was too late to unsee the file, to return to blissful ignorance. I could never unlearn what I knew.

Ember was the Elder Wyrm's vessel.

I felt my feet carrying me from my office, trekking the familiar path to the elevators, as I'd done countless times before. A senior executive, Mr. Roth, I thought, met me as he left the elevator box and asked a question. I answered without thinking, smiling, not even hearing what I told him. He nodded in return and continued down the hall.

Alone in the elevator, I stared at my reflection in the mirrored surface, still trying to process all that I'd learned. My sister and I were clones, created in a lab, just like the vessels. I was the heir of Talon, but only a fail-safe. Ember was the indispensable one. Now I knew why the Elder Wyrm was so determined to get her back.

The elevator dinged, and the doors slid open. In a daze, I walked past the front desk, turned the handle of the double doors and stepped into the Elder Wyrm's office.

"Hello, Dante." The Elder Wyrm's voice, brittle and cold, snapped me out of my trance. For a moment, I was certain she knew about the file and my conversation with Dr. Olsen. Her expression was hard, her eyes terrifyingly blank as she rose from her desk and came forward.

"We have a situation," she stated as I wondered, perhaps illogically, if she was going to kill me then and there. I forced myself to breathe, to appear casual, though a cold sweat had broken out on the back of my neck and my legs were trembling. Thankfully, the Elder Wyrm didn't seem to notice.

"Cobalt has struck again," the CEO went on, her voice filled with bridled rage. "I received word a few hours ago that he and a small regiment of soldiers stormed the breeder facilities, killed most of the guards there and escaped with the resident females. Director Vance was slain in the battle, as well as the oldest breeder, a pregnant female named Scarlett. We have lost the facility."

Stunned, I had to put a hand on the sofa back to steady myself. I knew what the facility was: a place where Talon's females could live and lay eggs without fear of discovery, but I hadn't known where it was located. Very few dragons did.

"How?" I asked. "How did they find it? And manage to defeat the security?"

"Reports are vague," the Elder Wyrm said. "It was chaos on the island that night, but there are accounts of several human soldiers aiding the outlaws, as well. It appears that Cobalt has recruited the help of a few rogue soldiers of St. George."

"What?" I gasped, appalled and horrified. "That's impossible. We destroyed them all. And the Order would never agree to help our kind. It goes against everything they've been taught."

"Yes," the Elder Wyrm agreed. "Unless, of course, their survival is on the line. Then they will agree to any alliance, make any deal to save themselves. It is human nature, something I have seen time and time again. There is nothing they will not do, no ideals they will not abandon, if their existence is threatened. Not even St. George is exempt from human frailty.

"Regardless." The Elder Wyrm's eyes narrowed, glittering dangerously. "Such a blatant attack on Talon facilities cannot be allowed to stand. Both groups have gotten desperate enough to unite against us, and that makes them dangerous, simply because they are willing to do anything to survive."

She walked to the window to stare down at the city. "We cannot afford any hiccups this late in the game, Dante. It is time we destroyed Cobalt, these rogue soldiers and whoever stands in our way." She paused a moment, her cold gaze scanning the city below. "We need to draw our enemies into one place," she went on. "Present them with something so huge they cannot ignore it, and then crush them once and for all when they appear."

My stomach dropped. I knew what she was talking about. Exposing it was risky, so very risky, but she was right; something so huge could not be ignored by Cobalt or the Order once they knew of its existence. Even if they knew it was a setup, they would come, drawn into the trap, and we would be there to destroy them.

Including Ember.

As if sensing my thoughts, the Elder Wyrm turned from the window, meeting my gaze head-on. Her eyes, ancient and all-knowing, glowed green in the shadows. "We are close, Dante," she said softly, her voice causing the walls to tremble. "So close to achieving our dream, a world where our kind can live freely. A world where dragons will never again fear the Order and all humans pushing us toward extinction. We cannot falter now. We must see this through to the end, no matter the sacrifices that will come of it. Do you understand?"

I took a deep breath so that my voice would be steady when I answered. "I understand. What would you have me do?"

EMBER

The first week back at the farmhouse was…interesting, to say the least.

Things were, of course, unbelievably crowded. With the arrival of the dragonells from the facility, the total number of rogue dragons on the property had exploded to thirty-eight, not counting me, Riley, Mist and Jade. It was a big house, but every available room, couch and sleeping bag had been taken over by dragons. Dragons who were exhausted, shaken, confused and understandably terrified. It had been a rough, painful trip back to the States. I hadn't been able to Shift at first due to that bastard Vance snapping my wing, and I'd spent two days in a dank shipping container with the four pregnant dragonells, drifting in and out of a fragmented sleep as my limb slowly healed. I'd sensed both Garret and Riley there several times, both of them worried as they hovered over me. Once, I'd thought Riley had a baboon mask on, but I was pretty certain that had been a dream.

By the time we'd reached the States, my wing had healed

enough for me to Shift back to human form, but I'd opted to stay with the dragonells for the rest of the journey. And so the final leg of the trip was made in the back of a semi truck, many hours from the coast to Riley's remote safe house, gritting my teeth against every bump, dip and pothole that jostled my still-aching wing. I'd never been so happy to be done with a trip in my entire life.

After the dragonells were settled in, we received a bit of a surprise. In a very short time, Jade had taken a group of chaotic, undisciplined young dragons and turned them into a well-oiled machine. There were hidden guards at the entrance and sentries around the perimeter. There were training exercises and morning meditations. Everyone had a job, from patrolling the yard at night to washing dishes and cleaning the rooms. Riley had been stunned. When Nettle told him that morning "reflection time" was her favorite part of the day, you could've knocked him over with a feather.

Unfortunately, Jade's disciplined regime sort of fell apart when we arrived with twenty-six more dragons *and* the Order of St. George. None of the various leaders trusted that a house full of dragons and soldiers of the Order would not erupt into bullets and flame. With the exception of Garret, the dozen or so soldiers had been regulated to an old but serviceable bunkhouse out back. It was a temporary solution, though after a week of healing, settling in, making sure everyone had medical care, food and their own beds, one thought was beginning to emerge in everyone's minds.

What now?

What was the next step against Talon and the Elder Wyrm? We couldn't stay here forever; sooner or later, the organization would find us. We had done the impossible in reaching the facility and freeing the breeder dragons, but even after that, even with help from what was left of the Order, our small, ragtag group couldn't stand against Talon's massive army of soulless dragon clones. All it would take was one push, one surprise attack in the middle of the night, and we would be finished.

We couldn't stay here. But one thing was certain; Talon wouldn't wait for us to decide what we were going to do. Their plans, whatever they were, were very likely in motion now, and we were running out of time.

One morning, about a week after we'd arrived at the safe house, I awoke early and couldn't go back to sleep. After pushing back the covers of my sleeping bag, I rose quietly and minced my way across the floor, careful not to wake the other four dragons who shared the room with me. Nettle and another girl named Iris slept in the twin beds along the wall, both of them snoring softly. Iris was a hatchling from the facility, and she had been extremely nervous about sharing a room with so many strangers. I'd given my bed to her on the first day to help her adjust, taking one of the sleeping bags on the floor. Usually, I'd be so exhausted by the end of the day that the thin mattresses on the hardwood floor didn't even register, but it did make it challenging to sleep late.

Gliding downstairs, I saw that Jade was already up, drinking a mug of tea at the kitchen table. Morning meditations, where the Eastern dragon gathered all the original rogues on the back porch and had them meditate until sunrise, began in a half hour. She claimed it cleared everyone's minds, preparing them for the day. I didn't know what to think about that, but the rogues were certainly more organized than they had been, even under Riley.

"Morning, Jade," I greeted, covering my mouth to mask a yawn. The Eastern dragon nodded in return.

"Good morning, Ember." Jade put down her mug and gave me a mildly concerned look. "You are up early again. Are you still having trouble sleeping?"

I shrugged. "Nightmares," I explained, trying to sound unconcerned. Every night, my brain would recount what had happened on the island, the fight with Director Vance, and the death of Scarlett. Sometimes it added scenes that hadn't happened, mostly involving Garret and Riley dying in front of me, torn apart by bullets or in the jaws of the director. "It's nothing serious."

She shook her head. "So young," she murmured, mostly to herself. "Everyone here is so young, and yet they have been forced into a life of war. Youth should be a time of learning, of growing up at your own pace. Of discovering the mysteries and wonders of the universe, and deciding where you fit in. This life changes you, forces you to grow up too soon, to make decisions you are not yet ready for." Her eyes crinkled with sympathy. "My heart bleeds for everyone here. You will not see the scars until many years down the road, but they will always be there, deep in your soul."

"We don't really have a choice, do we?" I said sadly. "It's either fight or conform to Talon. Even if we run, the organization will just hunt us down. We have to fight."

"Yes," Jade agreed. "In this, we have little choice. Though I would rather return to my homeland and forget this struggle. If left unchecked, Talon will consume the world." She frowned and took a sip from her mug before looking at me again. "Remember, though. You do not struggle alone. Meditation has been known to help with nightmares. Perhaps you should join

Mist and the others for morning devotions, since you are up this early, anyway."

"*Mist* is doing meditations?" I asked, smiling as I pictured the aloof Basilisk sitting cross-legged on a pillow, breathing deep. "I wouldn't have expected that of her."

"Indeed." Jade smiled back. "She learns quickly and is quite the devoted student. I believe her own words were, 'If I am going to continue to be around Cobalt, I need all the patience I can get.'"

I laughed. "I can see that. Well, maybe I'll join you sometime."

"Whenever you feel ready," Jade said, sipping her tea. "I think it would be a great boon to you, as well as your fellow rogues. You know they see you as the leader of this resistance, just as much as Cobalt."

I blinked. "Really?"

"Mmm." Jade put down her mug, regarding me seriously over the table. "It was you who put out the call to fight," she said. "Who led them into battle to aid St. George. You are at the head of every charge, every assault on Talon. They see your willingness to fight, to not run away or surrender, and it gives them courage. Cobalt might be the brains of the resistance, but you are its heart. And you will be the one who will change things in the end."

I swallowed hard. "I hope so," I whispered. I hoped we could change things, for everyone. I didn't just want to survive anymore. I wanted dragons to be able to live without fear of Talon or the Order of St. George. I wanted this stupid war to end, but I was afraid of what we'd have to do to make that happen. And who I was going to lose before it was over.

Jade gazed into her mug as if she could see the future floating in the leaves. "I think," she said slowly, quietly, "that, one way or another, we are reaching the end of this struggle. Whether it is a good or bad thing is undecided, but one thing is certain. The final battle is approaching. I only hope we are ready."

My stomach twisted in on itself, and I took a breath to calm it down. "I'm going to check on Autumn and the others," I muttered, stepping away from the kitchen. The four pregnant dragons who couldn't Shift now resided in the barn, which was off-limits to everyone but the various leaders of the underground: Riley, Garret, Jade and myself. And for the past two days, one of the Juveniles named Autumn had been acting strange, lying in her stall and refusing to eat. I had a feeling I knew what was wrong, but I hoped she wasn't getting sick.

Jade only nodded, returning to her tea, and I slipped out of the farmhouse into the predawn darkness.

The barn glowed softly in the distance as I walked across the yard, with the moon and stars glimmering overhead, unfiltered by streetlamps and city haze. A breeze ruffled my hair, smelling of dust and leaves, and a few yellow fireflies winked lazily in the pasture. It was always quiet out here; no traffic, sirens, crowds or blaring horns. No sounds except the crickets and the buzz of cicadas in the trees. I wanted to call it peaceful, but I was afraid of how suddenly that could change. How quickly this serene farm could erupt in an explosion of fire, bullets, screaming and death. I could blink, and everyone I knew would be gone.

A lump caught in my throat, and I jogged the rest of the way to the barn, pushing back the door as quietly as I could.

Garret knelt in the straw at the entrance to the last stall, speaking quietly to someone I couldn't see. He glanced up as the door opened, a faint smile crossing his face as I stood there in shock. Before I could say anything, he put a finger to his lips and rose, holding out a hand. Bewildered, I closed the door and padded across the dirt to join him. The rest of the barn was quiet, the other three dragonells curled up in the straw, sleeping soundly. The air was filled with the sound of dragons breathing and the faint smell of sulfur.

"What's going on?" I asked softly, putting my palm in his. He smiled and drew me close, nodding to the back of the stall.

"See for yourself."

I gazed into the shadows. Autumn lay at the rear of the stall, curled up in the hay with her tail around herself and her wings pressed close. A single white oval lay in the curve of her body, shining faintly under the lamps.

I gasped, and felt Garret's smile behind me. "When did this happen?" I asked, keeping my voice low so I wouldn't disturb the sleeping dragons or the new mother before me. Autumn watched me from the straw, protective but not alarmed, her breaths slow and deep.

"About twenty minutes ago, according to Autumn," Garret replied. "I was just about to go find you and Riley, but I wanted to make sure she had everything she needed."

I squeezed his hand, then smiled at the dragon curled around the egg. "Congratulations," I told her. "Are you okay? Do you want anything?"

The orange dragonell with the yellow stripes down her back shook her head. "Thank you," she murmured, and her voice was slightly choked. "I'm okay, it's just…" She blinked rapidly and raised her head, gazing at the egg lying beside her. "This is my second," she admitted. "My first… I wasn't even allowed to see it. As soon as it was laid, Director Vance's men came and took it away. I didn't want them to, but we were told that dragons who resisted or tried to fight back were severely punished." Her eyes darkened, as if reliving that moment in time. " After it was gone, I was horribly depressed for over a month," she continued. "I remember asking a couple of the older dragons if it ever got easier, and they said no, it really didn't. You learned to harden your heart, to suppress all the instincts telling you to fight, to not grow attached to the egg growing inside you, because you were just going to lose it in the end."

She lowered her head back to the straw, a small, peaceful smile crossing her face. "I'm so thankful to be out of there." She sighed. "To know I might actually see my egg hatch, and watch my baby grow up, free of Talon. It makes everything we're doing worth it." Her gaze shifted to us, golden and serene, as I swallowed the lump in my throat and blinked back tears. "Thank you," she whispered. "Both of you. I'm so grateful for everyone who rescued us. Cobalt, Mist, even the soldiers of St. George. Without them, I wouldn't be here now. Even if we die and Talon wins, I'm glad I got to experience this moment."

I don't think I could have said anything without breaking down, but a second later, the barn door slid back with a thump, and a new voice ruptured the peaceful quiet.

"Firebrand? St. George? You in here?"

"Shh!" I hissed at Riley, who furrowed his brow as he stepped inside, but closed the door quietly behind him.

"You two going to tell me what's going on?" he asked, though his voice was softer as he approached, and he moved almost soundlessly through the straw. "What you're doing, out here all alone? Some might think you... Oh."

Whatever he was about to accuse us of faded away as he reached the front of the stall. For a moment, he stared at the dragonell curled protectively around the egg. Then he blew out a short breath that turned into a genuine smile.

"Autumn," he said as the dragonell met his gaze calmly. "I didn't realize your time was so close." He glanced at the egg, as if making certain it was really there, that he really saw it, before turning back to the mother. "Are you all right? Do you need anything?"

"No," Autumn replied, shaking her head. "Like I told Ember and Garret, I'm fine. I have everything I need right now."

Riley nodded. "I'll post a guard outside the door," he said. "If you want something, no matter how small or insignificant, just tell him. I'll make certain he reports to me or someone in charge right away."

"Thank you, Cobalt." The dragonell smiled and let her eyes drift shut. "Right now, it's enough to know my egg will be safe. That I can go to sleep knowing it will still be here when I wake up."

"Count on it," Riley almost whispered. He watched the dozing dragon a moment longer, then turned and jerked his head at us.

We tiptoed out of the barn and pulled the door shut behind us. Riley was smiling in a way I'd never seen before—with happiness, relief and pride, but also fierce determination. "So it's happened," he murmured, gazing at the barn door as if he could sense the dragons beyond. "The first egg laid outside of Talon in a long, long time. We have to make sure it has a chance to hatch, that it grows up knowing its mother, and that it doesn't have to worry about the organization forcing it into the role they want. No matter what the cost." He seemed to be talking to himself now, bracing himself for what needed to be done. Garret and I exchanged a glance, right before Riley straightened and turned to us.

"You two need to see something, right now."

GARRET

"An anonymous email?" Tristan remarked, crossing his arms as he gazed at the laptop on the table. "Well, that's not suspicious at all."

Riley eyed him wearily, but was apparently too tired to argue. In the dim light of the tornado shelter, the soldiers of St. George stood uneasily around the table, watching the dragons on either side. Riley had gathered the leaders of both factions for this meeting; even Lieutenant Ward stood beside Lieutenant Martin, glowering at the rest of the room. There were nine of us altogether: me, Ember, Riley, Wes, Jade, Mist, Tristan and the two lieutenants of the Order. It was a tight fit, with five humans and four dragons trying not to bump elbows as we huddled around the table.

"What's this about, dragon?" Martin asked calmly. Riley's jaw tightened, but at least Martin called them *dragon* and not the more derogatory *lizard*. "If you've called all of us here at once, I assume it's for something important."

"Yeah." Riley ran his fingers through his hair, gazing around at us. In the dim light, he looked pale and grim, almost shaken. Glancing at Wes, who was standing beside him with his laptop open on the table, he gave a solemn nod. "Wesley, why don't you show them what you showed me this morning."

The hacker nodded. "Right," he said, and turned the laptop around to face us. "My email is locked down tight," he began, "but I keep a couple channels open, for runaway hatchlings and those looking to get out of Talon. If they know anything about Cobalt, they can contact us, even if they don't know where we are. This," he went on, "is from an email I received early this morning. No name, no return sender, nothing. Not even a bloody message. What it *did* contain...was this video."

He pressed a button on the keyboard, changing the view to full screen, and I leaned in as the video began playing. It was shaky and poorly lit, obviously taken from a phone or similar handheld device. At first, it showed only a pair of shoes walking across a concrete floor, indicating the camera was pointed straight down, perhaps hidden, when the video began. Voices murmured somewhere off-screen, snatches of conversation that were too garbled to make out. There was the creak and groan of a heavy door opening, and the shoes stepped through the frame onto a metal walkway. And stopped.

Slowly, the camera rose, shook, came into focus. I drew in a slow, horrified breath, feeling Ember stiffen beside me, feeling the shock and disbelief of everyone around me seep into the air.

"Mother of God," Martin whispered.

The camera showed a room that stretched back farther than the eye could see, a dark, seemingly endless cavern that had been suffused with a subtle green glow. That glow came from hundreds upon hundreds of enormous vats, marching in rigid rows through the cavern. They were massive, towering. It was difficult to tell with the poor video feed, but it looked like they were at least fifty feet tall, maybe taller.

And each one contained a dragon.

Vessels. Not hatchlings or Juveniles, but enormous, fully grown Adults. Dragons who, had they been normal, would have been several hundred years old. They floated behind the glass, unmoving, an army of savage, unstoppable killing machines, awaiting the day Talon would wake them up and send them into the world.

The video froze, and the screen went dark. For a moment, no one said anything. I could feel Ember shaking against me, realizing, as we all did, what this meant. What Talon's plan had been all along.

Finally, Tristan sucked in a breath and let it out slowly, composing himself as he did. "How long do you think we have before those things wake up?" he asked.

"Not long enough," Riley answered grimly.

"We have to find it." Ember raised her head, eyes glowing green in the shadows, her voice horrified and determined. "We can't let Talon start a war," she whispered. "Before that army wakes up, before Talon launches whatever they're planning, we have to find this place and destroy it."

"Destroy it?" This came from Mist, standing beside Jade at the far end of the table. "I think we have larger problems to worry about." She stared at the dark computer screen, her lips pressed into a thin line. "This is obviously a trap. If we go storming that lab now, Talon will be expecting us."

"Of course it's a trap," Riley growled. "Of course they're going to be expecting us, that's why that video found its way here. Because they know we can't ignore it." He sighed, stabbing his fingers through his hair again, raking it back. "And we can't," he muttered. "Not something like this. We can't ignore what it means, for us and the rest of the world. Talon is everywhere—their reach expands the globe. If those vessels wake up, it really will be the dragon apocalypse. I don't want to live in that kind of world, do you?" Mist dropped her gaze, her expression dark, and Riley's voice softened. "We don't have a choice, Mist. Believe me, I know it's a trap. I am well aware that if we go looking for this place, we'll be walking right into the jaws of death. I wish I could stick my head in the sand and pretend I never saw that video, but none of us can claim ignorance anymore. Once Talon takes control of that army, the entire world is going to erupt in war and dragonfire. There won't be a place left for us to hide." He narrowed his gaze, a muscle working in his jaw. "I'd rather die than live like that. I'd rather my entire underground be wiped out than have them exist in a world where Talon rules everything."

Mist didn't say anything, but the shadows on her face and the hard set of her jaw said she knew he was right.

"Do you know who sent this?" Lieutenant Martin asked, glancing at Wes. "Were you able to trace it?"

"Yeah." The hacker sounded weary as he turned the laptop around, tapping something on his keyboard. "It was pretty bloody easy actually. Whoever sent the video didn't do a damn thing to cover their trail, which makes it even more likely that this is some giant trap, lovingly prepared to destroy us all. But…here." He turned the laptop around to face us. A satellite image showed a swath of mountains and wilderness, with a pulsing red dot in the very center.

"The email was sent from a computer pretty much smack dab in the middle of the Appalachian Mountains," Wes said.

Beside me, Ember straightened, as if that had triggered a memory. Riley noticed, as well, and nodded.

"Yeah, Firebrand. The lab. I remember."

"Remember what?" I asked.

"There's a rumor in Talon," the rogue explained, his expression darkening with anger. "Of a laboratory where Talon sent the nonfemale dragons whom the organization had deemed 'unworthy.' Either they were sickly or crippled or weak in some other way. No one knew what happened to them, but if you were sent to that lab, you were never seen again." His brow furrowed, a shadow of pain crossing his face. "As one of my rogues once put it, the laboratory was a place they sent dragons 'to be sliced and diced and turned into something new.'"

"Something new?" Tristan shook his head. "Something new is a dragon that can also Shift into a motorcycle. Not an army of mindless dragon clones. Sorry, mindless *Adult* dragon clones." He shook his head in disbelief. "Shit, we barely held off a swarm of hatchlings...can you imagine a few hundred thousand Adults raining fire down on everything?"

"Like I said—dragon apocalypse." Crossing his arms, Riley stared at the rest of us. "So the question becomes, how are we going to storm another massive, heavily guarded Talon compound—one that is expecting us, by the way—and what are we going to need to have half a chance in hell of pulling this off?"

"A fucking miracle?" Tristan muttered.

Riley arched a brow at him. "Not terribly helpful, St. George, but I'll take it under consideration."

"We need more people," I said.

All eyes turned to me. "We don't have enough bodies," I went on. "Not for something like this. We barely had enough people for the assault on the facility. I'd expect this to be much larger and well guarded. Even if they weren't expecting us, we need a far bigger force to have any hope of success."

"I'm afraid Sebastian is right," Lieutenant Ward added, surprising us. His voice was grim as he gazed around the room. "This is their army, the dragons they've grown and bred to launch an attack, to declare war on their enemies and the entire human race. There will be more security in that spot than any other Talon facility in the world. We don't have the numbers for this." His voice grew even darker. "I don't think *anyone* has the numbers for this."

"Then we get more."

Ember stepped forward, raising her head as she faced the table of men and dragons. "We get more," she repeated firmly. "We put out the call to oppose Talon, once and for all. Lieutenant Martin, Lieutenant Ward, there *have* to be other survivors from the Order, other soldiers that are scattered or in hiding. Call them here. Make them understand what must be done, that allying with us is the only way to stop Talon. Jade…" She looked at the Asian woman, silently watching from the corner. "Rally the Eastern dragons and all their followers. I know there are more of them out there—they called a council a few weeks back. Convince them to fight with us. I know the Eastern dragons are reclusive and would rather not get involved, but the time for hiding is past. If we lose this battle, Talon will come for them, too."

Jade offered a slight, solemn bow to the other dragon. "I will try, Ember," she stated, raising her head. "I do not know how many of my people I can persuade—as you say, they have spent thousands of years in isolation, remaining neutral to the troubles of the outside world. But, in this, you are correct. We cannot hide any longer. This must become our fight, as well."

Ember nodded. "Mist," she went on, and the silver-haired girl raised an eyebrow at her.

"You're going to ask me if I can convince Basilisks who are still in Talon to join us," she said dryly. "To go rogue and fight the organization."

"Not just the Basilisks," Ember replied. "Any dragon or human who is unhappy with Talon, who hates what they've done but has been afraid to oppose the Elder Wyrm. I'm not saying we should alert the Vipers to our presence, but I trust your judgment, Mist. You must know of a few who would be willing to go rogue, to fight Talon with us."

Mist offered a grim, mysterious smile. "I think I might know a few."

"Good. You handle that, then." Ember paused, then took a deep breath and turned to the front of the table. Her voice, once firm and confident, went a little bit softer. "Riley..."

He held up a hand. "I know, Firebrand," he said before she could say anything. "You don't have to convince me this time. We're going to have to fight. All of us, everyone who can hold a gun or breathe fire. So don't worry." He shook his head, a rueful smile crossing his face. "It's either make our final stand here, or burn with the rest of the world when Talon wakes those things up."

He took a deep breath, then let it out and grinned savagely around the room. "All right," he said in an overly grand voice. "There's not much time left, and we have work to do. The dragon apocalypse is coming."

PART III

Inferno

RILEY

Ten days.

That was the countdown. We couldn't wait much longer.
Ten days to plan, to prepare, to wait for reinforcements to show
up. That first afternoon passed in a flurry of confusion, questions and fear. When the video was shown to everyone, the
soldiers of the Order had reacted with indignation and out-
rage, the rogues with horror and fear, but in the end, a steely
resolve had settled over both groups, tinged with quiet resignation. Everyone knew what would happen if Talon's mindless clone army was awakened. We'd all seen it firsthand, on
a much smaller scale. We knew that if we didn't destroy that
army now, we wouldn't have a chance when they woke up.

The soldiers of St. George arrived first. A few days after the
meeting, Martin and St. George took the jeep away from the
farm and returned that evening with a pair of grim-faced soldiers in the backseat. The following day, they did the same and
brought back another three. Over the next few days, a handful of soldiers trickled in, all with the same story. They were

the only survivors of their various chapterhouses, or they had been away on a mission when the Night of Fang and Fire hit and had returned to find that nothing remained of their home but cinders, ash and the bones of their comrades.

Naturally, everyone was extremely cautious of the newcomers. Dragons and soldiers alike eyed each other with suspicion, loathing and fear, uncertain whether or not the other would attack. I, St. George and both lieutenants strove to make it *very* clear that no one was allowed to harm or threaten *anyone* on the property, no matter who or what they were. The rules were nonnegotiable. If anyone had a problem working with each other, they were welcome to leave and take their chances with Talon, alone. If there were incidents of violence, if anyone—dragon or human—hurt or threatened anyone on the property, they would be driven to the nearest town and left there. No trial, no questions asked. We were all under the same banner, and those who could not get along were liabilities. It was harsh, but the situation was too grave to have to worry about infighting. Fortunately, the near-destruction of the entire Order of St. George had shown the soldiers exactly what Talon could do, and how dire things really were. They were much more willing to ally with dragons, now that there was no other way they stood a chance against the organization. Funny how things like that worked.

One evening, a little more than a week into our preparations, Wes and I were huddled over his laptop, trying to pinpoint exactly where the laboratory was, when there was a tap on the doorframe. Jade stepped into the room.

"I must go," she announced without preamble.

I straightened. "What the hell? Now?" I stared at her, feeling the inevitable tick of the clock counting down the seconds.

"Dammit, Jade, why do you always skip out on us when something big is going down? If you haven't noticed, we're about to start a war with Talon."

"That is why I must leave," the Eastern dragon said, unconcerned with my anger. "And I am not, as you Americans would put it, skipping out. But I know my people. They will not hear me if I plead with them from the other side of an ocean. I must go to them directly and speak with them face-to-face. It is the only way to make them understand."

"And how long is this going to take? Weeks? Months?"

"I do not know," Jade said. "Hopefully, it will not be that long." I gave a sigh of frustration, and her eyes narrowed. "I have watched over your underground, Cobalt," she reminded me. "I have fought with you in battle, time and time again. And I have always returned when I said I would. Can you not give me the benefit of the doubt in this? Do you think that I do not understand what is at stake, what will happen to us all if Talon wins?"

"I know." I held up a hand. "I'm sorry. You're right—you've always come back. It's just…" I shrugged helplessly. "This is the big one, I think. If we don't succeed here, the world is going to burn when that army wakes up. And you're our heavy hitter, Jade. Against Talon, we're going to need all the help we can get."

"Which is why I am going," the Eastern dragon returned. "The dragons of the East cannot remain neutral in this war any longer. I hope to bring back a few of my kin, at the very least. Even if I must drag them here by their overly elegant whiskers." Her eyes glittered, and the statement would've been funny if Jade herself wasn't so terrifying. "But you are wrong in saying that I am your 'heaviest hitter,' Cobalt," she went on. "Physical strength is not the most important aspect in this war. If you want the true warriors, look to those whose hearts burn with passion, loyalty, justice and courage, for they will be the ones who will lead us to victory. You won't have to look far."

I gave a resigned nod. "Do the others know you're leaving?"

"I've told the soldier. He has already wished me luck." She stepped back and hovered in the doorway. "I'll return as soon as I can," she said. "Don't wait for me here—I will find you again. Oh, and if you would, please tell Mist to lead the morning meditations in my absence. I don't want the hatchlings to neglect their inner reflections, especially now."

"Right." I dredged up a smirk. "I'll do that. Well, good luck to you. Hopefully, we'll see you soon, with a giant army of Eastern dragons behind you."

"I will try." Jade nodded as she stepped away. "We will see who can be more stubborn but, as you Americans would put it, do not hold your breath. Until we meet again, Cobalt. Wesley." She nodded to the human at the desk. "Keep him out of trouble."

Wes snorted. "Right. Don't ask the impossible or anything."

Jade smiled. Then, as she had done several times before, she turned and walked away, vanishing from our lives for a little while. I hoped we would see her again. If she could convince the Eastern dragons to fight, if they would stand with us against Talon, I'd lead those morning meditations myself.

Mist entered the room, her footsteps silent as always. I felt that weird twist in my stomach again, my senses perking to life when she was around. "Is Jade going somewhere?"

"Only back to bloody China," Wes answered. "Again. Says she going to try to rally the Eastern dragons to fight, but bloody good luck with that. You know what those old wankers are going to say, right?" He raised a hand like he was holding a teacup, lifting his pinky finger into the air. "Let us now meditate upon the world going to hell."

"Don't be an ass, Wesley." I sighed. "Jade knows what she's doing."

"Oh, well, pardon me. I was just a wee bit worried that we're all going to fucking die in the next few days, that's all. That some wanker is going to aim the whole bloody lot of us at Talon and get us all killed." Wes was in rare form this evening, and my own anger stirred in response, fed by the fear and stress and exhaustion of the past few days. "Hey, remember the island? Remember the bloody Adult dragon they had guarding the place? Know what would've been nice to fight that thing? Another bloody Adult dragon."

I reached down, grabbed him by the front of the shirt and yanked him out of the chair. "There was another Adult dragon on that island!" I snarled in his face. "Her name was Scarlett, and she *died* to make sure we got out safely. So don't bitch at me like I have no clue as to what's going on. Like I don't know what this really is, that it's a fucking suicide mission. I already know, better than anyone." I released his shirt and pushed him back to the chair, glowering down at him. "My underground is probably going to die," I said, voicing the words that had been haunting me ever since that video came to light. "Everything I've worked for, everyone I've protected, those kids I promised to save from Talon…they're going to be marching straight into their jaws. Same with the dragonells. We rescued them from the island only to throw them right back at the organization. So yes, Wesley, I realize that having an Adult around would be nice. I realize that our numbers right now aren't going to be enough to take on the organization. I know everyone is terrified but trying really hard not to show it. Because there's no one else who can do this. It's just us. We *are* the resistance, and if we can't stop this, the world is screwed."

Wes stared at me with hooded eyes. "You done, mate?" he finally asked. I resisted the urge to yank him to his feet again and throw him through the window.

"Yeah," I growled shortly. "Something more you wanted to add?"

"After that little scene? Fuck, no."

"Good." Raking a hand over my scalp, I stepped away from him, feeling that if I didn't get some air I might start putting holes through walls. Mist was watching me from just inside the door, her expression carefully neutral. For some reason, I was suddenly embarrassed that she had seen me lose control, and then I was annoyed about being embarrassed. "Keep researching the laboratory," I told the sulking human. "I'll...be back in a second."

I swept out of the room before either of them could say anything.

The living room and kitchen were full of young dragons, sitting at the counter talking, playing cards, reading or gathered around the one television in the house. Phones, tablets and personal computers had been strictly forbidden for security reasons; the only computer allowed on the property was Wes's laptop, and it was probably more secure than the Pentagon. This did make for some very bored hatchlings—how did kids ever function before smartphones?—so we had to come up with other ways to keep them entertained. Nettle, perched cross-legged on the sofa, looked up from a hand of UNO cards and waved as I stalked by. I paused a moment to watch her and four others, including a pair of hatchlings from the facility, toss cards into the pile in the center amid much laughing and good-natured taunting. The game ended with one of the dragonells shouting "UNO!" as she threw down her final card, and the rest of the table exploded into loud groans and laughter. Nettle looked back and grinned at me.

"Hey, Cobalt," she called, and waved a hand at the table. "Wanna play? We have room for one more, and someone has to stop Sera's four-game winning streak."

"Maybe some other time," I said, and the girl bobbed her head before returning to the game. I watched them a moment longer, glad to see the grin back on Nettle's face as she began shuffling the deck. After Remy's death, she had become angry at the world, making snarky, acidic remarks to anyone who tried talking to her. After this resulted in a near-fight with one of the boys, Jade had stepped in and taken the furious, grieving hatchling into another room. Two hours later, Nettle had emerged wet-faced and puffy-eyed, but gradually began acting like herself again. And after that, morning meditations became a regular thing.

I gazed around the room, taking in every dragon there. Realizing that it would never be like this again.

I turned away and slipped outside.

Putting my hands in my jacket pocket, I began walking down the driveway, not really knowing where I was going. In the distance at the edge of the fields, I saw the barn silhouetted against the navy blue of the evening sky, orange light glimmering through the cracks in the wood. Autumn would be in there now, curled around her precious egg, two more lives that were depending on us. I wanted Autumn's baby to be the first US dragon who would hatch and grow up away from Talon, who wouldn't know the organization at all, who wouldn't have to fear what they would do if he or she didn't meet their expectations. I wanted my hatchlings to be free, to not know war and death and suffering. That's why I'd taken the hits for them in the past, why I worked so hard to be a pain in Talon's ass—so Talon would concentrate on me and leave my underground alone. But now...

I stopped in the middle of the driveway, feeling the truth start to claw its way out of my head, unwilling to stay buried. I couldn't protect them any longer. Everyone here would be drawn into the final battle with Talon and, win or lose, the casualties were going to be tremendous.

"Dammit," I whispered, closing my eyes. "Is this what we really have to do? Do we all have to die so the rest of the world can be safe?"

"Cobalt."

I turned. Mist stood a few yards behind me, pale and almost glowing under the light of the moon, her silver hair falling down her back. She regarded me solemnly, the echo of a silver-white dragon watching me from the center of the drive, and my heartbeat picked up in return.

"What do you want, Mist?"

She tilted her head, and the echo of the silver dragon became even stronger, watching me curiously across the gravel. "I don't really know," she said, walking forward. "I can't figure you out, Cobalt. You were a Basilisk. You worked for Talon. We've been trained to see everything, everyone, as tools. When did that change?"

I shrugged. "I got tired of it," I said. "I got tired of the casualties, being expected to turn a blind eye to what I was doing. I got tired of being used for Talon's dirty work, and seeing people suffer because of me. I guess somewhere along the way I grew a conscience."

"That seems very human."

"Maybe." I looked behind her at the house, where lights glowed through the windows and the echo of laughter reached me over the wind. "Or maybe we're not that different. Maybe that's something Talon has tried to extinguish, because if we let ourselves care for anything, eventually we realize how soulless the organization really is. Or maybe, over the generations, we really have become more human." I remembered the words of a certain red hatchling when she faced me in the shadows of the barn, her eyes bright with very human tears. *Dragons can love. We are quite capable of every emotion the organization has tried to stamp out.* "I don't know what happened to me," I said with a shrug. "I can see why Talon doesn't want us to have attachments—they're messy and complicated and painful as hell when you lose them. But I'll take that over what Talon wanted me to become. Ruthless. Someone who didn't care if their enemies *or* allies died, if it benefitted the organization. I just couldn't do that anymore."

"And what about me?" Mist asked.

The question was so unexpected that I didn't understand it for a moment. "What do you mean?"

"I mean…" She crossed her arms and looked away, frowning. If I didn't know better, I would say she was almost…embarrassed. "You said that you don't want any of your allies to die. Does that include a Basilisk who is only here because she was ordered to help you? Or a former enemy who had every intention of killing you in the past?"

"Mist…" I gazed at her in sudden understanding. "We've both done horrible things for Talon," I said softly. "Ember doesn't really get it. Neither does St. George, or any of the hatchlings. Sure, they know I used to be a Basilisk, but none of them really understands what that means. What I used to do." I thought back to those long years I worked for the organization. The missions that required me to destroy lives, careers and dreams, all in the name of profit for Talon. "Wes is probably the only one who knows about my past," I went on, "but there are things I haven't told even him, things only another Basilisk would understand. You're an exceptional agent, Mist," I said. "And I can see why the Archivist chose you. But you're still young. There's no mission you've completed for Talon that I haven't done several times over.

"So, to answer your question...yeah, it would bother me." I caught her gaze as I said this, looking her in the eye. "You might've been an enemy in the past, but hell, so was St. George. And Martin. And *all* the soldiers here, come to think of it. Believe me, I won't shed a tear if any Order fanatics go and bite the dust, but that's one less warm body that can hold a gun for our side, so I won't be dancing in the streets, either."

"Hmm. Well, it's nice to know I'm in the same boat as the soldiers of St. George."

"It's different with you." The words were out of my mouth before I could stop them, making her cock her head. "You're one of us, but even more than that, you're a damn good agent who is probably my equal in everything that matters. You kept your word when you helped us escape Talon. You were essential in getting us to the facility. And I wouldn't have trusted just anyone to lead the dragonells to safety. Even when you're driving me nuts, pulling shady shit and never giving me the whole story, I know that you'll come through for us in the end. If you died..." For some reason, that made my stomach churn a little, and I shook my head. "You're not in the same boat as the soldiers, I can tell you that."

She sighed. "Sometimes, I do hate you, Cobalt."

Stunned at the abrupt change of heart, I blinked at her. "O...kay," I stammered, utterly confused. "That came out of nowhere. Why?"

"Because I knew who I was before I met you." She shifted to stare at a point over the distant hills. "I was what Talon required, a Basilisk who didn't need to know the whys of my missions, I just needed to complete them. No questions, no doubts. Now..." She shook her head. "Now, I have no idea who I am, or what I'm supposed to do when this is all over. You're making me question everything, and I hate it, because it's something I can't seem to control."

"Yeah." I nodded. "Sucks, doesn't it? Welcome to my world. That's what happens when you grow a conscience."

"No." She took a short breath, regaining a little of her composure. "It's more than that. It's...you, Cobalt. For some reason, my distaste of you has grown tremendously."

My brows arched. "Oh?"

"Yes." Mist crossed her arms, still not looking at me. "You are constantly on my mind lately," she said. "I cannot think when you and I are in the same room. Your presence haunts me even when you are out of sight. It is irritating, and I don't know how to stop it." She gave a short huff and glanced at me, defiant. "Do you have any suggestions, since you seem to be more adept at these kind of things?"

I swallowed the sudden dryness in my throat. *No*, I thought furiously. *I don't want this. I've already been through enough with Ember. This can't be happening to me again.*

But it was different this time. There was no heat in my

veins, no fire consuming me from within. No savage, almost painful yearning from Cobalt toward the echo of the white dragon in the drive. Whatever this was, it was nothing like the *Sallith'tahn*. Whether through time or the knowledge that Ember had chosen someone else, I barely felt the life-mate bond anymore. If I concentrated on it, it was still there, weak and painful. And though my dragon side still keened the loss of his mate, my human self was...almost relieved. I was free. I could finally make my own choice, without following the instinctive pull of the *Sallith'tahn*. And, maybe, that was what Ember had wanted all along.

The only question was...did I want *this*?

I sighed. "I don't know, Mist," I told her truthfully. "I think we both know what's happening, but I honestly couldn't tell you where to go from here. I have absolutely zero experience with this type of thing, and really, I don't even know if I want to try. We've both seen it happen. We both know how screwed up it can get. I mean, hell, look at Ember and St. George. A dragon and a human?" I shook my head. "If that's not messed up, I don't know what is."

"It shouldn't be possible," Mist argued. "We're dragons. We're not supposed to feel like *they* do."

I almost smiled at how much she sounded like me. And how much *I* was starting to parrot the exact same things Ember had said. "Maybe it shouldn't be possible," I said, shrugging. "But it is. At least, it is for me. I've been around Ember long enough to know that it can happen, and that it's damned hard to ignore. Ember chose the human knowing what it meant, that they'd only have a short time together. She would rather spend a few years with him than a few centuries with another dragon. That's how powerful it can be."

"I don't see how they do it," Mist remarked. "Or why. It's completely illogical."

"Yeah. I guess it is." We were dancing around the words, as if not saying them out loud would somehow make it less real. The things that dragons did not experience. Emotion. Attraction. Love.

Mist looked down with a sigh. I watched her, noting how the moonlight shimmered off her hair, seeming to glow in the darkness. "So, what now?" I asked, feeling a strange pull in the pit of my stomach, urging me toward her. "What do we do about it?"

Mist didn't reply. Her brow furrowed, and she seemed perched on the razor edge of a wire, able to fall either way. I found myself holding my breath, waiting for her answer, hoping that she would... Actually, I didn't know. What was I hoping for here?

The Basilisk raised her head, letting out a long breath. Before she could say anything, however, my phone buzzed in my jacket pocket, sounding urgent.

"Dammit. What now, Wes?" I pulled it out, seeing a new text flash across the screen.

Did you fall down a rabbit hole? Where the hell are you?

Well, that was a mood killer. I rolled my eyes and hit Reply on the screen. Bitchy much? I texted back. I took a walk, where do you think I am?

Certainly not here, was the almost instant reply. Going over the blueprint the bloody Archivist sent us. Didn't Mist tell you? I thought that's why she went out there.

What? I looked up at the Basilisk, narrowing my eyes. "Why would the Archivist know what we're doing, Mist?"

"Because I sent him the video from earlier," she explained, as if that was obvious. "I also gave him full details of what was happening, and that we were planning to assault the lab to take out the vessels. He thought we could use all the help we could get."

"And you didn't tell me this earlier?"

"I didn't want to spend a half hour trying to convince you that the Archivist isn't going to sell us out to Talon," Mist said reasonably. "Besides..." She shrugged, unrepentant. "I'm a Basilisk. We don't ask permission. When something needs to be done, we trust our own judgment. You should know that just as well as me."

I shook my head. "And this is why Basilisks don't play well together." Stuffing the phone in my pocket, I started back toward the farmhouse. "Come on, then. Let's go see if your boss has any info that will make this less of a suicide mission."

GARRET

"An abandoned mining facility," Lieutenant Ward remarked.

At the edge of the table, Riley nodded, gazing at the sheets of paper scattered on the surface before him. "Yeah," he said. "According to the information we received from Mist's contact, the laboratory is located in what was once a large mining facility in the middle of the Appalachian Mountains."

"So, deep underground," Lieutenant Martin mused. "Which is why they haven't showed up on satellite or radar. And why no one has been able to find it until now."

"An underground compound is pretty defensible," Tristan said. "It's going to be hard breaking in. And once we're inside, it's going to be even harder getting out."

I looked at Riley. "But we know the layout of the facility, correct? And where the targets are located?"

Riley pulled a large sheet of paper from the pile and set it in the center of the table. It was a meticulously sketched map, almost a blueprint, that showed a complex underground facility with dozens of rooms, halls and stairways. "Right here," the rogue said, pointing to a truly enormous room near the back. "That's our target, where the vessels are being kept. We have to break in, get to that room and blow the whole thing to hell."

"Oh, is that all?" Tristan muttered. "Sounds easy."

Riley ignored him. "The main entrance will be heavily guarded," he said, tapping the paper. "And according to this, they have watchtowers set up so they can see anyone coming up the road. We won't be able to approach the main gate without tipping them off that we're coming. But apparently this was a huge mine once." His finger traced the surface to a different point on the map. "There's a second entrance into the facility near the back of the mine. There are no roads that lead to it, and it isn't well used or as guarded. Hell, they might've forgotten it's there. If we take that route, we might be able to surprise them."

"Why don't we just collapse both entrances?" Lieutenant Ward said, pointing a thick finger at the edge of the map. "It'll be easier to get to, easier to accomplish, and once the roof caves in Talon will have lost the compound."

"No." This from Ember, standing beside me. "This is Talon," she went on, gazing around the table. "We can't take any chances. We have to make sure that army is destroyed, and the only way to do that is to get to that chamber and personally bring it down."

"You realize that what you're talking about is basically a suicide mission," Martin told her. "Once Talon realizes why we've come, what we're after, they'll send everything they have to stop us. Whoever you send into the compound, if their mission is to blow it up from the inside, that team isn't coming out again."

"I know," Ember said softly.

A heavy feeling spread through me as I realized who that team would be. Casting a glance at Riley, I saw he was thinking the same. Three of us, then—me, Riley and Ember—to lead the charge into the laboratory, find the room with the vessels and destroy it.

"There should be two teams," Riley said after a moment of silence, staring down at the map. "A large force to assault the main entrance, to draw away as much enemy fire as they can, while the second goes in the back." He glanced at Ember, a wry grin stretching his mouth. "Hopefully, the infiltration group can sneak through and get to the target room before Talon even knows they're there."

"Seems tactically sound," Martin said, nodding. "It worked on the island. The challenge here will be dealing with a much larger, well-armed force. How many men do we have to assault the compound?"

"Not enough," Ward growled, and Martin looked at him sharply. "We've fought Talon before," he said, not backing down. "To take out even one of their small compounds, we'd need at least twice the soldiers we have now."

"Don't forget about us, Lieutenant," Ember said. "There are a whole lot of dragons here who are willing to stand and fight."

"Kids," the lieutenant said. "And females. How many of them have even held a gun? How many of those 'breeders,' as you called them, have recovered enough to participate in battle? An untrained soldier is more a liability than a help, even if that soldier is a dragon."

"Kids?" Riley's mocking voice drew our attention to the rogue, who stood with his arms crossed, smirking at the lieutenant. "That's an entirely different tune than what you sang earlier, Lieutenant," he challenged, making Ward's jaw tighten.

"Which is it? Either they're helpless kids or soulless demons— they can't be both."

"Riley," Ember said before Ward could erupt. "We're not here to fight each other. And he does have a point. Lieutenant Ward," she continued, staring the man down, "I understand your concern, but our options are limited. None of the hatchlings or dragonells has been trained like your soldiers, but they *are* dragons. And more important, they are all willing to fight. They've seen battle before, and they know what they're going up against. At this point in the game, with the numbers working against us, we can't be selective. The question is, will you and your soldiers be willing to work with them? Are you willing to accept that most of your troops will be dragons?"

I watched her, feeling proud as she stood up to the Order's most infamous lieutenant. A few days ago, I expected Ward to argue, just for the sake of disagreeing with anything a dragon said. But that was before Ember had stood between him and the killing flames of an Adult. It was difficult to despise someone who had saved your life, even if they were supposed to be your mortal enemy. As she had done with me, Ember was challenging everything the Order thought about her kind. If she survived the upcoming battle, she would be vital in bridging the gap between dragons and the rest of the Order of St. George.

Ward gave an annoyed sigh. "Yes," he snapped. "With how important the mission is, I suppose having dragons fighting alongside my troops is unavoidable. But what of the lizards? Will *they* accept orders from us?"

"Don't worry about that," Riley broke in. His mouth was set in a grim, determined line as he faced the officers. "I'll be there. No offense, but I'm not willing to leave them in the hands of the Order. I'll lead the assault on the main gate. You just worry about backing us up."

"Cobalt, no." Shockingly, it was Mist who spoke, the first time she'd said anything at any of these meetings. Pushing herself off the wall, she stepped up to the table, narrowing her gaze at the other Basilisk. "You're going to die if you charge at Talon head-on," she told him, and the worry in her voice surprised me. "You're a Basilisk—you're better off leading the infiltration into the laboratory."

"These are my hatchlings," Riley said. "My underground. I won't leave them to die at the hands of Talon." Mist started to protest, but he overrode her. "I might've been a Basilisk, but first and foremost, I am the leader of this resistance. My responsibility will always be to them.

"Besides," he went on, his voice softening, "we already have a Basilisk who will go with the infiltration team. And she'll do just as good a job as me, maybe even better." Mist blinked, and he offered a smile. "You don't need me there—Basilisks always work best alone. Just support and help the team like you've always done. I know I'll be putting them in good hands."

Mist sighed and glanced at Ember. "I have a feeling I know who'll be leading it."

Martin's gaze slid to me. "And what about you, Sebastian?" he asked. "You've been very quiet over there. What are your thoughts on this operation?"

"I'm just a soldier, sir," I replied. "I'll go where I'm needed. And I'll do what has to be done." Though I already knew my part in the operation, where I would be. At Ember's side, fighting to get her and the others into the room with Talon's vessel army, making sure they had a chance to save us all. Martin seemed to realize this, as well, for he gave a faint smile and shook his head.

"So, it's decided," Riley announced. "We have forty-eight hours to get ready. Get everyone together, gather all the supplies and weapons we need, make sure everyone knows the plan. In two days, this is going down. And we'll either succeed and stop Talon from taking over the world, or we'll die trying."

Silence fell over the room as Riley finished. As we all realized what we were up against, and what it would mean for everyone. This was it. The final confrontation. The last battle with Talon, where the only outcomes were victory, or death. Retreat was not an option. No matter how much opposition we faced, no matter how grim the odds, we could not leave until we finished what we came to do. Talon's army had to be destroyed.

Even if that meant the death of every last soul in the resistance.

★ ★ ★

"Crazy times, ain't it?" Tristan muttered.

I nodded absently. We were sitting on the roof of the farmhouse, Tristan's rifle over his knee, gazing over the endless fields, forest and pastureland surrounding the property. It wasn't Tristan's turn for guard duty, but this was his favorite spot: high overhead, lonely and isolated, where he could see everything for miles.

"I was wondering..." Tristan mused again, looking down at the yard, where a duo of soldiers passed a small group of rogues headed for the farmhouse. The two groups nodded stiffly to each other, and then continued on their way. "Let's say a miracle happens. Let's say, somehow, Talon crumbles and we actually win this war. What's going to happen to the Order, now that we've fought beside 'the enemy'?" I can see the council demanding that we turn around and slaughter every dragon here, but I know that some of us—hell, maybe most of us— are going to have a problem with that. If St. George decides not to kill dragons anymore, what's going to become of the Order? Where will we fit in?"

"I don't know," I answered truthfully. "I've been wondering the same thing myself, and there's no good answer, for either side. I just know the Order has to change. We can't continue as we've always done, not with what's happened."

"Yeah." Tristan sighed. "Guess we can worry about it when it happens. If it happens. Because, let's face it, we're probably all going to die when we assault that laboratory. I can't imagine Talon is going to leave those things unguarded, even if they aren't expecting us." A smile crossed his face as he looked toward the distant hills. "It's going to be huge," he said in an almost wistful voice. "This battle, it's more important than anything we've ever done. At least we'll go out in a blaze of glory."

I didn't answer, and he gave me a sideways look, a grin tugging at one corner of his mouth. "Don't tell me you're nervous, Mr. Perfect Soldier," he said teasingly. "You're the reason we're in this mess in the first place."

"I'm not nervous."

"No?"

"No." I was, but not for the reasons Tristan thought. Constant fighting and the teachings of St. George had effectively smothered any fear of dying in battle. We all accepted that death was a certainty, a fact of life for the soldiers of the Order.

We had all been trained to give our lives for the cause, and to have no regrets.

I had regrets. I regretted all the senseless killing I had done. I regretted that I wasn't able to save more of us, and that most everyone I knew would probably die in battle, as Tristan had said. We were both soldiers. We knew the odds. I wished it hadn't taken the Order of St. George being nearly wiped out to convince them they needed help, that the only way to stand against Talon was to ally with their greatest enemies.

But mostly, I wished I could've had more time with a certain red-haired girl. Not that we hadn't seen each other lately; Ember had taken it upon herself to train the hatchlings to both fight and use a weapon, and had recruited me to help. I had spent the past two days going over gun safety, how to reload and how to shoot, while Ember took them through sparring as both a human and a dragon. A few hours of training wasn't ideal, but it was better than none at all. At least they wouldn't be going into battle completely unprepared.

So Ember and I had spent quite a bit of time together, preparing for and getting our side ready for the assault. We'd had a few quiet moments alone, stolen between mission briefings, updates and day-to-day tasks. But with our base of operations so crowded with dragons, soldiers and rebels, even those moments were few and far between.

I wondered what she was doing now. After dinner I'd gone looking for her, only to find a scowling Nettle barring the door to the room they shared. The black dragon had informed me that Ember had passed out on her bed from exhaustion, and that I could just keep it in my pants until she woke up again. Not wanting to disturb her, or argue with a bristling dragonell, I had retreated.

Tristan was still watching me with a dubious look on his face. "I'm not afraid," I said, staring out over the fields. "I just... Ah, it's not important. Forget it."

"Uh-huh," Tristan said, and I heard the grin in his voice. "I see."

"What?" I muttered.

"Oh, nothing," Tristan drawled. "Just... I remember the Garret from two years ago. All you talked about was guns, bullets and killing things. You were about as fun as a used dishrag, and the only thing that scared you more than inactivity was talking to a girl." Leaning back on his palms, he regarded me with a lazy smirk. "You really are head over heels, aren't you? It's kind of adorable."

"Shut up before I push you off this roof."

He snickered, and I looked away to hide my burning face. Silence fell, the two of us quietly perusing the countryside, keeping watch as we'd done countless times before. No more words were passed between us; we already knew exactly what the other would say.

"There you are."

The familiar voice made my senses flare to life. I glanced over to see Ember sticking her head through the attic window Tristan and I had used. Ducking to avoid the frame, she slid gracefully through the opening and walked over the shingles to where we sat in the middle of the roof. For a second, she stood behind me, gazing at the landscape stretching away below us.

"Wow, you can see everything from up here," she murmured before glancing down at us, a smile crossing her lips. "So, what were you two discussing so intently?"

"Oh, not much," Tristan said in a gleefully smug voice that fooled no one. "Certainly nothing that would make the Perfect Soldier want to hurl me off the roof." Abruptly, he rose, yawning and stretching his long limbs. "Well, I'm tired of sitting in one place," he announced, which was a bald-faced lie; Tristan's specialty was remaining motionless for hours on end, waiting for his target to show itself. Something he not only excelled at, but actively enjoyed. "Think I'll patrol the grounds for a bit, see if the guards are keeping an eye out. You two have fun up here."

He gave me a very unsubtle grin, nodded to Ember, then turned and walked along the roof until he reached the window. After carefully maneuvering his rifle through the frame, he slipped through the opening and closed the panel behind him, leaving Ember and me alone.

Silence fell, broken only by the cicadas and the wind in the trees. Ember gazed down at me, and for a moment, I could see the outline of her other self in the moonlight, eyes glowing green, wings partially outstretched for balance.

"Huh," she remarked, cocking her head. "Listen to that. You can actually hear it."

"What?" I asked, bewildered.

"Absolutely nothing," Ember said.

Smiling, I held out a hand. She took it and carefully stepped over my legs to sit down between my knees. I wrapped my arms around her and leaned close, feeling her body against mine, the warmth of her in the cool night air. She relaxed against me, and I closed my eyes for a moment, letting myself sink into the feeling of peace. Tomorrow, we went to war. Tomorrow, we would lead a group of soldiers and dragons into battle with Talon, a battle in which many of us would die. Tomorrow.

"Well," Ember mused after a moment of peaceful quiet. "This is it, isn't it? The *Very Last Battle*, in capitals and italics. If we

win, Talon's army will be gone. They won't be able to do…
whatever it is they're planning. Which is probably try to take
over the world, knowing the Elder Wyrm. If we lose…"

"We won't be around to regret it," I murmured.

She shivered, though her voice remained contemplative.
"Are you scared?"

"Yes," I said quietly. "But not for me. For everyone we could
lose tomorrow." Reaching up, I ran my fingers through her hair,
brushing it from her neck. "For you."

"I'll be right beside you, soldier boy," Ember said, leaning
into my touch. "If we die, we go down together."

"No," I whispered, making her tense. Closing my eyes, I
pressed my forehead to the back of her neck, willing her to
understand. "Ember, my life isn't important. If I die, nothing
will change. The Order will either rebuild itself or be broken
completely, and Talon will continue on as it's always done.
The loss of a single soldier will mean nothing in the long run.

"But you," I went on, before she could mount a protest,
"you'll be the one to change things, Ember. Riley, Jade, even
Mist…they'll all play a part, but if we survive, the one who
will determine the future of Talon and St. George will be you.
I don't think Riley could do it—he still doesn't trust the Order,
and his underground will always come first. Jade craves the
isolation of her homeland, and Mist is more comfortable in
the shadows than in the thick of things. You're the bridge between us, dragon girl. We're all here because of you."

Ember gave a short, humorless laugh. "No pressure or anything," she muttered. "But you're wrong, Garret. It's not just
me. I might be the dragon who started questioning the way
things were, but I could do that…because I met you. Because
I fell in love with you, a soldier of St. George, when it was

supposed to be impossible. If we never met, I might still be in Talon. I could be a Viper now, killing for them, hunting down innocent dragons. *Everyone* here would be a target." She shuddered. "Actually, no, scratch that. I wouldn't even be a Viper, because the freaking *Elder Wyrm* would be living in my head right now." She clenched a fist on my arm, and my stomach curled. "I wouldn't even be myself anymore. I'd be *her*. The enemy of everyone here."

Ember took a shaky breath, pressing closer to me. "If things had gone differently in Crescent Beach," she whispered, her voice trembling, "we wouldn't be sitting here now. If anything, you're the reason I'm not on the other side of this war, that I'm not the enemy of the rogues and the Order, and maybe the whole world. *I'm* here, Garret, because of you."

Turning in my arms, she gave me a fierce glare as a lump rose to my throat. "So don't you dare say your life isn't worth anything," she finished, staring me in the eye. "And don't you dare go into battle tomorrow with the intent of charging off into some ultimate noble sacrifice." One hand rose, caressing the side of my face, as she gave a faint smile. "Your past has been forgiven, Garret. Those years with the Order—you've redeemed yourself a hundred times over. Now, you just have to forgive yourself." Her other hand came to rest against my cheek as she leaned in and touched her forehead to mine. "We end this together, like we've always done. And maybe, somehow, we'll beat the odds and win one more time. But I'm not going to do anything without you, so you'd better be there. Besides…" The smile curled at one corner, becoming teasing, though her eyes were dark with emotion. "You still have a wager to lose, soldier boy. How am I going to kick your ass in surfing if you're gone?"

Something hot slid down my cheek, even as I smiled back. "You're awfully confident about that," I said, and my voice came out slightly choked. Ember gave me a defiant grin.

"Prove me wrong, then."

"I will," I promised, and kissed her. She slid her arms around my neck and pressed close, and for a few fleeting heartbeats, with the moon shining down on us and stars fading from the sky, the past and future disappeared, and the present was the only moment that mattered.

Pulling back, Ember shifted and curled up against me, resting her head on my chest, as we gazed at the horizon. Overhead, the moon climbed ever higher, ticking down the minutes until dawn. It wouldn't be long now; a few hours, and then nothing would be the same. Not for the rogues, the Order, perhaps even the rest of the world.

Ember reached back to slide her fingers into my hair. "Can we stay like this a little while?" she asked. "It's so crowded downstairs, and I'm not going to get much sleep tonight, anyway. It's nice to be away from everything for a few minutes."

"Yeah." I nodded. "We can stay here." *All night if you want to.* Lowering my head, I kissed the side of her neck, making her sigh, and wrapped my arms around her. "If you get tired," I told her, "go ahead and sleep. I won't let you fall."

She chuckled softly. "That would be the height of embarrassing—a dragon breaking its leg by rolling off a roof. Riley would never let me live it down." She paused, lightly tracing my arm with her fingers. "We've come a long way," she mused. "And we've done so much in a such a short time. The Order and the rogues are working together. Riley finally got to the facility and rescued everyone like he wanted, but more important, we wouldn't have succeeded without St. George's help.

There's hope for us, for dragons and the Order, I can feel it. I just…" She lowered her head, her next words almost inaudible. "I wish Dante was here to see it, too."

DANTE

"Are you ready, Dante?" asked the Elder Wyrm.

Standing in the Elder Wyrm's new office, I took a breath to calm the emotions churning in my stomach, and nodded.

Everything was in place. The men, the security, the special "surprises" we had planned. All was foolproof. Nothing would slip past us this time. When Cobalt and the Order of St. George finally made their move, no matter what they had prepared, we would be ready for them.

And when Ember inevitably showed up, when I stood face-to-face with my twin once more, I knew what I had to do.

"Yes, ma'am," I said confidently. This was it, the end of an era. It was time to stop these games, once and for all. "I'm ready."

EMBER

In military terms, the darkest hour before dawn was known as Before Morning Nautical Twilight. Historically, according to Garret, it was a favorite time to launch a surprise attack on enemy forces, because it was the time when the human body was at its least alert. It also gave you a full day of war during which, hopefully, you could press your advantage and leave the enemy scrambling for control the rest of the battle.

That was the theory, anyway.

I sat beside Garret in the back of the semi truck, feeling every bounce and rumble of the gravel road through the metal walls of the container. Outside, it was dark; the only light came from a couple lanterns set on the floor of the semi, but at least it wasn't cold. Not with the amount of bodies surrounding us.

Beside us, covering nearly every square inch of the container, a small army of dragons waited in silence. Hatchlings, Juveniles and dragonells sat quietly along the wall, their expressions grim with anticipation. A few were asleep, curled up in corners or leaning against a friend, and I envied them

the few hours of oblivion. We'd been traveling through the
night, and even with several pillows, blankets and mattresses
scattered about, the bed of a semi truck was not comfortable.
Riley was up front driving the rig, with Wes and Mist beside
him in the cab, and I also envied them the additional comfort of padded seats. But I had volunteered to stay in the back
with the rest of the hatchlings and dragonells, so I couldn't
complain. At least there were no soldiers of St. George in the
container with us—well, besides Garret. The rest of the Order
were trailing behind in a second semi, and it was a relief not
to have to worry about certain soldiers taking offense over
sharing space with dragons.

Though, there being less of them, they probably had a lot
more room in the back of the truck. Stupid St. George preju-
dices. We were allies, yes, but there was still a long way to go.

Beside me, Garret was calm. He was dressed like a soldier,
in a black armored vest, gloves and combat boots, with a va-
riety of weapons holstered to his belt or across his chest. I was
dressed similarly, with a vest over my Viper suit, an M4 over
my shoulder and a pistol holstered to my belt. His gloved hand
was curled around mine in the space between us, and I could
feel the easy rise and fall of his breath.

I wished I could find some of his tranquility. For the past
hour, I'd been trying to calm myself, to ease the frantic writhing of nerves in my stomach the closer we got to our destination. I knew the hatchlings and the dragonells were just as
scared, probably more so, and they were all holding up remarkably well, considering the situation. But to me, gazing over the
crowded container, they all seemed very young. Which was
silly, as most of the hatchlings were my age or older, and some
of the dragonells were Juveniles. They had their whole lives

ahead of them, centuries of living left to do. But, for some of them at least, it was all going to end today.

I shivered, and beside me Garret turned his head, a worried look on his face. "You all right?" he asked.

I nodded, shoving my worries, regrets and doubts to the back of my mind. "How much longer?"

He glanced at his watch. "Another fifteen minutes," he murmured, making my stomach want to crawl up my throat. I shoved it down with the rest of my fears. "We're nearly to the stopping point."

And then, the hand that had been laced with mine disengaged, and he curled his arm around my shoulders, pulling me to him. I didn't resist, and he shifted slightly to draw me to his chest, wrapping both arms around me. I tucked my head under his chin and closed my eyes, knowing the hatchlings and dragonells were watching, not caring what they thought. Garret lay his cheek atop my head and tangled his fingers in my hair, but didn't go any further than that. We held each other in silence, listening to our hearts thump quietly together. *Last time*, his pulse seemed to whisper to me. *Last time, last time, last time*.

The semi shuddered once and rumbled to a stop. I felt Garret take a deep breath, felt his arms tighten almost painfully for a moment, before he let me go and stood, the steely soldier's mask falling into place. I rose, as well, and watched the others climb to their feet, their faces pale but determined.

The doors creaked open, and Riley stood there, eyes glowing yellow against the darkness. A pine-scented breeze drifted into the container, and I breathed in the fresh air as it drove away the smell of rust and fear and too many bodies packed in too small a space.

I hopped down from the truck, and my boots squelched in mud as I surveyed our surroundings. We were on a narrow dirt road in the middle of a vast forest, and with the upward cant of the ground, it felt like we were on a hill or mountainside. It was very quiet, and overhead the sky was still bright with stars.

Blinding lights announced the arrival of the other semi, and I winced, shielding my eyes until the massive truck stopped a few yards away and shut off the headlamps. As Martin dropped from the driver's seat and walked toward us, Garret and Riley joined me at the edge of the road.

"All right," Riley began as we gathered in a loose circle, two soldiers and two dragons—Martin and Garret, me and Riley. The rest of the hatchlings, dragonells and soldiers clustered around the trucks, waiting nervously, as the team commanders met for the last time. "We're about five miles from the mining facility, according to Wes. This road goes to the front gates. Which means that the second entrance is around that peak, due west from the gates. If you head straight that way—" he nodded toward the forest "—you should walk right into it."

"I have it marked on my GPS," Garret said. "We'll find it."

Martin nodded and gazed up the road. "We'll be waiting about a half mile from the front gates," he said. "Barring complications, it should take you an hour to reach the second entrance. Radio us when you get there—that will be our signal to start the attack."

"After that," Riley added, "we'll cause as much of a ruckus and buy as much time as we can for you to find the chamber with the army and blow it sky-high."

I swallowed hard. Riley was counting on us, as were the rogues, the hatchlings, the dragonells and the rest of the Order. We couldn't screw this up. We had to reach the vessels and destroy the army, otherwise the sacrifices of everyone here would be for nothing.

"We won't fail," Garret promised, echoing my sentiment. Riley gave a tired nod, as if wanting to believe him but knowing that we were probably going to lose a great deal before it was over.

"All right," Martin said. "Then, if we all know what to do, I suppose there's nothing left but to get this mission started. Sebastian..." He looked at Garret, an almost fatherly affection going through his eyes. "Be careful in there. Come back alive, if you can. That's an order."

"Yes, sir," the soldier answered quietly.

"Ms. Hill," Martin said, and with a shock, I realized he was talking to me. Though his tone was a little stiff, he looked me straight in the eye as he spoke. "I don't know if I'll see you again, or what will happen afterward, should this mission go as planned. I do want you to know that, whatever the result, I am committed to seeing the Order change. It will take time, there will be heavy resistance, and in the end I am not certain what the Order of St. George will be, how it will continue to exist. But there will be change. There *must* be change. You—all of you," he added with a brief glance at Garret and Riley, "are proof of that."

A lump rose to my throat, and my insides curled. I didn't know what touched me more: that he was finally saying the words I'd longed to hear the Order admit for so long, or that he was giving me his promise because he thought we weren't coming back. Granted, he was only one man, and his position in St. George would be tenuous at best, but it was a start. "Thank you, Lieutenant," I whispered. "I hope that I...that we *all* will see that happen one day."

"I hope so, too." Martin gave a resigned smile. "Good luck to us all," he said, and walked back toward the truck, where Lieutenant Ward and the rest of the soldiers waited for him. As Martin approached, the second officer's gaze flicked to mine, grim and unsmiling, but not hostile. He gave me a single nod, then turned his back on us to speak to his men.

Riley sighed. "Well," he said, looking at me and Garret, "guess this is it. I have to get our side ready for the assault, and I hate long goodbyes, so..." A shadow of pain crossed his face before he looked at me, forcing a defiant grin. "Good luck in there, Firebrand. If anyone has a chance of making this happen, it'll be you. I hope I'll get to see you blow Talon's shit to kingdom come, but if...if I don't make it, just know that you've made my life infinitely more exciting. I know that we've had some rough spots, and I wish some things could've gone differently, but I'm glad we met. And I think that goes for everyone." He glanced at the soldier watching quietly on my other side. "None of us would be here now if we hadn't met you."

My eyes prickled. "Stop talking like we're never going to see each other again," I told him. "This isn't goodbye forever. You're going to get through this, like you've always done."

This time his smile was wry. "If you say so, Firebrand." Stepping close, he gazed down with intense gold eyes, and Cobalt's presence surrounded me, the echo of the blue dragon so clear it was like I was staring right at him. "But in case the worst happens," the rogue dragon murmured, "and I go out in a blaze of glory and dragonfire, I don't want you beating yourself up over it. I regret nothing between us, Ember. Everything we've done, everything that's happened, has been worth every pain and fear and drop of blood. And if we do get through this, I can't wait to see what will happen next. It's been a good fight."

"Yeah." I blinked back tears. "A great fight."

"Then let's finish it," Cobalt said. "Once and for all. St. George?" He grinned at the human then, shocking us both, held out a hand. "I trust you're going to do what you do best, and fuck up Talon's plans to hell and back?"

Garret's mouth curled, and he gripped the offered hand firmly. "I'll do my best."

"Good. Try not to die in there."

Two more soldiers broke away from the second truck and came forward, dressed in all black, the remaining members of the infiltration team. They were, according to Martin and Ward, the best soldiers from each of the chapterhouses, and each had volunteered to back us up on the mission. One of them was Tristan, who gave me and Garret a brief nod as he stepped up. The other, unfortunately, was Peter Matthews.

I bit back a grimace. I didn't know why he had volunteered, but I suspected he wanted to be on the mission that was the most important. Or maybe the thought of blowing up a roomful of Adult dragons appealed to him. I hoped his tendency to be a douche would not interfere in the middle of the mission, or I would be tempted to set him on fire.

"This everyone?" Matthews commented as he and Tristan joined us. The soldier's gaze lingered on me and Riley and his jaw tightened, as if he wanted to say something, but he kept his opinion to himself. "The whole circus team?"

"Almost," I replied, determined not to let him get to me. "There's one more. She should be here anytime."

Tristan blinked and frowned at Garret, who was watching with a raised brow and the hint of a smile on his face. "Something you want to say, Sebastian?"

"Just surprised that you're here," Garret replied, "and not

crouched behind that huge gun we lifted from the train. I was sure you'd be the one to volunteer for the prototype."

"Oh, believe me, I wanted to." Tristan shrugged. "I'm already kicking myself for not being the first one to fire the Dragon-killer. But, the way I see it, this is probably our last mission together. And I promised Martin I'd watch your back, make sure a lizard doesn't drop onto it while you're trying to save the world." He smirked at Garret. "So don't make me regret that decision, partner."

Mist appeared behind Riley like a ghost, soundless and graceful, her pale hair tucked under a dark cap. She carried a pair of backpacks in each hand, and gingerly handed one to each of us. "Be careful," she warned as I hefted mine onto my back, feeling something large and rectangular inside. "There's enough explosives in each of these to bring down the whole cave system. So I would try very hard not to jostle it around."

"All right. Then we're ready." Looking around at the small group of three soldiers and two dragons, Garret nodded and stepped back toward the trees at the edge of the road. "Dawn is an hour away," he announced, slipping into the role of squad commander like it was nothing. "And it'll take that long to reach the second entrance. Let's go."

As we started off, Riley suddenly reached out, catching Mist by the arm and making her turn. For a moment, the two of them stared at each other, seeming to forget the world around them. My pulse skipped a beat at the emotions flaring between the two, at the way Riley gazed at Mist like he would never see her again.

Could he be…? My heart throbbed as I hurried after Garret and the others, but not in the way I thought it might. Though the tug of the *Sallith'tahn* was still there, weak but persistent, both sides of myself had chosen the soldier. Dragon instincts stirred, more curious than jealous at the thought of Cobalt with another dragon, but mostly I was happy for them, for Riley in particular. The worry on his face, and the way Mist gazed back at him—it was more than concern for a teammate. They might not know it themselves, but they felt something for each other, something more than friendship, trust and the begrudging respect each had for the other Basilisk.

But I knew why they would resist getting close to anyone right before the final battle, and I ached for them both. Nothing about this was certain, except the knowledge that there would be casualties before the night was over. I desperately hoped they would survive. We had all suffered, but Riley had experienced so much loss in such a short time; he deserved to find happiness with someone.

"Be careful, Mist," I heard him whisper as I entered the trees after the soldiers. "Come back alive."

"I will," Mist answered quietly, "but only if you promise to do the same."

Riley's answer was too soft for me to hear, and I didn't want to stop to look back at them, so I continued to follow Garret and the soldiers. A few seconds later, the Basilisk appeared beside me, her expression somber. She caught my gaze and raised a brow, but I didn't say anything about the conversation with Riley, and neither did she.

Together, we slipped through the shadowy undergrowth of the forest toward our final destination.

GARRET

"There it is."

Crouched behind a tree at the base of the mountain, I raised my night-vision goggles and scanned the area. At one point, part of the forest had been cleared away, as a large swath of land in front of the mountain was flat and empty of trees, though nature was steadily creeping back again. Debris was scattered throughout the area; tires, car parts and rusting metal barrels lay in the dirt, covered with weeds and vines, and a badly decayed wooden cart was overturned in a ditch, falling to pieces. Past a faded, nearly unreadable Danger! No Trespassing sign at the entrance, a gaping oval tunnel had been carved into the side of the mountain.

"Well, we found it," Tristan muttered after taking the night-vision goggles from me and sweeping the area himself. "I don't see any guards, though I'm not certain if that's a good thing or not."

"It's not." Mist crouched beside us, peering at the entrance with narrowed blue eyes. "Talon doesn't leave anything unguarded," she said, taking the goggles from Tristan. "Especially if it's an entrance to one of their top-secret laboratories. I'm guessing this isn't an entrance so much as an exit—a bolt hole, should they need to get out quickly. There might even be several of these scattered throughout the mountain." She lowered the goggles and gave me and Tristan a sideways look. "In case St. George comes storming through the front door."

Behind us, Peter Matthews snickered. "So even way out here in the middle of nowhere, with an underground lab and an army of giant demon lizards waiting to take over the world, Talon is still scared of us. Good to know they have their priorities straight."

I ignored him. "Do you see any cameras or security?" I asked Mist, who continued to scan the area with the night-vision lenses.

She shook her head. "No. Nothing." Frowning, she handed me the goggles again. "That's...worrisome. An iron padlocked gate can't be the only thing between us and the entrance to the lab."

"So what if it isn't?" Matthews snapped. "Just give the assault team the signal to go. They attack the front gates, fire a couple rockets, and Talon won't be looking at its back doors for long."

"No," Mist said calmly. "Once the attack begins, Talon will go into lockdown mode. We can't risk tipping them off until we're sure we can get inside, or the attack out front will be for nothing."

"All right, lizard. So how the hell are we going to do that exactly?"

She gave him a brief, disdainful look and stepped away. "Wait here. I'll check it out myself."

"You?" Matthews voice had a hard edge to it. "I don't

think so. Like we're going to let a former Talon spy tell us if the entrance to their top-secret facility is safe to approach." There was a metallic click, as if he had raised his gun. "You're staying right here, where we can see you."

"Matthews," I growled, turning to glare at him. "Stand down. You don't make that decision. I do."

He glared back at me, his mouth twisting in a sneer. "Commander," he said, making the word sound like an insult, "you're not seriously thinking of letting this lizard go off on her own? She could waltz right into the lab to let all the guards know we're right behind her and to shoot us as soon as we come in."

"Wow," Ember commented, looking at Mist. "That is one elaborate plan. You've been with us all this time and went through all this trouble, just to betray us in the end. You should have just shot us all in the back while we were on our way here and saved Talon the effort."

"Indeed," Mist deadpanned. "Why didn't I think of that earlier?"

Tristan snorted, sounding like he was trying to cover up a laugh, and I narrowed my eyes at Matthews. "Mist," I said, not taking my eyes from the soldier. "Go ahead. We'll wait for you here. Just be careful."

Matthews made a disgusted noise but backed off. Mist nodded once to me, turned and slipped into the darkness like a ghost. I raised the night lenses again to scan the entrance and surrounding area for guards, cameras or hidden threats, but continued to see nothing.

I didn't see Mist, either, though I knew she had to be approaching the mine shaft. As we waited, the minutes ticked by, and the Basilisk did not return.

Matthews gave a soft, menacing chuckle and shook his head.

"I told you, Sebastian," he said, his voice full of ugly triumph. "The bitch has gone to warn the rest of Talon that we're here. You can't trust a lizard."

Ember growled softly. "Give her time. She'll be back."

"Says the *other* dragon in the party," Matthews sneered. "And we don't have time. The assault team is waiting for our signal to start the attack."

Tristan gave him an annoyed look, but then glanced worriedly at the sky. "Garret, I hate to say this, but he's right. Martin told us an hour, and it's almost dawn. We need to move."

I sighed. "Two minutes," I said. Matthews's jaw tightened, and he took a breath to argue, but I overrode him. "That's an order, soldier."

"Fine, Sebastian," Peter Matthews said in a hostile voice. "But I hope you remember this when the lizards fuck our entire mission in the back. Tell your dragons hello when they send you to hell."

"Tell them yourself," said a voice, and Mist materialized behind us. "Because you would be the first to go. Sorry it took a while," she told me, ignoring the glare from Matthews. "I ran into something...well, not unexpected, but troublesome."

"What happened?" I asked her. She frowned.

"Better that you see for yourself. There are no cameras or guards, so we're safe for the moment."

I nodded and glanced at the others. "Let's move." We hurried across the clearing, prioritizing speed now rather than stealth, and ducked into the mine entrance. Inside, a rusted iron gate blocked the way forward, but the chain that held the door shut had been cut through, probably by Mist. After pulling the door back with a squeak, we entered the darkness of the tunnel.

"Ooh, a chain on the door," Peter Matthews mocked, his voice echoing quietly. "That must've been a bitch to get through."

"Maybe for certain oblivious humans," Mist replied. "But that's not what I was talking about." She stopped and gestured down the shaft. "See for yourself."

I shone my flashlight into the darkness, and my heart sank. About fifty yards ahead, the tunnel had been blocked by a massive pile of rocks and dirt. Judging from the size of some of the boulders and the way everything seemed to have settled, this cave-in must have happened months, if not years, ago.

"Dammit." Tristan shook his head, giving the rock pile a look of dismay. "Well, that's going to screw things up for us. No way we're getting through that." He shoved his fingers through his hair and looked at me. "Don't suppose you know of another way in? Otherwise this mission is screwed."

I didn't, of course, and was racking my brain to come up with an alternate plan when Ember made a thoughtful noise and stepped forward.

"No," she murmured, narrowing her eyes at the cave-in. "This isn't a mistake. This is what Talon wants you to see. There's no way into the cave, so intruders will turn around and leave."

"Exactly," Mist said, giving Ember an approving nod. "Talon excels in hiding in plain sight. If they had high-tech security guarding this place, anyone would become suspicious. So I did some digging. It took me a while—I had no real clue of what I was looking for, but in the end, I finally found this."

Reaching down, she grabbed one of the mine cart rails and pulled. An entire section of track swung up like a trapdoor, revealing a concrete shaft and a metal ladder that went straight down into darkness.

Peter Matthews gave a soft chuckle. "Sneaky bastards," he muttered. "I keep forgetting how shifty these things are." He glanced at me, a wide, somewhat evil grin crossing his face. "Well, Commander? Door's open. Let's get in there and slaughter some lizards."

I didn't like the zealous gleam in his eyes, or the bloodlust, but here we were. The door was open and the mission had to go on.

"Lieutenant," I said into my mic. "We've reached the back entrance."

"Copy that, Sebastian," Ward replied. "We'll begin the assault." There was a pause, then he added, "Good luck and Godspeed to you all."

His voice cut out, and I switched channels to our support, who was overseeing the operations of both teams. "Wes. You there?"

"About bloody time." The hacker sighed. "Yes, I'm here. I take it you've found the other way in?"

"Yes."

"Right. I'll guide you through best I can, but remember, I only have the blueprint. I can't account for enemy guards or killer dragons ambushing you. You're on your own then."

"Understood. Just get us to that chamber, Wes. We'll take it from there."

A sudden flash came from outside, followed by the muffled but unmistakable sound of an explosion. We all looked toward the tunnel entrance as distant gunfire sounded over the trees.

"It's started," Ember breathed. Her expression was dark but determined, and for a moment, I saw the outline of her real self, a fierce red dragon with eyes glowing green, as she turned to me. "I'm ready," she said. "Let's end this."

I nodded. "Move out," I ordered, and we started down the ladder into the depths of a laboratory of monsters, ready to destroy them all and save the world.

Knowing full well we weren't coming out again.

RILEY

Okay, that's bigger than I thought it would be.

I crouched in dragon form at the edge of the rise, digging my talons into the edge of the cliff, gazing down the slope at our target. The entrance to the laboratory sat at the bottom of a rocky bowl, surrounded by mountains on all sides. I could see a gaping cavern large enough to drive a truck through cut into the side of a slope—the original entrance to the mine, if I had to guess. The land around it had been cleared and stripped of all vegetation, leaving the area barren and rocky. Several long gray buildings sat in rows off to one side, and a yellow backhoe, bulldozer and other construction equipment sat silent and empty near a gravel pit. A chain-link fence surrounded the entire area, with watchtowers flanking either side of the road that led through the gate and up to the entrance.

And there were a lot of humans standing guard outside. Humans with combat vests and very large guns, who didn't look at all like scientists or corporate employees, but trained militia.

In fact, this whole operation didn't look like a mining facility so much as some kind of top-secret government organization.

"They're expecting us, all right," Martin said behind me. I scooted back from the edge and rose, watching as he scanned the area with a grave expression. "No need for that many guards unless you know something is coming."

"Guess we shouldn't disappoint them, huh?"

He sighed. "Are the communications working?"

"Yeah." I wore a headset with an earpiece and mic that had been specially modified for a dragon. The bud had been shoved into my ear canal and was uncomfortable as hell, but it would allow me to keep in contact with both lieutenants. Wes was supporting Sebastian's team, and was responsible for leading them through the laboratory to the stasis chamber, so his attention would be elsewhere. I would never admit it, but it was strange, having someone else's voice buzz through the earpiece. It just wasn't the same without a sarcastic English accent. "I hear you loud and clear, Lieutenant."

"Martin." Ward's voice crackled in said earpiece, sounding urgent. "Sebastian just reached the back entrance."

"All right." I ignored the painful churning in my stomach. It was time. How many would I lose before this was over? How many would I watch die, to defend a world that didn't know we existed? "We're ready."

Martin nodded and stepped back. "Good luck then, dragon," he said in a grave voice. "See you all on the battlefield."

I watched him stride away, back to the soldiers of St. George, and glanced at the small army that waited behind me. On the ledge, dozens of glowing, reptilian eyes watched me, wings and tails fluttering anxiously in the predawn stillness.

I swallowed, knowing I should say something to them, that

they were all looking to me for encouragement, on the last day some of us would be alive. Speeches were never my forte, but I stepped forward and took a breath, bringing their attention to me.

"It's okay to be scared," I told the thirty-plus dragons who watched me with solemn eyes. "This is Talon, and we all know what they're capable of. We've all suffered under the organization. We know the cruelty and depravity they're capable of, even to their own kind. You have every right to be afraid, and for that, I want you to know that I am proud of each and every one of you." Some of them blinked, raising their heads, as I smiled grimly. "You chose to fight, to be here now. Because you know that without us, Talon will sweep the world and turn it into a living hell for both humans and dragons. Well, that's not going to happen. Today, we strike back at the organization, and we send a message to the Elder Wyrm that we will never accept her world." I gestured down the slope, to the massive facility at the bottom, and bared my teeth in a smile. "The Elder Wyrm's plans are going to go up in flames, but they need us to make it happen. We have to strike so hard and fast, and rain so much fire down on Talon's heads, they're going to believe it really is the dragon apocalypse. Think we can do that?"

At the front, a small black dragon raised her head, yellow eyes flashing in the darkness. "Hell, yeah," Nettle said, her crown of spines bristling with anticipation. "The bastards won't know what hit them. I'll tear them all a new one. For Remy."

"For Scarlett," another growled, one of the dragonells from the island facility.

"For Isaac," Kain muttered in the back.

I closed my eyes. *Too many to name,* I thought as faces from the past flickered through my head. *For everyone I've lost, everyone who won't survive this. And for those who will. I'll give you a better world, I swear it.*

"Okay." Opening my eyes, I turned to face the laboratory, resolve settling over me. Even from here, I could easily see the entrance, and the dozens of humans milling about, unaware of an impending attack from the sky. I took a deep breath, filling my lungs, feeling the heat and fire within surge to every part of my body. If these were my final hours, it was fitting that I should spend them as a dragon.

A flash of red lit up the sky, and the distant roar of an explosion echoed into the silence, as an RPG slammed into one of the watchtowers and blew it sky-high. Almost instantly, a siren blared, spotlights flashing on to sweep the ground, as the guards rushed to engage the soldiers charging in the front gate.

Here we go.

Rearing onto my hind legs, I gave a booming, defiant roar, and the dragons behind me took up the battle call, a few dozen Draconic voices rising into the air. Springing from the ledge, I opened my wings and plunged into a steep dive, hearing my army do the same, and we swooped toward what could be our very last battle.

EMBER

I hit the bottom of the ladder and quickly stepped aside for the others to come down, gazing around warily. We'd landed in what looked to be another mine shaft, with natural stone walls held up by thick wooden timbers, and a track stretching past us into the dark. I shone my flashlight in one direction and saw that it ended in a solid wall of rock and collapsed stone; either from a natural cave-in or one that Talon had orchestrated.

"Well," I muttered as Garret landed beside me, "at least that makes one choice easier."

We followed the tracks, taking the only direction that we could. They didn't go far. Maybe a hundred yards from the ladder, they curved around a bend and ended at a door. And not just any door. A large, thick barrier of solid steel, set into a wall of iron. A keypad glowed green at the edge, though the screen was covered in a film of dust, indicating this had not been used in quite some time.

"Ah," Mist said, sounding triumphant and awed at the same time. "*There's* the high-tech security I was expecting."

"Can you get us through?" asked Garret.

"I should be able to." Mist stepped forward, frowning as she approached the massive door. "We'll see if the codes the Archivist gave me will work."

"And if they don't?" Matthews asked.

"Then there will likely be an alarm, and the mission will be a failure," the Basilisk stated bluntly, making him scowl. "To prevent that, I will need absolute silence to concentrate. So perhaps you could refrain from making any noise until I am finished."

I bit my cheek to stifle a grin at the real meaning behind her words—*please shut up and go away*—and took a step back with Garret to give her some room.

"Hope this works," Tristan muttered, his voice pitched very low. "Otherwise this is going to be a very short mission."

"If it doesn't," I whispered back, "we'll just have to find another way in. Or we'll fight our way through the guards when they come." It didn't matter how we did it, but we *had* to get inside to destroy the vessel army. We couldn't fail. Riley, Martin, the rogues, everyone—they were all out front, fighting and dying to give us this chance.

Fortunately, it was only a few seconds before the door gave a soft beep and clicked as it swung back. Relieved, we started forward, but Mist stood in front of the now-open door, a slight frown on her face as we joined her. Another tunnel, this one made of tile and concrete and lit with overhead lights, curved away past the frame. "Something wrong, Mist?"

Mist shook her head. "I know I got the codes from the Archivist, but…it shouldn't be this easy," she murmured. "This is Talon we're talking about—there's no such thing as luck."

The Basilisk crossed her arms and glared past the frame. "I don't like it. It smells like a trap."

Garret moved up beside me, also peering through the door. "Luck or not, we have to move on," he said. "We can't abandon the mission, even if there is a trap waiting for us inside. There's no choice but to continue."

Warily, we started down the corridor, following the lights and the piping that ran along the wall. I shivered as I trailed Garret, hugging the wall and feeling highly exposed with all the lights and no cover whatsoever. There were no cameras in the hall, no guards or security. When we came to an intersection, Garret paused, speaking quietly to Wes through the com. After a moment, he nodded and jerked his head down the passage to the right, and we continued.

The hallway ended at another heavy-duty steel door, though this one had a small square window near the top. As we approached, I could see flashing red lights through the glass, and heard the shrill howl of an alarm. Pressing against the frame, Garret and I peeked through the window and saw that the room beyond, though filled with pipes and gauges and strange blocky machines, was empty of people.

"Looks like the assault outside is doing its job," Tristan muttered, his face lit by the eerie, flashing red lights. "Let's hope they keep it up."

I glanced at Garret. "The chamber with the vessels isn't far, right?"

He shook his head. "According to Wes, it's directly below this floor. We'll have to find a way down, either by stairs or elevator."

I looked through the glass again. Beyond the window, a man in a white coat rushed past the door, looking panicked or in a hurry. A couple of armed guards followed him as the alarm continued to blare and the lights flickered on and off, adding to the chaos.

Riley, I thought. *I hope you're okay. Wherever you are, keep it up for just a little while longer.*

"Wes," Garret said into the com. "Find us a way down. Once we're through this room, we can't stop for directions. Just get us there as quickly as you can." He paused another few heartbeats, then nodded. "Understood. Heading there now."

He looked at me, and I took a deep breath. Together, we pulled the door open and slipped into the flashing, blaring chaos of the lab.

We hurried through the halls of the laboratory as swiftly and quietly as we could, passing rooms of shelves, counters and strange equipment, going deeper into the lab. The lights and alarms continued to sound, and after a few minutes, I started to feel a headache throb behind my eyes. We saw very few people on our way through the corridors, and the ones we did see were either running away or huddled in a room, looking confused and scared. We didn't slow down. Garret led us through twisting hallways and narrow corridors without hesitation, following instructions from Wes. Once, we turned a corner and ran into a trio of guards, who shouted and raised their weapons, but were swiftly gunned down by the soldiers before they could respond further. Another time, a pair of humans in white coats barged out of a room, nearly running into us, and rushed off down the hall without looking in our direction. Peter Matthews raised his gun to shoot them in the back, but was stopped by Garret's sharp order to stand down.

After several tense minutes, we turned another corner and

came to the end of the hallway. A pair of elevator doors stood in front of us, open and blinking red inside.

Mist balked when she saw what lay at the end of the hall. "I really don't like the idea of using the elevator," she remarked, gazing at the metal box with suspicion. "It might not even work, now that the alarms have sounded. Can we find a staircase?"

"Not according to Wes," Garret told her. "The nearest staircase is on the other side of the laboratory. But this will take us to the lowest floor and will be the closest point to the target room." Shouts echoed down the hall, making us all jerk up, and Garret's jaw tightened. "There's no time for anything else. Let's move."

We crowded into the elevator, and Garret slammed his thumb into the button for the last floor. The doors hissed shut, cutting off the alarms and flashing lights, and the elevator started to descend.

I forced myself to breathe, tried to calm my pounding heartbeat. Almost there. Almost to our destination, the room that held Talon's vessel army, hundreds, maybe thousands, of Adult dragon clones. I felt the weight of my pack on my shoulders, the bag that held a scary amount of explosives, enough to collapse a room by itself. Garret, Tristan, Peter Matthews, they all carried the same in their own packs, but would it be enough? Could we really destroy that massive army, make it so they could never rise to threaten the world? And, if we did, how many more lives would be taken when the lab went down? I thought of the scientists we'd passed on our way here, the humans who would be trapped in this laboratory when everything detonated. They would all be killed, along with any dragon who happened to be here when the explosives went off.

This is war, Ember. The elevator came to a smooth halt at the bottom of the shaft. *If we don't stop Talon now, the fighting will never be over. You know this has to be done.*

I set my jaw and took a deep breath, gathering my resolve, as the elevator doors hissed and slid back.

Revealing Dante's smiling face on the other side. And a dozen armed human vessels behind him, all pointing guns into the elevator.

RILEY

So far, so good.

I spun around for another pass at the base, dodging a purple hatchling as she soared by, and angled myself into a dive that would take me close to the ground. The sky was filled with dragons, swooping from above and breathing jets of flame onto enemy guards. The ground in front of the laboratory smoldered, scattered fires burning across the scorched earth, sending columns of smoke billowing into the air. When the soldiers of St. George had first swarmed the yard, the guards had been so focused on the attacking humans they hadn't seen the small army of dragons descending from the sky until it was too late and flames had exploded around them. Since then, it had been utter chaos, with bullets and dragons flying through the air, screaming humans and the roar of flames and gunfire, all mixing into a hellish cacophony that pounded my eardrums and vibrated through my teeth.

But it seemed that we were actually winning. I didn't want to get cocky, but it looked like there were more enemy guards lying on the ground, and hardly any dragons or soldiers of St. George. The remaining guards had taken cover behind whatever obstacles they could find, but we were slowly driving them back toward the lab and the enormous steel doors of the entrance.

"They're on the retreat!" Lieutenant Ward's voice crackled through the bud that had been jammed into my ear canal. "All squads, press forward. One last push should finish them—"

With an earsplitting groan, the enormous steel doors of the laboratory creaked open. I paused in midair, beating my wings to keep aloft, as the huge barriers swung slowly back.

Uh-oh. That's a bad sign...

With a sound like the buzzing of a million locust wings, a swarm of metallic gray dragons flew out of the opening and took to the air. Hissing and snarling, they coiled upward in a glittering cloud, before turning and descending on us like a storm.

"Shit!" I surged into motion again, flapping my wings hard, as the army of clones set upon hatchlings and the soldiers of St. George alike. Now our soldiers were forced back, diving behind cover to avoid gouts of flame, as vessels swooped overhead. They swarmed into the air, slamming into hatchlings and dragonells, and several bodies plummeted to the ground.

Roaring, I dove into the fray, ripping a vessel away from a hatchling and sending it careening into one of its fellows. The vessels tumbled from the air, but another slammed into me from the side and sank its talons into my back. We dropped from the sky in a tangle of wings and tails, snarling and raking at each other. At the last second, I managed to bring my back feet up and kick the thing in the stomach, shoving it off me. Quickly, I opened my wings, enough to turn my freefall into a dive and skim the dusty ground as I regained my aerial balance. The vessel couldn't react fast enough, however, and crashed full force into the rocks with a thud and a sickening crack of bones.

Climbing into the air, I gazed around in dismay. There seemed to be a lot more metallic gray bodies than my own dragons, and the mood of the battle had become even more frantic. Vessels chased their bright counterparts with predatory skill and latched on to them to bring them to the ground, seeming not to care about their own safety. Lieutenant Ward's voice barked in my ear, shouting commands to the men on the ground. The soldiers of St. George had regrouped and were doing what they did best, which was kill dragons, but they had their hands full with the sheer amount of vessels swooping out of nowhere.

A booming retort, more like cannon fire than a gunshot, rang out from somewhere far behind me, and one of the vessels simply exploded in midair. One second there was a dragon swooping toward me, the next it had vanished into a cloud of blood, bone and scales.

"Nice shot, Nicholas!" came Martin's voice through the earpiece, and I realized they had finally brought out the prototype we'd stolen from the train. The Dragonkiller, as it was aptly dubbed. "Keep it up," Martin encouraged as the echo of the retort finally died away, "but don't fire willy-nilly! We don't have a lot of ammo for that thing."

Also, please don't hit any of us, I thought, wondering, for a split second, what this would mean for the future of the Order. A gun like that would certainly change things, for both St. George and Talon, provided any of us survived this. It was certainly powerful, but there were swarms of small, fast-moving vessels that were difficult to hit with any single firearm, and a lot more clones than there were bullets. We couldn't count on the Dragonkiller to turn the battle. It was up to us grunts, on the ground and in the air.

A dragonell shrieked as she plummeted past me, two vessels clinging doggedly to her back. With a snarl, I dove after them. Sinking my claws into one clone, I wrenched him off the other dragon as the dragonell twisted and managed to shove the other away. But the vessels recovered, beating their wings to stop their downward plunge, and came back for us. We flew higher with the clones in hot pursuit, and I whirled to face them, roaring a challenge as the two abominations came at me with teeth bared.

Ember, St. George, I hope you're almost done in there. Because I don't know how much longer we can keep going.

EMBER

"Hello, Ember."

Dante's voice was emotionless, his smile chilling, as he gazed at me over the threshold. I felt my companions stiffen in place as a couple dozen gun barrels were aimed right at us. The shock lasted half a second and was immediately followed by anger and bitter resignation. There was nowhere to go, no place to hide or take cover. We were caught, and the mission was over.

"Dante," I whispered as my twin stared at me with hard green eyes. "You were waiting for us."

His smile widened. "Who do you think sent that video?" he said in a low voice, making Garret and the others straighten. "Of course we were waiting for you. Of course we knew about the other tunnel into the lab. All of this, every part of your plan, was not only expected, but partially orchestrated by myself and the organization. You've made it this far because I allowed it."

"And who the fuck are you?" Peter Matthews demanded.

My brother gave him a look of disdain. "You wouldn't understand the significance even if I told you," he said in a cold voice that was nothing like the Dante I'd known. "That said, I'm the one who holds your life in his hands. Keep talking to me like that, and I'll have every one of you executed right here. Take them," he told the vessels, and several closed in. Swiftly, we were disarmed, handcuffed and herded out of the elevator. A few stripped us of our packs, making my heart sink even lower. One vessel handed my bag to Dante, who unzipped the top and peered inside. His brows arched and he chuckled, shaking his head.

"Well, you certainly came prepared. I guess the Order doesn't do anything halfheartedly." Closing the pack, he carefully handed it back to a vessel, who swung it over his shoulders. "But I'm afraid you're not going to be blowing anything up tonight. Tomorrow, the Awakening begins, and there will be no one left to stop it. The Order, Cobalt's rogue underground—in the next hour, all of Talon's enemies will be no more."

"So why the elaborate ruse?" I asked. "Why didn't you just kill us when you had the chance?"

"Because I want you to see our victory." Dante turned cold green eyes on me. "Because I want you to watch as I destroy Cobalt and the rebellion. I want you to fully understand that there will be no one left to challenge Talon, and the only way you will survive is by joining us."

"You don't understand, do you?" My voice came out shaky, remembering the lab, the scientists and the Elder Wyrm gazing down at me with alien green eyes. "I can't go back, Dante. You don't know what the Elder Wyrm wants, what she'll really do to me."

Dante gave a small, sad smile. "Yes," he said quietly. "I do."

Stunned, I could only gape at him for a moment. "I know

that you're her vessel," Dante went on, "and that she'll be using you to live forever. I've known for a while now."

"And...you're okay with that?" I finally stammered. Not truly believing it. Dante was my enemy, the heir of Talon, and was responsible for countless deaths and suffering on our side. But even through all that, I couldn't accept that my brother would willingly stand by and watch the Elder Wyrm kill me to extend her own life.

"We all have sacrifices to make, Ember." Dante's voice was flat, unemotional, and sent an icy lance through my stomach. "I've accepted mine. It's time that you did the same."

"Dante..." I stared at him, too horrified to say anything. Dante gazed back, utterly impassive, and a sick feeling spread through my body. This was the heir of Talon, the Elder Wyrm's second in command and, next to the leader of Talon herself, our greatest enemy within the organization. My brother, the twin I'd known and loved, the sibling who'd looked after us both all the years we were growing up, was truly dead.

"Let's go." Dante turned, and the vessels surrounded us, silent and threatening as they closed in. "The Elder Wyrm is waiting."

RILEY

Things weren't going well for us.

Too many. There were too many of them. Around me, the air was filled with darting, swooping dragons, but many of them were the metallic gray, silver-eyed clones who never gave up and never seemed to get tired. My own dragons were putting up an incredible fight; after the initial shock, the hatchlings and dragonells, instead of meeting their enemies head-on, began using teamwork and group tactics against the single-minded, predatory clones. They even began using St. George to their advantage, luring a vessel into chasing them, only to fly close to a group of soldiers, who would immediately gun the enemy dragon down. The Order had retreated behind crates and vehicles and whatever obstacles they could, taking cover against enemy dragonfire. They were doing a good job of picking clones out of the sky, but they, too, had been pushed to the defensive. It was only a matter of time before raw numbers overwhelmed us.

But we had to keep fighting.

I gave my tired, aching wings a flap and dove toward a pair of vessels pursuing a hatchling, slamming into one from above and sending it crashing to the ground. The other turned on me, whipping around like a damned snake, and lunged. Its jaws closed on a wing joint, and I snarled, ripping and snapping at it as we plummeted from the air. At the last second, the dragon's jaws loosened and I shoved it away, but barely had time to open my own wings to slow the fall before we both crashed into the ground. The impact snapped my jaws together and drove the breath from my lungs, forcing me to lay there for a moment, dazed and gasping.

"Riley!" a voice snapped in my ear, small and artificial sounding. After a confused moment, I realized it was Martin, speaking to my through the earbud. "Get up, dragon!" the lieutenant barked, making me frown. "You have hostiles closing on your six, and none of the men are close enough to help. If you can hear me, respond!"

Gritting my teeth, I pushed myself upright, and found myself surrounded by clones. Four of the bastards had closed in and were tensing to pounce.

My chest ached, my wings shook with exhaustion and I could feel the sting from a dozen or so gashes all over my body, but I planted my talons and snarled a challenge. *Come on then, you bastards. If I die here, at least I'll take all of you with me.*

"My God." Martin's voice was a breath in my ear. He sounded stunned, but I didn't dare take my attention off the circle of dragons closing in on me. "I don't believe it."

The first vessel lunged with a howl, jaws gaping...and was abruptly snatched out of the air as a forty-foot scaly body passed overhead, casting me in its shadow. Eyes wide, I looked up as an enormous Eastern dragon curled effortlessly into the sky, the twitching carcass of a vessel in its massive jaws. Tossing the body aside, Jade coiled around and flew back with a roar, smashing aside two vessels that leaped at her and catching a third in her jaws as she streaked past.

My pulse spiked, and a tiny ray of hope pierced the darkness of my mood. "About time you got here!" I called as the Eastern dragon circled around again to hover several feet overhead. "I swear you disappear just so you can come back at the most dramatic moments, don't you?"

I didn't know it was possible for a dragon to raise an eyebrow, but somehow the Eastern dragon managed it. "And you have the strangest way of showing appreciation," she replied in that cool, slightly lofty voice. "Especially since—what is the Western term for it?—the cavalry has arrived."

With a roar and a blast of wind, two more long, snakelike bodies soared overhead, manes and whiskers trailing behind them, to join the battle in the sky. One of them, a dragon with gleaming red scales and a golden underbelly, was slightly smaller than Jade. But the other, a turquoise-blue male with onyx horns and ridiculously long whiskers, was enormous, probably sixty feet from nose to tail tip. They sailed past us, momentarily blocking out the sun, and continued toward the fighting.

I gaped at the two behemoths, then glanced back at Jade, who gave a faint smile. "I made a promise, did I not?" she said. "I said I would return with help, if I could. Granted, only two of my kin decided to make the journey overseas, but three *shenlung* are certainly better than none. Certainly, we are more than a match for these abominations. Now..." She raised her head, eyes glittering as she stared at the vessels, who had certainly noticed the appearance of three huge Eastern dragons and were whirling around to attack. "Let us see if we cannot turn the tide against Talon. I assume Ember and the others are already inside the laboratory?"

"Yeah," I said, and opened my wings, ready to launch myself into battle once more. "Hopefully by now they've made it to the main chamber and are setting up the explosives. We just gotta keep Talon off their backs till then."

EMBER

I followed Dante and his vessels down the long, dimly lit corridor, despair and resignation making me feel hollow inside. We had failed. We had given this our all, and had come up short. Talon had been one step ahead of us at all times, and now, everyone I knew was going to die. Riley, the hatchlings, the dragonells and the Order; they were still out there fighting Talon, not knowing that we had been caught. They would keep fighting until Talon killed them all, down to the last hatchling, and I couldn't do anything to stop it.

Something touched the back of my arm, soft and hesitant. I glanced over and saw Garret's bleak, tortured expression as he gazed straight ahead.

"I'm sorry," he whispered, not meeting my eyes. "I couldn't get us there. I should've seen this coming, found another way."

"No." Raising both my cuffed hands, I clutched his sleeve, clinging to him like he was a lifeline, keeping me from drowning. "This isn't your fault, Garret. We all knew the risks going in. But…" I stole a glance at Dante, walking several yards in front of us, and lowered my voice to be certain only Garret could hear. "Don't hate me for this," I whispered, forcing my voice not to tremble, "but I need you to promise me something, Garret."

He gave me a puzzled look, and I swallowed hard. "The Elder Wyrm," I went on shakily. "I can't be a vessel for her. If she wins, and takes over my body, she'll live for another thousand years. If...if there's a chance, if you see an opening, I... I want you to—"

Garret's voice was strangled. "You can't ask me to do that."

"Please, Garret." My vision blurred, and I blinked hard, forcing the tears back. "I don't know if I can do it myself. But I can't let her extend her life. If I'm going to die, anyway... I'd rather it be you. There might not be an opening, but if there is...please end it. Before it's too late for everyone. Promise me."

His eyes closed, an anguished look crossing his face. "All right," he whispered. "If there's a chance, I'll do it. But you have to promise something in return. The Elder Wyrm—if you see an opening to take her out, do it. Don't worry about me or the rest of us. Like you said, we're going to die, anyway. But if there's the slightest chance of getting to the Elder Wyrm..."

A lump rose to my throat, and I nodded shakily. "I'll give it my all."

Dante led us down several more hallways, then through a pair of double doors that opened into a large chamber. It was dark, the only light coming from several huge screens that hung on the far wall. There was no sound, but the screens flickered and pulsed, each showing an image of the chaos outside. Dragons zipped through the air, men scurried over the ground and gouts of flame lit up the room. The enormous body of a strange Adult Eastern dragon coiled through the air, being pursued by a half dozen vessels, and my heart leaped. It looked like Jade had come, after all, and had brought reinforcements. Though it wouldn't matter now; we hadn't been able to complete the mission that everyone was dying for. Desperately, I looked for a dark blue dragon among the frenzied swarms, but if Riley was still alive out there, I couldn't see him.

Beneath the flickering screens, an enormous desk sat on a raised dais, two stone-faced vessels standing guard at the bottom of the steps. The tall leather chair behind the desk was turned away from us. I felt the enormous power radiating from that seat, and knew who sat there even though I couldn't see her.

Dante led us across the room and came to a stop at the edge of the steps. For a moment, there was silence. The presence in the chair didn't speak, continuing to watch the atrocities play out on-screen. Then her voice drifted up, quiet and calm, but seeming to vibrate the room with power.

"Why did you bring them here?"

My insides recoiled, cringing back in both revulsion and terror, as the familiar voice of the Elder Wyrm rang through my head.

"I ordered that only my daughter be taken alive, Dante," the Elder Wyrm went on, still not turning to look at us. "The rogue Basilisk and the soldiers of St. George are of no interest to me. Why did you not kill them?"

"Forgive me, ma'am," Dante said in a solemn yet unruffled voice, his gaze on the back of the chair. "I thought you might want to look upon the faces of your enemies and destroy them yourself. To let them know the true power of Talon, and why no one can stand against us."

"Do not presume to know what I would want, Dante." Without a squeak, the chair swiveled, revealing the woman behind the desk, and the piercing intensity of the Elder Wyrm's gaze hit us full-on. Tristan whispered a curse, and Mist's breath escaped her as she sank to her knees, as the massive presence of the Elder Wyrm filled the chamber from floor to ceiling. Only the vessels seemed unaffected, their guns steady and unmoving, their expressions blank even in the presence of the oldest dragon in the world. Dante bowed, his gaze on the tile, as the leader of Talon rose and walked around the desk, observing us like she would a dirty spot on the floor.

"Daughter." Her gaze found mine, ancient and terrifying, and I had to force myself to keep breathing. "Here you are again, defying me. Only now, you commit the greatest atrocity of all and stand with the Order of St. George." She shook her head almost sadly. "Disappointing. But I will deal with you momentarily."

Her cool gaze shifted to the soldiers, to Garret, Tristan and Peter Matthews, and hardened with darkest hate. "St. George. It has been many, many decades since I have laid eyes on any of you. And now, you stand before me, in the company of dragons. Dragons you have allied with, even though the revered Code of St. George strictly forbids associating with demons. How quickly you humans seem to break your sacred oaths when you are in danger of extinction."

"You bitch," Peter Matthews growled, though his voice came out shaky. "We were right to hunt you. If we had managed to exterminate all you lizards back then, we wouldn't be here now."

The Elder Wyrm turned her cold gaze on the soldier. "As ever, you humans remain blatantly shortsighted and ignorant," she remarked. "It was *St. George* that caused me to form Talon

all those years ago. It was the human's persecution of dragons that caused us to band together for survival. Because you
could not see beyond your own hate and fear. Because you
were convinced dragons were monsters, and thus needed to
be exterminated." She pointed a manicured nail at the defiant solder. "*You* are responsible for Talon, you and the rest of
your kind who would hate us because we are not human. And
you are accountable for what will happen to the rest of humanity. The death of every human, every soul who opposes
Talon—be it man, woman or child—is on the head of the
Order of St. George."

Peter Matthews didn't answer, but from the corner of my
eye, I saw Tristan stagger, as if the Elder Wyrm's words hit him
hard. "You can't do that," he protested. "You can't declare war
on the entire human race."

"Why not? St. George certainly had no compulsions against
declaring war on us. What made you think we would not retaliate?" She smiled again, her eyes glittering green in the
shadows. "You are weak, St. George," she stated. "The entire
human race is weak, violent, hypocritical and prone to self-
destruction. Through the long ages I have been alive, I have
seen it time and time again—the war and devastation humans bring, even to their own. Those who are different, who
see life in ways other than yours, you declare 'evil,' and use
that as an excuse to persecute and destroy. It has been this
way since the beginning. And it will not change without intervention. Well…"

The Elder Wyrm turned and gazed at the screens again.
"Intervention has come," she stated. "We will bring a new age
to humanity, one where they will live in peace with dragons,
because we will *force* them to. That is the only action humans

understand, and if we must slaughter half the human race to make them see reason, so be it. But first, we must destroy the traitors within our own race to proceed. Dante."

At the base of the steps, Dante looked up, his face expressionless. "Ma'am."

"Have you seen enough of the battle? Do we know where the sniper fire is coming from?"

Tristan jerked as Dante nodded once. "Yes. I've determined the trajectory—it's coming from the eastern side of the mountain, about half a mile away."

"Then launch the second phase." Her cold gaze found mine. "As long as they are here, I want them to see their rebellion die. I want my daughter to understand why she should never have opposed us."

I locked eyes with my brother, pleading. He met my stare, his expression as remote as ever, then reached into his suit jacket and pulled out a phone. "Lilith," he said, holding my gaze as he spoke into the device, "the sniper fire is coming from the east. Remove it, kill the Eastern dragons and destroy the rest of the attackers. Leave no one alive."

RILEY

Something was about to happen, I could feel it.

The fight was going...okay. With the arrival of Jade and the two Eastern dragons, it had definitely shifted to not completely hopeless. But there were a lot of vessels, and even their smaller forms could overwhelm a larger dragon if they ganged up on it. I didn't know how many dragons and soldiers were down, but it seemed like half our forces had been depleted, though the number of clones was finally dwindling, as well. I didn't want to think about the hatchlings I'd lost until the battle was over, but I hoped at least some in my underground would survive this.

A shout below me drew my attention to the ground. Two vessels had a soldier of St. George by the legs and were dragging him across the stones on his stomach, with the soldier desperately trying to bring his gun around to shoot. I dove toward them and dropped onto a vessel's back with all my weight behind me, crushing it to the earth. At the same time, the soldier finally managed to flip over, raise his M4 and shoot the second clone in the head and neck.

Panting, the soldier scrambled to his feet, nodding at me. "Thanks, lizard," he barked out, and limped for cover once more, dodging a gout of flame from a vessel that swooped by. I had just tensed to leap into the air again when a shudder went through me, starting from the ground and shivering all the way up my spine. My stomach dropped, and for a split second, everything froze, the sounds of battle muted for a single heartbeat.

With a chilling, earsplitting groan that seemed to echo over the battlefield, the front doors of the laboratory creaked open again. Whispering a curse, I darted behind a vehicle and peered beneath the undercarriage, watching the iron barriers push outward. Of course Talon would have another surprise planned for us. What kind of monstrosities would pour forth this time?

The ground under my feet trembled, and three massive shapes prowled out of the shadows to step into the light. My heart nearly stopped. I huddled close to the ground, curling my tail around myself, as I fought back the despair and sudden terror.

Three Adult vessels. The same metallic gray of their smaller counterparts, but fifty times bigger. Their chests and forepaws were huge, their necks thick with muscle, and jagged, bony spines bristled from their shoulders and down their backs. They stalked forward, blank silver eyes blinking in the light, gazing emptily at the chaos surrounding them.

One of the Eastern dragons, the smaller red female, soared overhead, and the first Adult vessel reacted instantly. Shockingly fast, it leaped into the air, powerful wings unfurling, to slam into the other dragon. Clamping thick jaws around the slender body, it dragged the Eastern dragon out of the air and used its larger bulk to pin it to the ground. The Eastern dragon shrieked, thrashing and writhing in its grip, coiling her long body around the monster like a python, but the vessel did not relent.

With twin howls, the remaining Adult vessels launched themselves into the fight, unfurling huge leathery wings and taking to the air. Hatchlings and dragonells fled as the two behemoths began their pursuit, snapping and clawing at any dragon that came within reach. Thankfully, the hatchlings were small and quick, and the vessels' enormous bulk weighed them down. But there was no way any of my dragons were going to bring down those monsters.

With a roar and a streak of green, Jade flew toward one of the vessels like an arrow, smashing into the huge body with a crunch that sounded like a pair of semis colliding. The Adult vessel screamed and tumbled down in a flurry of wings and tails, taking the Eastern dragon with it. The rumble as they struck the earth vibrated the ground and made my teeth chatter.

Okay, St. George, I thought, and leaped into the air once more, praying that my hatchlings would be smart enough to get the hell out of the way. If I couldn't take those monsters down, at least I would be a distraction for the rest of them. *If you ever needed a reason to use that damned rifle, here it is. You won't ever hear me say this again, but shoot those things already!*

But seconds ticked by, measured by the screams of dying dragons and the roars of those still living, and the shots never came.

EMBER

I watched the horror unfold on-screen, watched one Adult vessel pull a red Eastern dragon out of the air and tear it apart with brutal efficiency, while the other two set upon Riley's dwindling forces. We had failed. They were all going to die, but worse than that, their sacrifice would be in vain, because we were unable to uphold our end of the bargain.

"Your friends are lost," the Elder Wyrm stated, watching me from the top of the steps. "The alliance between dragons and St. George is finished. Everything you have done up until this point has been for nothing. We will rise, and humans will fall before us, as it should have been from the beginning."

"No," I whispered. "Please stop this. There's been so much death and suffering already. We can end the war. It doesn't have to be this way."

"You have lost," the Elder Wyrm repeated, her voice a terrible drone in my head. Dante walked up the steps to stand behind her and did not look at me. "And now, I will take back what is mine, what I had created specifically for me. Vessel 176, bring me my daughter."

One of the vessels stepped forward and grabbed my arm. Instantly, Garret turned, bringing both cuffed hands up, and smashed them into its nose, sending it reeling back. In that split second of shock, I made my decision.

I leaped through the ring of vessels, Shifting forms in mid-air. The cuffs burst open as I landed at the base of the steps in dragon form. We were all going to die, Talon had won this round, but at least I could take the Elder Wyrm down with me. Gathering myself, I tensed my muscles and sprang for the woman at the top of the steps, aiming for her slender white neck. *Garret, Riley, I'm sorry. But maybe this will be enough to change things. See you on the other side.*

"I think not," the Elder Wyrm said quietly.

She took one step back as I came in, sweeping her arm up, blindingly fast. I barely had a chance to register that she'd moved before she backhanded me in the temple, right below my horns, and my head felt like it imploded. My vision fractured into shards of pain, and I was hurled away, hitting the floor with a jolt and rolling to a painful stop.

My head throbbed, feeling like it would split open at the slightest movement, and spots of darkness floated before my eyes. Dazed, I looked up to see the Elder Wyrm walking toward me, a faint smile on her lips. Behind her, the vessels had forced everyone to their knees, the muzzles of their rifles shoved into the base of their skulls.

"Foolish hatchling." The Elder Wyrm loomed over me, ancient and unamused. Her eyes glowed green, and her presence pushed down on me like a boulder, crushing the air from my lungs. I couldn't move as the oldest dragon in the world turned the full power of her gaze on me. "Did you think I would be weak as a human? That this pitiful body would be easy to destroy?" She raised an elegant, manicured hand, the nails as red as blood. "I have but a fraction of my true strength in this form, but that is still enough to crush your skull with my fingers. There is no one strong enough to challenge me face-to-face.

"Now." The Elder Wyrm took a step back, her eyes hard. "It is time to end this little game, once and for all. But don't worry, daughter. Soon, all your memories of this day will be erased, along with everything else. In some ways, I would think it a blessing. Vessels," she called as Garret's bright, soulful gaze met mine across the floor. "Kill the—"

A shot rang out, echoing off the rafters. My heart stopped, and I stared frantically at the group surrounded by vessels, expecting one of them to topple forward.

The Elder Wyrm made a tiny choking sound above me.

Stunned, uncomprehending, I looked up. A bright red stain was oozing through the front of her white blouse and spreading over her chest. Gingerly, she touched the crimson mark, then stared at the blood on her fingers, her expression one of shock.

Slowly, she turned…to reveal Dante standing behind her, the muzzle of a smoking pistol aimed at her chest.

"Dante," the Elder Wyrm breathed as I gaped at my sibling, unable to move. "You…?"

"I'm sorry." Dante's voice was conflicted, though his expression was resolved, his mouth set in a grim line. His eyes glittered in the shadows as he stared down the Elder Wyrm. "I would have done anything for Talon," he said as the Elder Wyrm took a staggering step forward. "I would have sacrificed everything to see our race thrive. I've played the villain, slaughtered innocents, supervised the creation of atrocities and sent those abominations into battle, all for the good of our kind." For just a moment, his gaze flicked to me, and a shadow of anguish crossed his face. "But there's one line I will not cross, and one piece of my life I will not sacrifice. I'm sorry it's come to this, that it's taken me this long to see what you really wanted."

"Very clever, Dante." The Elder Wyrm, amazingly still on her feet, put a hand to her chest. "I suppose I cannot be too surprised. You are...of my blood, after all. But you're wrong if you think...I would hand Talon over to you."

Dante's gaze hardened. "I'm afraid you'll have no choice," he said, and raised his head. "Vessels," he called, without taking his eyes from the Elder Wyrm. "To me. Release the prisoners and stand down—"

The Elder Wyrm moved. One moment she was standing in front of me, her blood dripping in slow puddles to the floor. The next, she had lunged forward impossibly fast, toward the boy with the gun a few yards away. At the last instant, Dante saw the danger and fired several shots at the approaching Wyrm. A fine spray of blood erupted from the Elder Wyrm's back, misting into the air, as she grabbed Dante's shoulder, wrenched him close and drove her clawed hand into his chest, sinking it past her wrist.

Time stilled around me. I watched, frozen in place, my brain refusing to accept what had just happened. Dante's mouth gaped silently and a thin stream of red ran down his chin. The Elder Wyrm yanked her arm free, her hand covered in red halfway up her forearm, and Dante staggered, still looking stunned. He swayed on his feet, the pistol clattering sharply to the floor, and the world unfroze.

I leaped upright with a screaming roar and lunged at the Elder Wyrm, whose hateful green eyes snapped in my direction. Grabbing Dante by the collar, she yanked him around and shoved him at me. Dante staggered and fell forward, and

I instinctively Shifted to human form, catching him before he could hit the floor.

Gently lowering him to his back, I looked up to see the Elder Wyrm vanish through a door in the far wall, leaving a spattered red trail behind her. As she passed through the frame, a metal barrier dropped down, cutting off pursuit.

Numb, I looked down at my brother. He lay there gasping, the front of his suit jacket a mess of blood. One hand was pressed to his middle, and blood pooled between his fingers, staining his shirt and spreading rapidly from his chest.

"Dante," I whispered as my eyes started to burn. "You idiot. You always have to try to save me." I couldn't look at the gaping wound in his chest, fixing my gaze on his face, on his eyes as they sought mine. "Why?" I choked out. "Why now? What made you change your mind?"

"Didn't...you hear me?" Dante looked up with a wry smile, though his face was tight with pain. "I said...there were some things I wouldn't sacrifice, even to the Elder Wyrm. That some things are sacred. You...are one of them. The only sacrifice I couldn't make." His eyes closed, and my heart gave a violent lurch, but he just sighed and continued in a voice of dark regret. "I never changed my mind," he whispered. "I just... I wanted to be free. I thought...if I reached the top, I would have made it, that power equaled freedom. But I was wrong. The Elder Wyrm...had no intention of ever stepping down." He opened his eyes, and they were hard, glassy with pain, anger and revulsion. "Do you know how much worse it would've been, had she been ruling Talon from *your* body? Reminding me...that I *had* a sister, once, and I had failed her? I wouldn't be able to live with myself."

A shudder went through him. Blood bubbled from his lips

as he coughed, and I gripped his hand. "Dante, don't try to talk. We'll get you out of here—"

"There's not...much time left." Dante's words were forced, as if he was rushing to get them out. One bloodstained hand reached into his jacket, withdrawing a plastic key card. "Take this," he said, dropping it into my palm. "That will get you through every...door in the laboratory. The hall on the left... will take you to the stasis chamber. Destroy it, and the clones, before she can declare war on humanity." Something exploded on the screen behind me, lighting the room for a split second, and Dante winced. "Go, Ember. Before it's too late."

"I'm not leaving you here!"

"It's all right." His fingers weakly squeezed my palm as he settled back. His green eyes stared up at the ceiling, tired and, strangely, at peace. "I'm finally free," he whispered, almost too soft to hear. "You were right, you know. About Talon, and the Elder Wyrm, and everything. But I'm glad... I got to see you again. That I could protect you one last time." He chuckled, barely a breath in the stillness of the room. "You were always like that," he murmured. "Always the impatient sister that needed saving. I don't know how...you made it this far...without me..."

"Dante."

No answer. My twin stared up at the ceiling, his expression vacant and unmoving. I shook my head, unwilling to believe, and squeezed his hand.

"Dante." I reached out and shook him, watching his head flop limply, eyes staring straight ahead. "Dammit, say something! Don't you dare fucking die, not now, not with everything we went through to get here. Answer me! *Dante!*"

"Ember!"

Garret knelt beside me, stilling my arm, his gaze solemn as he pulled me back. "He's gone."

No. I slumped, a thousand emotions raging inside, making me want to scream, to Shift and rip something to pieces. Tears blurred my vision and crawled down my face, and I could barely speak through the sudden fury. "Dammit, Dante," I choked out, gazing down at the still form of my brother, lying motionless on the tile. *Gone.* He was really gone. I'd never see him again. "Why didn't you believe us earlier?" I whispered. "Why didn't you just listen? We could have saved you."

"Ember." Garret's voice was soft, hesitant. I glanced at him with tear-streaked eyes, and he gently put a hand over mine. "I'm sorry," he said, his eyes bright with sympathy. "But we have to move. The Elder Wyrm could be rallying her forces against us right now. We still need to find the stasis chamber, plant the explosives and get out of here."

Dammit. Screw the mission. For a moment, a part of me rebelled, hating everything that had brought us here. I didn't want to think about the clones, the attack or the mission. I wanted to find a dark, empty room, curl up in a ball and sob out my anger and grief, and maybe blast a few things with fire. I wanted to grieve the brother I had lost, the twin who had been with me most my life, whom I had always believed we could save in the end.

But the Elder Wyrm was still out there. Gravely wounded, perhaps even dying, but still an unknown. Still a threat. And we had a whole lot of people and dragons who were counting on us. Riley, Martin and everyone outside wouldn't retreat or back down. The longer I sat here, the greater the casualties, and even more would die because of me.

With a shaky breath, I accepted Garret's hand, letting him

pull me upright. At the bottom of the steps, Tristan, Mist and Peter Matthews were gathering our packs and confiscated fire-arms, warily eyeing the vessels, who were now staring straight ahead without expression, ignoring the movements around them. Their last command, I remembered, was "Release the prisoners and stand down," which they had done. Without someone to direct them, they were on standby, awaiting further orders. Orders that would never come—unless the Elder Wyrm or another Talon dragon returned.

I looked at Dante one last time, memorizing his face, remembering the last words he'd said to me. Not as a rival or an enemy or the heir of Talon, but as a brother. I didn't want to leave him here, in this dark, cold room that would eventually explode in a blaze of fire and destruction if we managed to complete the mission. But there was no way we could take him with us, and time was dangerously short. The sudden thought that this was really the last time I would see him, ever, hit me hard, and fresh tears threatened even as I took a step back.

Garret took my hand, squeezing gently, and I turned away before I really broke down. We left the lair of the Elder Wyrm—me, Garret, Tristan, Mist and Peter Matthews—hoping to make it to our destination before the alarms were sounded. I looked back only once, glimpsing my brother's limp body lying on the stage, and bit my lip to keep back the sob.

Goodbye, Dante. If there is an afterlife for dragons, I'll meet you on the other side. Maybe sooner than we both thought.

RILEY

I hit the ground hard, rolled and managed to get to my feet, just in time to meet the vessel who had slammed me out of the air. Dodging two raking claws to the face, I ducked and clamped my jaws around its throat, then held it down until it stopped moving.

Panting, I looked up. Dead dragons surrounded me, littered across the rocky ground, both vessel and hatchling alike. Scattered among them were the bodies of soldiers and guards, sprawled limply in the dust, either shot or torn open or blasted with fire. Looming over them all were two giant, motionless forms: the long, limp body of the red Eastern dragon, and one of the Adult vessels, as well, courtesy of a furious Jade tearing it apart.

We couldn't go on like this. Almost all of my dragons were gone, and only a handful of soldiers remained, firing on the swooping vessels. Jade and the other Eastern dragon were both fighting for their lives with the Adult clones, and I didn't know how badly the battle was going for them.

And then, a shot rang over the battlefield, making my ears throb, and the male Eastern dragon screamed. Stunned, I looked up to see the huge serpent falling slowly from the sky like a deflated balloon, seemingly unable to stay aloft. It wobbled in the air, trying to stay afloat, before an Adult vessel slammed into it and bore them both to the ground with an earthshaking crash.

My heart plummeted. That had been a shot from the Dragonkiller, which had been unnaturally silent until now. There was no way the sniper had hit the Eastern Adult by accident, not a dragon the size of a small airplane. That shot had been deliberate, and now the biggest dragon on the battlefield was fatally wounded.

"Dragon!" Martin's voice crackled in my ear. "Dragon, come in. Cobalt, are you there?"

"Yeah," I snarled. "I'm here. What the hell just happened, Lieutenant? I just watched your sniper shoot one of our dragons out of the air!"

"I know." Martin sounded frustrated, as well. "Something must be wrong. I've been trying to contact Nicholas since those damned Adults showed up, but there's been no response. We need to get to that ledge to see what the hell is going on. I'm heading there now—join me if you're able."

"What? Wait a second—" But the line cut off, and I snarled a curse.

Dammit. Gazing around at the frantic movements of vessels and hatchlings, I ground my teeth. I didn't want to leave my underground to fight alone. The ledge in question was on the other side of the bowl, through a whole lot of dragons and gunfire.

An agonized wail shivered through me, coming from the

male Eastern dragon as the Adult vessel tore into him relentlessly, and my stomach turned. If we took another hit like that, if *Jade* was shot down, then it really would be over.

"Cobalt!"

There was a streak of darkness, and Nettle landed beside me in a cloud of dust. The black dragon was panting hard, and red streaked the scales along her flank and shoulders, but a savage grin stretched her narrow muzzle as she gazed up at me.

"I think we're putting a dent in the clones," she said, making me blink in astonishment. "Kain is rallying who's left, and we're about to launch a counterattack with the rest of the soldiers. How are you holding up, leader?"

I shook myself out of my split-second daze. When the hell had my dragons turned into full-blown soldiers? "I have to check out something with Martin," I replied. "But I'll be back as soon as I can. You got this?"

She nodded and stepped briskly away, unfolding her wings. "Go. We'll keep them off your back."

Bounding forward, I launched myself skyward and headed for the cliff face.

Even knowing vaguely where it was, the exact location was difficult to find. They had set up the massive rifle behind camouflage, covering the metal to prevent reflection. Still, once you got close, it was fairly obvious: an enormously long barrel sitting atop a ledge overlooking the laboratory. From this vantage point, I could see the whole battle, the flashes of dragons as they darted through the air and the bursts of gunfire coming from the ground. But the gun sat empty, abandoned. There was no body, living or dead. No blood or churned earth indicating a struggle. No footprints or scorch marks or scrap of clothing. Nothing that pointed to what had happened here.

Footsteps shuffled behind me as Martin climbed the rise and strode across the rocks to stand beside me. I frowned at him. "That was fast."

"I was close. Ward and I were near the gate, covering the wounded soldiers' retreat." He, too, frowned in confusion, gazing around for the missing sniper before looking at me. "Did you see anyone else?"

I shook my head, and the scowl deepened. "Impossible." Walking to the edge of the cliff, he peered out at the battle, then spun back. "Something was here," he insisted. "Shooting at our forces. They must've run when they saw you coming, but—"

I felt the ripple of energy go through the air, and my adrenaline spiked in warning, but it was too late. Behind Martin, a head rose on a long, snaking neck, as a familiar green dragon grinned down at the unsuspecting human, eyes glowing demonically as she towered over him.

"Martin, behind you!" I shouted, just as Lilith's jaws closed over the human's upper body. Martin's legs jerked as the Viper lifted him into the air and shook him like a dog with a toy.

I roared and tensed to spring at her, but from within the dragon's jaws, three shots rang out, making the Viper recoil with a shriek. Somehow, the lieutenant had the presence of mind to fire his weapon even while halfway down a dragon's throat. Eyes blazing, Lilith turned her head and hurled the body over the cliff. The lieutenant arced lazily into the air, seemed to hover for a split second, then plummeted out of sight, falling several hundred feet to the rocks below.

I hurled myself forward, Shifting forms as I did, and collapsed beside the Dragonkiller, swinging the huge barrel toward the Viper. Lilith roared as she turned on me, blood streaming from her nose and mouth, one eye bulging out of the socket as she lunged, desperation and rage making her fast, but not fast enough.

"Eat this, bitch," I growled, and pulled the trigger.

The boom from the huge rifle made my eardrums explode, and the recoil knocked me back a couple feet, nearly dislocating my shoulder. Pain flared, my head, shoulders and chest feeling like they'd been kicked by a Clydesdale. But the two-foot, armor-piercing, solid length of metal hit the Viper point-blank in the chest and went out the other side, leaving a massive hole behind. For a moment, Lilith gaped at the wound in her armor, clearly stunned. Her jaws moved, probably cursing me, though I couldn't hear anything through the painful, high-pitched ringing in my head.

Then her wings shuddered and went limp, her eyes glazed over and her body slumped, sliding a bit on the rocks before losing balance entirely. With a last defiant cry, the leader of the Vipers tumbled backward off the cliff face and disappeared. I felt, rather than heard, the moment when she hit the ground, a shudder that rippled through the air and vibrated the earth.

As I lay on my back beside a gun called the Dragonkiller, waiting for the throbbing in my ears to go away, I allowed myself a small smile. In the split second before I'd pulled the trigger, when Lilith's jaws had been a fraction too slow to end my life, someone's face had flashed through my mind. Oddly enough, it wasn't the face I would have expected.

"Dammit," I sighed, my voice sounding muffled in my own ears. "I'm turning into a walking cliché. Mist, you'd better come back alive so you can taunt me about this later."

GARRET

I peeked around a corner and immediately ducked back as a hail of bullets shot toward me, peppering the corridor walls and sparking off the floor.

"Looks like security's been alerted," Tristan muttered, pressed into the wall next to me. Matthews, Ember and Mist huddled behind us as gunfire continued to ring through the corridor. "How many?"

"Two," I answered, and raised my weapon. "Cover me." I ducked out, firing down the hallway while Tristan and Matthews popped around the corner and did the same. The pair of guards in the corridor jerked and fell, guns clattering to the floor, and I turned to the others. "Clear, let's go!"

As we reached another intersection, I turned the corner, and a pair of double doors loomed ahead, ominous and important looking. A squad of six human clones waited in front of them, three kneeling and three standing over their shoulders. As soon as they saw us, the three standing opened fire, while the ones kneeling Shifted forms—becoming sleek gray dragons—and charged.

I ducked behind a thick metal pipe across the hall as Tristan and Matthews jerked back around the corner. "Ember, Mist!" I barked. "Take out the vessels. The rest of us will cover you."

The two didn't hesitate. As the vessels drew close, a bright red dragon and a silver-white dragon bounded into the hall with a roar and pounced on the clones. As the snarls and shrieks of angry dragons filled the air, the rest of us ducked out of cover and fired into the remaining guards. I felt a bullet graze my arm, taking a chunk of skin with it, but the three human vessels fell back and slumped lifelessly against the doorframe.

I looked to where the fight between dragons still raged in the middle of the hall and raised my weapon to help, but it wasn't necessary. Mist had one vessel pinned and was finishing it off with her jaws around its throat, and a few yards away Ember stood over two lifeless, bleeding dragon bodies, panting and glaring down at them. Her wings shook, either with fury or adrenaline, and her front talons were covered in blood. Tristan whistled softly.

Carefully, I approached the red dragon. "Ember," I said, making sure she heard me before touching her shoulder. "Are you hurt?"

Her head came up, green eyes wide and a little glassy, and my worry for her spiked. Losing Dante was hitting her hard, and she was taking out her rage and grief on whatever she could. I wished I could comfort her, but there was no time, and we both knew it.

"No," she whispered, and Shifted to human form. Blood stained her fingers and was spattered across her face in ribbons, but she didn't seem to notice. "I'm fine. Let's keep moving."

We turned to the heavy double doors. They were locked, but Ember slid the card she'd gotten from Dante into the slot below a touch screen, and the red window above it blinked from red to green. The doors groaned as they swung back, and a billow of warm, damp air hit us in the face as we stepped inside to gaze around in horrified awe.

"Son of a bitch," Matthews commented, craning his neck up toward the ceiling.

The stasis chamber from the email video stretched away before us, massive and towering. The vats containing the Adult clones marched in neat rows into the dark, and the dragons inside seemed even larger up close and personal. I felt a shiver go through me as I stared at the sleeping army. So many. If they woke up, it would be hell on earth.

A shot rang out behind us, and a bullet ricocheted off the doorframe about an inch from where Tristan stood. The two of us turned and fired, and a pair of guards crumpled to the floor. But footsteps echoed through the hall, a moment before an entire squad of vessels rounded the corner and raised their guns in our direction.

"Close the doors!" I shouted, firing as I leaped back. The roar of assault rifles filled the hall, and we ducked behind the metal barriers, straining to push them shut. They closed with a moan and a loud clang, and the window above the touch screen on the inside flashed red, locking automatically. Raising my gun, I fired several rounds into the screen, until the touch pad was a smoking, sparking mess of wire and broken glass.

"That won't stop them for long." I shrugged off my pack, removed the case and yanked it open, revealing the deadly packages inside. Four each and, according to Mist, created with a special combination of explosives and dragonfire that would devastate everything around them. "Split up," I told the group. "Try to cover as much of the room as you can. Pay special attention to structural features that could collapse the ceiling, but don't spend too much time on any one thing. Regroup near that big central column when you're done. We'll have to do this fast."

They nodded and melted into the room, vanishing between endless rows of vats. I followed, pausing only to attach a bomb to the first glass cylinder I passed. The device stuck easily to the glass, and when I pressed the button on the side, a row of numbers flashed to life on the screen.

Fifteen minutes, counting down.

A hiss behind me turned my attention to the entrance, where a thin line of blowtorch smoke was drifting up from the locked doors. Snatching the case from the cement, I slipped farther into the chamber.

"Stop!"

The shout came as I was planting the last explosive on a vat in the center of the floor. I whirled, raising my weapon, as a man stumbled out from behind a pillar and hurried forward, eyes wild. He wore a white lab coat and glasses, had thinning brown hair and looked like all the other scientists I'd seen in this room tonight. But instead of running from me, he rushed the vat where I'd just set the last charge, throwing out his hands as if to protect it.

"What are you doing?" he demanded, gazing up at the sleeping vessel, as if making sure it was all right. "You can't be in here! Get out!" Suddenly catching sight of the bomb, counting down the seconds in ominous red, his face went pale. "Oh, God. What have you done?"

"You need to leave," I told him. "This whole place is rigged to explode. If you tamper with the devices they'll just go off sooner. There's nothing you can do now."

"Dr. Olsen!" Pounding footsteps rang out behind us, and a younger man came to a gasping halt at the bottom of the vat, his white coat fluttering wildly. "Sir, we have to go!" he cried. "The vessels are coming, and those people have set bombs through the whole chamber. We have to leave while we still can."

"No," rasped the other scientist as my heart skipped a beat with the realization. "I won't leave. You can go, but this is my life's work! I won't abandon them."

Olsen. Something clicked in my head, a memory from not very long ago. Myself, and Martin in his office, staring at a name on a yellowed birth certificate.

Lucas knew your mother, Garret. That's why he took you that day. Before he became a soldier, before she married a scientist and started working for the organization, they knew each other.

"John Olsen," I said quietly as the younger scientist hesitated a moment longer, then fled, vanishing between rows of vats. I barely noticed him go. The older man looked up, and his gaze narrowed briefly in my direction.

"Do I know you, St. George?" he snapped, and when I didn't answer, he dropped his attention to the panel again. "Look, whoever you are, you've done enough. If you're going to kill me, then kill me. If not, I suggest you leave, before the vessels get here and bullets really start flying."

I took a steadying breath. "You might know me," I told the scientist in a voice that shook only slightly. "My name is Garret Xavier Sebastian. But I had another name once, a long time ago. Garret David Olsen."

The scientist's fingers froze over the panel. Slowly, he straightened and turned, as if seeing me for the very first time. Finally, one corner of his mouth twitched in a wry, ironic smile.

"Damn." He sighed, shaking his head. "They told me you were dead. That you and Sarah had died in the raid. If I had known..." He trailed off.

"What?" I challenged. "Would you have done anything? Would you have searched for me? Tried to get me back?" I nodded to the huge tanks surrounding us, the Adult clones that hovered beyond the glass. "Or would you have kept working for them? Knowing that you were helping the Elder Wyrm take over the world? You must've known what she was doing. You can't claim ignorance when you helped create this."

"*Helped* create?" Dr. Olsen gazed up at the vessels, smiling. "You don't understand," he murmured. "These are my greatest achievements. The cumulation of my life's work. Science and magic, blended together to create something entirely new. I would sell my soul, again, for the opportunities Talon afforded me." His gaze swept to me again, hardening. "I will not see them destroyed by the boy I'd given up for dead!"

"Garret!" Ember rushed up, followed by the other three. "The vessels have blocked that side of the chamber and are heading in this direction." She panted. "We can't go back the way we came."

I turned to the scientist. "Dr. Olsen," I began, unable to call him...that other word. "You need to come with us. This place is going to blow in a few minutes. There's no time—"

"No." He shook his head, and his eyes were a little glassy now. "You don't understand," he went on, turning back to the panel. "This is my life's work. I can't leave them. I might be able to save a few."

"You can't save them," I argued, suddenly furious. "If you stay here, you're going to die, along with everything else in this room."

"Garret," Tristan said in warning, just as a shot rang out. Lightning fast, Mist turned and fired her pistol at the vessel who appeared between the vats, and it collapsed to the cement. But more were coming; I could see their shadows moving across the floor, blurry shapes of both human and dragon sliding behind the vats.

Torn, I gave the scientist one last, desperate look. He ignored us all, fiddling with the panel, muttering to himself. A light at the top suddenly flashed on, blinking red in warning, and an automated voice announced: *Warning, system override in process. Awakening procedure starting in five...four...three...*

"Dammit, we gotta move, Sebastian," Matthews snarled at me. "Now!"

With an inner curse, I turned and fled with the others, pushing farther toward the back of the chamber. I didn't know where we were going exactly, or how we would escape.

"Garret!"

I turned back to see Dr. Olsen watching me, illuminated red in the flashing light of the tank.

"Take the emergency elevator in the back left corner," he called, his voice barely audible over the warning buzz coming from the vat. "It will take you up to the first floor, provided you have a key card to operate it." He gave a half smile and mouthed something that I couldn't hear, but in the dim light of the chamber, I could almost imagine it was, *Good luck, son.*

I spun and ran for the corner as shots followed me into the dark.

"Dammit," Tristan muttered as I caught up to the group, taking cover behind a pair of large columns. "They keep pushing us back. I don't see any way to go around them." He glanced at the pillar, where one of the explosives stared back, blinking ominously. "Less than eight minutes to go." He sighed. "At least it'll be quick."

"Fuck that," Peter Matthews sneered, and raised his weapon. "I'm not going to sit on my ass and wait for it to explode. If I'm dying here, I'm sure as hell taking as many lizards with me as I can."

"No one is dying," I said firmly, meeting Ember's gaze from where she huddled behind the second pillar. "There's an emergency elevator that will take us to the surface if we can reach it. Ember, do you still have the key Dante gave you?"

She nodded, took the card from the cord around her neck and tossed it to me. "In case I have to Shift again," she said, her voice strangely calm.

"Here they come!" Mist snapped as a half dozen gray dragons bounded toward us through the aisles. Gunfire followed them, sparking off pillars and ringing through the air. The tank above us cracked, leaking greenish fluid that steamed as it trickled down the glass.

"This way!" I called, and we ran for the back of the room, keeping our heads down, hearing the shrieks of the vessels as they gave chase. Ember and Mist Shifted while running, giving them greater speed and a little protection from flying bullets, while the rest of us wove around columns and tanks, trying to keep obstacles between us and the advancing guards.

There was a sound above me, the faint flap of wings overhead, making my blood chill. I glanced back to see a pair of vessels swooping toward us through the aisle, weaving around vats.

"Incoming!" I called, and spun around to fire at one vessel lunging in from the air. It shrieked as it flew into a hail of bullets, and I ducked out of the way as it crashed, fracturing one of the tanks as it did. Greenish fluid hissed to the floor and over the body of the vessel, filling the air with steam and a foul, almost fishy smell.

A yell rang out through the aisle, jerking my attention around. Peter Matthews lay on his back with a dragon atop him, biting and clawing. As I started toward them, the vessel's head snaked toward Matthews's face, and the soldier gave a ragged scream as narrow jaws closed around his neck.

With a flash of scales, both Ember and Mist slammed into the clone, knocking it away. It tumbled to the floor, bounced upright with a snarl and then jerked wildly as Tristan and I put several rounds into its body.

"Matthews," I called as the vessel slumped lifelessly to the ground. "You all right?"

A raspy gurgle was my response, making my blood run cold. The soldier tried to sit up but slumped back as we hurried over. One look at his face told me everything. Blood soaked his collar and streamed from the side of his neck where the vessel had savaged his throat. With the amount of blood he was losing, he had a few minutes at most.

"Stupid," he rasped, glaring at me as we eased him into a sitting position against a vat. "Why're you still here, Sebastian? Get going, the elevator is just ahead."

"Dammit." I rose, hating myself. I'd never liked Matthews, but he was still part of my team; I was responsible for all the lives under my command. "I'm sorry," I told him, backing away. He sneered.

"Don't be. I get to see the end." He raised his weapon, bloody lips curling in a smirk. "I get to say I saved your sorry ass from the lizards, one more time." His gaze flickered to Ember, standing at my shoulder, and he gave a tiny nod. "Try not to eat too much of his soul," he told her. "You'd probably choke on it."

More shots echoed around us, and Tristan cried out and slumped to one knee. Heart racing, I dropped to his side, and Matthews swore.

"Dammit, get the fuck out of here, Sebastian! I'm tired of seeing your face. Go!"

Slinging Tristan's arm over my neck, I went, Ember and Mist at our heels, as Peter Matthews's defiant voice rang out behind us, punctuated by the sound of gunfire.

"Yeah, you like that? Come on then, you ugly bastards! Come get some!"

"There's the elevator," said Mist, still as calm and practical as ever. It sat in the corner, a small metal box surrounded by iron lattice, a relic of the coal-mining era. Ancient-looking, except for the modern keypad near the doors. As Ember and Mist Shifted back, taking Tristan's weight, I stepped forward and shoved the plastic card into the slot. The keypad blinked on, and with a groaning and squeaking of gears, the elevator began to descend. Slowly.

"Garret," Ember called, and I turned back to face a swarm of dragons closing in from all sides. As the elevator clanked slowly overhead, I stepped forward and raised my gun, firing into the horde, hearing Ember and Mist do the same.

"Let me go," Tristan ordered, a second before his shots joined ours. Vessels screamed and collapsed, but more crept forward to take their place, blank silver eyes glowing in the shadows. The four of us stood back-to-back, holding our ground, but the swarm of dragons still pressed closer. A shot echoed from the darkness, and something hit me in the thigh, making me stagger.

Behind us, the elevator doors opened with a ding.

"Fall back!" I gasped, and we edged backward, still firing into the horde. I felt another bullet graze my arm, and then we were inside the box. Mist slammed her thumb into the door panel, but just as the doors were sliding shut, a scaly head burst through the opening and latched on to my leg, pulling me off my feet. I was yanked partway through the doors before Ember stuck her arm through the opening and shot the vessel cling-ing to me point-blank in the head. As it reeled away, several hands grabbed my arms and vest, dragging me back into the elevator. The doors finally closed, shutting out the chaos be-yond and plunging the box into darkness.

Panting, I relaxed against the press of bodies that surrounded me, feeling their harsh breathing match my own.

"Everyone okay?" I finally husked out. "Tristan?"

"I'll live" was the strained reply. "But you're not looking so hot yourself, Garret. At least I'm not the one bleeding all over the floor."

"Nothing serious," I said, though standing up seemed hard right now. Ember's grip on me tightened, and I put a hand on her arm, squeezing gently to reassure her. The box inched upward, creaking and rattling. "How much time do we have left?" I asked Tristan.

He gave a dark chuckle. "You don't want to know."

Not enough, then. I slumped against Ember, feeling a peace-ful resignation creep over me. So, this was it. After everything we'd been through, all the narrow scrapes and traps and close calls, our time had finally run out. I would die in an explosion of my own making, along with Talon's army of vessels that were meant to take over the world.

All in all, not a bad way to go, I mused, feeling the heat from the dragon beside me, the warmth of her against my back. At least my death would mean something. There was a moment of regret, where I wished Ember could have seen the end of this war. But at least, for the dragons and humans that came after us, the world would be a little safer.

"Just out of curiosity," Ember asked, "what will happen when this place explodes? Will it reach all the way up here?"

In the corner, Mist raised her head. "The explosion itself won't reach us," she replied, "but the fires will shoot up the elevator shaft and bring the entire thing down. Not even a dragon could survive that fall. We could fly, but that would mean leaving the humans, and I know you're not going to do that."

"You could go, Mist." Ember gave the other dragon a nod of understanding. "Riley is waiting for you, isn't he? No need for all of us to die here."

"No." Mist shook her head and looked away with a sigh. "I wouldn't be able to face him if I left you now. It seems his disturbing sense of loyalty has rubbed off on me. So..." A faint smile crossed her face, as if she couldn't believe herself. "I guess we're all going down together."

My earpiece suddenly sputtered, and Wes's voice crackled in my ear.

"St. George? Are you there? Can you hear me?"

I straightened, causing Ember to draw back slightly, and sat up, putting a hand to my ear. "I'm here, Wes."

"Bloody hell, where the fuck have you been?" the hacker spat at me. "I've been trying to contact you for over thirty minutes. What the hell happened in there?"

"They were waiting for us," I told him. "They must've jammed all communications on the last floor. We just got out a couple minutes ago."

"Dammit," Wes muttered. "I knew this was a trap, I just knew it. Damn it all to hell, Riley, why do you never listen to anything I tell you?" He gave a sigh that sounded more weary than angry. "So, the mission was a bloody catastrophe, is what you're saying. You didn't get the explosives planted."

I took a deep breath. "The mission was a success. We found the stasis chamber with the Adult vessels and planted all the explosives, as planned. Give the signal to retreat, Wes. It's going to blow in..." I glanced at my watch, and closed my eyes. "Fifty-eight seconds."

"Shit," Wes breathed. "Right, sending the signal now... Wait, where's your team, St. George? Are you bloody still in there?"

"We'll be fine," I said wearily. "Sebastian out." And, ignoring his horrified protests, took the mic and earpiece out and let them fall.

For a moment, the four of us sat there in silence, lost in our own thoughts as the final seconds ticked away. At my back, Ember pressed close, slipping her arms around me, and I curled my fingers over hers. Tristan leaned against the wall, his blue eyes dark and far away, and I wondered what was going through his head. As for me, I had no regrets. This was a good death, saving the world. You really couldn't ask for a better one.

Then Ember jumped to her feet, eyes blazing green in the

darkness of the box. "Dammit," she growled. "I am *not* dying here. Everyone, get up! We're getting out of this place, all of us, right now!"

RILEY

A flare streaked across my vision, cutting a bright orange path across the sky.

I leaped to my feet, watching as another followed, then another, arcing through the sky and leaving trails of smoke behind them.

Damn, that's the retreat signal. They did it!

Shifting immediately, I launched myself off the cliff and flew as fast as I could toward the laboratory. As I drew close, I saw that most everyone was in full retreat, falling back to the front gate. I saw soldiers helping the wounded across the field, while hatchlings and dragonells covered their escape, engaging or intercepting the vessels that still pursued. Lieutenant Ward staggered toward the gate with a half-burned soldier leaning on him, still shouting orders to his men. And overhead, a very bloody, angry Eastern dragon swirled back and forth, keeping the rest of the clones busy while our forces escaped.

"Jade!" I swooped to meet her, dodging the end of a long thrashing tail. She coiled around to face me, dropping the carcass of a vessel as she did. Her scales were streaked with red, deep puncture wounds covering her body, and she held one foreleg tight against her stomach. "St. George and the others," I panted, rearing back and beating my wings to hover in front of her. "Do you know if they got out?"

She shook her head. "I haven't seen them. But we cannot look for them now. Our job is to make sure everyone else gets away safely."

"Dammit, I know that! I just…" I gritted my teeth, glancing toward the laboratory, where several men and women in white coats were fleeing through the front doors. "I hope they got out in time," I muttered.

Another flare streaked across the sky, leaving trails of smoke behind and making us both look up. "That's the final signal," I growled. "And we've saved all that can be saved. Let's get out of here."

Turning, we fled across the barren yard, and not a moment too soon. With a flash and a rumble that shook the ground, the entrance behind us exploded in a howl of flame, rock and debris. Fiery bits pelted my scales as I soared away, dodging falling rocks as best I could, feeling the immense heat of the explosion behind me. The energy blast nearly knocked me out of the air, but I stayed aloft with a few desperate flaps and soared toward the edge of the yard.

A raucous cheer went up as Jade and I joined the others in front of the gate. Soldiers and dragons alike stood side by side, giddy with triumph and relief. Our numbers were smaller, I noticed; a quick head count revealed that twelve dragons had survived, with only a handful of St. George soldiers still on their feet. Better than I had hoped for, really, and given what we'd just been through I was happy that *anyone* made it out.

But every loss hurt. Especially as I gazed around and realized several key players were still missing.

"Dragon!"

Lieutenant Ward stepped forward, pushing his way between a soldier and a hatchling, to face me. "Have you heard from Martin?" he asked brusquely. "Or Sebastian's team?"

I swallowed hard. "Martin is dead," I said gravely, and his expression darkened. "He died...saving my life from a Viper. And I haven't heard from any of the others."

Ward sighed, gazing back toward the lab entrance, which was now impossible to see beyond the billowing cloud of smoke rising into the air. "Your hacker friend says he lost contact with them while they were still in the lab," he said, making my heart plummet. "Given that, we can only assume that they didn't make it out." His jaw tightened, his next words spoken with grudging respect. "They knew going in that it was a suicide mission. They died bravely, saving the world from Talon."

Numb, I backed away from him. It didn't seem possible that Ember, St. George and the rest of them were gone. I knew the odds had been against us, but hell, they always were. Somehow, no matter how hopeless the circumstances, Ember would always pull out of it; she was just too damn stubborn to die. If obstinacy failed, St. George usually had something up his sleeve that could turn the tables. And Mist was too slippery to let Death catch up to her.

You weren't supposed to die, I thought furiously. *Damn every one of you, we were supposed to come out of this together, or not at all. I can't be the only one who survived.*

"Riley," said Jade, raising her head. Her voice was full of wary hope as she gazed back toward the lab. "Look."

I spun. Two dark shapes were winging their way out of the

smoke, gliding toward the ground. They wobbled in the air, and they were so covered in soot and ash it was almost impossible to tell their color, but I thought I saw a glint of crimson, of silver-white scales, as they half soared, half fell toward the rocks.

Forgetting everything else, I sprang forward, hearing the rest of the hatchlings and soldiers follow. Trailing smoke and ash, the two dragons glided toward us, but were either too hurt or exhausted to make a landing and collapsed as they hit the ground, rolling several feet in a tangle of limbs and wings. The humans were thrown off and went tumbling over the earth, as well, until they, too, came to a painful stop.

"Ember! Mist!" Skidding to a halt, I nudged one of the bodies anxiously, heart pounding wildly in my ears. The white dragon lay on her stomach, sides heaving, her scales covered with soot. With a groan, she shifted her weight, and then two crystal blue eyes cracked open, blearily gazing up at me.

"Cobalt," she murmured, blinking as if she couldn't quite trust herself. "You...you're still alive."

I exhaled a gust of air, nearly collapsing in relief beside her. "Surprised?" I choked out. She smiled.

"A little. I was certain at least one of us wasn't going to be able to keep our promise." Grimacing, she pushed herself to a sitting position. A few feet away, Ember groaned as she raised her head, and the two soldiers of St. George began to stir, helped upright by a few of the other men. A huge weight seemed to lift from my shoulders, taking the fear and pain with it, and suddenly everything was fine. "I really expected it to be you," Mist went on, "but I keep forgetting you have the devil's own luck."

"Speaking of luck." I glanced at Ember, who shook herself

with a flap of her wings, scattering soot everywhere, then looked around for her human. "How did you guys get out?"

"We flew up the elevator shaft."

I blinked. "With the soldiers?"

"Well, *they* certainly couldn't fly out." She gave me her patented disdainful look, then glanced at Ember, who had stumbled over to make sure St. George was all right. "It was her idea," she said quietly. "She was bound and determined to get us out, even though our chances of making it in time were virtually zero. We nearly suffocated when the explosion went off, and barely beat the flames out while we were fleeing the shaft, but we made it, after all."

"Yeah." I let out my breath in a rush and pressed my forehead to hers, closing my eyes. "We made it," I breathed as she trembled and leaned against me, lowering her walls for just a moment. "We actually won."

And then, a tremor went through the earth under my claws, and a hollow boom echoed in the direction of the lab.

I froze, as did everyone else. Slowly, we turned to stare at the billowing cave mouth as a chill I'd never felt before slithered up my back. The boom came again, followed by another, and then the ear-piercing groan of metal being twisted and wrenched out of the way.

Inside, something was screaming at me to move, run, but I was rooted to the ground, paralyzed with everyone else. The ground shook, and rocks crumbled from the cave mouth, falling away and bouncing off each other, as something emerged from the smoke.

A massive talon smashed to the ground in front of us, and a wall of dark red scales pushed through the billowing smoke and rose to an impossible height. Shaking, I craned my neck up as a head emerged, bristling with horns, towering several stories overhead. Blazing green eyes glared down at us, wings unfurling to block out the sun, as a lesser god opened her jaws and made the whole earth tremble with her roar.

The Elder Wyrm had arrived. And we were going to die.

EMBER

The Elder Wyrm. To date, I had seen three ancient dragons, and though only one had been in his true form, all had been impressive and awe-inspiring in different ways. Certainly, the meeting with Ouroboros had been terrifying and memorable, as it was hard to imagine anything bigger than the ancient rogue.

There weren't words to describe the complete, utter terror of the Elder Wyrm.

She towered over us, over everything, rising to an impossible height and casting all in her shadow. She was probably more than one hundred feet from nose to tail, with curved black talons half as long as a man and jaws that could swallow a hatchling whole. Her scales were the color of old blood, gnarled and thick with age, and her wings were tattered. She loomed before us, a mountain come to life, green eyes glowing with hatred and fury, before she let out a roar that vibrated my bones and made my ears ring.

"Fall back!" Ward cried over the shouts and curses of men

and dragons, scrambling to get away. "Soldiers, spread out and sweep around to flank—!"

"No!" I yelled, interrupting him. "If you do that, she'll pick you off one by one. Stay together! All dragons, protect the humans when she breathes—"

The Elder Wyrm unleashed a hellstorm of dragonfire, a roaring wall of flame that rushed toward us like an explosion. I yanked Garret to the ground and curled my wings around his body, feeling the inferno shriek around us. It burned hotter than anything I'd ever felt, a maelstrom of heat and fury that singed even my protective scales. I heard cries of pain and terror from both human and dragon, but I couldn't see anything beyond the howling flames.

When the firestorm finally stopped, I peeked up and blinked in surprise. Nearly all the hatchlings and dragonells had moved to protect the soldiers in some way. Riley stood in front of Tristan, wings spread wide to guard the soldier, who crouched behind him looking stunned that he was still alive. Jade had coiled herself around several of the humans, including Lieutenant Ward, her long body protecting them all from the flames. I smelled burned hair and clothes, as none the soldiers had escaped that inferno unscathed, but it was better than our whole human force being incinerated in one breath.

The Elder Wyrm snarled in fury and stalked forward, her thunderous footsteps shaking the ground. We scrambled to our feet and fell back as the soldiers opened fire, filling the air with the howl of assault rifles. The Elder Wyrm didn't even flinch as she walked into the bullet storm, the shots sparking off her horns and thick chest plates, doing nothing. One of the men either panicked or tried to find a better position, breaking rank and darting around toward her side, even as Ward yelled for him to stop. The Elder Wyrm's head shot down, huge jaws closing over the human in one bite, and the soldier vanished instantly.

"Dammit, we're dead if she gets close to us," Riley snarled as the Elder Wyrm raised her head, the unfortunate human sliding down her long throat. She seemed to smile at us across the rocky ground, knowing there was little we could do to stop her. "And your guns aren't going to do a damn thing against her, not unless..."

He jerked up as Tristan straightened at that exact moment. "The Dragonkiller," the soldier gasped, and turned to Ward. "Sir, where's the prototype? Do we still have it?"

With an ominous rumble, the Elder Wyrm started forward again, stalking us across the yard. We scrambled away like mice fleeing the cat.

"I know where it is," Riley gasped, looking at Tristan. "I can take you there, but we'll have to move fast. And someone will need to keep the Elder Wyrm off our backs."

"Leave that to me," Jade said. The Eastern dragon's voice was weary but determined as she raised her head and watched the approaching Wyrm. "I can at least slow her down."

"No!" I snapped, leaping forward. "Jade, if you fight her, you're going to die. No grand sacrifices, I forbid it!" I glanced at the Elder Wyrm as she prowled forward, patient and calculating. She was in no hurry, knowing we couldn't fight her, and was content to stretch the terror out as long as she could. "We'll keep her distracted," I told everyone. "If we work together, we might survive this. Jade..." I turned to the Eastern dragon. "Can you pull down a thunderstorm, make it hard for her to see fast-moving targets in the rain?"

"Yes." The Asian dragon gave a solemn nod. "This I can do. Give me but a moment."

With a streak of pale green, the Eastern dragon shot skyward. The Elder Wyrm watched her go, and a chilling smile stretched her huge muzzle—probably she thought Jade was fleeing, abandoning us to our fate. That was fine; it would give us the few seconds we needed to pull this off.

"Garret." I lowered my wings, and the soldier swung onto my back without hesitation. "Keep moving," I told everyone. "Keep flying. We don't have to fight her, we're just keeping her distracted until Tristan can fire the gun. Watch her head—she's quicker than she looks. We might be able to stop her yet."

"You heard her," Ward snapped at the rest of the soldiers. "St. Anthony, get going. We'll keep her distracted long enough for you to take the shot."

The Elder Wyrm's massive shadow fell over us as she lunged forward with a roar. Everyone scattered. The soldiers flung themselves atop dragons taking to the air. With a howl, I launched myself right at the Elder Wyrm's gaping jaws, breathing a gout of fire into her face, hoping to surprise her at least. She wasn't surprised or fooled in the slightest. Her huge maw came at me through the flames, and I veered away, barely avoiding the snapping jaws. Garret fired several rounds at her head as we soared by, the bullets sparking off her horns and scales, and she turned on us with an annoyed growl.

I banked sharply, flying higher, avoiding the snapping jaws a second time. It was like flying around a large scaly mountain, one that was trying to crush you and was shockingly fast at the same time. I didn't have to worry only about her head; her talons, tail, even her wings were weapons that she used to try to swat us from the air. I saw a hatchling and rider veer away to avoid her claws only to be caught by the Elder Wyrm's long lashing tail, which smashed them from the air and into the side of the mountain.

With a flash and a crack of thunder, the skies opened up, and the rain came down in sheets. The hatchlings and riders vanished in a haze of mist and rain, and the Elder Wyrm became a blurry red shadow moving through the storm. She was so huge that it was impossible not to see her even in the haze. But the dragons buzzing around her were at least a little harder to catch as they swooped and soared through the rain.

As I circled around, the Elder Wyrm's piercing green eyes locked on me, and I saw the rage in them as the massive dragon spun, jaws opening to snap me from the air. As she did, she turned her body away from the eastern cliff, presenting her side to the sniper waiting in the trees.

The shot boomed through the air, the retort cracking like a whip over the storm, making my eardrums ring. The Elder Wyrm jerked, throwing her up head and staggering back a few steps. Desperately, I looked to her side as I flew past, hoping to see a gaping hole where the Dragonkiller had punched through.

My heart sank. A few of her scales were dented, and a couple of them looked cracked, but other than that, she didn't have a scratch on her. Shaking her head, the Elder Wyrm snarled angrily and turned, searching for whatever had hit her. Our best shot, our best weapon, had only pissed her off even more.

"No good," Garret panted behind me. "Not even the prototype can get through her scales. Either she needs to be closer, or Tristan has to find some kind of opening in her armor. And even then, he'll need to hit something vital if we're going to have any chance of killing her."

With a hiss, the Elder Wyrm snatched a dragon from the air and shook it vigorously before slamming it and its hapless rider to the earth at her feet. I cringed. Sooner or later, she was going to tire of swatting insects and go hunting for the one thing that had any hope of hurting her. We were running out of options, and the Elder Wyrm seemed invincible.

A tiny shout came through the storm, and I turned, blinking water from my eyes. At the edge of the trees, a skinny figure stood alone in the rain, waving his hands over his head, like he was trying to flag us down. Garret followed my gaze and straightened in surprise.

"That's Wes," he muttered.

"What is he doing out here?" I wondered, banking sharply and winging toward the hacker. Wes *never* got this close to the battle, being content to stay as far away as possible from guns, bullets and things that could kill him. A giant demigod of an Elder dragon certainly qualified. "Wes, what do you think you're doing?" I snapped, landing a few feet away. "Don't tell me you suddenly got the urge to be a hero."

"Bloody…hell…finally," Wes gasped. "I've been trying to get *somebody's* attention for the past five minutes, *and* not be noticed by the giant lizard of death over there." He doubled over, panting. "And no, I certainly do *not* have any suicidal urge to be a hero, thank you very much. I wouldn't even be here if you wankers weren't all about to die."

I was about to ask what he thought he could do about it when I spotted the black case clutched in one skinny hand, and my stomach dropped. "Wes, is that…?"

"Yeah, it is. Here." He stepped forward and shoved the case at Garret. "I kept an extra one, for an emergency," he said as Garret pushed back the lid, revealing a familiar device that set my heart to pounding. "Don't know how you'll get close enough to use it," Wes went on, "but if you can, that's nasty enough to ruin even the Elder Wyrm's day."

"We can get there," Garret muttered, and looked up at me, eyes hard with determination. "Ember?"

I nodded. "Yeah," I said breathlessly. "I'll get us in. How much time do we have?"

"The timer is set for thirty seconds," Wes answered. "So don't bloody push the button until you're sure you can stick it to the right spot."

Garret gave a brisk nod. "Give us two minutes," he told the hacker, tossing the empty case to the ground, "and then signal Ward to sound the retreat. We don't want anyone else caught in the blast when it goes off. Ready, Ember?"

I opened my wings in reply and launched us into the air. Wes's outline got smaller and smaller as I climbed steadily through the rain and turned toward the huge red blur that was the Elder Wyrm.

"Where are we going, Garret?" I asked, beginning the dive toward our enormous enemy. Garret bent low over my neck, his gaze on the massive red form below us. The Elder Wyrm was still pursuing the smaller dragons that darted around her, swatting or snatching them from the air. A vivid green hatchling and its rider tried swerving out of the way, but those huge jaws whipped around and closed on them both with the snapping of bones.

"Around to her left," Garret muttered, and I heard the warning beep as he started the countdown, the bomb flaring to life in his hands. "Fly low, get behind her foreleg."

I realized what he was aiming for and took a quick breath. "All right, here we go!"

We dropped fast, dodging a huge wingtip as the Elder Wyrm spun around. I saw my reflection pass through her blazing green eyes, and she roared, lunging at us with a maw like a black hole.

I twisted desperately, barely clearing those jaws as they snapped shut, making my insides shriek in fear. "Hang on!" I cried to Garret, spiraling away, trying to get behind her again. She followed, and I darted up as fast as I could, avoiding her fangs by a hairbreadth, feeling hot breath blast my scales.

"Fifteen seconds, Ember!" Garret warned.

Dammit, we weren't going to make it. I spun and angled my body into a final dive, knowing I might be flying straight down the Elder Wyrm's throat. As the enormous head rose to meet me, there was a streak of blue from the side, and Cobalt flew right into the Elder Wyrm's face. The dragon flinched, shaking her head, and we soared past her snapping jaws even as she snarled in fury and flung Cobalt away. I banked up, flew past her chest plates, and soared alongside her ribs as Garret reached out and pressed the device to her scales, right behind her foreleg.

"Go!" he yelled, and I swerved away, not daring to see how much time we had left. But as I swooped low to the ground, I had a split-second glimpse of something big and red coming at me before it hit me with the force of a wrecking ball. I smashed into the rocky ground and rolled, the world spinning around me, before coming to a painful stop.

My entire body blazed with pain. Gasping, I raised my head. Garret was lying next to me, tangled in one shredded wing, looking as bruised and dazed as I felt. Blood streamed down his face from a gash on his temple, and one eye was swollen shut as he looked back across the yard.

The ground trembled as the bleary form of the Elder Wyrm lurched toward us through the rain.

"One," Garret whispered, and turned away.

The Elder Wyrm's side exploded. There was a split-second flash, and then a shock wave of heat and energy ripped through the air as a burst of fire, blood and smoke sent the Elder Wyrm staggering sideways. She screamed, a horrific, piercing wail that stabbed through my eardrums and made me want to bury my head in the dirt, and then the ground shook as she collapsed, sending tremors and a billow of dust into the air.

In the few heartbeats of silence that followed, as the smoke began to clear and the dust began to settle, I started to breathe again, to believe that it was actually over.

And then, the Elder Wyrm moved, shifted and, unbelievably, got back to her feet.

No way. Numb, I stared at the mass of dark red scales, unable to move, as the Elder Wyrm clawed herself upright, panting. Blood streamed down her side, running in rivulets to the ground as she turned, revealing the mangled, bloody mess where the bomb had exploded. Her scales had been blown away, leaving a gaping hole behind, and glimmers of bone peeked through burned, angry flesh.

But she was still alive. Impossibly, she was on her feet. And as pissed as hell. Her gaze, livid and terrifying, found me across the yard a moment before she gave a furious, screaming roar and lurched forward. She limped across the ground, leaving behind a trail of red, a demon of rage and destruction come to crush me once and for all.

"Tristan," I heard Garret mutter, even as I braced myself to die. "Do it, now."

The shot boomed over the yard, as sharp and distinct as

cannon fire, the retort echoing off the cliffs. From my position on the ground, I saw something hit the Elder Wyrm in the side…and pass right through in a spray of blood.

The Elder Wyrm staggered to a halt a few yards away. For a moment, we stared at each other, unmoving, her burning green gaze locked with mine. I gazed at her, frozen, wondering if she would just shake off the injury and continue. If she was truly immortal, after all.

With a rumble of a landslide, the Elder Wyrm finally collapsed. Her massive head struck the ground a few feet from mine, slitted green eyes rolling up toward the sky. Blood pooled from her side and spread over the rocky ground in a grim flood as the Elder Wyrm shuddered, gasping for breath as her life bled away.

I pushed myself to my feet and, though my ribs felt like they would explode out of my body, forced myself back to human form. Taking a few steps forward, I came to a stop at the head of the Elder Wyrm, feeling the gravity of the moment press down on me as I watched the passing of the oldest dragon in the world. Her jaws moved, a small, incredulous voice emerging from within.

"Daughter," it whispered. "What…have you done?"

I swallowed hard. "What I had to," I whispered. "I've put a stop to your plans to rule the world, to declare war on humanity. They don't deserve it. Dragons and humans can learn to live together. Look at what we've done today, with the Order of St. George. We just had to find that common ground."

The Elder Wyrm gave a weak, raspy chuckle. "Foolish," she whispered. "You…you are just like me. Not only in blood. We are one and the same. I once thought to change the world, to make a difference for our kind. You will see…in time. If you live as long as I, you will come to know mankind's true colors. And you will have to make a decision, as I did."

A shudder went through her, and she made a strangled noise and gazed up at the sky. "How?" she whispered. "How can this...be? I should have been immortal. I was supposed to live...forever."

Then the brilliant light faded from her eyes, her body stilled and the whole earth seemed to shiver as the Elder Wyrm, the founder of Talon and the oldest dragon in existence, finally moved no more.

I took a deep, cleansing breath, feeling something hot run down my cheeks to mix with the rain. Overhead, the clouds parted, the storm faded away and the morning sun shone over the battlefield, glittered off scales and armor and the massive body of the Elder Wyrm in the center of it all.

A lump caught in my throat. I watched as the rogues and soldiers of St. George began clustering around us, cheers and shouts of triumph rising into the air. I closed my eyes, as a swirl of emotions rushed to the surface. Relief that it was done, that we'd made it. Anger at what we'd had to sacrifice to win. And a deep, bone-numbing grief for everyone we'd lost. For friends and allies who gave their lives for our victory, and for a sibling who couldn't be saved, but who had come through in the end, as he had always done.

"Ember."

I turned. Garret stood behind me, blood trickling down his face, his combat vest torn and shredded. He held out an arm, and I stepped into him, pressing my face to his chest as he hugged me tight. And for a moment, we just stood there, numb with relief, dazed with the realization.

It's finally over.

There was a blast of wind, and Riley landed close, breathing hard. With a ripple of energy, he Shifted back to human form and staggered toward us.

"Hell," he whispered, gazing up at the massive corpse. His voice was laced with both amazement and unrestrained glee as he shook his head. "We did it. We actually fucking did it. The Elder Wyrm is gone." Laughing, he turned and threw his arms around us, pulling us all into a manic group hug. "Talon is dead," he whispered fiercely. "The organization will be nothing without the Elder Wyrm. After all these centuries, we can finally start to breathe again."

No, I thought as Riley pulled back, the rogue too elated to be embarrassed. We weren't done yet. The Elder Wyrm and her army might be gone, taking with them her plans to rule the world, but the work was far from over. With the death of its leader, Talon would be in shambles, the Order was a mess and the future of both was uncertain. Neither organization would just go away; Talon was too big, its reach too extensive for it to simply vanish. Despite the Elder Wyrm's plans, it was still the only place where dragons could exist without fear. And I realized what had to happen, what that would mean for all of us.

Talon had to continue. Too many dragons depended on the organization to keep them safe—maybe not from the Order, but from the rest of the world. We weren't quite ready to reveal our existence, and the world wasn't ready for us even if we were. Talon and the Order both had to change, that much was certain. But with the Patriarch, the Elder Wyrm and the heir of Talon all dead, who would step up to take their places?

I swallowed hard. *Well, Dante,* I thought as Garret slipped his arms around my waist from behind. *Looks like you got your wish, in the end. I'll be going home, after all.* I took a deep breath and swiped a hand over my eyes. *I just wish you were here with me.*

"Hey," Garret murmured in my ear, and I peeked back at him, feeling a tear slide down my cheek. He gave a sad smile and brushed a fingertip over my skin. "Don't think about it, dragon girl," he whispered, drawing me closer. "There'll be time to mourn everyone soon enough. We won, and we're alive. Savor this victory, for what it's worth."

I smiled shakily and looked back at the cheering, celebrating soldiers and dragons. Soldiers grinned and slapped each other on the back, while hatchlings bounced around each other and the humans, uncaring that they were once their greatest enemies. Wes had ventured close and gave a yelp of surprise as Nettle pounced on him in ecstatic glee, knocking him on his back. His cursing demands for her to get off were lost in the chaos around him, until a soldier pulled him upright and gave him a hearty slap on the arm, making him wince.

A pale-haired girl walked around the body of the Elder Wyrm, coming to a halt at the edge of the crowd. Mist watched the celebrations with an amused detachment, a faint smile on her lips, though her blue gaze scanned the area, searching for something.

Breaking away from Ward, Riley turned around, strode across the yard and, without hesitation, pulled her into a deep kiss. Mist's eyes went huge, her body stiffening. Most of the hatchlings stopped what they were doing to stare and, after a moment, began cheering Riley instead. When he finally pulled back, Mist's eyes were still wide as she stared up at him, and for a moment, we all held our breath, wondering if she would slap the rogue or shove him away. Riley offered a tiny, crooked grin, and Mist's jaw tightened, right before she grabbed the back of his head and pulled him down again.

I smiled and leaned into Garret, feeling his arms tighten around me, the solid thump of his heart echoing mine.

The Elder Wyrm was dead.

Time for a new beginning.

EPILOGUE

RILEY

Two weeks later...

"I bloody can't believe I have to do this."

I watched Wes stuff his laptop into a bag and zip it shut with a fierce exasperation. His scowl was even deeper than normal as he swung the bag onto his shoulder and turned to glare at me. "I once promised myself that I would never go back there," he said. "I don't even know why they want me to attend—it's not like I'm the bloody war hero."

"You were part of the final battle," I told him. "You were my second in command for years. According to most, you *are* a bloody war hero."

Wes snorted. "Yes, well, the day I start taking the masses seriously is the day I set fire to my computer." He shook his head and scowled out the door. "I was supposed to be on a plane to London right now," he muttered. "You know, back home, to see the folks who thought I was dead for nearly a decade? And now I have to postpone the thing I've dreamed about for years, because some bloody hatchling decided she needs to hold a meeting *right now.*"

"You'll get your chance to go home." I sighed. "That 'bloody hatchling' has even agreed to pay for it, and to provide information for whatever cover-up story you're going to tell them. Which you're going to need. I trust you're not informing them that you've been working for dragons for the past several years."

Wes's look of blatant disgust could strip paint from the walls. "Yes, Riley, that's exactly what I'm going to do," he scoffed. "Just waltz in and say, 'Oh, hi, Mum, hi, Dad. Yeah, I've been gone a bloody long time, haven't I? Well, funny story—I've been helping these rogue dragons wage a war on an oppressive organization that is also run by dragons. Sorry I didn't call.'"

I rolled my eyes. "So stop complaining," I said. "You'll get to go home soon. You've been away for nearly a decade, another day or two isn't going to matter."

"I'm a bloody war hero. I'm allowed to complain."

With a rustle of cloth, Mist walked into the room and my senses prickled. The Basilisk was dressed in heels and a dark skirt, and her silver hair was pinned atop her head. She did not look like the quietly aloof girl of the past few days. She looked poised, elegant and businesslike, and gave my jeans, boots and leather jacket a critical raised brow. "You're wearing *that* to the meeting?"

"What?" I grinned at her. "I'm wearing a nice shirt. Besides, everyone there knows who I am. Why spoil their expectations?"

Wes shook his head. "I'll wait in the car," he muttered, and swept by with a last rueful look at Mist. She waited until he had left the room and the farmhouse door had closed behind him before turning back to me with a pained smile.

"I spoke to the Archivist this morning," she said, and her voice was subdued. "He...relieved me of my duties to him. I'm no longer part of that circle. Or welcome back in the Vault."

I frowned. "Any idea why?"

"Apparently, he believes I can do more good here, with you. That my Basilisk training will better serve this new faction he and the CEO have implemented." She wrinkled her nose. "Of course, with the upheaval and the restructuring of every existing department within Talon, no one is really certain what is going on. I imagine it will be months before the Basilisks are truly back on their feet. And even then, I doubt we'll be doing the same things that we've done before. No more stealing company secrets or blowing up buildings, not with the new management.

"So..." She shrugged. "Until that time, or until Talon calls for me again, I guess I'm stuck with you. Lucky me."

I sobered. "You can leave if you want, Mist," I told her, though I wanted to kick myself for saying it. "No one is stopping you. You're not beholden to Talon, the Archivist or anyone now. I would hate it, but...you truly have that choice. If you want to leave and see the world, that's up to you."

Her lips twisted in a half smirk. "That's assuming I know what to do without Talon," she admitted, a strange note of bitterness in her voice. "You forget, I'm not like you and your band of outlaws, Cobalt. Talon, my job with the Basilisks... that was my whole life. Without the organization... I'm not really sure what I'm going to do."

I took two steps forward, closing the distance between us. She peered up at me, wary but almost defiant, and I smiled back. "Well, it *is* lucky for you that I happen to be an expert on life without Talon," I told her. "If you like, I'd be happy to show you."

Her brow arched sardonically, making me shrug. "Up to you, of course," I went on. "But I don't expect I'll be babysitting the hatchlings forever, now that there's no need to hide from the organization. And I've seen a fair bit of the world myself. Someday, I'd like to get out there again, without having to worry about my network and keeping everyone alive."

I reached down and took one of her hands. A shiver ran up my arm as her fingers curled lightly around mine. "I'd… be happy to have you along, Mist," I said quietly. "There are places in the world where we can both be ourselves, with no humans around to see. I'd love to show them to you."

"Mmm." The Basilisk gave me a scrutinizing look, but didn't pull back. "And the new CEO of Talon isn't going to want you around to help rebuild?" she asked. "The hero of the final battle? The leader of the free dragons?"

"I'm sure I can convince her that I've earned a vacation."

She laughed. Inside, Cobalt stirred lazily, content to let me take the lead on this. There was a dull ache whenever I thought of Ember, but it was barely noticeable now. I still wasn't sure if dragons could feel the same emotions humans did, but…what the hell. If this was the start of something bigger, so be it. I didn't think I would ever get a second chance.

"Well, then," Mist said, smiling up at me. "I guess we'll have to see where this goes."

GARRET

When I walked into the room, the line of soldiers waiting for me snapped to attention.

"At ease," I told them, and they relaxed, including Tristan, standing at the head of the line. Coming to a halt in front of the men, I took a moment to study each of their faces, evaluating my forces, the ones who had survived.

Eleven soldiers. That was all that was left of the Order of St. George. On this side of the world, anyway. If any of our neighboring chapterhouses had survived, we hadn't heard from them. The Order had shrunk from a few hundred individuals from chapterhouses across the United States, to these eleven soldiers before me. Talon's devastation had been almost absolute.

Almost.

"Lieutenant St. Anthony," I said, glancing at Tristan. "Have the men been informed of the situation?"

"Yes, sir," Tristan replied in a tone that made me wince inside. I was still getting used to being called *sir* by everyone, including my former partner. But after Lieutenant Ward had suddenly and unexpectedly resigned, claiming he no longer had a place in this new world where dragons were not monsters, the vote had been unanimous: I was the new commander of the Western Chapterhouse. Which meant, unless someone of higher rank showed up to challenge me, I would lead the United States Order of St. George.

Such as it was.

I wished it didn't have to be me. I wished Martin had survived; he was the best suited to lead the Order. After the assault on Talon, the lieutenant had been brought home and buried with the rest of the fallen, his cross rising above the others in the cemetery, somber and proud. I wished he was here now, to tell me how a true leader should act. But St. George needed someone, someone who knew dragons, and who would make decisions based not on fear, but on understanding. The Order needed me, but more important, the dragons needed someone to be their voice. I couldn't falter now.

I faced the men before me, recognizing each of them. They had all been there, in the last, terrible battle. They had all seen the horror of the clones and the terror of the Elder Wyrm. And they had all stood with a hatchling or rogue dragon fighting beside them as an ally. They were ready to begin something new.

"Today is a new day for the Order," I began. "Today we will take the first steps toward peace with those we once considered enemies. Today, Talon and St. George will finally reach an accord. I know this goes against everything the Order taught us, but everyone here has seen the truth, just as I did. They're not monsters. Just like humans, they're individuals with their own fears, ambitions, regrets, everything. Most important, they don't have to be our enemies. We can learn to work together, but the Order has to change to see that happen. I'm committed to seeing that change, but know that if you stay, we will face opposition. It will be a hard road at first, and if there are other survivors within St. George, some of our own will certainly challenge us." I paused, and saw some of them nod; they knew, as well as I did, the minds of the Order would not be changed overnight. "But we must stand firm," I went on. "We cannot let blind hatred drive us any longer. This is just the first step toward peace with dragons—it will take all of us to make it last."

"Sir." One of the men stepped forward; I recognized him as a soldier named Alexander, maybe two years older than me. He'd been part of Ward's group, but had yet to develop the sadistic hatred the Eastern Chapterhouse soldiers were famous for. "I have a question," he continued as I nodded at him. "Sir, what will happen to the Order if we're not at war with the dragons? What will be the purpose of St. George, if we are no longer called to fight? Will the Order eventually be disbanded?"

"No." I shook my head. "Not yet. Not for a long while. Perhaps, someday in the future the world will no longer need the Order of St. George. But right now, we are the only human organization who is aware of the existence of dragons. We will provide...not opposition, but a counterbalance to Talon. There will be dragons who share the Elder Wyrm's view, who might wish to harm the organization or humanity itself. Talon will call on us if they need the Order's help to deal with problem individuals within the organization. And as we grow and rebuild our numbers, the Order of St. George will stand vigilant, ready to act should Talon attempt a hostile takeover once more."

He nodded gravely. We might not be at war any longer,

but we all knew the threat the organization represented. I didn't want to think it could happen, but if the worst came to pass and another Elder Wyrm rose to power, the Order of St. George was still humanity's best defense against Talon and the threat of dragons.

I hoped it would never come to that.

"Are there any more questions?" I asked, and when no one answered, I turned to Tristan, standing rigidly beside me. "Are we ready to go, Lieutenant?"

"Yes, sir," Tristan replied. "The car is waiting out front now."

"Dismissed," I told the soldiers before me. "Alexander, you're in charge until we return. Contact me if anything unusual happens."

"Sir."

"Let's go," I told Tristan, and we left the room, heading outside into the hot Arizona sun.

★ ★ ★

"Damn," Tristan muttered a few hours later. He craned his neck, gazing up at the skyscraper towering overhead. It loomed against the evening sky, a monolith of glass and steel rising into the twilight. "To think, an office of the Elder Wyrm was right here, and we never realized it."

"Good thing we didn't," I replied as we walked toward the front doors. A security guard opened them for us with a nod, and we ducked into the air-conditioned building. "I can't imagine going head-to-head with her again and not being completely obliterated."

"God, that was a fight, wasn't it?" Tristan agreed, keeping his voice low, as our footsteps echoed across the spacious lobby. "One thing that confuses me, though. How did *you* become the leader of St. George when, technically, *I* was the one who killed the freaking Elder Wyrm?"

I shot him a glance and saw that he was grinning. "You want the job?" I asked, heading toward a trio of well-dressed humans who looked like they were expecting us. He snorted.

"Fuck, no. But a plaque on my office door would be nice. Tristan St. Anthony, Slayer of the Legendary Elder Wyrm, has a nice ring to it."

"I'll see what I can do," I muttered, and then fell silent as the trio of smiling humans came forward, shook our hands and requested that we follow them to the meeting.

The elevator took us to the very top floor, and when the doors finally opened, a wall of windows showed off open sky with a few dotted stars, and the glittering city streets very, very far below. A pink tinted cloud floated in the sea of navy blue, and for a moment, I felt a sudden, irrational urge to stand at the very edge of the building, as close to the sky as I could get.

"The meeting is about to start, sir," one of the humans said, gesturing at a large wooden door at the end of the hall. "Please, go on in."

Tristan and I pushed open the doors, and walked into a roomful of dragons.

Everyone had arrived before us, it seemed, though we had arrived early. Across the table, Riley and Mist sat side by side, with a very bored-looking Wes lounging over his laptop. Jade and another Eastern dragon, a slender man with a white mustache down to his waist, perched at the other end. Both wore elegant robes, and Jade's hair was pinned up with ivory chopsticks, adding to her unruffled mystique. The older Easter dragon's eyes were closed, either in meditation or trying very hard to appear serene, given the final dragon in the room. At the head of the table, the Archivist, the ancient Wyrm who guarded Talon's Vault, stood beside an empty chair, a sheaf of papers in both wrinkled hands. His pale blue eyes met mine as we entered, and he inclined his head.

"Commander Sebastian," the ancient dragon greeted, his quiet voice making the tiles shiver under my feet. "Lieutenant St. Anthony, welcome. We are glad you could join us."

"Thank you," I said, and seated myself at the end of the table, Tristan beside me. The Archivist leaned over and pressed a button on the phone in front of him, speaking into the receiver.

"The Order of St. George has arrived, ma'am."

My heart beat faster as a door opened on the opposite wall, and Ember came into the room. Gone was the girl in jeans and a T-shirt, a firearm hanging at her waist and her hair standing on end. Now, she wore a dark green suit jacket, a matching skirt, and her hair was brushed back, looking almost manageable. For just a heartbeat, I felt a flicker of apprehension at how similar she looked to Dante. Maybe not her clothes, but her posture and appearance spoke of the same cool, businesslike attitude I'd seen in her twin and many of the other Talon dragons.

But then our gazes met and she gave me a smile, instantly becoming the Ember I'd always known, and I relaxed. Despite the expensive clothes and sudden acquisition of an entire multi-billion-dollar company, she was still the same.

"Everyone." She took her place at the head of the table and gazed around at the assembled humans and dragons. For a moment, she seemed to gather herself, to collect her thoughts or her composure, to act in the way the new CEO of Talon should. Then she smiled, and it filled the entire room.

"This hardly seems real, doesn't it?" Ember regarded the table with shining green eyes. "I never really thought that, in my lifetime, we would see the end of the fighting between Talon and the Order of St. George. But here we all are." She raised her hands, indicating the table, though her gaze lingered on me. "Alive. At the end of the war at last. Though it's been hard getting here. I know we all lost something to finally see this day come."

A shadow crossed her face, and my heart ached for her, knowing she was thinking of Dante. Her sibling's body had been lost in the lab explosion, and Ember had taken that hard, not being able to say a proper goodbye. I understood. I, too, had left someone behind in the explosion, someone I'd never imagined running into. Seeing him in the depths of Talon's laboratory, knowing exactly what he had become, what he had turned into, hadn't made it any easier. It was painful, but the last piece of my past was truly gone; I was Garret Xavier Sebastian, Commander of the Order of St. George, and now, I would look only to the future.

"But regardless," Ember continued, taking a short breath to compose herself. "We're here. And we can't cling to the past. So, unless anyone has any questions, we should get started."

"Actually, I do have one question, Firebrand," Riley said, making the old Eastern dragon blink at him, perhaps startled by his nonchalance in addressing the new leader of Talon. "I was going to ask you later, but what the hell, we're all friends here. I'll bring it up now. Are you sure you want this? Being the new CEO? Taking over the Elder Wyrm's job?"

"Yes," Ember said seriously. "I'm sure. The executives have accepted my position, or at least, they were forced to accept my position. As daughter of the Elder Wyrm, I am the rightful heir to Talon now that Dante is gone. And the Archivist fought for me. He's offered to be my mentor and assistant, until I can run company affairs on my own."

"That's not really what I meant," Riley said, making the Archivist frown at him. "I've worked for Talon. I know how they do things. Not that I doubt your abilities, Firebrand, but Talon has been unchanged for centuries, and a lot of the members are not going to want to try anything new. It's going to be a fight every step of the way, and you're still just a hatchling. Are you sure you want this? To give your entire life to the organization?"

"If not me," Ember said softly, "then who?" He didn't have an answer for that, and she nodded. "This is why I'm here, Riley. I wanted our race to be free, to not live in fear of Talon."

"At the cost of your own freedom?" Riley asked grimly.

Ember gave a sad smile. "Dante once told me that sacrifice is necessary," she said. "He was right. There are too many people and dragons who are counting on me to make a difference. So many things need to change. I know it's going to be an uphill fight all the way, but I have to do it." Her smile became wistful. "Maybe someday I can retire, but right now, this is my place.

"I hope we can make this work," Ember went on, and paused. "No, I am committed to making this work. Talon *will* change, I promise to see that happen. But there's still a lot of work to do, and we need everyone's help to make the transition as smooth as possible."

"That is why we are here," the Archivist broke in, and stepped forward. "Ma'am, if I may?" he asked, looking at Ember, who nodded.

"I take it you have all reviewed the treaty?" the Archivist

continued, placing the documents on the table in front of us. His pale eyes shifted to me behind his glasses. "First and most important—Talon and the Order of St. George will agree to an immediate cease-fire, and the Order will abstain from killing any members of Talon, dragon or human, without reasonable cause. Which are clearly documented on page two, paragraph 4B. Likewise, all members of Talon will follow the same procedures when dealing with the Order and its members. Does St. George have any questions or concerns, Commander Sebastian?"

"No," I replied. I'd reviewed the treaty earlier and found no discrepancies or loopholes; with a few corner cases, it basically stated that Talon and St. George were at peace, and members of both sides were not to harm the other unless their lives were threatened. At the behest of Tristan, I did add a clause that, should any member of Talon attempt a global hostile takeover, or mean obvious harm to a human being, the Order would be free to act on their own judgment and respond accordingly. I was told that many Talon executives weren't happy with that clause, but Ember and the Archivist had agreed to it.

The Archivist nodded. "Agent Cobalt," he went on, looking at the former rogue. "You have agreed to head the new branch Talon plans to open. Is this still acceptable? For hatchlings who do not wish to directly serve the organization, your division will be responsible for placing them in homes where they will be safe, and monitoring their progress until they come of age."

"Basically, what I do now," Riley answered with a wry grin. "That's fine with me."

"But they would have a choice," Ember said. "That's the difference. They don't have to work for Talon—they can choose what path they want for themselves. Talon will, of course, provide a full education should they decide to stay with the organization, but for the first time, that choice will be theirs alone."

"Personally, I don't see many of them leaving Talon, at least not permanently," Mist broke in. She sat next to Riley with her chin resting on her laced fingers, looking thoughtful. "When you've been raised as part of something bigger, even if you have that choice, it's hard to break away and try to make it alone."

"They'll never be alone," Ember said, and Riley nodded. "We will always be here for any dragon, member of Talon or not. Which is why I'm very happy to be allying with the Eastern council. Mr. Lei," she went on, turning to the old man beside Jade. "I know your people crave isolation, so thank you for agreeing to this partnership, and for allowing Jade to represent the Eastern dragons. I promise we will stay out of your affairs as much as possible."

The old man narrowed his eyes. "It was as much for our own survival that we agreed to ally with Talon," he said in a breathy but powerful voice, causing a shiver to run up my spine. He wasn't as old as the Archivist, but he was an old dragon all the same. "Your organization has proven how dangerous and devious they can be, and in this, we feel we have no choice. At least with Jade keeping an eye on things, we will not be taken by surprise again."

Ember bowed her head. "I hope to change your opinion," she said quietly. "I hope that, someday, you will come to see the Western dragons as friends, and not as a threat."

The old dragon sniffed. "We shall see," he said imperiously. "Let us hope you will show better judgment than those who came before you, hatchling."

Ember didn't answer, but Jade caught my gaze across the table and rolled her eyes, making me bite back a smile. Whatever their opinion of Talon, at least we had one ally who would defend us. I suspected we hadn't seen the last of the wise, witty Eastern dragon who had kidnapped me, and I had no complaints about that.

"Then," said the Archivist with the note of drawing the meeting to a close, "if we are in agreement, all that remains is for the treaty to be signed by the respective parties. Once signed, it will be effective immediately." He flipped to the last page of the documents and slid it over to Riley, who made a show of scrutinizing the last words before scrawling his name on the first of four lines, with Mist acting as witness. It then crossed over to Jade and the Eastern dragon, who did the same. Finally, it came to me. I signed my full name on the given line and passed the treaty back to the Archivist, who placed it before Ember and handed her a pen.

"Ma'am," he said quietly. "Yours is the final signature."

As Ember took the pen, her gaze met mine for a brief moment, her eyes shining with triumph, and hope. *We did it*, they said. Everything we'd been through, all the sacrifice, losses, struggles and heartache—it all came down to this.

The daughter of the Elder Wyrm added the final signature to the document, and the treaty was complete.

Ember took a deep breath and straightened as the papers were taken away. "It's done," she whispered, and rose from her seat, gazing around the table. "Thank you," she said simply. "All of you. You don't know how happy I am that we've finally come to an accord."

Riley pushed back his seat, prompting the rest of us to rise, too. "So, what now, Firebrand?" he asked. "We defeated an army, killed the Elder Wyrm and ended a war. Where do we go from here?"

"Forward," Ember replied. "Always forward. It's a new day, and anything is possible."

"Well," Riley said, gazing around at the rest of us. "I've got somewhere to be soon, but I'd say this calls for a celebration, drinks on me." His gaze fell on me and Tristan, and he grinned. "What'dya say, St. George? Not opposed to throwing a few back with a bunch of lizards, are you? If anything, I'll bet money I can drink both of you under the table."

Tristan scoffed. "You're on, lizard," he began, and caught himself. "Uh, that is, if the commander is up for it."

I grimaced. This commander thing would take some getting used to. "We have nowhere to be until tomorrow," I said. "I'd say establishing relations with our new allies isn't a bad idea." I shot Tristan a sideways look. "Though I'll leave the drinking to you, Lieutenant. I still remember the last time you convinced me to 'loosen up.' My stomach still hasn't forgiven you for that."

"Suit yourself, Commander. Guess I'll just have to drink for the both of us."

"A fine idea," Jade put in, standing up in a fluttering of robes. "Mr. Lei will be returning to the hotel room, but I believe I will join this wager, as well. In the name of strengthening alliances, of course."

I blinked in astonishment, and Riley did the same. "Wait, you're in, too?"

"Of course," Jade replied, and gave him a tranquil smile. "What, did you think that all I drink is tea?"

Mist chuckled, nudging Riley's shoulder. "Don't take this the wrong way," she mock whispered, smiling up at him, "but my money is on her."

I grinned at the genuine fear on Riley's face, and looked

across the table. "Ember?" I asked gently. The new CEO stood beside the Archivist, watching us all with a wistful smile on her face. "What about you? Will you be joining us?"

She shook herself. "Um, give me an hour," she replied with a rueful look at the Archivist. "Apparently, I have some other things to sign and contracts to review that cannot wait until tomorrow. But yes, afterward, I would love to join you all. Especially since this will probably be the last time I'll ever see the light of day."

Riley curled a lip in sympathy. "Yeah, welcome to the corporate world, Firebrand. Now you know why I left. Well, if you ever need someone to come crashing into a board meeting to shake things up, you know my number."

Ember smiled. "I'll remember that. Commander Sebastian," she went on before we could leave. "Could I have a moment? It won't take long." She stepped back and indicated the door on the other side of the room. "Please see me in my office when you are finished here."

My heart jumped. I turned and nodded to Tristan, who had a knowing smirk on his face. "Go on," I told him. "Don't wait up for me. I'll join you when I can."

His grin told me he wasn't fooled in the slightest. "As you say, *Commander*. I'll 'uphold relations' until you return. Feel free to take your time."

Jade offered a slight bow in my direction. "Until we meet again, Commander Sebastian," she said solemnly, and left the room with the other Eastern dragon.

Mist gave me a nod as she went by, and Wes followed her with a muttered, "Drunk lizards, this should be interesting." They filed out of the room and shut the door, until it was only me and Riley left.

"Well." The former rogue dragon sighed and glanced out the window, where the moon hovered over the city like a glowing golden eye. "Interesting times ahead, huh, St. George? You, the leader of the Order, me heading this new branch of Talon. And Ember sitting up here as the CEO."

"Things will definitely be different," I agreed. "We're all going to face some strong opposition, but the three of us should be able to handle whatever comes up."

Riley snorted. "Compared to what we went through this past year, I say bring it on," he muttered. "Though Talon politics are a special kind of torture that makes you want to stab forks through your eyes. I just hope Ember can handle wrangling an entire company of fickle, ambitious, backbiting dragons. We can be ruthless dicks sometimes, if you hadn't noticed."

"If anyone can do it, she can. And she won't be alone."

"Yeah." His yellow gaze slid to me, a grin curling one side of his mouth. "Well, then, you'd better get going, *Commander*. Don't want to keep the new CEO of Talon waiting."

I extended a hand. He gripped it firmly, watching me over our clasped fingers. "See you around, Riley."

"Later, St. George. Looking forward to actually working with the Order. That'll be a nice change." He turned and sauntered toward the door, but paused after a few steps. "Oh, and tell Ember that I don't care how much the Archivist glares at me, I'm not calling her *ma'am* or Madam President or anything similar. If he doesn't like it, he can suck my tail."

"Making friends already, I see."

"Hey, I keep things interesting. See you around, human." With a final grin, the former rogue leader stuck his hands into his pockets and slipped out the door, leaving me alone in the room. I smiled, shook my head and turned toward the office of Talon's CEO.

EMBER

A quiet knock echoed through the office door, and I looked up from where I was leaning against the front of my desk. "Come in."

The door swung back without a squeak, and Garret entered the room, sending a flutter through my insides. The new commander of St. George was dressed in "civilian clothes," as they called them—slacks and a collared shirt, as they couldn't parade through a major city in the Order's black-and-gray uniform without drawing attention to themselves. Strangely, in the meeting only a few minutes ago, everything about him—his posture, words, the way he acted—spoke of a person of authority. But Garret had always been a leader; even among dragons, rogues and hardened soldiers, it came naturally to him. It seemed logical that he would take over what remained of the Order. He had proved himself time and time again, and his men, the soldiers of St. George, respected that.

I hoped I would prove to be as worthy.

He smiled at me as he approached, but paused a few feet

away, sweeping his gaze around the room. "I'm...not entirely sure how to address the president of Talon in her office," he said in a low voice, as if people could be listening. "I wouldn't want rumors to spread, especially if their president is alone with the commander of St. George."

"Don't worry about that," I told him, waving an airy hand. "I had the Archivist do a thorough check. No cameras in the Elder Wyrm's office, no security devices, and the walls are completely soundproof. What the president of Talon does in her private chambers is no one's business but her own."

His smile widened. "Good to know," he said, and closed the distance between us. I wrapped my arms around his neck as he slipped his around my waist, pressing us close. As his lips met mine, I closed my eyes, breathing him in, savoring the moment as long as I could. With all the changes to Talon and the upheaval within the organization and St. George, I hadn't seen Garret in over a week, and I'd missed him more than I'd thought possible. It had killed me a few short minutes ago, glimpsing him over the table, knowing I couldn't go over and hug him or even talk to him like I wanted to. No, I was the CEO of Talon now, and I had to behave accordingly, even among my closest friends.

Pulling back, Garret regarded me with solemn eyes, his pupils contracted until they were thin black lines against the gray. My heart sped up, and Garret must've sensed it, for his brow furrowed, and he gently stroked my cheek. "What's wrong?" he murmured.

I shook myself. "Nothing," I replied, seeing my reflection in those silvery irises. "It's just...hard to believe that we're here. That we're alive, and together, at the end of everything." He bent forward and kissed me again, long and lingering, and I sank into his touch.

Several minutes passed, and the windows along the wall were in danger of fogging up, before I forced myself to pull away.

"Garret, wait. There's something I have to show you. I didn't call you in here just for…this." He cocked his head, looking puzzled, and I felt color creep up my face. "Not that I'm complaining, at all, and what the CEO does in her own office is not anyone's business but her own, but… I'm going to stop talking now, because the CEO of Talon does not stutter like a vapid teenager." I frowned at the grinning soldier. "And you will tell no one what transpired here, especially the Archivist."

Garret chuckled and released me. "Of course not, Madam President," he said, looking far too innocent as he stepped back. "The CEO of Talon and the commander of St. George are nothing but professional. In public."

Firmly telling myself not to blush, I walked around my desk, pulled open a drawer and withdrew a large manila envelope.

"These are the results of the tests you wanted," I told him, sliding the envelope across the desk. "I had our scientists run a thorough examination of your blood, and you were right." I paused, swallowing hard, as Garret picked up the envelope and pulled out the papers inside. "There is a large percentage of dragon DNA in your blood," I told him, "and traces of it throughout your body. From the tissue samples they took, the scientists were able to conclude that your cells regenerate at an amazing speed, almost identical to a dragon's healing capabilities. They've never seen anything like it before. A couple of them wanted to know your identity so they could 'detain' you for further study. I told them absolutely not, your identity would not be revealed, and I would eat them if they asked me again."

Garret smiled at this, still studying the documents. "But you're in no danger of this killing you, Garret," I continued. "Quite the opposite, in fact. The scientists noted that the dragon DNA continuously regenerates and heals the human tissue, to the point where it actually seems to prevent normal human aging."

Garret blinked and looked up, a frown crossing his face. "What does that mean?"

"They're not sure exactly," I admitted. "It's all theory at this point. But they've posited that you could have a longer life-span than an average human. Much...longer."

Garret's voice was quietly awed. "As long as a dragon's?"

"Maybe." I took a breath, trying to control both the fear and wonder that had been hovering inside ever since I'd heard the news. "Like I said, they're not really certain. They would have to run more tests, but it will likely be years before they have any sort of real answer. But I did want you to know that there is the possibility of you living...for a very long time, Garret. Maybe as long as a dragon."

Garret didn't answer right away. He stared back down at the papers with an unreadable look on his face. "I hope this doesn't come as too much of a shock," I said at last, wondering what was going through his head. "And I hope this won't threaten the truce between Talon and St. George. The Order might get suspicious if they notice that the commander never seems to age."

He gave his head a little shake and tossed the envelope back on the desk. "I'm sure the Order will have a few questions," he stated softly before giving me a faint smile. "In a decade or two."

I cocked my head at his nonchalance. "You're not worried about this?"

"About spending a few centuries with you? I think I'm okay with that." The faint smile turned into a full-blown grin that lit up the room. "Though Riley might have something to say about it."

My heart swelled like a balloon, even as a lump caught in my throat. Turning, I walked to the enormous windows lining my office wall, and gazed out at the sky. Far below, the city glittered with a million blinking lights, but I looked toward the distant horizon and the final sliver of sunlight sinking into the dark.

"Everything is changing," I murmured, feeling Garret slip his arms around me from behind. "There's so much to do, and we'll both be so busy. I have to lead Talon, and you're the commander of St. George. I don't know what's going to happen to us."

"I don't, either." Garret bent close, resting his head on my shoulder, as we both gazed out over the city. "But I spent the last year thinking that I was going to die. Now that the war is finally over and we're both still alive, I don't want to waste a single moment of the time we've been granted. Especially now." His arms tightened around my waist, his breath warm on my cheek. "I love you, Ember," he whispered. "No matter what happens, I'll be here. And who knows? Maybe it will be longer than we thought. Maybe it'll be forever."

"Forever," I mused, as the last sliver of sunlight finally vanished into the dark. "Forever sounds good. Let's go for forever."

★ ★ ★ ★ ★

AUTHOR NOTE

When I was in high school, I wrote a fantasy about a cold, hardened dragonslayer who met and fell in love with the dragon he was hunting. The setting was different; it was a typical medieval world with castles and knights and swords, but those two characters—Ember the dragon and Garret the dragonslayer—stayed with me for years and years. I'm thrilled that I finally got to tell their story.

Dragons have been my favorite mythological creature since before I can remember. When I was a teen, all I read was fantasy, and most of my books had a dragon on the cover. In fact, if there was a dragon anywhere on the book, it was pretty much guaranteed that I was going to pick it up and look at it. When I started writing *Talon*, I wanted to do something different. Dragons have always been a staple of medieval worlds, either as villains for the brave knight to slay, or wise and powerful creatures that the hero implored for help. And while I loved reading those stories, I always wondered what would happen if dragons lived in modern times. Dragons are long lived, powerful and supremely intelligent; if they existed today, they wouldn't be sitting in caves guarding treasure, they would be the CEOs of billion-dollar companies. And if dragons evolved with the times, surely the knights that hunted them would adapt, as well. They would no longer use swords and lances, not when they could be hunting dragons with machine guns, sniper rifles and modern weapons of destruction. And a story about modern knights fighting dragons in this day and age just seemed really cool.

But, at its core, *Talon* is a story about "othering," and how we perceive those who are different than us. Those who look different, talk different, see the world differently—we don't understand them, and so they must be "bad." When, if we just sat down and had a real conversation, we might discover that we're much more alike than we thought. Ember and Garret both challenge the beliefs they were raised with, finding friendship, acceptance and love with someone their society believed was "evil." If we could do the same, if we could all take that first step toward acceptance and understanding, we might make the world a kinder place. Think of all the things we could learn, if we saw the world through another's eyes.

That's not to say we'd discover dragons have been living among us all this time...

But you never know.

HQ Young Adult
One Place. Many Stories

The home of fun, contemporary
and meaningful Young Adult fiction.

Follow us online

 @HQYoungAdult

 @HQYoungAdult

 HQYoungAdult

 HQMusic